CROSS OF FIRE

Paula Grey's German girl friend, Karin Rosewater, is strangled on the Aldeburgh marshes in England. Twenty-four hours later – in Bordeaux, France – Tweed's agent, Francis Carey is strangled. The killing technique? Exactly the same.

Tweed faces imminent catastrophe as one murder follows another. Bob Newman, foreign correspondent, flies to discover the sinister secret of Bordeaux. He meets General Charles de Forge – pseudo-de Gaulle and commander of a huge army. Has he walked into a trap?

Savage riots break out in France, calling for expulsion of foreign elements. The mob brandishes blazing Crosses of Lorraine. Europe trembles. Is a new Reign of Terror about to assume power? Who is the mysterious enemy destabilizing the continent?

What part is played by Lord Dawlish in his mansion near Aldeburgh and the weird marshes? By de Forge's flamboyant English mistress, Jean Burgoyne? By Isabelle Thomas, fiery girl friend of the murdered Carey? There are new victims. Who is the ghost-like strangler, Kalmar?

Other characters appeal in the tangled web Tweed struggles to unravel. Captain Victor Rosewater, British Army officer, husband of the dead Karin; the ruthless Major Lamy; Lieutenant Berthier – sighted in Aldeburgh.

The action sweeps from Britain to Switzerland, Germany, France. Tweed races to Paris, becomes the key to saving Europe – collaborating with the French premier, the German Chancellor. Or is he too late?

Events move at breakneck speed. Tanks begin to roll. Paula and Newman are in great danger. Assassination is the spark exploding crisis into catastrophe. The *Cross of Fire* erupts into volcanic inferno.

Forbes has written his most epic and panoramic novel to date.

CROSS OF FIRE

Colin Forbes

BCA

LONDON · NEW YORK · SYDNEY · TORONTO

AUTHOR'S NOTE

All the characters portrayed are creatures of the author's imagination and bear no relationship to any living person. Also, the mansion, Grenville Grange, is non-existent.

A Pan original

First published 1992 by Pan Books Ltd,
Cavaye Place, London SW10 9PG

This edition published 1992 by
BCA by arrangement with Pan Macmillan Ltd
CN 2722

© Colin Forbes 1992

Photoset by Parker Typesetting Service, Leicester
Printed and bound in Great Britain by
Mackays of Chatham plc, Kent

FOR JANE

CONTENTS

Prologue

November. Paula Grey was fleeing for her life . . .

Under a stormy sky, in Suffolk, England, she ran across the spongy marsh towards a dense copse of evergreen trees. Above the whine of the wind coming off the sea she heard again the baying of the hounds, the shouts of the men pursuing them.

She glanced over her shoulder. Her friend, Karin Rosewater, was some distance behind her, having trouble negotiating the treacherous ground. Paula thought of going back, urging her to hurry, but the sinister men chasing them were closing in.

'Head for the trees, Karin,' she shouted.

But her voice was carried away on the rising wind. She ran on, ran all-out, gasping for breath, with fear. Then she was inside the shelter of the black firs. Clad in denims and a windcheater, she ran deeper inside the small wood. The barking of the savage dogs was closer. There was no escape.

There *had* to be. Hidden inside the firs she looked up at a giant spreading its branches like hands reaching out to grasp her. Her denims were tucked inside leather boots with indented rubber soles. She grabbed at a low branch, hauled herself up the huge trunk, forcing herself to move fast. Her boots were wet from splashing through a creek a short distance back. She continued her climb like an agile monkey, thanking God she was slim and fit.

Near the top of the fir, which rose above the surrounding trees, she perched herself, legs straddled over a branch, back leant against the trunk as she waited to get her breath. Looking down, she saw she was concealed from the ground except for one small gap. She stared out across the marsh towards the river Alde as dusk descended. To her horror, she saw Karin running in the open, heading for a small boat moored in a creek snaking in from the yacht basin. Close behind her followed the hunters. Paula heard a sound below, glanced down, stiffened with fright.

A large Alsatian, released by its handler, was sniffing round the base of the fir. She waited for its head to lift, to stare up at her refuge. Two of the pursuers appeared. Tall men wearing Balaclava helmets with slits for vision, camouflage jackets tucked into military-style boots. Both men held rifles.

Paula reached quietly into her shoulder bag, took out her .32 Browning automatic. Then she heard the sound of more men treading through the undergrowth. She was out-numbered. The Alsatian was moving in circles as though baffled. It ran away out of sight. Paula remembered the creek she had splashed through by chance. The beast had lost her scent. The two hunters moved away. She let out a sigh of relief.

Still seated, she stretched up to her full height, gazing in the direction of Aldeburgh, the strange town by the sea. Its huddle of rooftops had disappeared in the dark. She had a brief glimpse of a belt of sea with whitecaps and then that, too, disappeared in the moonless night.

Where is Karin? she asked herself.

As though in reply to her anxious question she heard a penetrating scream piercing the silence of the marshes. It came from the direction where Karin had run for the boat. The agonized scream was choked off. The return of silence sounded dreadful. God! Had they reached Karin? What had they done to her?

Shivering with cold, she buttoned the windcheater up

2

to her neck, checked the time by the illuminated hands of her watch. 5.30 p.m. Experience warned her she must wait inside her refuge. The hunters knew there had been two women. And she still caught the distant sound of a dog barking.

Her legs were beginning to ache – reaction from the desperate run across the marshes, from the strain of keeping still, straddled over the branch. The wind stirred the smaller branches, brushed her face with prickly twigs. She waited until 6.30 p.m. before hauling out the mobile phone from her windcheater pocket. There had been no sign or sound of the hunters for three-quarters of an hour. She was frozen stiff as she dialled the number of SIS headquarters at Park Crescent.

Robert Newman, world-famous foreign correspondent, drove his Mercedes 280E at speed through the night along the A1094, hardly slowed as he turned into Aldeburgh High Street, which was eerily deserted. By chance he had called in at Park Crescent when the phone message for help had come through from Paula.

Beside him sat Marler, slim, compact, small, and the most deadly marksman in Western Europe. His Armalite rifle rested on his lap. In the rear sat Harry Butler, in his thirties, clean-shaven, well built, and a man of few words. Beside him sat his younger partner, Pete Nield, slimmer, a snappy dresser with a neat black moustache.

In a shoulder holster Newman, of medium height and in his early forties, carried his favourite Smith & Wesson Special. Butler was armed with a 7.65mm Walther, and Nield also had a Walther.

Newman was the only member of the team not permanently employed by the Secret Service, but was fully vetted and had helped with a number of dangerous missions. He was also fond of Paula, another member of the SIS.

'You'll wake the dead,' Marler drawled in his upper-crust voice.

3

'At eight in the evening the place is dead,' Newman snapped.

'You seem to know your way,' Marler observed.

'I should. I've spent time here recuperating. Most of it walking. I reckon I can take us straight to that copse of trees Paula described over the phone . . .'

'If she's still there. It's a God-awful night. Wind howling like a banshee. Wonder what it's all about.'

'We'll know when we find her,' Newman said grimly and hoped Marler would shut up.

Newman was driving with his headlights undimmed. In the beams Marler saw the High Street as a collection of shops and houses, old and with the roofs going up and down. A weird atmosphere.

'Dotty sort of place,' he commented.

'Quaint is the word,' Newman growled. 'We're nearly at the end of the line for driving. We hoof it from the end of the town, which is here . . .'

The road surface beyond where the town stopped abruptly had deteriorated. In the headlight beams it was a wide track of gravel. As they alighted they heard above the wind the boom of surf waves hitting the unseen beach. It was a wild night. Newman checked his watch. 8 p.m. It had been about 6.30 p.m. when Paula had phoned.

'Where does that track lead to?' Marler enquired. 'And what is that huge bank with cranes atop it?'

'Reinforcing the sea defences. If it breaks through it will flood the marshes we have to cross.' He switched off the headlights, locked the car, stood for a moment to get back his night vision. 'The track leads to the Slaughden Yacht Club. Slaughden village slid into the sea years ago. Like Dunwich further up the coast. I can see the copse of firs. Let's pray to God Paula is still there. Alive . . .'

He led the way off the road down on to the marsh. The other three men automatically spread out to make a difficult target. In her brief message Paula had warned of

4

men with guns. Using a powerful flashlight, Newman picked his way across the ooze, stepping from grassy stump to grassy stump. One wrong step and he'd sink into the slime of mud.

The night air was bitterly cold but Newman had called at his flat to put on ankle-length boots. Like the others he wore a padded windcheater. Torch in left hand, revolver in the other, he was the first to reach and enter the fir copse. He began to call out softly. 'Paula . . . It's Bob . . . Paula . . .'

His boots pressed down the mush of dead bracken. He swivelled his torch upwards at the foot of a giant fir. The beam shone on his face. He stiffened as a fragment of the fir fell to the ground.

'Bob! I'm up here! I'm coming down. God! It's freezing . . .'

He was carrying an overcoat he'd grabbed during the brief visit to his South Ken. flat *en route* to Suffolk. He wrapped it round her as she jumped to the ground. She threw her arms around him and he hugged her tight.

'It's all right now, Paula.'

'There were men with rifles . . .'

'And we have men with guns. Myself, Marler, Butler, and Nield.'

'We must look for Karin at once.'

'It's dark. Pitch-black . . .'

'We *must* look,' she insisted, freeing herself from his grip. 'I saw the direction where she went. I know the area. Give me the torch. *Please*, Bob . . .'

They emerged from the copse and Newman's three companions were waiting for him. Shining the flashlight downwards Paula moved stiffly but at surprising speed across the marsh towards the yacht basin where a number of craft were moored to buoys, their hulls covered with sheeting for winter.

Aching in every limb, Paula gradually loosened up as she pressed on over the grassy tufts, avoiding pools of oily water. The others followed, using their own flashlights. Within five minutes Paula had scrambled up the embankment hemming in the anchorage. Switching off the flashlight, she stood on the narrow footpath following the ridge of the embankment. Her eyes swiftly became accustomed to the dark, and her sense of direction had been good. She was close to the craft she had seen Karin running towards before that hellish scream.

Switching on the flash again, she hurried along the footpath. Every step was an effort after her long vigil up in the fir but her determination carried her forward with Newman close behind. The elevated footpath was even more exposed to the wind blowing in from the sea. Out in the anchorage the masts of the moored craft swayed back and forth. She stopped, directed the beam down towards the small craft moored in a creek some distance from the main river.

'What is it?' Newman asked, raising his voice.

'Look. That craft is empty. That was the one she was running towards.'

'You heard a scream,' he reminded her quietly. 'I don't want to assume the worst, but it will be easier to search the area in daylight.'

'I'm going down there,' she replied stubbornly.

Before he could grab her arm she had scrambled down the wet grassy bank to the edge of the creek. He looked back quickly. Marler was crouched further back on the footpath, Armalite held at the ready, scanning the whole marshland. Butler and Nield were similarly crouched, spaced well out. Their rear was safe. He scrambled down after her.

'I can't understand it,' Paula said, half to herself.

She was gazing at the empty hull, moving the beam back and forth. Newman stood beside her, began playing

6

the beam of his own flash over a wider area. The beam passed over another nearby creek, then swivelled slowly back.

'Go and join Harry and Pete,' he advised in a sombre tone. 'Tell Marler to come and join me now.'

'Whatever it is I must see it. I'm a big girl now. So, what is it?'

Newman switched off his flash. Tucking it inside the pocket of his windcheater, he cupped his hands to call out to Marler.

'Leave Harry and Pete where they are. Come down here quickly . . .'

'What is it, for God's sake?'

Paula tugged at his sleeve in frustration. He ignored her until Marler had joined them. As always, Marler was calm and controlled.

'Something up? If so, what? If I may be so bold as to enquire.'

'Come with me. Stay back, Paula . . .'

Switching on his flash, he trod carefully at the edge of the marsh towards the next isolated creek. Marler kept close to his heels and Paula followed him. Newman stopped, looked back at Paula, shook his head in resignation, aimed his flash.

At the edge of the creek of stagnant water covered with green slime were the relics of a rowing boat. Most of its structure had rotted away and it was half buried in mud. The basic structure stood out like the ribs of a prehistoric beast. Reeds had recently been torn up and thrown over the ruin. Newman steadied his torch. Paula gasped, then got a grip on herself. At the prow nearest to them a pair of training shoes projected, toes pointed at the sky. Newman knew the trainers had to be occupied by a pair of feet.

Marler moved forward after handing his Armalite to Newman. He used his bare hands to remove the mess of

7

reeds carefully from the stern. By the light of Newman's steady beam they saw dark hair exposed, a white blotchy face staring upwards, the tongue protruding horribly from the half-open mouth. Marler continued removing more reeds, exposing the torso clad in a dark blue windcheater. Then the boat lost balance, toppled the corpse out sideways.

A macabre movement, the body rolled as though alive, ended up on its back, lying on damp reeds. Paula sucked in her breath. By the light of Newman's flash Marler bent over the pathetic figure clad in denims below the windcheater.

'It's Karin,' Paula whispered. 'She's dead, isn't she?'

'Fear so,' Marler answered quietly. 'Dead as a door-nail,' he added under his breath.

'How did she . . .' Paula began.

'Strangled,' Marler replied.

The flashlight focused on the girl's bruised, swollen throat. The protruding tongue flopped over the lower lip. Newman put his arm round Paula, forced her back up to the footpath on the embankment.

'We'd better get back to the car. I need my mobile phone to call the police.'

'You've forgotten – I've got one.'

Paula pulled her own instrument from underneath her windcheater. She handed it to Newman as she stood very still, staring down where Marler, realizing he could do no more, had stood up, was brushing stray reeds off his raincoat.

'Then I can call from here,' Newman said, taking hold of the phone.

'You won't know the number.'

'On the way I stopped briefly at a call box, checked the number of Ipswich police headquarters. Your message to Park Crescent mentioned a scream which was choked off. I suspected we might face something like this.'

8

He pressed buttons after extending the aerial. He had to wait a minute before the desk sergeant answered.

'I want to report a murder. Location . . .'

PART ONE

Nightmare for Paula

1

'I sense a crisis situation in Germany,' Tweed said, to take his mind off his anxiety about Paula. He paced the floor of his first-floor office at the Park Crescent HQ.

The Deputy Director of the SIS was of medium height, well built, ageless. He wore horn-rims and could pass people in the street without being noticed – a trait which had so often helped him in his job.

The only other occupant was his faithful assistant, Monica. A middle-aged woman with her grey hair tied in a bun, she sat behind her desk as her chief continued. He checked his watch. 10 p.m.

'Thank God Paula is safe. That call from Newman was brief. If she's injured he'd keep it from me until they get back here. I wonder what happened up in Suffolk.'

'You'll hear when she gets back and tells you. What made you use the word crisis about Germany?'

'The urgent call from Chief Inspector Kuhlmann of the German Kriminalpolizei. His request for me to meet him in the utmost secrecy in three days' time in Luxembourg City. Why there? I could have flown to his HQ in Wiesbaden.'

'Again, you'll only know when you meet him.'

'What could have gone wrong in Suffolk?' Tweed repeated. 'Paula only dashed off up there because she knows I am investigating the disturbing rumours from France. Karin Rosewater told her she was on the track of a connection with the rising chaos in the French Republic. What connection could there be between Suffolk and France?'

'Maybe all three situations are linked,' Monica suggested. 'Suffolk, France, and this trip to see Kuhlmann.'

'That I find in the realms of fantasy.'

It was a remark he was to regret later. The phone rang, Monica took the call, looked pleased, said come up now.

'Paula, Newman, and Marler have arrived . . .'

'Bob must have driven his Merc to the limit . . .'

As the trio came into the room Tweed noticed Paula's grim expression. Nodding to him she said nothing as she sagged at her desk. Marler perched on the edge of her desk, giving her moral support. Newman threw his windcheater over the back of a chair, sat down, began to talk while Monica hurried out to make coffee. Tweed leaned back in his swivel chair, listened without interruption, glancing occasionally at Paula.

'. . . so, after we found the body I called Ipswich police,' Newman continued. 'We left Butler and Nield to show the police the location when they arrived. We took Paula to the local hotel, the Brudenell, booked a room so she could have a hot bath, then drove straight back here. That's it.'

'Not quite all, I suspect.' Tweed looked at Paula. 'I must first say how very sorry I am about the fate of your friend, Karin Rosewater.'

'It was cold-blooded murder. I'm all right now. The hot bath revived me. Like you, I'm an owl, so we can get on with it now. You'll have questions.'

'Why did Karin come over to see you?'

'She knew I was employed by what she thought was a highly organized security service. She didn't know I was SIS, of course. She said she had been asked by what she called the authorities to investigate the deteriorating situation in France. She asked me to go with her to Dunwich in Suffolk. A tiny scrap of a village down the coast below Southwold.'

'I know Dunwich. Why there?'

'Then you probably know most of Dunwich is buried

14

under the sea – erosion over the years. At her suggestion we hired wet-suits and drove up there. Some organization is exploring underwater, trying to locate and map this sunken village. I thought she was crazy, asked her why. She said she couldn't say but would I help? She said there was a connection with what is happening in France.'

'Did she elaborate on that odd remark?'

'No. I was going to pump her later during dinner but as it turned out . . .' She paused, swallowed. 'Karin phoned ahead before we left London to someone she knew in Southwold. When we arrived at Aldeburgh a seaman was waiting for us with a rubber dinghy with a powerful outboard engine. Karin took us up the coast over a calm sea until we were opposite Dunwich, then cut the engine and we went over there in our wet-suits.'

'How far offshore?' asked Newman.

Paula drank half the large mug of coffee Monica had served. 'About half a mile, maybe less.'

'Go on,' urged Tweed. 'Anyone else about when you arrived?'

'Absolutely no one. There was a long rope curled up in the dinghy with an iron hook at one end, the other attached to the dinghy. Karin threw it overboard, then said we could find our way back up to the dinghy fast if we had to. And by God, later we had to.'

'What happened underwater?' Tweed prodded.

'To start with it was fascinating. Horribly cold but there are surprisingly well-preserved relics of the sunken village. Even an old church tower, which was upright, which I thought strange. We swam among the relics and the rocks and then I thought I saw a great white whale. I nearly jumped out of my wet-suit but it remained quite motionless, as though it was anchored. That was when the floating cavalry appeared – men in wet-suits, one with a knife between his teeth.'

'You mean they were hostile?' Marler drawled.

15

'I mean they were trying to kill us, for God's sake. We managed to evade them by swimming fast among the relics. Karin led me to where the iron hook rested – she'd attached it to a window in the church. We shinned up the rope, climbed back into the dinghy and had the shock of our lives.'

'Have more coffee,' Tweed advised.

He was watching closely for signs of reaction. She'd had a punishing experience and he was ready to send her home. But she seemed determined to tell her story.

Even under stress, she was attractive. In her early thirties, she had raven-back hair, good bone structure, was slim with an excellent figure and of medium height. She put down her mug.

'The sea was no longer deserted. Not far from our dinghy a large vessel was floating. Weird. I've never seen anything like it. Beautiful lines but something sinister about it. Not like an ordinary ship.'

'Hovercraft?' Newman suggested.

'Absolutely not. High out of the water. Something odd about the hull.'

'Hydrofoil?' Marler queried.

'No!' She waved an impatient hand. 'I know what both look like. The hull seemed to be split in two.'

'Why not tell us what happened next?' Tweed coaxed.

'Three of the men in wet-suits came up to the surface close to the dinghy. Karin slashed the anchor rope, I started up the outboard, and we beat the hell south for Aldeburgh.'

'Why go all that way?' Tweed asked.

'Because I'd left the car in a public car park just outside Aldeburgh near the marshes. I thought we could just make it before night came. Luckily we had a good start on the hunters. When we reached the beach at Aldeburgh we had another shock.'

'More coffee.' Monica had refilled her mug. Paula had

16

another drink of the hot, soothing liquid. Eyes half-closed, Tweed waited and watched her as she continued.

'That peculiar ship had caught up with us. Again it was lying about half a mile out as we hit the beach. We saw them lowering dinghies with outboard motors as dusk came. No one was about. We stripped off our wet-suits, dropped them on the beach and pulled on our everyday clothes we'd left there. The dinghies were closing in when we started running for the car park. I glanced back and saw them scrambling ashore – this time men wearing Bala-clavas and carrying rifles. No time to get the car open and started. I ran faster than Karin, heading across the marshes for the copse of firs . . .'

Sipping more coffee, her voice lowered as she described the last horrific scenes – Karin making the mistake of fleeing for a boat, the dreadful scream . . .

'Shouldn't we stop now till the morning?'

Tweed made the suggestion as Paula paused for a couple of minutes, staring into space.

'No. Ask me questions. Please. I don't want to be alone yet. It helps me to talk.'

'As you wish. Tell me something about Karin Rose-water. Why the mix of nationalities in her name?'

'She's married to an Englishman, Victor. He's a captain with the British Army in Germany. Military Intelligence. He's liaison officer at a Nato air base near Freiburg in southern Germany. Has an apartment in Freiburg.'

'And Karin was German?'

'Her mother was French, her father German. She's from Colmar in Alsace.'

'Everything close to the Swiss border,' Tweed mused.

'What's the significance of that?' Paula asked.

'Probably nothing. Just a geographical comment. Were you close friends?

17

'Yes and no. I met her during that holiday I took in Germany. We got on well. Seemed to be on the same waveband. We agreed to keep in touch.'

'Exactly how and where did you meet?'

Tweed was becoming intrigued. He felt something important was eluding him.

'At a party at the air base. Lots of people there. Oh, I've just remembered. Otto Kuhlmann was there. We had a long chat. He explained he was there on duty, but didn't say why.'

'What about her husband, Victor? You met him?'

'Yes.' Paula pulled a face. 'I didn't like him too much. I'm not sure why.' She stifled a yawn. 'Just not my type, I suppose.'

'And while you were with Karin over here did she tell you what "authorities" – that was the word you used – had asked her to investigate the deteriorating situation in France?'

'No. She didn't refer to it again. And afterwards we were preoccupied with what happened.'

'When you first met her did you get any inkling whether she had some sort of job?'

'No, I didn't. I thought she was a housewife. I feel I'm being interrogated. Not that I mind. But that's how it feels.' She managed a wan smile.

'You *are* being interrogated. You may know more than you think you do. Now, it's late. I really think you ought to go home. Marler, would you escort her?'

'My pleasure. You've really put her through the mill.'

'That's all right,' Paula assured him as she stood up and slipped on her windcheater which had been drying on the radiator where Monica had placed it. 'There's something funny going on, isn't there? I don't just mean the brutal murder of Karin – that is bad enough. But why was she interested in the underwater exploration of a sunken village?'

18

'You need sleep. Don't worry about it. You've done wonderfully well in a desperate situation.'

It was unusual for Tweed to pay her such a compliment. She smiled gratefully, said good-night, and left the room with Marler.

'There is something funny about this whole business,' Newman said grimly, repeating Paula's thought.

He was alone with Monica and Tweed, who had resumed pacing slowly round the large room. He was frowning and Monica kept quiet, knowing he was thinking hard.

'You're right, Bob,' Tweed said eventually. 'One key question I'd like to know the answer to – were those killers trying to liquidate only Karin, or Paula as well? The answer to that would tell me not only what happened. But *why*.'

'From what she told me in the car they were after both of them,' Newman responded.

'And the other mystery is what is the link between Suffolk and France? Karin told Paula she was hired by authorities to report on the French situation. Also, who owns that strange ship – and what kind of a vessel could it be?'

'Lots of questions,' Monica commented, 'and absolutely no answers.'

Tweed paused, looked down at Newman. 'You left Butler and Nield to cope with the police. What story will they tell them?'

'I covered that carefully, not knowing what we'd got ourselves into. I had to warn them to tell the truth – up to a point. That Paula and Karin were interested in underwater exploration, that they travelled to Dunwich in the outboard, went under the sea, were chased by men with knives, fled back to Aldeburgh where they'd left their car, hadn't time to use the car so they fled over the marshes.'

19

'So far, so good. It covers all the evidence the police will unearth. The two wet-suits left on the beach, the abandoned outboard. Even the car parked near the marshes.'

'I had to think fast and that's the way I thought. But I left out this business of Karin investigating the situation building up in France, that she was working for someone unknown. You'd better warn Paula in the morning – she's bound to be interviewed by the police soon.'

'I'll call her tonight by the time she's just reached her flat in Putney. Just in case they discover her address and tackle her there.'

Tweed resumed his slow pacing, hands clasped behind his back. Monica realized he was staring into space.

'What's on your mind?' she enquired after a moment.

'Those men in Balaclava helmets – with guns and savage dogs. That suggests a high degree of organization. I just wonder who is behind all this, who is their employer. Bob, while I'm in Luxembourg City, would you please drive back to Aldeburgh, make a few discreet enquiries. Don't forget Dunwich. The trouble started there. Why?'

'I might take Paula with me. She needs some action to get her mind off her awful experience.'

'I may need to leave her here.' Tweed paused. 'There is something you don't know. I've sent the new man, Francis Carey, into France to nose around.'

'After only six months with the SIS?' Newman sounded doubtful. 'Has he enough experience in case he walks into a dangerous situation? What qualifications has he for such a mission?'

'His father was English but his mother French. He spent part of his childhood in Bordeaux. He can pass easily for a Frenchman. He's cautious by nature, but persistent. He's attractive to women – Paula would confirm that. So he'll probably pick up a girl friend. A couple is less conspicuous than a single man.'

'Theoretically, it sounds a perfect choice.' Newman

20

shook his head. 'But I've met him, talked to him. In an emergency I think he could panic.'

'I wish you hadn't said that . . .'

'Which means you don't disagree.'

'Well, he's there now with a transmitter. He's sent several coded reports from the Bordeaux region. There are serious and growing riots – over the issue of deporting foreign immigrants. Someone is stirring up hatred of the Algerians, for a start. There is a lot of talk in the bars that men high up are plotting a coup. I might just know when I get back from Luxembourg City. In the meantime we'd better get some rest. Tomorrow may hold some unpleasant news. I just have that feeling . . .'

2

The following evening it was bitterly cold in the old city of Bordeaux, a port situated inland on the wide Garonne river. In the Bar Miami Francis Carey looked at his watch. 10.30 p.m. Soon he'd be able to go off duty and hurry back to his cheap apartment.

He had got himself a job as barman at the Miami, which was always crowded, after making casual enquiries about the place in his fluent French. It was one of several bars he'd checked out before taking the job. He had heard this bar was popular with low-ranking officers of the French Army who regularly patronized the Miami.

At that hour – and because of the weather – the long room parallel to the bar was packed. Every chair and stool was occupied, many stood with their drinks. The noise was deafening as Frenchmen talked and joked. Carey, a thin man in his late twenties, with dark hair and a long lean face, polished glasses rapidly for new customers as he mentally wrestled with two problems.

He had found himself a French girl friend, Isabelle Thomas. She had a job in an advertising agency, long titian hair, a pallid complexion, a good figure she liked to display to advantage. She appeared to have fallen for him heavily, which had not been his hope when he picked her up as good cover. And any moment now she would walk in so he could take her out for a quick meal. He dreaded her arrival. And he wanted to postpone their date.

Returning to his modest apartment in a large old block on the rue Georges Bonnac after a shopping trip that morning, he'd detected traces of the place being searched. The compact transmitter he used to send coded signals to Park Crescent had been concealed inside a battered old suitcase hidden on the top of the huge museum piece of a wardrobe. Before leaving for the supermarket in the Mériadeck Centre Commercial, a vast newish concrete complex, he'd attached a hair to the suitcase. When he'd returned he'd had trouble opening the door. His first suspicion that something was wrong.

A closer check on the apartment inside confirmed his suspicions. The hair half-inserted inside the suitcase had vanished. At first he'd assumed Madame Argoud, the mean old biddy who ran the *pension*, had been nosy. But Argoud was short and fat. Carey was tall and still had had to stand on a chair to reach the suitcase pushed out of sight on top of the wardrobe.

Now he was wondering whether he should have packed up, left the *pension* that morning and moved to another part of the sprawling city. All his training with SIS had emphasized this point. *You never take one single unnecessary risk in hostile territory. You act to remove the risk instantly . . .*

Had he left it too late? Continuing to polish glasses at

speed, he checked over the crowded room again. No one who seemed out of place. And had he been wise to trust Isabelle to send the message if anything happened to him? 'If I disappear and don't phone you,' as he had put it.

Two Army lieutenants came in, walked straight to the bar, ordered drinks. He served them as they talked, paid, and drank.

'Soon we'll be drinking in Paris, Anton. They say the women there are quite something.'

'Paris? You mean on leave? We haven't any due.'

'So they haven't told you? Well, I am in a specialist unit. Forget what I said.'

The officer turned to stare at Carey. The barman was using a cloth to wipe the counter.

'Haven't seen you here before,' the lieutenant said.

'It's a new job,' Carey answered easily. 'My girl friend moved, so I moved to be close to her.'

'And I'll bet you're very close to her at night!'

The officer grinned lewdly, finished his drink, the two men left. An odd remark that – about Paris – Carey thought. I'll quote it in my next signal. He froze as he saw Isabelle pushing her way through the crowd towards him, a wide smile on her full red lips. A fat man leaning on the bar belched and Carey forced himself not to show repugnance. A mixed stench of garlic and anisette turned his stomach. He'd gone off French smells after his years in England. Isabelle perched on a stool and he poured her a Pernod.

'Will you be free soon?' she asked eagerly. 'I know a small restaurant where we can get a super meal.'

'Pay for your drink. The boss is looking. I'll give it to you later.'

'No need. You can buy the dinner. Here it is.'

Further along the counter the chief barman, a short fat man with greasy hair, a long moustache and a stomach which bulged against his apron noted the transaction with

23

satisfaction. No free drinks in his bar – not even for Henri's bedmate.

'Just a few more minutes and we can go,' Carey said, automatically polishing the counter.

He glanced at the door, wondering why a hush had descended on the room. Everyone was looking at two men who had just entered. Both wore belted grey trench coats with wide lapels, trilby hats pulled down over their foreheads, and dark glasses. Why in winter and at night would they sport tinted glasses? Carey was suddenly afraid as they pushed their way steadily towards him.

'Get well away from me, Isabelle,' he ordered. 'No questions. Just move – and take your glass with you.'

Unlike some women she did exactly what he told her to without asking any questions. She had melted into the crowd by the time the two men reached the bar opposite Carey. The crowd, still silent, continued to watch their backs.

'DST.' The taller of the two heavily built men flashed a folder. 'You are Henri Bayle?'

DST. *Direction de la Surveillance du Territoire* – French counter-espionage. And they had the name he had assumed, the name on his papers skilfully forged in the Engine Room in the basement at Park Crescent. He nearly produced his papers to confirm his identity and then decided that would be a mistake at this stage. He continued polishing the counter as he replied.

'That's me. What can I do for you?'

'You are coming with us. For interrogation. Where is your jacket and coat?'

'I only have a jacket. It's out at the back. I'll go and fetch it.'

'Stay where you are,' the taller man snapped. He looked at the chief barman who had edged close. 'Go and bring this man's jacket. He's leaving with us . . .'

'You have a problem?' Carey enquired.

24

'No. You are the problem.'

Carey put on the jacket his boss had thrown on the bar counter, walked to the flap exit, lifted it and walked out with an escort on either side. He was careful not to look for Isabelle. As they came close to the door he rammed his elbow into the stomach of the man on his left, shoved his way through the crowd and out into the bitter night air. A foot reached out, tripped him up. The foot was planted on his back as he lay on the flagstones, trying to get his breath back.

'Stupid, that,' the tall man remarked as he came out.

Carey looked up and saw two more men similarly dressed. They had been waiting for him outside. Hauled to his feet, he was thrown into the rear of a parked Citroën. As the car moved off one man sat on either side of him. Their two companions occupied the front seats. They arrived at the Gare St Jean and the Citroën turned down the deserted ramp leading to the quiet station entrance below street level.

Behind them as they drove away from the bar Isabelle followed on her moped, easily keeping the Citroën in view along the dark empty streets. She was puzzled when the Citroën disappeared down the ramp. Where were they taking Henri? Could they be moving him somewhere by train? If so, why? She parked her moped by the station wall, attached the safety chain, clasped her windcheater close to her neck against the bitter wind off the Atlantic.

As the Citroën descended down the ramp Henri gritted his teeth to conceal his fear. It was like entering a dimly lit cavern. No passengers were about at that hour. The tall man repeated for the third time the question he had asked as they drove to the Gare.

'Who were you communicating with when you used that transmitter we found in your apartment?'

'I'm a radio ham. I talk to other hams all over the world.'

'You're lying. That's the last time I'm going to ask.'

25

'How did you get into my apartment?' Henri demanded.

'Haven't you heard of skeleton keys? I'm sure you have. This is the end of the line. Get out.'

The Citroën had parked near the entrance to the ticket hall. Behind, the cavern was disturbing darkness. Carey followed the shorter man out on to the sidewalk. His arm was gripped in a vice. The tall man stayed inside the car, pointed an automatic at him.

'Get rid of him, Louis. He isn't going to talk.'

'You can go now,' Louis told Carey. 'You get out to the street that way. Shove off before we change our minds.'

Carey walked into the deep shadow and stopped as something moved, a shadow among the shadows. Hands grasped him round the neck. Carey tried to kick his attacker in the groin, slipped and fell. The shadowy figure knelt on top of him, hands still grasping his neck, thumbs pressed expertly on his windpipe. Carey tried to scream. Only a gurgle emerged as the remorseless pressure increased. Carey began to lose consciousness. He choked for dear life, his clenched fists hammering futilely against his assailant. Even when Carey had gone limp the strangler continued exerting pressure. When another minute had passed he rose to his feet, vanished into the darkness.

Louis pressed the button on his flashlight, walked forward, bent down over the prone form, checked its neck pulse. He strolled back to the car, climbed back into the rear.

'No neck pulse,' he reported to the tall man.

'Kalmar – whoever he may be – did another good job. For a big fat fee, I'm sure. What will we get? A pat on the back.' He addressed the driver. 'Back to the barracks.'

Isabelle pressed herself against the wall at the top of the ramp as the Citroën drove off. She had caught a glimpse of Henri getting out of the car by the glow of the courtesy light

26

inside the car when the rear door was opened.

She crept slowly down the ramp, stopped to listen. The silence frightened her. She pulled out the flashlight her mother insisted she carried, switched it on, walked on to the bottom of the ramp. Swivelling the beam, she ventured into the shadows.

She almost tripped over the body, gave a little cry as she aimed the beam downwards. Henri was on his back, his tongue protruding obscenely from his slack open mouth. His throat was badly bruised.

She forced herself to kneel beside him, felt his wrist pulse. But she knew he was dead. Numb with terror and grief, she felt inside the breast pocket where he kept his papers, his wallet. Both had gone. She had no way of knowing that within minutes Kalmar would be throwing them from the bridge into the Garonne.

She kissed the cold head, her eyes closed to avoid seeing the distorted face. Standing up, she stumbled back up the ramp to where she had left her moped. She was unlocking her moped chain when a drunk holding a bottle staggered across the wide *place* from the Bar Nicole. Tears were streaming down Isabelle's face as she began to wheel her machine to the street. The drunk leered at her.

'Lost your boy friend, girlie? Maybe we could have fun together . . .'

'*Drop dead.*'

She started up her moped and rode off towards her home. The wind raked her damp face as tears continued to pour down her cheeks. She remembered what she had just said to the drunk. It was poor Henri who was dead and she had been in love with him.

At least she could do one last thing for him. Carry out his request if anything happened to him. On her way to work the following morning she would phone the London number he had given her in secrecy, would tell whoever answered what had happened to him.

27

3

'Kuhlmann has changed the rendezvous at the last moment,' Tweed announced to Monica and Paula. 'That is quite out of character. He must be a very worried man. Geneva – not Luxembourg City – is the meeting place. Tomorrow morning at the Hotel des Bergues.'

'What time would you like to leave?' Monica asked, her hand poised over the phone.

'I'd like to leave this evening.' Tweed turned to Paula. 'Yesterday was a bit gruelling for you – I spent most of the day drilling you in what to say to Chief Inspector Buchanan.'

'And I'm grateful. I'm sure I'm word perfect. It was clever of you to tell Buchanan when he phoned I was out of town and you didn't know where . . .'

She broke off as the door opened, Newman and Marler came in, sat down and looked at Tweed. As Monica lowered her voice on the phone Tweed warned Newman quickly.

'Bob, I've got a bit of a shock for you. The man who is investigating Karin Rosewater's murder is our old friend, Chief Inspector Roy Buchanan.'

'He's no friend of mine. The last time we met he had me marked as number one suspect in a murder case. May I look forward to a repeat performance?' He frowned. 'Just a minute. Buchanan is Homicide, New Scotland Yard. There hasn't been time for the locals to request the Yard's aid. It was only the day before yesterday we found Karin's body.'

'I asked Buchanan that very question when he phoned to come and interview Paula yesterday. Apparently he'd just solved another murder case in Suffolk and was still there. Most of the senior officers at Ipswich HQ are down with flu. Hence the Chief Constable asked Buchanan if he'd stand in temporarily.'

'What lousy luck . . .'

'And he's on his way here now. Which is why I left a message on your answerphone to get here as early as you could this morning. Both you and Marler have a lot to grasp before Buchanan descends. Yesterday Paula and I went over how she would handle it – his questioning. Briefly, no mention of Karin being hired by some mysterious authority to check the state of France. Just a friend of Paula's who shared her interest in underwater exploration. I'm going to point Buchanan in the direction of Paula so he questions her first. You two can then follow her lead. Volunteer nothing – answer any questions he asks and shut up.'

'I say,' Marler protested, 'we're not exactly amateurs at this game.'

Tweed leaned forward over his desk. 'And neither is Buchanan, so don't you forget it . . .'

The phone rang, Monica took the call, listened, grimaced at Tweed, who nodded and relaxed in his chair.

'They're on the way up,' Monica said as she replaced the receiver. 'The Heavenly Twins – Chief Inspector Buchanan, with his ever-faithful sidekick, Sergeant Warden.'

'We must welcome them. Make coffee, if you would.'

Tweed rose behind his desk as Monica opened the door and two men entered. Buchanan was a tall slim man in his forties with a deceptively relaxed manner which had trapped more than a few suspects. Warden, an inch or two shorter, had a poker face and rarely showed any kind of reaction. He carried a notebook. Greeting them amiably,

29

Tweed ushered them into two chairs he had earlier placed so they half-faced Paula and himself.

'We are all ready for you,' Tweed began amiably, 'and Paula is ready to answer your questions.'

'Really?' Buchanan's tone was cynical as he glanced round the room. 'You mean you're going to co-operate without waving the Official Secrets Act in my face? Something General & Cumbria Assurance have been known to resort to.'

Tweed smiled at this reference to the cover name for the SIS, the name on the brass plate on the front door.

'Monica will be bringing coffee,' Tweed continued his welcoming act. 'It's a raw day.'

'It must have been a raw day, Miss Grey, when you went scuba diving at Dunwich. At least that was the story Mr Harry Butler told me at Ipswich police headquarters two days ago.'

'Miss Grey?' She gave him her best smile. 'I recall it was Paula last time we met.'

'This is a formal inquiry into a cold-blooded case of murder. How do you think she was killed?'

He's going for the jugular for openers, Tweed thought. Trying to throw her off balance with a brutal approach.

'She appeared to have been strangled,' Paula replied quietly.

'By an expert. One might almost say a professional.'

'What makes you say that?' Tweed interjected sharply.

'The autopsy report. It was carried out by Dr Kersey. You may have heard of him – one of the leading pathologists.' Buchanan jingled loose change in his pocket.

'What does he base that conclusion on?' Tweed persisted.

Buchanan faced him and his alert grey eyes showed a trace of amusement. He was well aware Tweed had intervened to take the pressure off Paula for a moment.

'The way the strangler had used his thumbs to press on

30

the windpipe to bring about death as swiftly as possible. Kersey suspects some of the bruising was inflicted after death – an attempt to cover up the skill with which the strangulation was carried out. Now, if you don't mind, I'd like to continue asking Miss Grey certain questions. After all, she was at the scene of the crime. You weren't.'

'I wasn't actually at the scene of the crime as you said,' Paula contradicted him. 'I was shivering with cold and fright near the top of a fir tree.'

'But you saw the murder take place?'

'I did not. Would you like me to explain how Karin and I came to be there?'

'You're willing to make a statement?'

Buchanan glanced at Warden who sat with his notebook on his lap, then at Tweed, expecting opposition. Tweed, playing with a pen, merely nodded.

Paula told her story tersely and without a wasted word. While she talked Buchanan never took his eyes off her but she stared back. The Chief Inspector crossed his legs, perched the cup and saucer Monica had given him on his knee, sipped the beverage as Paula concluded.

'. . . I wish to God now I'd insisted Karin and I spent the day shopping in London.'

'I hadn't heard you were interested in underwater exploration,' Buchanan remarked.

'But you don't know all that about me. I've made my statement.'

'And these mysterious men in disguise who hunted you with rifles . . .' There was a hint of sarcasm in his tone and he paused, hoping Paula would rise to the bait. When she remained silent he pressed on. 'Who could they have been? Why would they want to kill the two of you? When you were racing back to Aldeburgh with the other outboard dinghies in pursuit why didn't you head for the shore earlier and run for it?'

Warden smiled to himself. A typical Buchanan tactic.

Without warning he was putting on the pressure to break her down with a barrage of queries. Pressure had broken many witnesses before.

'I've made my statement,' Paula repeated. 'In that statement I answered all but one of those three questions but I'll humour you. You don't mind if I repeat myself, Chief Inspector?'

'Not at all,' Buchanan replied agreeably.

'I've no idea who the killers were. I've no idea why they came after us. The third question was not covered in my statement. If you knew that part of the world you'd know that south of Dunwich is one of the loneliest stretches of coast in the world. I felt we had to get to the parked car to escape.'

'And the three dinghies these men used to pursue you at sea had appeared after you had dived below the surface?'

'I refer you to my statement.'

'Karin's husband, Captain Victor Rosewater, is stationed at a Nato base in southern Germany. Someone will have to tell him what's happened.'

'I've already done that. It wasn't a pleasant duty.'

'You left that out of your statement,' Buchanan pointed out.

'It's been added to the statement now.'

'How did he react?'

This was the unexpected question she'd been dreading. Something which hadn't arisen when she'd had her long session with Tweed. She hesitated for a second, used her hand to straighten a pleat in her blue skirt.

'He expressed complete disbelief. I don't think he'd taken it in by the time the conversation ended.'

Buchanan smoothed his brown, neatly cut hair, stroking the back of his neck. Warden recognized the gesture: frustration. Buchanan suddenly looked over his shoulder at Newman.

'Have you anything to add to the latter part of Miss

32

Grey's statement? After all, you were there at the crucial time. I have a further question when you've explained your own version of events.'

'I have nothing to add to Paula's very lucid description of what took place. And your other question?'

'The timing seems wrong. I was at Ipswich police HQ when your call came through. I was passing the duty sergeant's desk and he'd also gone down with flu. So I took your call . . .'

'Funny, I didn't recognize your voice,' Newman interjected, playing for time.

'Probably because I used my official voice. I recognized yours. The call was timed at exactly 8.20 p.m. From Miss Grey's account you must still have been on the marshes. So how did you know the right number to phone?'

'Driving out to find Paula we passed a call box. I stopped the car, went back, checked the number in the phone directory.'

'Why? At that stage?'

Buchanan's tone was whiplash. Newman smiled, lit a cigarette, blew smoke rings.

'I refer you to Paula's statement. You're a detective. You should have worked that out for yourself. When she called for help she mentioned hearing Karin scream. I feared the worst, thought we might need the police.'

'I see.' He turned suddenly to Paula. 'Were you carrying a weapon?'

'No,' she lied promptly.

'What about you, Newman – and the others?'

Buchanan had twisted round in his chair again. His gaze swept over Marler, rested on Newman.

'We were all armed. I don't have to explain why, do I?'

'What weapon were you equipped with?'

Buchanan was addressing Marler who had been sitting

33

like a statue. He was smoking a king-size cigarette. Marler flicked ash from the cigarette into a glass bowl, looked at Buchanan with amusement.

'For the record,' he drawled, 'as if it mattered, I had my favourite weapon. An Armalite.'

The cup and saucer on Buchanan's knee jiggled. Warden, intrigued, leaned forward. It was the first time he had ever seen his chief rattled. Buchanan recovered quickly, nodded in response before he replied.

'A strange weapon to be hawking round the countryside.'

'You think so?' Marler's tone was still bantering. 'I would have thought it logical when we'd heard the men hunting Paula were carrying rifles. I'm quite a fairish shot, you know.'

Buchanan put down his cup and saucer on a table. Standing up, he addressed Paula, his tone neutral.

'We'll have your statement typed out and then maybe you would be good enough to drop in at the Yard to sign it.'

'Have it brought here,' Tweed said quietly. 'Something urgent cropped up yesterday. Paula will be occupied for some time to come.'

'As you wish.' Buchanan walked to the door Warden had opened. He turned round before leaving. 'I would like to thank everyone for their co-operation. And yours especially, Tweed . . .'

He said nothing more until he had climbed behind the wheel of his Volvo parked further along the Crescent. He was fixing his seat belt when Warden asked his question.

'What do you think, Chief?'

'Paula Grey was lying.'

'Really? I didn't get that impression.'

'She was lying by omission. Her statement bore all the hallmarks of having been carefully rehearsed. Probably with Tweed. There's a lot they haven't told us. You noticed Newman said very little? Just said he agreed with Paula's version. Not like him to keep so quiet.'

'That Marler is a saucy sod.'

'Oh, that was a clever tactic. A way of terminating the interview.'

'And you let him get away with it? Not like you.'

'I realized we'd get no more out of them at this stage. We'll leave them alone for a while, let them think we swallowed it, hook, line and sinker.'

'What about the mysterious men in Balaclavas carrying rifles? Sounded a load of codswallop to me.'

'There you could be wrong. It's so bizarre I do believe it happened. I think we may have stumbled on to something big. We'll go back to the Yard, you pick up your own car, then we drive back to Suffolk. Separately, we scour the area, ask questions – especially about underwater exploration. Even with the two of us we'll have our hands full. It's a very large area . . .'

'Well, that went well,' Newman commented after their visitors had left.

'You think so?' Tweed queried. 'Buchanan wasn't fooled. He'll be back. What we've gained is a breathing space so we can get to the bottom of what is happening – here and in France. Where were you yesterday, Bob?'

'Marler and I went to Aldeburgh. We avoided the marshes where the police have cordoned off the killing ground. And someone is financing a new expedition to explore that sunken village of Dunwich. Ever heard of Lord Dane Dawlish?'

Tweed ticked off items on his fingers. 'Self-made millionaire. Has armament factories in Scotland, at Thetford in Norfolk, in Belgium, and at Annecy in southern France. Made his original fortune out of the property boom in the eighties. A tough ruthless character. I suppose he had to be to get where he has. That's it.'

'I think I ought to try and get an interview with him,' Newman suggested.

'I might do better at that,' Paula intervened. 'I hear he has a soft spot for girl friends.'

'How could you present yourself?'

'I know the editor of *Woman's Eye*. I could go as a reporter to write an article on his achievements.'

'Hold off, Bob,' Tweed advised. 'For the moment. I'll decide who goes when I get back from Geneva – and Paula is coming with me. One step at a time. I want to hear what is disturbing the Germans first.'

The phone rang, Monica answered it, saying it was General & Cumbria Assurance. She listened for a short time, then put her hand over the receiver and looked at Paula.

'Could you take this? It's a girl. Speaking in French.'

Paula took the receiver, perched herself on the edge of Monica's desk. She spoke in French.

'This is General & Cumbria. Who is this?'

'My name is Isabelle Thomas.' There was a choking sound. 'I'm sorry about that. I'm upset. Do please excuse me. Did you know Henri Bayle?'

Paula put her hand over the receiver. 'Henri Bayle?'

'Francis Carey, the undercover man I sent to the south of France,' Tweed confirmed.

'Sorry,' Paula continued, 'the line crackled. You did say Henri Bayle? Yes, I work with him. I know all about him. I'm the General Manager . . .'

'Henri is dead . . .' Isabelle's voice broke again. 'It was awful. He's been murdered . . .'

'Isabelle, where are you speaking from?' Paula enquired quickly.

'From the main Post Office.'

'That's all right. Sorry to interrupt. Do go on,' Paula said in a businesslike tone. 'This is appalling news. I

36

need to know as much as you can tell me.'

She listened while Isabelle, calmer under Paula's controlled reaction, related her story, starting from the arrival of the DST men at the Bar Miami. Paula was scribbling in shorthand on a pad Monica had pushed in front of her. The room had gone quiet. Everyone sensed the tension in the conversation as Paula encouraged the French girl to go on. Eventually she started checking Isabelle's story.

'You did say two DST men? Your *Direction de la Surveillance du Territoire*?'

'Yes, it was them. I was close enough to Henri in the crowded bar to catch what they said. I don't understand why they would . . .' Another choking sound. 'I was in love with Henri.'

'So you're very upset – as I would be.' A vital question: 'Have you informed the local police?'

'No. Should I?'

'Under no circumstances. Don't do that. Tell no one.'

'I haven't even told my mother. I'm so confused.'

'I can understand that. I may know what happened,' Paula lied. 'Whatever you do, tell no one,' she repeated. 'We will try and send someone to meet you. He will introduce himself as . . . Alain Dreyfus.' The first name which came into her head. 'Have patience, Isabelle. It could be a short time before we can contact you. Now, would you give me your address and phone number?'

She wrote the details down carefully, asked Isabelle to repeat the address to make sure she had it down correctly.

'Isabelle, have you got a job? I see. Don't throw it up. Carry on your life as usual – as far as you can, considering the terrible bereavement you have suffered. And no police. Why was Henri working for an insurance company? He was checking on a suspicious death where a claim for insurance had been made.'

'I must get back to my job now,' Isabelle said in a

37

lacklustre voice. 'I have at least done what Henri asked me to if something happened to him.'

'You did the right thing. We will investigate. But, don't forget, no police . . .'

She put down the phone and sighed heavily. She was wearing a white blouse with a pussy bow. She fiddled with the bow before she looked at Tweed.

'God! I hope I handled that reasonably well. You do realize what has happened?'

'With no time to think you reacted brilliantly. And am I right in assuming Francis Carey is dead?'

'Yes. Murdered through the agency of two DST men who took him from a bar to the Gare St Jean late in the evening yesterday. In Bordeaux . . .'

She gave a terse account of what Isabelle had told her. Tweed listened with an expressionless face. When she had finished he drummed the fingers of his right hand lightly on the desk top and looked at Newman.

'I fear you were right. Carey was too inexperienced to send him on that mission. My deadly mistake.'

'Rubbish!' Newman snapped. 'Not too long ago Harry Masterson, an area chief in Europe, experienced as hell, was also murdered. It's part of the risk run by anyone belonging to SIS. I'm sure you warned Carey before he agreed to go. So stop blaming yourself.'

Tweed was suddenly galvanized into action. 'Two DST men? It's unbelievable. Monica, try and get me René Lasalle on the scrambler now. We'll soon find out the truth . . .'

There was silence as Monica dialled the number. Paula sat at her desk, plucking at the pleats of her skirt, playing back in her mind the conversation with the distraught Isabelle. Monica nodded to Tweed, indicating the DST chief in Paris was on the line.

'René,' Tweed began in a decisive tone, 'Tweed here on scrambler . . . You are too? Good. I sent an agent to the south of France as we agreed. I've just heard he was murdered last night in Bordeaux – at the main station. After being hustled out of a bar by two men who said they were DST . . .'

'Good God! You did say DST? That's impossible. No DST men are operating in the Bordeaux area. I should know.'

'Then they were impersonators . . .'

'That I will not tolerate. As soon as this call is ended teams will be flown to Bordeaux to investigate. But I need more information, if you are willing to reveal that.'

'Certainly. The agent was masquerading – with papers – under the name Henri Bayle. He was working as a barman at some dive called the Bar Miami. From the timing I was given the murder must have taken place something in the region of 11 p.m. Apparently in some underground entrance which is reached by a ramp. Someone other than the two fake DST officers actually committed the murder.'

'And who told you this?'

'An informant whose name I would sooner not give. The informant sounds reliable. Carey was due to transmit a radio signal last night and nothing came. I assumed it was inconvenient.'

'And you heard this news when?'

'Five minutes ago.'

'My teams will be flying there immediately. Tweed, I would appreciate it very much if you could fly to Paris to see me. There are developments you should know – and they may be linked with this assassination. I send you my sympathy. But, most important, can we meet?'

'Yes. Very soon. I have to fly elsewhere in Europe first. May I call you as soon as I can come on to Paris?'

'Please do.' Lasalle's tone became grim. 'Events here are taking a desperate turn. A crisis is upon us. Hurry, my friend. *Au revoir . . .*'

Tweed stared into the distance after putting down the

phone. He seemed to have forgotten the presence of everyone else in the room.

'Any instructions?' asked Monica.

'Yes. I've decided Paula is coming with me to Geneva and then to Paris. Book another room at the Hotel des Bergues in Geneva, get her a ticket on my flight. Get us both open air tickets from Geneva to Paris. Book two rooms at that small hotel in Paris, the Madeleine. It's fairly close to the rue des Saussaies – to Lasalle.'

'What is this Lasalle business?' Newman asked.

'The second man who has used the word crisis in the past few days. First Kuhlmann, now Lasalle. Something explosive is building up in Europe.'

'I've just remembered something Karin said,' Paula reported. 'It was while we were hurriedly changing into our clothes after hitting the beach at Aldeburgh with those men coming after us. Drove it out of my mind.'

'What was it?' Newman asked.

'She said the French Army was the danger. The units stationed in the south. In our anxiety to escape it completely slipped my mind. I was never able to ask her what she meant.'

'My next objective,' Newman decided. 'While Tweed is haring over Europe.'

'What objective?' Tweed asked.

'To interview the commander of that army . . .'

4

Gun barrels. Row upon row of lethal firepower projecting menacingly from the huge assembly of tanks Newman was escorted past by a French Army lieutenant.

He had driven from Bordeaux to the heavily guarded entrance of the Third Corps. After flying to Bordeaux he had been surprised by the speed with which the commander of this great battle array had agreed to an interview.

'You represent *Der Spiegel*, Mr Newman? Then I am sure the General will be pleased to see you,' the suave voice had responded. 'I am Major Lamy. You are in Bordeaux? Shall we say 2 p.m? Yes, today. That is agreed . . .'

GHQ, Third Corps, was located in hilly country east of Bordeaux. During his drive in a hired Citroën Newman had passed through fields laid out with grids of vineyards, a distant view of the turrets of a large chateau.

'This way, Mr Newman,' the lieutenant said in French, walking between four lines of tanks, gun barrels precisely aligned parallel to each other. Uniformed soldiers ran in the distance. Newman had an impression of a highly organized military machine run by a man who tolerated no waste of time. Escorted inside a single-storey building guarded by sentries, he was led along a wide corridor to a heavy wooden mahogany door, elaborately carved with Napoleonic-style eagles. More like the door he'd expect to have seen inside the chateau he had passed.

'The General is expecting you. Just walk in,' the

lieutenant invited, taking hold of the handle.

'How does he know I've arrived?' Newman enquired.

'The officer in the guard room had obtained a newspaper photo of you from the library. When you got out of your car he radioed to the General's aide-de-camp.'

'Radioed? Haven't you heard of the telephone?'

'Phones can be tapped.'

'And why was I body-searched before I was permitted to enter?'

'More security. You were checked for weapons, for a concealed tape-recorder. Normal procedure against the danger of saboteurs. The General is waiting . . .'

The door was closed behind him as Newman walked alone into a long room with a polished woodblock floor. A very long room with a large Louis Quinze desk at the far end. Behind the desk sat a stocky figure wearing the uniform of a full general. Standing behind the tall-backed Louis Quinze chair was a thin erect man, also in uniform and with the rank of major.

But what caught Newman's attention was the framed silhouette hanging from the wall behind the chair. A large black silhouette, unmistakably of General Charles de Gaulle, head and shoulders, in profile and wearing his képi.

'Welcome to Third Corps, Mr Newman. Please do sit down. I hope you won't mind but we checked with *Der Spiegel* that you were reporting for them.'

'General Charles de Forge?' Newman enquired, remaining on his feet.

'Of course. This is Major Lamy, my Chief of Intelligence.'

De Forge had a strong hawk-like face, longish and with a firm jaw. His eyes were a piercing blue and he stared penetratingly at Newman as he rose, extended a hand. His grip was so firm Newman's fingers would have suffered had he not been prepared for it.

42

Lamy sported a dark smear of a moustache and his expression was sardonic as he nodded to Newman who now sat down.

'I can't interview you, General, with someone else present.'

De Forge, his manner aloof, stared at Newman. Leaning against the imperial high-backed chair, he exuded dynamic energy under the control of an iron will. There was something almost presidential about his manner.

'Major Lamy is one of my closest associates.'

'Nevertheless,' Newman insisted, 'I made it quite clear on the phone – and the call was with Lamy – that the interview was to be personal. That means alone.'

'Lamy, you'd better leave us. Reporters seem to think they out-rank generals.'

'I have heard rumours,' Newman began after the Intelligence officer had shut the door, 'that you have strong views on the present position in France. When I was at the gate I was body-searched. The lieutenant used a word I didn't quite grasp. Saboteurs.'

'The scum are everywhere. France is polluted with alien elements that should be removed. Algerians, Arabs – God knows what else.'

'That sounds like the programme of the new party, *Pour France*, an extremist group akin to *Action Direct*.'

Newman's French was fluent. He thought he detected a hint of surprise in the penetrating eyes. De Forge waved a well-shaped hand.

'I am a servant of the Republic. Politics does not interest me. But I must correct you. *Pour France* is a party whose popularity is growing hourly. If their views coincide with mine, that is irrelevant.'

'You're not concerned in any way with politics, or so you say. Have you any views on the new Germany?'

It was like pressing a button. De Forge leaned forward,

gesticulating with a clenched fist. But his voice remained calm as he launched his attack.

'We have to be on our guard. The present Chancellor is a man of peace, but who follows him? A new Bismarck who will attempt to use the tremendous power of unified Germany to take back Alsace-Lorraine from us again? I draw your attention to the *Siegfried* movement which is growing stronger daily. An underground organization which may surface at any time. France must be prepared for a fresh onslaught. I repeat, *Siegfried* is a great menace to us – to your own country. We must be strong. You want to see how strong we are?'

'I did see your tanks . . .'

'I refer to our methods of training an élite army – ready for any emergency. Come with me, Mr Newman . . .'

De Forge stood up, placed his képi over his high forehead. He glanced at the silhouette of General de Gaulle and smiled coldly.

'He was a great man. Maybe it is time for a second de Gaulle to arise. Come!'

De Forge led the way from his office out of the building to where a vehicle like a jeep was parked. Jumping with agility behind the wheel he beckoned for Newman to join him in the passenger seat. Curious, Newman climbed up. He had barely sat down when the vehicle began moving at high speed.

Uniformed men on motor-cycles appeared as outriders with sirens screaming, ahead of the General and behind his vehicle. The racing cavalcade swept through the gates of the main entrance which had been opened, continued into the countryside.

Newman, holding on with his right hand to avoid being tipped out, glanced at the General. His hawkish profile was calm despite the fact that he obviously enjoyed moving at high speed. The cavalcade swung off the road up a track across a field towards a forest, slowed down.

'Just where are we going?' Newman demanded.

'To show you the punishment well. Men have to be tough to form an élite strike force. Discipline, order, and stability are our watchwords.'

'I seem to recall the leader of *Pour France* used the same slogan.'

Swivelling the wheel, de Forge stared at Newman and his expression was bleak. He stopped the vehicle in the middle of the evergreen forest in a clearing. There was something sinister about the atmosphere, the way the outriders formed a circle a distance away from an old stone well.

'This part of the interview is off the record,' de Forge ordered.

'I didn't agree to that condition earlier. You can't impose it now.'

De Forge paused as though about to change his mind, to drive back to GHQ. Newman, sensing the change of mood, jumped out of the vehicle, strode over to the well. De Forge followed him. He wore riding boots polished so they gleamed like glass. In his right hand he carried a whip which he slashed against the boots. Newman had to admit it was an impressive performance. Whatever else the General was, he was a natural leader.

Newman examined the ancient well. The main structure had crumbling walls but the windlass, operated by a handle, was brand new. Attached to one end of the windlass was a gauge measured in metres. Two ropes dangled tautly into the depths. Newman picked up a small stone, dropped it down the side. It seemed for ever before he heard a faint distant splash.

'Don't drop a large stone,' de Forge warned and smiled his cold smile. 'You might hit the prisoner.'

'Prisoner?'

'This is the punishment well. If a soldier fails to carry out an order – or doesn't perform up to scratch on the obstacle

45

course – he spends some time down the punishment well. A defaulter is now suspended just above the stagnant water.'

'Why two ropes?'

'One is attached round his neck like a noose. It has a special adjustable slip knot which can be tightened or loosened from here. He is in no danger. Just a touch of terror.'

'And the second rope?' Newman asked in a tight voice.

'Attached to a harness round his chest. The main support between the defaulter and eternity. Later he will be hauled up by the harness rope.'

'And that gauge?' Newman persisted.

'That tells us how close to the water the prisoner has been lowered.'

Newman peered over the rim into the black hole. It was so dark he could see no sign of the poor devil hanging in space. He heard an engine sound. Out of the corner of his eye he saw Major Lamy arrive in another jeep-like vehicle, the sardonic officer crouched over the wheel like a bird of prey.

De Forge strode over to him. There was a brief conversation. Lamy picked up a microphone. An aerial extended upwards automatically. Lamy was speaking into the mike, then replaced it and drove away. De Forge strode back.

'You see now how we have built the most powerful army in Europe.'

'I think it's barbaric . . .'

Nothing further was said between the two men while de Forge drove Newman back to GHQ. The sinister outriders, wearing tinted goggles, accompanied them. Racing up to the entrance, de Forge stopped with a jerk which would have hurled Newman to the ground had he not been prepared for just such a manoeuvre. De Forge stared straight ahead as he spoke.

'You leave here.'

Newman jumped out, de Forge raced into GHQ through the gates which had been opened at his approach. Walking towards his parked Citroën, Newman had to pass between the circle of outriders who had remained. Behind tinted glasses unseen eyes stared at him. Careful not to touch a motor-cycle, he slipped through a gap, took out his key and inserted it into the lock of the Citroën.

The key did not slip in easily as it had done earlier. Newman grunted, punctuating his thought. He opened the door, slipped behind the wheel, closed the door, started the engine. The accelerator seemed slower to respond. He drove off, waited until he had rounded two distant bends, well clear of GHQ, parked on the grass verge.

Getting out, he extracted his pencil flash, crawled under the chassis, examined it carefully. No sign of a bomb. It would have been a bomb activated by remote radio control – he had realized earlier there would be no danger of an explosion with the motor-cyclists so close. I'm getting paranoid, he thought. De Forge is just an egomaniac who likes to show off.

He drove on towards Bordeaux. Five minutes later, moving along the deserted road, he saw a black Berliet van, a large wide vehicle, appear in his rear-view mirror. The type of vehicle used by the CRS, the French para-military police brought in to quell mob violence. Surely de Forge hadn't managed to persuade them to become his allies? Then he recalled the phoney DST men who had taken Francis Carey from the Bar Miami. Had the vehicle been hijacked?

It was closing up on him rapidly, huge in his mirror. In the cab sat the driver and two men wearing Balaclavas which concealed their faces. One held what looked like a long truncheon. Standard CRS equipment for beating back a seething mob.

Newman had an excellent memory for routes. He had only to drive along a new complex route once to be able to remember every detail on the return trip. He rammed his foot down and again there wasn't the normal reaction he'd experienced when driving out to the GHQ, the same burst of speed.

Newman knew exactly what had happened. He recalled the change in de Forge's manner when he had refused to accept the 'off the record' condition imposed so belatedly. The arrival of the cynical Lamy, de Forge's conversation with him, Lamy's use of the radio to send back a message. They had used skeleton keys to open his car, had tampered with the accelerator. He glanced in the mirror again. The black Berliet van was moving like a shell from a gun, was almost in his boot.

He pressed his foot all the way down, coaxed more speed out of the damaged mechanism. Newman swung round a bend, sped on, recognizing exactly where he was. Could he reach the bridge in time? It would be a matter of seconds. No bookmaker would give odds on him for this race for survival.

The two Balaclava-masked passengers in the cab leaned forward. Newman could sense their savage eagerness to get at him. The gap between the two vehicles had temporarily widened with his recent pressure on the accelerator. Two more bends.

The Berliet was closing the gap again, filling his rear-view mirror like a mobile hulk. He swung round the first bend, his foot pressed down with all his strength. Ahead lay the last bend. It seemed to creep towards him as the Berliet almost touched his rear bumper. He swung the wheel, negotiated the last bend and the narrow hump-backed stone bridge was a hundred yards away. Newman tightened his grip on the wheel, forced himself to ignore the mirror.

On his outward journey he had slowed to cross the narrow bridge, just sliding both sides of the car between the stone walls without scraping the Citroën. Now he had to judge in centimetres, taking the bridge at a belting speed. He risked a brief final glance in the mirror. The Berliet was about to ram him. The wheels of the Citroën mounted the near side of the hump-back, raced over the crest. The solid stone walls flashed past him in a blur. He gripped the wheel more firmly as he felt the Citroën descending. He almost lost control but his nerve held. He was beyond the bridge.

In his rear-view mirror he saw the Berliet reach the bridge. Because he'd had plenty of time Newman had not taken the main road to Third Corps GHQ; he had driven along a more devious route to see the vineyards and maybe a chateau. The driver of the Berliet saw the bridge too late. The wide van roared up the near side, metal screaming as it grated against the stone. The van stopped abruptly, jammed between the walls. The left-hand wall broke under the pressure, fell into the gorge below and took with it a portion of the floor of the bridge. The Berliet swayed, hung tilted at an angle over the drop for a fraction of a second, then followed the wall, turning over in mid-air, smashing into the rockstrewn gorge with a noise like a bomb detonating.

Newman stopped the Citroën, jumped out, climbed a bank which gave him a view down into the gorge. The Berliet lay motionless. Nothing moved. No one emerged from the metal coffin.

Newman shrugged, got back behind the wheel and drove on to Bordeaux. When Tweed heard he was flying to the city he had given him the address of Isabelle Thomas, Francis Carey's girl friend. It was time someone paid her a visit to see how she was bearing up – and perhaps gain more information.

5

The first surprise Tweed and Paula had when they arrived in Geneva at the Hotel des Bergues was the sight of Chief Inspector Kuhlmann sitting reading a newspaper in a chair near reception. He had arrived much earlier than they'd expected.

The second surprise was his reaction. He glanced up and then ignored them, turning to a fresh page of his paper. Paula looked at Tweed.

'Don't say a word to him,' he warned. 'And don't look at him again . . .'

Tweed registered for his room. When Paula followed his example Tweed wondered why she stood well back as she filled in the form. The receptionist handed her a key.

'What room did you say?' she asked in a loud voice. 'I have left my reading glasses behind.'

'Room Number 135,' the receptionist repeated in an equally carrying voice.

Tweed hurried to her room as soon as he had swiftly unpacked. Her room was also a large double – the only rooms Monica had been able to reserve. Situated at a corner overlooking the rue du Mont-Blanc on one side and the river itself across the street where the main entrance was located, it was more like a suite.

'Very de luxe,' Paula glowed. 'And look at the lights across the river.'

Beyond the uncurtained windows neon of various colours illuminated the distant buildings in the dark, the signs reflected like coloured snakes in the water. Tweed nodded appreciation, his thoughts elsewhere.

'Otto Kuhlmann has already phoned me,' Paula went on. 'He asked when we would be leaving for dinner, said he'd be waiting in the lobby, then rang off abruptly.'

'He's acting mysteriously. Maybe he's going to join us so I think we need somewhere discreet.'

'I'd already caught on to that. I hope you don't mind, but after his call I booked a corner table for three at Les Armures. It's a fashionable restaurant in the Old Town, near the Cathedral. I hope you approve.'

'An excellent choice. Do you want to change?'

'I want food. I'm hungry. And I sense Otto is wanting to see us urgently. He used that word when he called me.'

'Put on your coat and let's move . . .'

Kuhlmann was standing just outside the entrance, wearing a black overcoat and a black wide-brimmed hat pulled down over his broad forehead. Short in stature, he had very wide shoulders, a large head and reminded Paula once more of old films she'd seen of Edward G. Robinson. The same tough face, firm mouth, the suggestion of great physical and mental strength. Again he ignored them as he stood under the canopy, peering to left and right as though waiting for someone else.

Paula approached the Mercedes cab which drove forward. As the driver darted to open a rear door for her she spoke in a clear penetrating voice.

'Could you take us to Les Armures, please? It's a restaurant in the Old Town near the Cathedral.'

'I know it well, Madame . . .'

She settled back in the warmth of the car with Tweed beside her as the car left the kerb. It had been freezing cold even during the short time she had stood on the pavement. A raw east wind was blowing from off the lake – probably from Siberia, she thought.

'I hope he caught on,' she whispered.

'Oh, he'd catch on, if that is his idea . . .'

51

Crossing the wide Rhône bridge, the car followed a zigzag course to the restaurant. It had begun to drizzle. The cobbled streets had a greasy shine under the glow of the street lamps. The Old City was perched on a hill facing the main part of Geneva across the river. It rose steeply, climbing to the summit, the Cathedral. The car continued its swerving pace round hairpin bends between rows of old houses huddled together. Tweed glanced at Paula.

Her reaction to the dreadful experience in Suffolk had been remarkable. The way she had taken command of the situation back at the hotel, relaying to Kuhlmann her room number. And later when they left she had cleverly informed him of their destination.

He knew what she was attempting and admired her for it. She was proving to him that despite her ordeal she was capable of doing her job.

Paula stared out of the window as the Mercedes continued its endless ascent of the narrow cobbled streets. At night the Old City had a sinister atmosphere. No one about. Shadowed alleyways and the occasional flight of precipitous staircases.

The Mercedes slowed, stopped close to a narrow street running alongside a large raised platform supporting old cannons. The driver twisted round to speak.

'It is only a short walk under the Arsenal,' he said, indicating the platform.

'I know,' Tweed said and paid him.

The driver ran to open the rear door, Paula stepped out, followed by Tweed who stood in the drizzle, pulling up his overcoat collar as the Mercedes drove off. He appeared to be listening to the heavy silence which had fallen.

'Trouble?' Paula enquired, sheltering on the platform.

'No. I wanted to make sure we hadn't been followed. 'Let's get inside and hope Kuhlmann joins us . . .'

Les Armures, 1 Puits-St-Pierre, showed a welcoming glow of light behind old windows. They entered through a

52

revolving door, passed a bar with wood-topped stools. Paula revelled in the sudden warmth, took off her coat and handed it to a waiter who hurried forward. The room was packed with tables, most of them occupied. A babble of voices mingled with the clink of glasses.

'You have a table for three. The name is Grey,' Paula told the waiter who was relieving Tweed of his coat.

As the waiter escorted them Paula had a glimpse through an archway into another room, the *Salle des Artistes*. Elephant tusks decorated the wall of the inner room. Paula had requested a secluded table and they were shown to a corner table with crossed muskets on the wall. She sat in a chair, leaving the corner chair for their guest while Tweed occupied the flanking seat.

'This place is just as I remember it,' Paula remarked before studying the large menu. 'And still popular.'

'A good place to talk,' Tweed replied.

The warmth, the babble of voices created an atmosphere of people enjoying themselves. Mostly locals, Tweed judged. He was studying the menu when Paula saw Otto Kuhlmann enter. He paused by the bar, scanning the crowded room. She guessed he had checked the faces of everyone in the room before he handed over his coat and hat and joined them in the corner chair.

'I had company,' the German began in English, explaining his precautions. 'A motor-cyclist tagged my cab.'

'How did you shake him?' Tweed asked.

'By directing my cab to stop at the tunnel of steps below the Cathedral. Then I ran up the steps and he was unable to follow on his machine. He's lost.'

'Something to drink,' Tweed suggested.

'Let's start with Kir Royale,' Paula said promptly and Kuhlmann nodded agreement as he produced his trade-mark, a large cigar.

'Down to business. I hope you don't mind the cigar – I

53

have denied myself since leaving Wiesbaden, hoping to avoid identification. Somewhere I slipped up – but the people we are dealing with are ruthless and thorough.'

He paused while Tweed gave the drinks order. They were served almost at once. Paula drank half the mix of champagne and blackcurrant liqueur, put down her glass.

'I needed that. Now, Otto. And do smoke your cigar.'

'As I said on the phone, Tweed, a crisis is building in the new Germany. We have a dangerous enemy we can't locate. Extreme elements of the Paris press are painting a picture of an aggressive Germany which wishes to take revenge on France for historic defeats.'

'That's ridiculous, Otto,' Tweed protested. 'We know Germany has the most peaceful intentions of any nation in Europe.'

'True, but there is a brilliantly orchestrated campaign to portray us as dangerous.'

'Under the present Chancellor? That's absurd.'

'I know. The propaganda is insidious, worthy of the infamous Goebbels. It is suggested a new Bismarck may take over later. That he will want to take back from France Alsace-Lorraine – which Germany annexed in 1871.'

'Surely such an obvious lie can be countered.'

'There is more.' Kuhlmann drank the rest of his Kir Royale, paused while Paula ordered another round. 'I have to tell you there is a new underground movement being organized by someone outside Germany. Organized in cells made up of terrorists. Where they are coming in from we can't trace. It is called the *Siegfried* movement. And has extreme right-wing characteristics. We know arms and explosives are being smuggled in and stored for future use on a large scale. Again, we can't detect the source.'

'You must have some idea who is behind this conspiracy,' Tweed said quietly.

'As I said earlier, certain extremist elements of the Paris

54

press are stoking the fires.' He puffed at his cigar as they ordered food, said he would have the same. 'All this is very confidential, you will have realized. Even more top secret is the fact that I've travelled here as the personal representative of the Chancellor.'

Paula stared at him over the rim of her second Kir Royale. With his thick dark hair, equally dark eyebrows, his wide mouth clamped tight on his cigar, Kuhlmann looked very grim.

'I see, Otto,' Tweed said quietly. 'Have you an idea of the view of the President of France?'

'He can't believe there is any such conspiracy. He is extremely annoyed at what certain French newspapers have said. He thinks it best not to comment – that would draw more attention to their aggressive statements. Also, he has his own problems.'

'Which ones are you referring to?' Tweed pressed.

'The growing popularity of this new party, *Pour France*. They advocate deporting all foreigners – Algerians, etc. That strikes a chord with many and he doesn't know how to react.'

'So I come back to my earlier question. Who exactly in France is behind this conspiracy, all these lies about Germany?'

'Emile Dubois, driving force behind *Pour France*, is one, I would guess. But there are disturbing rumours that some Cabinet Ministers in Paris support Dubois secretly. There is a fog over France and it is very difficult to penetrate it, to find out what is really happening. Which is why I have taken the enormous risk of sending in an agent secretly to investigate.'

The *émince de veau Zürichoise* with *rosti* had been served after Kuhlmann had revealed his role as representative of the German Chancellor. Now Paula sat very still, food poised on her fork. She was wondering whether Tweed would tell Otto about Francis Carey. 'Define the risk for me,' Tweed said.

'Supposing he was caught, his mission exposed. Can you imagine what the French press would make of it? *German Secret Agent Spies On France*. I could write the headlines myself.'

'You must be – determined – to take that risk.'

'Maybe desperate would be a better word.' Kuhlmann waved his cigar and grinned for the first time. 'His real name is Stahl. He has entered France from here – Switzerland – under an assumed name with forged papers. He may escape undetected. Stahl's mother was French, his father German. And he comes from Alsace which, as you know, is a real hotch-potch of French and German names.' He turned to Paula. 'Hotch-potch? Is that right?'

'Perfect, Otto.' Paula placed a reassuring hand on his thick wrist. She knew he prided himself on his English, on mastering colloquialisms. 'Just as all your English has been since we started talking.'

'Why are you telling me all this?' Tweed asked briskly. 'Why me?'

'Because I know you have established an excellent network of agents inside France. There you are ahead of us. I'm hoping if Stahl fails you will succeed. Providing you agree to help.'

'I agree. Paula, show Otto that photograph you have of yourself and your friend.'

Paula blinked, opened her shoulder bag, took out an envelope from a zipped pocket. Inside the envelope was the only photo she had of Karin Rosewater – taken while she had spent time with Karin on holiday in Freiburg near the Black Forest. She passed over the envelope to Kuhlmann.

He extracted the photograph, held it in the palm of his large hand. The only reaction was his teeth clamping tighter on his cigar. He looked at Tweed, at Paula.

'You know the girl with you in this snap?'

'Do you, Otto?' Tweed asked quietly.

Kuhlmann stubbed out the cigar, began to eat the superbly cooked veal and the speciality Swiss potato which was so crisp and tasty. He drank some of the champagne Tweed had ordered earlier. Paula pursed her lips, glancing at Tweed. Kuhlmann put down his knife and fork, wiped his mouth with his napkin.

'Yes, I know her,' he said eventually. 'What puzzles me is how you know her. It seems an amazing coincidence.'

'I have bad news for you, Otto.'

'Tell me.' Kuhlmann put down the glass he had been about to drink from.

'She is dead . . .'

Kuhlmann listened with an impassive expression as Tweed related tersely what had happened in Suffolk. He also referred to the mysterious 'authority' Karin had mentioned to Paula.

'She was talking about me,' Kuhlmann said grimly. 'I remember now, Paula, you were at that party at the Nato base in southern Germany when Karin was there. That was why I was also there. To protect her cover she never came near Wiesbaden. We'd meet for a few minutes at a party – prearranged. Chat like acquaintances for just a short time. She reported to me, I gave her fresh instructions.'

'You weren't going to mention her,' Tweed commented. 'Only Stahl.'

'Deliberately. I was fond of her – and she was a brave lady. Want to hear how I recruited her?'

'I'd like very much to hear that,' Paula broke in.

'She was a brilliant linguist. Her husband, Victor Rose-water, is with British Military Intelligence. He has had occasion to visit Wiesbaden in connection with his work. I was invited to their home. One day when I arrived Karin was on her own. She told me she'd worked for the BND at Pullach near Munich . . .' Tweed glanced at Paula. The BND was German counter-espionage. 'She pressed me to let her help with my work,' Kuhlmann continued. 'Karin

57

could be very persuasive. And I was needing an operative to back up Stahl. She seemed the perfect choice. I regret I hired her to check on the situation in France – working with Stahl.'

'Did her husband know what she was doing?' Tweed asked.

'Victor Rosewater? I warned her not to tell him. And there the arrangement fitted so well. Rosewater spends a lot of time away from home – tracking the IRA units operating in Germany, I gathered.'

'Anyone else except yourself and Stahl know what she was doing?' Tweed persisted.

'No one. Security seemed watertight.'

'Why didn't the Chancellor involve the BND in this?'

Kuhlmann waved a dismissive hand. 'They are up to their necks checking dubious characters infiltrating from Eastern Europe since unification. Also, for some reason the Chancellor seems to trust me. God knows why.'

'Because you're so reliable, like a bulldog which never gives up,' Paula said and gave him her warmest smile. 'Now do get on with your meal.'

'We'll do what we can to unravel this mystery,' Tweed assured. 'If you want to let me know how we can contact Stahl it would be helpful. It's up to you.'

Kuhlmann took out a notepad, tore off a sheet, rested it on the cardboard back so there would be no impression, wrote rapidly, gave the folded sheet to Tweed.

'Thank you for your offer of help. We need it. That gives you Stahl's present address, the name he's operating under, his phone number. The codeword which will identify you as safe is Gamelin. Now maybe we can relax – even if only for tonight. I return to Wiesbaden tomorrow. One more thing – Stahl reports *Siegfried* have hired the most ruthless assassin on the continent. Someone called Kalmar.'

'That's a new name.'

'To me, too. And Stahl said contact between *Siegfried* and Kalmar is maintained here in Geneva. Now, I'm going to finish this excellent meal . . .'

At Kuhlmann's suggestion they left separately as they had arrived. Tweed asked the waiter to phone for a taxi. Paula kissed Kuhlmann on the cheek, told him to take care of himself. Just before they left, Tweed leaned close to the German, whispered.

'Warn Stahl that however he communicates with you not to use a radio transmitter. Detector vans could locate him.'

'You have a reason for that advice?'

'I have . . .'

Kuhlmann left the restaurant ten minutes after Tweed and Paula were driven away in a taxi. Tweed had insisted on paying the bill. The German did not call for a cab. He walked in the drizzle through the silence and the dark of the Old Town. He chose to descend by a route opposite to the way the cab had brought him to the foot of the tunnel below the Cathedral. Walking down the deserted Grand Rue, his mind was full of the death of Karin Rosewater. But as he pursued a devious route through side alleys he kept a lookout for the motor-cyclist who had followed him earlier.

He had seen no sign of the tracker when eventually he crossed the Rhône footbridge to the Hotel des Bergues. Tweed had really said very little, but the German felt now resolving the crisis depended largely on the Englishman.

6

Seen on a street plan Bordeaux is a city going nowhere. Driving round the city Newman had the same impression. Moving along a main street leading from the Gare St Jean towards his hotel, the Pullman, small narrow streets led off on both sides, radiating like the sails of a windmill.

The ancient city comprised old blocks, five or six storeys high, built of grey stone. The walls were stained with the grime of ages, hadn't been cleaned for years. Shutters hung at drunken angles. Nowhere was there any sign of paint being used for a decade. Some were uninhabited ruins, stark walls which looked like the relics of bombing, but he suspected they were simply relics of neglect.

It was like driving through a monstrous prison as he jammed on the brakes once again. Traffic everywhere, filling the streets, parked nose to tail on the sidewalks. Most bore signs of collisions – dented chassis, battered doors. The leaden sky added to the atmosphere of dreariness.

Newman had a room at the Pullman, one of the better hotels. But he had also taken a room at a small dump of a lodging house where he'd been able to register in a false name. All the old biddy who ran the place wanted was money in advance. He had bought a shabby suitcase from a sleazy second-hand shop, had filled it with a selection of clothes taken from his suitcase at the Pullman, carried to his car in one of the ubiquitous plastic bags.

It was a precaution – taking a room at the lodging house. The murder of Francis Carey had made him take certain precautions. Now he was driving to a rendezvous with Isabelle Thomas, Carey's girl friend. He had phoned her at the address provided by Tweed, they had agreed to meet at a bar named by Isabelle, the Bar Rococo, at six in the evening. She had told him how she would be dressed. He turned down the street she had named, saw a car leaving a 'slot' on the sidewalk, drove in fast. A woman with a fur round her neck behind the wheel of a Renault leaned out of her window.

'That was my slot, you bastard. Get out of the way.'

Newman gave her a broad smile. 'First come, first served,' he rejoined.

He locked his car and waited to make sure she wasn't going to follow up her insult with physical damage to his vehicle. She made an obscene gesture, drove away. Bordeaux drivers' manners . . .

The Bar Rococo was of a higher class than he'd expected. Large bulbous pots stuffed with green ferns obscured a clear view inside. The tables had clean red check cloths. The waiters' green aprons were also spotless. He wandered among the ferns and stopped. She fitted her description, but again he was surprised – she was so attractive and well dressed. Could this be her?

'Isabelle Thomas?' he enquired politely in French.

'Yes.' Her tone was guarded.

'Good, I'm Alain Dreyfus,' he went on, giving the code name Paula had arranged with her from London. 'May I sit down?'

'Certainly, Mr Robert Newman. And we can speak in English,' she continued in that language.

It was his third surprise. She smiled as she saw his expression when he was sitting opposite her.

'Actually, I recognize you from pictures I've seen in the foreign press. You are Robert Newman, aren't you? And your profession?'

She was covering herself again, wondering if she had

61

made a bad mistake. He smiled reassuringly. Inwardly he felt annoyed she had penetrated his real identity so quickly.

'I am Robert Newman, foreign correspondent. Is it safe to talk here?'

'That is why I chose this rendezvous. It is early. We are almost the only people here. And, as you see, the heavy lace curtains conceal us from the street.'

She was more than attractive, she was beautiful, Newman was thinking. She had a mane of titian hair, a slim, tall neck, good bone structure, greenish eyes, and a clear complexion. Very little make-up: just a touch of red lipstick on her firm mouth. She struck him as a woman of character. In her late twenties. And what she said about the place was true – there was no one else anywhere near them.

'An aperitif?' he suggested as a waiter hovered.

'Why don't we go straight on to a bottle of wine? You choose. Doesn't matter what we decide to eat as far as I'm concerned.'

'We'll have a 1979 red Bordeaux,' he told the waiter in French. 'Leave the menu. We'll order later.'

'Pushing the boat out a bit, aren't we?' she teased him.

'I've had a long day.'

'Do you mind if I start talking about what happened?'

'I wish you would. But first, let me ask you something. Was Henri your first serious boy friend?'

'No.' Her expression changed, became intense. 'I was engaged to be married to a soldier with the Third Army Corps. A tank commander. It ended tragically.'

'You want to tell me how?'

'Someone should know about General Charles de Forge.' Her tone dripped contempt. 'Joseph Roux was his name, would have become mine – Roux. I have never told this to anyone. As a foreign correspondent you might like to add to your experience. It's a pretty horrific story. I don't want to spoil your meal.'

'I've developed a pretty strong stomach. Go on.'

'Joseph was very independent-minded. De Forge has what he calls the punishment well . . .'

'I've heard some details about it.'

'You have? Your contacts must be pretty good. Joseph was among a group of troops addressed by the General one day. De Forge likes the sound of his own voice. He was damning the Jews, said they ought to be eliminated from French life. After he'd finished speaking he asked if there were any questions. You're not supposed to react to that. Joseph did.'

'What did he say?'

'That he thought he was in the Army. That politics was nothing to do with the military. And in any case he had two good friends who were Jews. He said that anti-Semitism was a curse, that it was anti-French. De Forge was livid. He gave the order at once.'

She paused, drank some wine, her hand trembled slightly. She tightened her grip on the glass, was careful to stand it back on the table without trembling.

'What order?' Newman asked quietly. 'If you want to go on with this.'

'Now I've started,' she said firmly. 'They took him to the punishment well immediately. Joseph was hung in the well by his thumbs.' She leaned forward, her gaze intense. 'Can you imagine hanging for six hours by your thumbs? And Joseph was a big man.'

'Quite horrible – and barbaric.'

'That's how de Forge maintains what he likes to call iron discipline. Some of his officers call him the Iron Man.'

'Go on about Joseph. What happened next?'

'After the six hours they hauled him up out of the well. He was kept in the military hospital at GHQ and then discharged from the Army with a big pension.'

'What sort of state was he in?' Newman asked gently.

'I wasn't allowed to visit him in hospital. When he came

63

home both thumbs were horribly distended. My doctor examined him and said he would be a cripple for life. Nothing could be done for him. Joseph was a very active man and they'd reduced him to a wreck. That's what he said to me, "I'm a shipwreck for ever."'

'What did his parents say? Do?'

'Joseph was an orphan. We had been living together in an apartment. A very unpleasant officer, a Major Lamy, told him just before he left hospital that if he ever told anyone what had happened his pension would stop at once.'

'What was Joseph's reaction?'

'At first he thought we could get married and live on the pension.'

'Which is why he kept quiet about the atrocity?'

'There was more to it than that . . .'

She paused as the waiter served the grilled red mullet and *pommes natures* they had both ordered. Newman disliked the way the fish's head leered at him. He cut it off, hid it under the tail.

'You were saying?' he coaxed her.

'Joseph was very self-conscious about his handicap. He thought it made him look like a freak. The idea of being interviewed by reporters – then photographed – horrified him.' She gulped, drank more wine. Something even grimmer was coming Newman sensed. She ate for a few minutes, then put down her knife and fork.

'He became very depressed. There was so much he was unable to do for himself. I knew something was going to happen when we stopped making love. He said he was no good to me any more. I argued that was nonsense. One evening after dark he said he was going to go out by himself, to have a drink in a bar, to learn to lead a normal life. I was glad.'

She drank more wine and stared at Newman as he refilled her glass. She was nerving herself to tell him something. He let her take her time.

'Joseph fooled me with his story about going to a bar. He had secretly bought two heavy iron weights from a hardware shop. He drove to a bridge over the Garonne, got out, attached the weights with rope to each ankle, lifted himself and the weights somehow over the side of the bridge, and went down into the Garonne. Divers brought up his body later that night. A woman had seen him go over and called the police. So, you see, General Charles de Forge is a murderer.'

'How long ago?' Newman asked, for something to say.

'Two years. It seems like two weeks. I lived for revenge until I met Henri. And now Henri is gone – murdered by the Government's DST. What is happening?'

Newman changed the direction of the conversation, asking her about herself. She had returned to living at home with her mother in a Bordeaux apartment. At the moment her mother was visiting relatives in Arcachon, a port and seaside town on the Atlantic coast west of Bordeaux.

She worked as an account executive for an agency. Yes, she was young to hold such a job, but they had found women directors of client firms preferred dealing with their own sex. Especially when they were advertising women's clothes and underwear.

'You must earn a good salary,' Newman suggested.

'Far more than most girls my age. Which is perhaps why I have few friends.'

'Is there somewhere private we could go to chat and be sure we're not overheard?'

Newman looked round. The restaurant was filling up. At tables close by every chair was taken. He wondered why it was called a bar and voiced the question aloud.

'They have a large bar downstairs which is very popular. As to somewhere quiet . . .' She considered, watching Newman while she drank the rest of her coffee. 'I told you my mother has gone to Arcachon – so there is no one at the apartment. We could go there . . .'

At Isabelle's suggestion – when he said he disliked parking in the street – he drove the Citroën round the end of the grey apartment block inside an alley leading to a court-yard. He parked the car out of sight of the street.

She was waiting for him, one of the huge tall double doors unlocked, closed it behind him and led the way across an interior yard. The apartment was on the first floor at the top of a flight of bleak stone steps. He realized it overlooked the street when she ushered him inside. Lace curtains masked the tall windows.

'Don't switch on any lights in here,' he warned.

'OK. But why?'

'The place will look empty from the street. We need somewhere not overlooking it.'

'The kitchen. Then we can have more coffee . . .'

He perched on a stool at an island unit after taking off his trench coat. Underneath he wore an English business suit, a blue bird's-eye. The kitchen was a different world from the living room which was furnished with heavy, old-fashioned furniture; it was equipped with the latest facili-ties, including a hood over the cooker. He opened his onslaught when she had placed a brown mug of steaming coffee in front of him, had settled herself on a stool facing her guest.

'How many people knew of your friendship with Henri?'

'No one really. I told you I have few friends.'

'What about your mother?'

'Not her.' She made a move. 'We don't see eye to eye on many things. I never let her know what happened. She would have criticized my choice of a barman.' She warmed her hands round her mug, shapely hands. 'I did think it funny that Henri was just a barman – he seemed so

66

intelligent. When I said so he shrugged, said he was travelling round France to get experience of the world.'

'Are you actually saying that no one else in the whole world knew about you and Henri?'

'Yes. When we went out he asked me to choose places to eat I'd never been before. I didn't ask him why.'

'Someone must have betrayed Henri to the DST. From what you've said you're the only one who could have done that.'

Her face flushed. She stared at Newman as though unable to believe her ears. Newman stared back as he continued.

'How much did they pay you for your services?'

Her hand tightened on the handle of her mug. For a moment he thought he was going to get the contents in his face and prepared to duck.

'You swine!' she hissed in her well-modulated voice. 'I could kill you for what you've just said. Why? In the name of God, why do you say such terrible things?'

'Because you're the obvious betrayer. Making up to him, gaining his confidence – when all the time you were an agent of the DST . . .'

She slipped off her stool, ran swiftly round the island. On the way she tipped the contents of her mug into the sink. She was slimly built, almost as tall as Newman, wore a mini-skirt which exposed her excellent legs. She came at him like a tigress.

He stood upright just in time as she aimed the mug to smash it against his head. He grabbed her arms, forced them to her sides, surprised at her strength, her agility. She aimed her knee at his groin, he took the thrust in the side of his leg, held her prisoner until she stopped struggling, breathing heavily.

'And you're a damned good actress, I'll give you that,' he goaded her.

She dipped her titian-maned head, prepared to butt him

67

under the chin. He swivelled her through a hundred and eighty degrees, holding her arms against her sides, his head pushing against hers, pressing himself into her back. A faint whiff of perfume drifted to his nostrils. She relaxed, unable to fight any more. Her voice was controlled now, loaded with venom.

'Get out of here,' she ordered him. 'I never want to see you again. I thought you were a friend . . .'

'I am,' he said quietly, his mouth close to her ear, 'but I had to be sure of you. To test you to breaking point. I believe you now, Isabelle. Sorry I upset you, but I repeat, I had to be certain of you.'

She relaxed in his arms completely. Her tone held a hint of amusement.

'Maybe you'd better let me go. If anyone came in and found us like this they'd think we were lovers.'

'Not a bad idea – as far as I'm concerned. But I'm here for professional reasons. Behave? If I let you go?'

'If I must.'

She turned round and gave him a glowing smile, tears in her eyes. She collapsed with emotion, buried her head against his chest. He stroked her hair as she shook with relief, let her get it out of her system. She let go of him, ran to the sink, turned on the tap, splashed her face with huge quantities of cold water. Drying herself, she opened a drawer, took out a brush and attacked her mane with the aid of a mirror on the wall.

When she had finished smartening her appearance, Newman pushed his mug of coffee over the island.

'I've had enough. The rest is yours.'

She drank greedily, watching him over the rim as she had done in the Bar Rococo drinking wine. When she had emptied the mug she asked her question.

'Who, then, do you think could have betrayed Henri – if he was doing something against the French state?'

'Tell me why he chose to work in the Bar Miami,'

Newman suggested, folding his arms, leaning against the island.

'He never said. But I met him there often, sometimes sitting at a table while I waited for him to come off duty. A lot of French officers in the Army use that bar. I had the impression they interested him.'

'He asked them questions?'

'Sometimes, yes. Innocuous questions as though he was being companionable. Were they on leave? Things like that.' She frowned. 'I've just remembered something. Shortly before the two DST men arrested him he was serving two French lieutenants. I was out of sight but close. You know how in a crowded bar for no reason there is sometimes a brief hush in the conversation?'

'I know exactly what you mean.'

'That happened on that night. I heard one lieutenant tell his fellow officer he was with a specialist unit, that soon he'd be in Paris – and not on leave. Henri was intrigued by that remark.'

'So am I. But how could you tell Henri was intrigued?'

She looked wistful, had perched herself on a counter top, her long legs swinging.

'Because by then I knew him well. His every little gesture. Henri was polishing a glass. He was very quick. When the lieutenant made that remark for a second Henri stopped polishing the glass, then polished it furiously.'

'I see.'

Newman saw more than that. He thought he'd learned how Carey had been detected. A trifle too much enthusiasm talking to officers, asking the odd question. Someone had reported his interest.

'Let's go sit on the couch in the living room,' Isabelle suggested, her eyes smoky.

Newman frowned as she switched off the kitchen light before opening the door, followed her. She seemed to be interested in him. Business and pleasure didn't mix – and

69

he sensed that despite her outer poise she was in an emotional state. Little wonder after what he had put her through.

He kept close to her to avoid furniture until he became accustomed to the dark. Isabelle wandered over to one of the tall windows, glanced down through the curtains, stiffened. Newman saw how her silhouette froze.

'What is it?' he said and joined her quickly.

'Those two men standing in that shop doorway. They are the DST men who took Henri away.'

'How can you be sure?'

'The way the tall one moves. He turned to the shorter man to say something. It *is* them, Robert. I may call you Robert?'

Newman was staring down into the street. He knew the temperature outside was arctic, compounded by the wind-chill factor. So why should two men take up a position opposite the entrance to the apartment block? A couple of friends who had met by chance? Then they'd head for the nearest bar. Newman looked up and down the narrow street. Fifty yards away from where the men stood a solitary Renault was parked. The shorter of the waiting couple thrust gloved hands into the pockets of his wide-lapelled trenchcoat, huddled his shoulders, stared at the entrance opposite.

'I know it's them,' Isabelle insisted. 'I was close to them when they came up to Henri. That's how they were dressed then.'

'Does anyone at the Bar Miami know your address?'

'The chief barman. I left a silk scarf there once. I phoned him, he said they'd found it. He asked for my address – there was an expensive scarf ring attached to it. He made me repeat my address when I went to collect it.'

'And he'd know you were Henri's girl friend?'

'He could hardly avoid realizing that.'

'You have to leave here. Tonight. Can you go out to

70

Arcachon and stay with your mother? I'll drive you there. Do you want to pack? Urgently?'

'So many questions, Robert . . .'

'My friends call me Bob. Now, can you?'

'Yes. But not with my mother. I have a sister with an apartment there where I could stay – Lucille, my sister, is abroad and left me the keys. The advertising agency is having a slack time and owes me two weeks' holiday. I could phone them, say I'm leaving for San Trop. I can pack in ten minutes, maybe less.'

'Is there some way we can get to my car in the alley without using the main entrance? Those aren't real DST men – they're far more dangerous. DST don't go round murdering people.'

'Yes, Bob. There is a back way direct into the alley. I have a key.'

'Next point. Have you two sharp knives? I suppose you wouldn't have a French coat I could wear?'

'There is one which Henri left. He was about your size. In a wardrobe in the bedroom. And a hat, if you want one. We'll be lucky if that fits . . .'

Closing the door, when they were inside the bedroom, she switched on the light, went to a huge, old-fashioned wardrobe, took out a dark overcoat, a trilby hat – both shabby. Carey's method of passing for a Frenchman. Newman slipped on the coat, pulled up the collar. Rather tight under the arms but it would pass in the dark. He rammed the hat on his head, pulled the brim low over his forehead.

'It's not big enough,' Isabelle decided.

'Big enough at night. Now, the knives.'

She was a girl who never wasted time asking unnecessary questions, which impressed Newman. In the kitchen she opened a drawer, stood back, invited him to take his pick. The wooden box divided into compartments fitted snugly inside the drawer contained an amazing selection. He

71

chose two short-bladed knives with strong handles, slid them blade first carefully inside the coat pockets.

'Show me how to get out of the rear entrance. While I'm away do your packing. Oh, I suppose you haven't an empty bottle of wine?'

'Only in the trash can. I could wash and clean it thoroughly.'

'I'll be drinking out of it. Fill it with water . . .'

She led him down to the rear entrance, unlocked the door and he found himself in the alley leading to the main street.

A raw wind slashed at his face. Newman cowered under his floppy hat, staggering slowly along the sidewalk, waving the bottle with his left hand. The wind grew in fury, sheets of newspaper flew in the air, Newman leaned against a wall, tilted the bottle, drank from the neck. He stumbled into the deserted street closer to the parked Renault.

Behind him the two men in trench coats peered out at his erratic progress. Newman rammed the hat tighter over his head as the wind almost blew it away. He spun round in a drunken circle. The trench coat men had retreated deep into the shelter of their doorway.

He lurched across to the car, sprawled on the cobbles alongside the rear wheel of the Renault. Letting go of the bottle, he grasped the first knife, plunged the blade deep into the tyre, the handle protruding close to the cobbles in the direction the car would move. Swiftly he gripped the second knife, repeated his performance, driving the second knife alongside the first. The wind was blowing away the bottle when he grabbed it by the neck, staggered to his feet. No sign of Trenchcoats.

He began his weaving walk back the way he had come, watching the doorway from under the brim of his hat. Still no sign of the enemy. He resisted the temptation to move faster, arrived at the entrance to the alley, tottered out of sight.

Now he ran to the rear entrance in the alley, took the key Isabelle had handed him from his trouser pocket, and within a minute was back inside her mother's apartment. She was standing by the window in the living room, turning round as he entered.

'God! You just made it. They both peered out as you made the alley . . .'

'You're supposed to be packing.'

'I'm ready. Can we make a run for it now?'

'Now . . .'

She wrapped a silk shawl round her head, concealing her titian mane. A blue coat buttoned to her neck completed the transformation. As protection against the wind she had changed her mini for a knee-length blue skirt.

'My trenchcoat,' Newman reminded her.

'Packed in my case, plus Henri's shaving kit and the pyjamas he left behind – hidden where my mother would not find them. It will get you through the night in Arcachon . . .'

The alley was deserted as they hurried to the parked Citroën in the courtyard. They'd have the description of his car, Newman thought grimly – and its registration number. Plenty of time to record that while de Forge took him to see the punishment well. Undoubtedly passed to the phoney DST men. Best to assume the worst.

He drove out of the alley with Isabelle beside him. She was careful not to look towards the doorway sheltering the watchers as Newman swung the vehicle in the opposite direction. He glanced back, saw the two men running for the parked Renault.

The two men dived into the front of the car. Behind its wheel the taller man started up the engine, released the brake, pressed his foot down. The car sped forward maybe a dozen yards and then the rear wheel's tyre collapsed as

73

the knives penetrated it. The driver cursed as the car slewed towards the sidewalk, the wheel rims grinding on the cobbles.

Newman saw what happened in his mirror, increased speed along the deserted street as the wind hammered at the windscreen. With Isabelle's guidance, he soon left the outer suburbs behind and was racing along the N650 – towards the Atlantic, towards Arcachon.

'Has your mother friends in Bordeaux who could let enquirers know her address?' Newman asked.

'No. She doesn't like her city neighbours, lets them know nothing of her affairs. No one knows she has relatives in Arcachon. No one can say anything.'

It seemed she would be safe in Arcachon, Newman hoped. He was also wondering whether the police had acted on his anonymous call to the Prefecture in Bordeaux. His call had been made from the Post Office before driving on to the Bar Rococo.

He had told them about the CRS Berliet truck crashing into the gorge, had given them an idea of the location. Whose bodies would they find inside?

7

General Charles de Forge sat in his high-backed chair, his hands rested on the arms as he fired questions at Major Lamy, standing facing him across the large desk. It was early evening, the only illumination a desk lamp which threw Lamy's saturnine face into sharp relief.

'Most unfortunate about that Berliet truck. Has Newman got away?'

'Only for the moment, sir. We're watching the airport, the main rail stations – a small army of our men in plain clothes. All with his description.'

'And the Berliet?'

'Dealt with. The bodies removed to the usual place.'

'And that spy? Henri Bayle, wasn't that his name? I understand he had a mistress.'

'Her apartment is being watched. I hope to have news of her detention. After being questioned – if necessary under pressure – she will be disposed of.'

De Forge stood up, walked round his desk, hands clasped behind his back. He paced slowly up and down the long room.

'It is the details which have to be attended to. Never forget that, Lamy.'

'What I don't understand, General, is why you agreed to see Newman, then changed your mind about him.'

'Because I have a fingertip feeling about people. I hoped an article in *Der Spiegel*, angled my way, would add to the growing anxiety and confusion in Germany. Later, he seemed hostile. My decision, as always, was logical. Now, I will address my troops . . .'

The tank commanders assembled in the drill hall had been served a good meal. De Forge often quoted maxims of Napoleon. One of his favourites was 'an army marches on its stomach'. A loud cheer went up as de Forge appeared in full uniform on the raised platform at the end of the hall. Then the chant began.

'*Pour France . . . Pour France . . . Pour France . . .*'

De Forge silenced them by raising his right hand, palm open, shoulder high. The soldiers, who had jumped to their feet at his appearance, sat down and leaned forward. At the end of the front row a certain Lieutenant Berthier, lean and clean-shaven with fair hair cut very short, watched his commander intently.

'Soldiers of France,' de Forge began in his magnetic

voice, 'the time is approaching for action. Paris – not Berlin – will become the capital of the New Europe. It will be your skill, your courage which will bring all this about. And you are not alone – your help in bringing in the harvest assures us of the support of the farmers. And beyond that we have our friends in high places – in Paris. You are the iron barrier against which the foreign scum will break their unwashed skulls . . .'

He had to pause as his audience broke into a thunder of cheering and applause. He continued speaking for another half hour, a natural orator of compelling power. His climax, which lifted off the roof, was typical.

'None of this is for me, as you well understand. It is for France . . .!'

He acknowledged the three minutes of wild applause with a solemn, aloof expression, hands clasped behind his back, then walked off the platform, disappearing through a side door where Major Lamy waited.

'They would die for you, my General,' Lamy commented.

'They may have to. Now, drive me to the villa of Mademoiselle Jean Burgoyne. I need some active relaxation.'

De Forge was married but rarely visited his wife, Josette. She lived in an expensive apartment in Bordeaux where she held 'salons' – parties for influential and artistic celebrities. He had married her because she had been the daughter of the Minister of Defence at that time. A career move.

Jean Burgoyne was an attractive Englishwoman whose vitality had appealed to de Forge when he met her at a government reception in Paris. He always felt need of her when he had made a speech.

As Lamy drove him to the villa the Chief of Intelligence glanced at his chief. De Forge was staring ahead, presenting his famous profile to his subordinate.

'That reference, General, to friends in Paris was a clever remark. Most confidence-inspiring. And true.'

'What would not have been clever would have been a reference to an even stronger ally. General Lapointe, next to myself the most important member of the *Cercle Noir*.'

'Lapointe is vital,' Lamy agreed.

French military power rested on the *force de frappe*, the formidable group of long-distance rockets deep in silos on a plateau to the east. And the rockets were armed with nuclear warheads.

One of the soldiers who had listened most closely to de Forge's address did not immediately return to barracks with his comrades. Lieutenant Berthier, protected against the Siberian cold, walked by himself across the parade ground.

As he strode along Berthier repeated to himself the speech he had listened to word by word. He had an excellent memory but wished to be sure every sentence was imprinted on his brain. When the time came for him to report the contents of the speech he wanted to be word perfect.

Tweed moved fast the following morning. Paula found herself sitting next to him aboard Flight SR951 – bound from Geneva for Basle, the Swiss city at the north-west tip of the country where the French border meets the German frontier.

The flight took off promptly at 7.10 a.m., was due to touch down at 7.55. Paula glanced behind them, saw the seats were empty, as were the seats in front. No damn wonder: they'd had to get up at five in the morning. She still kept her voice low.

'Now will you tell me why – instead of flying direct to

77

Paris to see Lasalle of the DST – we're first meeting Victor Rosewater in Basle?'

'Because he was Karin's husband.'

Paula gritted her teeth. The previous night she had phoned Rosewater at his apartment in Freiburg, asking if she could meet him in Basle, that maybe he'd like to hear from her exactly what had happened to his dead wife as she'd been with Karin. Rosewater had agreed at once and they'd arranged to see each other at the Hotel Drei Konige. Now, from Tweed's terse reply, she realized he was going to tell her nothing more after instructing her to make the call the previous evening. What was Tweed playing at?

'After we've seen Rosewater we'll fly straight on to Paris,' Tweed remarked. 'When you'd fixed up this meeting with Rosewater I called René Lasalle in Paris. He seemed very anxious to see me at the earliest possible moment. Events appear to be moving out of control. Confirming Kuhlmann's worst fears. The momentum of events is gathering pace.'

'What events?'

Tweed handed her a copy of the *Journal de Genève* he had bought at the airport. The headline in large type jumped at her. She read it in French but thought of it in English.

SERIOUS RIOTS IN BORDEAUX. 1,000 CASUALTIES.

She read the article below. Large groups of men wearing Balaclava helmets had gone berserk, attacking pedestrians, wrecking shops near the Gare St Jean, painting anti-Semitic slogans on walls. The odd result had been no arrests were made: the police had been taken completely by surprise.

She glanced down out of the window. The aircraft had flown half-way along Lake Geneva, had now swung northwest overland. Below they were crossing the Jura

78

mountains behind Geneva. The range was like a whaleback and its summits were crested with snow. She shivered, handed back the paper.

'What is behind it all?' she asked.

'You should have asked "Who" – and I have no idea.'

She didn't believe him but said nothing. They'd be landing at Basle soon and she was bracing herself for talking to Karin's widower. What on earth could he tell Tweed?

At the isolated villa east of Third Corps GHQ, de Forge, wearing only pyjama trousers, jumped out of bed and ran to the shower. He turned on the cold water tap and stood quite still as ice-cold water sprayed his slim body.

Jean Burgoyne climbed out of the king-size bed more slowly, wrapped a towel round her nude body, opened the door and picked up the newspaper the maid had left on the floor. She perched on the edge of the rumpled bed as she read the headline, looked up as de Forge reappeared, dried himself, swiftly dressed in his uniform. She stood up, still holding the towel with one hand, the newspaper in the other.

Jean Burgoyne was five feet seven, about the same height as de Forge, had blond hair, good bone structure, long well-shaped legs. Her face was also longish with a firm chin and a flawless complexion which owed nothing to make-up. She handed the paper to de Forge. The headline was about the Bordeaux riots.

'Charles, this wouldn't have anything to do with you, would it?' she asked, her glance shrewd.

De Forge glanced at the paper. He dropped it on the deep wall-to-wall carpet. His right arm rose and he struck her across the face with the back of his hand. She reeled backwards under the blow, fell across the bed. The towel dropped, exposing her well-moulded figure. Her eyes stared at his as she reached for the towel, wrapped it round herself again, stood up.

Her voice was calm. She even managed a wicked smile.

'Charles, don't ever do that again. You may be a great man, but I doubt whether de Gaulle ever struck a woman in his life. Maybe,' she continued, 'this is why your wife, Josette, wants so little to do with you.'

He took a step forward, his eyes glowing with anger. She raised one warning finger, her voice now little more than a whisper.

'I said never again. I mean it. Now, that creep, Major Lamy, will be freezing outside. Duty calls, *mon Général*.'

He hesitated, unsure whether she was mocking him. Then, turning on his heel, he walked to the door and paused before opening it to leave.

'Jean, I will phone you again when I am available.'

'As you wish . . .'

But de Forge had gone. Outside the balustraded two-storey stone villa surrounded with evergreens a de luxe Citroën stood parked. Major Lamy was walking up and down, swinging his arms round his body, slapping his gloved hands against his greatcoat. It was even colder than the night before. De Forge glanced at the sky which was a low ceiling of sullen cloud. It looked like a threat of snow coming.

De Forge took the wheel: he loved driving at speed. Lamy sat by his side as de Forge sped down the twisting drive, spurting up showers of gravel until he emerged on to the road. He pressed his foot down as he queried with Lamy the general situation. He was still smarting from Jean's first remark: women were for only one purpose. They should bloody well never ask serious – even danger-ous – questions.

'Exercise General Ali is ready to start as soon as you reach GHQ,' Lamy informed his chief.

'That's routine. I see we've started in Bordeaux.'

'Only the beginning.' Lamy smiled, twisting his lips. 'More is on the way. Toulon, Marseilles, Toulouse.'

'Then Lyons,' de Forge continued. 'Make it look like the start of an uprising, a revolution. After that,' he said with satisfaction, 'the big one. Paris . . .'

Back at the Villa Forban Jean Burgoyne sat in front of her dressing table, using a pad of cottonwool dipped in wych-hazel to apply to where de Forge had struck her. She didn't think there would be a bruise but it was best to take precautions.

'And I think a brief holiday back home in England would be a good tactic,' she mused aloud. 'Charles can fret for me for a while. And I can spend a few days at my uncle's house in Aldeburgh . . .'

At 8.45 a.m. exactly Tweed hurried inside the Drei Konige – the Three Kings Hotel – in Basle. Carrying both cases with Paula at his heels, he handed them to the waiting porter, gave him a generous tip, asked him to store them safely.

'Victor's here already,' Paula whispered.

Facing the reception counter inside the main entrance was a well-furnished sitting-room area. A tall, well-built man wearing a German sporting jacket and slacks stood up from a deep leather armchair, came forward to greet Paula, hugged her, gave her a kiss on the cheek.

Tweed studied the Englishman, who had spoken in German, one of the several languages both Tweed and Paula spoke fluently. Tweed guessed Victor Rosewater was maintaining some kind of cover even in Switzerland.

In his thirties, Tweed estimated, Rosewater had an easy manner, was clean-shaven with the weather-beaten complexion of a man who spent a lot of time outdoors. He had a strong nose, shrewd brown eyes under dark eyebrows and a well-brushed thatch of thick hair. A good-looking man with a powerful personality.

'This is Tweed,' Paula introduced in German. 'He is in security,' she continued, following her chief's earlier instructions. 'Also a good friend.'

'Security?'

Rosewater's eyebrows rose a fraction, asking for further enlightenment.

'Security,' Tweed repeated and left it at that as he shook hands.

Rosewater had large hands, a strong grip. He smiled warmly and nodded, pressing Tweed no further. A natural probe on the part of a man engaged in undercover military intelligence, Tweed thought.

'They have a pleasant dining room overlooking the Rhine,' Rosewater suggested. 'Maybe you would like to take breakfast with me? I drove down the autobahn from Freiburg. It was no distance at all, but I skipped any nourishment. Personally, I'm as hungry as a horse . . .'

Tweed knew the room, had stayed at the hotel before, but he made no reference to this. Rosewater led the way to a table by one of the large windows overlooking a closed verandah where in summer the wealthy met for drinks and dinner.

Beyond the verandah the Rhine flowed swiftly, a muddy colour compared with the Rhône at Geneva. A barge train hauled by a stubby tug ploughed slowly upriver against the current. Rosewater sat facing his two guests, made the remark to Paula after breakfast had been ordered.

'I'm coming to terms with Karin's demise.' He glanced at the barge train. 'At least I kid myself I am. I suspect, frankly, I'm still in a state of shock.'

'Do you really want to hear about it now?' Paula asked.

'I think it would help me. My work is putting me under great pressure at the moment . . .' He looked at Tweed briefly. 'Not entirely divorced from your world of security. I can't make up my mind whether that's helping me or not.'

He looked at Paula. 'Just tell me how it happened. What shook me most was when you used the word murder on the phone. Why Karin?'

'That's what we would like to know,' Tweed intervened brusquely and then went silent, eating some of the excellent bread on the table.

Paula had just started talking and then trailed off into silence. She sipped her coffee slowly and took her time spreading jam on a piece of bread. Rosewater had switched his gaze to the far side of the restaurant and Tweed looked quickly in the same direction.

An attractive brunette in her thirties sat by herself at a table by the wall. She had crossed her shapely legs, her skirt sliding above her knees, stroking her tilted leg slowly with one hand as she looked straight at Rosewater. He watched her for a moment with an expressionless face, then stared at Tweed. He gave a broad grin to disguise from the brunette what he was saying.

'I've seen that woman before somewhere. I think I've been tagged, and God knows I'm careful.'

'Maybe she just likes you,' Paula teased him.

Rosewater, she realized, had a personality appealing to many women. He exuded good nature and a sense of fun. Rosewater's voice remained serious.

'I would doubt that. Once is a chance encounter – twice is a danger signal. I don't know whether Paula told you, Tweed, but I'm Military Intelligence.'

'She mentioned it in passing. You don't have to worry. In my job I have to be very discreet. Also at times I have a shocking memory.'

He sipped coffee, leaving the field to Paula. She was in a better position to ask questions. Rosewater persisted in addressing Tweed.

'You said your job was security?'

'Security,' Tweed agreed, and again left it at that.

'Would this be a good moment to tell you what

happened in Suffolk?' Paula intervened. 'Or would you sooner not have the details?'

'Tell me everything. I'll feel better for knowing . . .'

He turned to her, listened with an intent expression as she gave him an edited version, again leaving out any reference to Park Crescent, as she had with Chief Inspector Buchanan in London. Rosewater, ignoring his breakfast, watched her until she'd concluded.

'. . . so the police arrived and took charge. Eventually I drove back home to try and get my mind off the whole experience.'

'Did you see the murderer – even though I suppose he wore one of these Balaclavas?' Rosewater asked.

'I had a good view from the treetop. I'm not sure. I was busy trying to hide myself from the men with guns.'

'I see.' He broke a roll, automatically piled butter and marmalade on a chunk, chewed it with a thoughtful expression. 'I think I'll visit Aldeburgh as soon as I can,' he said eventually. 'I was appalled I couldn't attend her funeral. I was involved in a very important check on a possible suspect – a saboteur, I'll call him. That was inside Germany.'

'I was there,' Paula said quietly. 'I laid a wreath for you. Do you want to see her grave?'

'No!' Rosewater showed emotion for the first time. 'I don't think I could bear that. I want to remember Karin as she was. Are the police anywhere near tracking down the swine who killed her?'

'Nowhere near, as far as we know,' Tweed commented. 'I was wondering how you could visit Suffolk, tied down as you are in Germany. You could take leave, I suppose?'

Rosewater dabbed at his strong mouth with his napkin as he glanced across the room at the brunette and looked away. She was still staring at him, tilting her crossed leg provocatively up and down.

'I have a strange job, Tweed. You could call it a roving

commission. To locate the people I'm after I can travel anywhere in Europe, often incognito, as now. I shall make it my business to visit Aldeburgh as soon as I can.'

'When you do, Victor,' Paula suggested, 'call me before you leave Germany at this number.' She scribbled on a notepad she'd extracted from her shoulder bag. 'If I'm not in leave a message on the answerphone. If you want me to – but only if – I'll come with you to Aldeburgh.'

'Thank you.' He put his arm round her shoulder. 'I'd appreciate your company on such a trip. I will phone before I come.' He looked at Tweed. 'And where are you off to, now? Or does that question come under the heading of indiscreet?'

'Not at all. London,' Tweed lied smoothly. 'You say you travel all over Europe. What do you think of the trouble building up in France? Specifically, in Bordeaux?'

'Yes, Europe is my playground,' Rosewater agreed. 'A battlefield more than a playground. Germany is mainly my theatre of operation. As to Bordeaux, I haven't had time to read any papers.' He checked his watch. 'Soon I'll have to leave.'

'Just before we go,' Tweed said, leaning over the table, keeping his voice down. 'In my job I have recently heard rumours of an ace assassin operating on the continent. Name of Kalmar.'

Rosewater used one hand to scoop crumbs off the table into the other. He dropped them on to his plate and studied Tweed.

'So you've heard of him. They call him the Ghost in the Shadows. No one knows his nationality, where he's come from, where he's based – if anywhere. He reminds me of a moving target. I've a funny feeling that some time during my work I may encounter Kalmar. Twice I've just missed him by a whisker. Provided with an address, I go there and find the bird has already flown.'

'Interesting.' Tweed stood up, insisted on paying the bill.

'You've left your lighter,' Paula said as they began leaving. She picked it up.

'Observant lady, and thank you,' responded Rosewater, pocketing the lighter.

It was, thought Paula, the only outward sign that he had been upset by her story. He wasn't the kind of man who normally overlooked anything, she felt certain.

As they walked out of the restaurant Tweed glanced at the brunette who still sat smoking a cigarette with a cup of coffee in front of her. She stared boldly at Rosewater as they left. Certainly an attractive woman, Tweed thought.

The taxi he had ordered for the airport was waiting. They said goodbye to Rosewater, who hugged Paula and thanked her for her help. While the driver was walking round to his seat after opening the rear door, Paula glanced out at Rosewater. He was standing outside the entrance, tall and handsome. Tweed followed her gaze as Rosewater waved and she waved back, then the taxi was moving. Paula looked at the expression on Tweed's face.

'You're thinking what I am. Victor would make a good recruit for Park Crescent.'

'You will persist in believing you can read my mind,' he chided her. 'But he's bright. The way he dodged my question about Bordeaux. What you'd expect from a top flight Military Intelligence officer. I should know.'

'I wonder what he is really doing?'

'From the little he said, infiltrating the IRA cells operating against British bases in Germany. Now, we should find out what is really happening. Within a couple of hours we'll be in Paris. With Lasalle – I called him briefly from the airport after we landed from Geneva.'

'And I wonder how Bob Newman is faring,' Paula mused.

8

At Arcachon, about thirty miles west of Bordeaux, the anchorage, triangular in shape, is almost entirely closed off from the fury of the Atlantic by a narrow peninsula which forms a barrier. The only entrance, to the south, is a narrow opening between the tip of the peninsula and an island.

Isabelle was well muffled against the piercing wind, clad in a heavy knee-length trench coat and a hood pulled over her head. By her side walked Newman, wearing the new clothes he had purchased at several local shops. He wore a black beret, a dark French over-coat, and training shoes. They walked past the Casino de la Plage and out on to the exposed promenade. It was deserted and the gale beat at them with full force. Isabelle pointed to a jetty.

'The Jetée d'Eyrac. That's where in summer the boats leave for Cap-Ferret. Further along to the east is the port. You can see the boats sheltering there.'

Newman stared into the distance where a forest of masts swayed drunkenly under the blast of the wind. The previous night Isabelle had guided him to a small hotel near the Gare, had then been driven to her sister's apartment behind the front.

'Do you have to leave today, Bob?' she asked wistfully.

'Definitely. There are things I have to find out. I rely on you to stay here until I contact you at your sister's. On no account go anywhere near Bordeaux.'

'If you say so.' She jutted her chin against the wind to show her disappointment. 'In summer you wouldn't recognize the place. Luxurious yachts from all over the world come here with their rich owners. There is even one strange ship with its hull cut in two.'

'Cut in two?' Newman was instantly alert. 'Can you describe it more clearly?'

'I don't know much about ships. All I can say is it's a big luxurious job.'

'Name?'

'No idea.'

'How often does it come in here?' Newman persisted.

'I don't know. But I can tell you that unlike most of the millionaire-type private ships it doesn't just arrive in the summer season. I've seen it heading for the port at various times of the year. Including now – in November.'

'And that's unusual?'

'Very. Millionaire yachts turn up here in the summer. There's the right atmosphere. Topless girls on the beach – sometimes bottomless, too. The Casino is booming. And the night club, the Etoile. I went there once at my sister's insistence. Never again.'

'What happened?'

'An English lord made a heavy pass at me. Wouldn't take no. Seemed to think every French girl was just dying to get laid by his Lordship. I should be able to remember his name.'

They moved closer inland as waves began to hurl themselves against the promenade, splashing spume over the wall. Their force was so great Newman could have sworn the promenade shuddered when a storm wave hit.

'It's not usually like this,' Isabelle commented. 'I think we ought to get back.'

'I'm going to my car now. I have to move on. Stay in Arcachon, Isabelle.' He decided to drive home his plea regardless of her feelings. 'Remember what happened to

Henri in Bordeaux. And they know you exist.'

'Lord Dane Dawlish,' she said suddenly. 'That was the man who made a pass at me at the Etoile.'

Newman drove back to Bordeaux at speed under a sky heavy as lead. The low clouds scudded east like drifts of grey smoke. Before leaving his Arcachon hotel he had phoned the airport, booked a flight to Paris on his open ticket. He had also booked a flight from Paris to Heathrow. First, he'd call at the Pullman Hotel to pick up his case. He wasn't worried about the old second-hand case he'd left at the *pension*: also he had paid for his miserable room for a fortnight in advance.

He was approaching the Gare St Jean when he ran into a traffic jam. Vehicles, bumper to bumper, were not moving. He checked his watch. Reasonable time yet to catch his Air Inter flight to Paris. The driver of a car next to him leaned out of his window to speak to Newman.

'Don't go into the centre. A lot of trouble there.'

'What kind of trouble?'

The traffic was moving before the other driver could reply. Newman shrugged. Trouble was becoming a way of life in France. He had passed the Place de la Victoire when he saw there was no traffic ahead. Instead the street was filled with a sinister-looking mob. He swung his wheel, drove down a side street and parked his Renault well away from the main street.

Locking the Renault, he ran back the way he had come, peered out, saw the mob seemed even larger. A sign advertised a bar on the first floor. He ran up the steps, entered a crowded room, ordered a Pernod to have a glass in his hand, slithered between men and women chattering excitedly until he reached a window overlooking the main street.

Below a mob of Balaclava-masked men waving clubs

and bottles were shouting slogans. *Pour France . . . Pour France . . . Pour France? Oui! . . . Juif? Non!!!*

The inflamatory chant went on. *For France? Yes. The Jew? No!!!* Holding his glass, Newman went on watching. He had the distinct impression the chant was organized. The riot became more savage. Men stormed into a restaurant, tore down the lace curtains, upturned chairs with customers, throwing them to the floor. Men and women: it made no difference. Terror was loose on the streets.

Having wrecked the interior the rioters flooded out, seeking a fresh target. One man with an aerosol paint canister sprayed a word across the window from the street. In huge red letters the word *Juif!* disfigured the glass. On the fascia above was the owner's name. Bronstein.

Newman estimated over two hundred Balaclava-masked men were prowling the street when he saw the CRS van stop further up the street. The paramilitary had arrived to quell the berserk mob. Berserk? What followed was extraordinary.

The apparently wild mob moved into a series of separate units. Somewhere a bell like a strident alarm was bellowing its clangour non-stop. A warning? A signal? Instead of retreating, units of the mob ran towards the van where CRS men clad in black coats and visored helmets were emerging with clubs. Seven men in the mob produced stubby wide-barrelled pistols, aimed at the van.

The CRS troops were about to advance when the projectiles from the pistols hit the cobbles in front of them, sending up clouds of tear gas. The CRS men stumbled, coughing, some ramming their hands to their injured eyes. A second unit, also armed with similar pistols, aimed for the no man's land of deserted street between the CRS and the mob. More projectiles hit the area accurately. Black smoke billowed. Smoke bombs.

Below the bar inside which Newman stood a TV man with a camera was grabbed by two men, held as a third took the camera he hadn't yet used. The lens was aimed away from the mob, swivelled slowly across the wreck of shops, restaurants, bars. No pictures of the mob.

When he had finished using the camera, one of the thugs holding the TV cameraman clubbed the back of his head. The TV reporter was perched on the edge of the kerb. He slumped into the gutter. The camera was dumped into his lap.

The strident alarm bell had stopped ringing. The mob moved in ordered groups, like troops on an exercise, some vanishing down side streets. Others climbed inside large tradesmen's vans which had appeared from the direction of the Gare St Jean. The vehicles sped out of the area.

Suddenly the street was deserted. The CRS men, recovering from the tear gas onslaught, appeared through the curtain of smoke to find their targets gone. Newman opened the window cautiously, heard the boots of the CRS trampling across heaps of shattered glass. It looked like the aftermath of a battlefield.

There was a hush inside the bar as Newman sidled his way through the crowd, ran down the steps before the CRS arrived. He continued running up the side street, reached his Citroën, unlocked it, dived inside, drove away from the main street, heading for the airport.

He had intended calling at the Pullman Hotel to collect his few belongings. Now he decided to forget it. His one aim was to leave Bordeaux alive.

He doubted whether this was the only riot which was in full swing in the city. What he had seen had all the hallmarks of a carefully organized campaign of terror. Objectives: to scare the population witless. To demoralize them into a state where they would welcome any force which could bring strong government, law and

91

order. Anything which would allow them to live their normal lives in peace. It was a diabolical strategy.

He approached the airport cautiously, certain there would be watchers – even phoney DST men. And they'd probably have the registration number of his Citroën, which had to be handed back to car hire. Slowing down, he let traffic catch up with him. As he drove into the airport a queue of cars was ahead of him, disgorging passengers. Newman switched off, took out the keys, looked round.

Close by, a man in uniform stood waiting by an empty limousine. His cap band carried the name of a hotel. Newman reached for his case, climbed out, approached the chauffeur, speaking rapidly, a five-hundred franc note between his fingers.

'Excuse me, can you help? I'm going to miss my Lyons flight. I have to hand in that Citroën to the car hire people up there. Could you hand it in for me?' He winked. 'Trouble is I have the most accommodating girl waiting for me. She won't wait for the next flight . . .'

'What about payment?' the chauffeur demanded, eyeing the banknote.

'Nothing to pay. Paid in advance as usual . . .'

'Petrol?'

'I've used a lot less than I've already paid for.'

Newman extended the folded note.

'It's a lot but the smallest I've got. And what is waiting for me in Lyons is worth it.'

'My pleasure, sir . . .'

The banknote vanished inside the chauffeur's clothing. He ran to the Citroën and Newman hurried into the airport, then slowed down. Two men in trenchcoats with hats stood erect by a café. Stood too erect, more a military stance. With his beret pulled well down, Newman strolled to the counter, had his ticket verified, left his case at the check-in counter, walked to the departure point for his Paris flight.

He only relaxed when the Air Inter machine took off. And he had no intention of lingering in Paris. A flight straight back to London at the earliest possible moment. As the ground receded, a flat plain of green and grey segments, he hoped to God Isabelle would be safe in Arcachon.

9

The Paris headquarters of French counter-espionage – the DST – is located in an obscure side street few tourists ever notice. This is despite the fact that the rue des Saussaies, a narrow winding street off the rue du Faubourg St Honoré, is close to the Elysée Palace, residence of the President of France.

The entrance is a stone archway leading to a cobbled yard with only two uniformed policemen giving a clue that this building is the key to the protection of the French Republic.

Tweed and Paula were seated in the cramped office of the chief of the DST, who was standing while he poured coffee. René Lasalle was a tall, heavily-built man in his forties. A dynamo of energy, he placed the cups in front of his guests, darted round his desk to sit behind it. He studied Tweed from under thick brows through horn-rimmed spectacles, his eyes alert and quick-moving. 'A man for all seasons,' Tweed had once described him, 'and especially in a major crisis.'

'I'm glad you brought Paula with you,' Lasalle began. He gave her a half-smile. 'An experienced woman can detect something vital a man might miss.'

'What is the situation?' asked Tweed, determined to hear his host's comments before he made any of his own.

'Critical. Soon to be catastrophic. For France – and maybe for the whole of Europe.'

'You're not usually so melodramatic.'

'First tell me where you two have been,' Lasalle suggested.

'Geneva, then Basle. From Basle straight here.'

'So Robert Newman is operating on his own in Bordeaux.'

Tweed was rarely taken aback. Even now his expression gave nothing away. Paula was equally staggered and tried to keep her own expression neutral as she crossed her shapely legs.

'Is Newman all right?' Tweed asked quietly.

'I would say he is now. Two of my men spotted him as he boarded a plane at Bordeaux airport for Paris . . .'

He excused himself as the phone rang. Listening for a moment he said, '*Merci*,' and replaced the receiver.

'Newman is moving fast. I sent men to meet his aircraft here at Orly. He took a cab to Charles de Gaulle Airport and is aboard a flight for London.'

'You said *now* a few moments ago, referring to Newman. Why?' asked Tweed.

'When he arrived at Bordeaux Airport he was dressed like a Frenchman. My operative who spotted Newman had once met him. His clothing suggests to my suspicious mind he was evading pursuit by someone. Possible?'

'He flew to Bordeaux with a commission from the German newsmagazine, *Der Spiegel*. To interview General Charles de Forge.'

Lasalle raised his eyebrows. 'Our Mr Newman is a brave man. France is about to experience an earthquake. And I'm convinced the man organizing it is General Charles de Forge, who sees himself as the new de Gaulle. I would say a pseudo-de Gaulle.'

'Can you explain that in more detail?' Tweed asked. 'And did you find out why my agent, operating under the name Henri Bayle, was arrested by the DST?'

'One question at a time, please. Excuse me ...' He answered the phone again, then spoke rapidly in French. Paula got the gist of it. Lasalle was ordering a new team of twenty DST men to leave for Bordeaux at once.

'You're reinforcing your people in Bordeaux,' Paula commented. 'Sorry if I sound interfering, but I couldn't help hearing what you said.'

Lasalle smiled at her. 'Of course, the pressure is such I'd forgotten for a moment your French is better than my English.'

'Nothing wrong with your English. Again, my apologies.'

'Not necessary.' Lasalle waved his hands. 'Now your questions, Tweed. First, when Bayle was taken from the Bar Miami and later murdered at the Gare St Jean there was not one single genuine DST operative in the Bordeaux area. I should know – I'm aware of the location of every DST man under my command. The men who took Bayle were impersonators.' A bite came into his normally soft tone. 'I do not find that amusing – which is one reason why I am flooding that city with my men.'

'And the other reason?' Tweed enquired.

'May I come to that later. I have been in touch myself with the Prefect of Bordeaux. The police there have come up with nothing so far. But he told me a curious story. He had an anonymous phone call. It reported a Berliet truck of the type used by the CRS would be found at the bottom of a gorge well outside Bordeaux. With bodies inside. A rough indication of the location was given by the caller.'

'Curious, as you say,' Tweed agreed. 'They found it?'

'No! No truck, no bodies. But they located the bridge described ...' He arched his hand in a hump-back. 'The police found the bridge, partly collapsed and one wall in the gorge.' He paused. 'They also found traces of a very heavy tracked vehicle. The type of vehicle used by the Army. To be specific, by the Engineering Section of the Third Corps. Only such a machine would be able to lift and transport away a Berliet truck.'

'You're checking with General de Forge?' Tweed pressed.

'Why? I have no solid evidence. No witnesses. So it becomes merely another mysterious incident added to my dossier on de Forge.' He looked at Paula. 'Another fact in that dossier is the existence of de Forge's English mistress at the Villa Forban near Third Corps' GHQ. A Jean Burgoyne. Comes from some nowhere place I'd never heard of in East Anglia.' He checked the dossier. 'Here it is – Aldeburgh.'

Paula forced herself not to stiffen. She began reciting a catalogue of facts.

'Jean Burgoyne. A blonde beauty. Comes from landed gentry in Lincolnshire. Walked out of the London season because she said "London society is such a bloody bore." I quote her. Reputed to have a very high IQ. A bit wild and independent-minded. Likes adventurous living.'

'The Villa Forban,' Lasalle repeated. 'Owned by de Forge, used as a secret hideaway for meetings with the infamous *Cercle Noir*.'

'What's that?' Tweed enquired. 'And it sounds to me you have an informant planted in de Forge's camp.'

'Did I say so?' Lasalle raised his eyebrows. 'Now, we will take some lunch at a Swiss restaurant near the edge of the Place de la Madeleine. Afterwards I will tell you about the Black Circle . . .'

In her bedroom at the Villa Forban Jean Burgoyne sat in front of her dressing table, clad in only a silk dressing-gown, unbelted at her slim waist. De Forge, she guessed, was about to engage in some frenetic activity.

It was only midday and was his second visit to her bed in twelve hours – always a sign that something big was under way. It was as though he felt the need for her in times of crisis. On a drum table by the window lay his leather dispatch case.

De Forge emerged from the shower, completed towelling his lean frame. He dressed quickly in his uniform and then his eyes fell on the dispatch case. He froze for a second, then completed his dressing.

Normally he handed the dispatch case to Major Lamy before entering the villa. But it had started snowing when he arrived this time and he'd hurried inside, depositing the case on the table. He walked slowly to the dressing table, his hypnotic eyes staring at hers in the mirror. She ignored his gaze after a second, continued applying face cream. His hands gripped her shoulders, slithered the gown off them, exposing her well-rounded breasts as the cloth slipped to her lap.

'Not again, Charles,' she said in her slightly husky voice. 'Time you went. And I'm flying home for a few days in England. Today.'

The grip on her shapely shoulders tightened. Jean never showed any fear of de Forge, a quality she suspected which added to her attraction for him. His voice was dangerously quiet.

'I left my dispatch case on the table over there. It is not exactly in the position I left it. I have an eye for detail . . .'

'Your eye must be slipping.'

The grip tightened more, his fingers pressing through the white flesh to the bone.

'You looked at the papers inside while I was in the shower.'

'Take your hands off me, you fool,' she replied with equal quiet. 'You think I'm interested in your stuffy papers? You're becoming bloody paranoid – spies every-where. And,' she continued calmly, 'if you hit me again I'll sock you with this brush . . .' Her right hand grasped the handle. 'Now push off with that creep, Lamy, and play your silly war games.'

'Why are you flying to England?' he demanded as he released his grip, stood back away from her.

'Because I want to, Charles.'

This time she had insisted on using the shower first. Now she pulled on her tights, dropped a slip over her head, put on a black form-hugging knee-length dress, tucked her small feet into court shoes, fastened a string of pearls round her neck. All in record time.

'Why do you want to go back to England?' de Forge persisted. 'You're always flying off somewhere – like a dragonfly. I may need you here.'

'Because I like to visit my uncle, to see my home. You will just have to contain your desire. If you're desperate you could pay Josette a visit. How long is it since you've seen your wife? And when you do go to her apartment do you take that damned dispatch case there, darling?'

De Forge's mouth tightened. He moved towards her with a deliberate step. Again, she held up a minatory finger.

'Remember what I said when you struck me last time. I meant it. And why do you always choose women whose names begin with the letter "J"?'

De Forge asserted his natural will-power, refused to respond to her mockery. He was putting on his képi when someone rapped quietly on the door.

'Come in,' Jean called out to show who was in control.

The door opened slowly and Lieutenant André Ber-thier, fair haired and good looking, his képi tucked respectfully under his arm, stepped into the room, careful to look straight at de Forge.

'Excuse me, General, but Major Lamy sent me in as you asked to be reminded of the time.'

'Maybe the lieutenant would like a glass of champagne?' Jean suggested, moving towards the ice bucket beside the rumpled bed.

'He would not,' de Forge replied in a cold voice. 'He is on duty.'

'You do have some handsome men on your staff, Charles,' Jean whispered.

She stroked her blond hair across a shoulder, staring at Berthier. She studied his build, his strong young face. Berthier, aware of her scrutiny, stared at the wall.

'Competence is the only qualification for my choice,' de Forge responded in the same chilly tone.

He marched swiftly to the door, picked up the dispatch case. Her remark about taking his dispatch case to Josette's apartment in Bordeaux had alerted him: he *did* take the case with him on his occasional visits.

Jean watched him leave with grim amusement. Always arouse a little jealousy when your lover was departing – it kept you in his thoughts. Hearing the outer door close, she ran to the bedroom door, opened it a fraction. Yes, they had gone. She went to the phone, dialled a number.

Outside it was arctic cold as snowflakes drifted down. Standing by the bullet-proof limousine, Major Lamy reached out to open the rear door. It seemed to have iced up. His large strong hand gave it a powerful twist, the door opened, de Forge brushed flakes off his uniform, sat inside. Lamy closed the door as Berthier sat in the front passenger seat next to the chauffeur, ran round the back, climbed in beside de Forge. The limousine sped down the drive, the wheels spurting up gravel.

De Forge glanced at Lamy. The Intelligence Chief often reminded the General of a fox with his long face, his expression, his pointed jaw. De Forge closed the sliding glass panel, shutting them off from the front compartment so Berthier could not hear him.

'Why do you choose Berthier as bodyguard?'

'Because,' Lamy explained, 'he is an expert with machine-pistols. He has one now by his side. He scores higher than anyone else on the range.'

'Kalmar did a good job with that spy, Henri Bayle,' de Forge commented, switching the subject suddenly – a favourite tactic to keep his officers off balance. 'I wonder who he really is. You must have some idea.'

'No idea.' Lamy gazed out of the window where the snow had become a white curtain. 'He keeps his identity a close secret. Communication only by phone – between two public call boxes. Payment in Swiss banknotes. Inside an envelope placed inside a small leather pouch. Always a different drop for the pouch. Always at a remote spot in the country – a location which can be watched for miles all round.'

'You'd almost think he had military training,' de Forge decided. 'Still, he does a perfect job. That's all that matters.'

'I have a different problem you might wish to consider,' Lamy said quickly, changing the subject. 'We are running low on the secret projects fund. And we need more of the special missiles – and the nerve gas they are armed with.'

'Don't worry. I have received a coded signal from our supplier. More funds are on the way, more missiles, more nerve gas.'

'When will the ship arrive?'

'Soon. I will tell you when I have a definite date.'

'And the pick-up point is Arcachon? As before?'

'Yes, Lamy, it is. There is one more task calling for immediate action. I want Jean Burgoyne followed when she leaves the villa. Reports on where she goes, who she meets. A complete rundown. Berthier is fluent in English. Stop the car, give him my orders.'

100

'Why now, General? How can Berthier follow her in his uniform? She will recognize him.'

'Your brain is getting duller, Lamy . . .'

De Forge glanced behind the limo where outriders in uniform had joined the cavalcade to bring up the rear. More outriders preceded the car. They had taken up station as soon as de Forge's limo emerged from the entrance to the Villa Forban. Jean Burgoyne had complained she didn't want a lot of rowdy motor-cyclists on the property.

'She is leaving soon for the airport,' de Forge continued. 'Send one outrider back to stay under cover, watch the villa gates, and follow her discreetly if she drives away. He can use his radio to contact Berthier. What happens to Berthier? He takes over one of the motor-cycles, rides like hell to GHQ, changes into civilian clothes. I've seen him in mufti. He wears a hat which hides his fair hair, sports tinted glasses. Give him some money. Stop the car. *Now*, Lamy . . .!'

The major alighted from the car after telling Berthier to get out. He spoke rapidly to the lieutenant. With his back to de Forge, he took out his wallet, extracted three 1,000-Swiss franc notes. The equivalent of well over £1,000.

'That's dealt with,' he reported as he sank back into his seat, his face raw from the brief exposure to the elements.

The car with its outrider escort began to move again. De Forge was thinking he'd also have to arrange to have his wife, Josette, put under surveillance. In case Paris had infiltrated Third Corps the answer was more spies.

10

'General Charles de Forge is the most sinister political figure France has seen this century,' said Lasalle.

Paula looked at Tweed, who merely nodded, encouraging the DST chief to continue. They had returned from the Swiss restaurant and again sat in Lasalle's cramped office.

Paula had grasped Tweed's tactics. He was still at the stage of gathering data before returning to London, before deciding how to deploy his forces. A phase now familiar to her.

'He is inflaming French public opinion against Germany,' Lasalle went on. 'Dubois, head of the *Pour France* party, is his puppet, the ventriloquist's dummy. It is de Forge who supplies the angle for Dubois to take. It is outrageous – Germany is the most peace-loving nation in all Europe. De Forge is whipping up artificial fear of the new unified Germany.'

'Why?' Tweed asked. 'What is de Forge's objective?'

'To become the next President of France . . .'

'Has he a hope in hell? A general?'

Lasalle gave his wry smile. 'There is a precedent – General de Gaulle . . .'

'Who took power at a time of national emergency when the government became desperate.'

'Which is precisely the scenario de Forge is successfully recreating. Disorder, fighting in the streets. Clearly you have not grasped the significance of what has happened in Bordeaux.'

'Why Bordeaux?'

'Ah, Bordeaux! There you put your finger on it. You see, Bordeaux was the city which witnessed three French crises – and two humiliating defeats at the hands of Germany. In 1871 when Bismarck's armies destroyed us, annexed Alsace-Lorraine. In 1914 when the Paris government panicked, fled to Bordeaux temporarily. Above all, in 1940 when, as you know, the premier, Paul Reynaud, fled – again to Bordeaux – with his government. And surrendered to Hitler.'

'I still don't see why de Forge should launch his campaign from there.'

'He asked to be transferred to the command of the Third Corps, partly because it was based close to that city. De Forge is using Bordeaux as the symbol of French humiliation. What better city to launch a revenge campaign from? To make France the most powerful nation on the continent?'

'You said "partly". What was the other reason?'

'Because there he is close to his friend and ally, General Lapointe, commander of the *force de frappe* – France's atomic strike force.'

'And his request for this transfer was accepted?'

'Another ally is the Minister of Defence, Louis Janin. De Forge has Janin in his pocket.'

'Surely the President could do something, must know what is going on?'

'Ah, the Elysée!' Again the wry smile. 'The President is treading carefully. He cannot yet believe that a mere general would challenge him. And *Pour France* is worrying him with its growing popularity. Throw out the Algerians, the Arabs, Dubois thunders.'

'It has hardly become a national emergency,' Tweed insisted, determined to make Lasalle prove his case.

'We are close to it. The riots in Bordeaux. I hear that down there people . . .' He broke off as an aide rushed in, laid a long sheet of paper in front of Lasalle while apologizing for the intrusion, then rushed out after glancing at his chief's visitors. Lasalle's normally relaxed expression became grim. He looked at Tweed.

'You said there was no national emergency. This decoded fax has just come in. There have been major riots in Lyons. First reports indicate over one thousand five hundred casualties and the centre wrecked. Rioters were wearing Balaclava masks and not a single one has been arrested. The CRS were held back with tear gas, smoke bombs. Every hour it is coming closer to Paris.'

'So the plan is working.'

'Yes, Tweed. *De Forge*'s plan is working. He is destabilizing France, creating conditions for revolution. Who will save France? I give you one guess.'

'Tell me about the *Cercle Noir* you mentioned earlier.'

'The Black Circle.' Lasalle threw out both hands in a gesture of helplessness. 'A strong rumour that it is a small club planning all this. My investigations suggest – no proof – that its members are General de Forge, General Masson, Army Chief of Staff, General Lapointe, Louis Janin – Minister of Defence here in Paris. And Emile Dubois.'

'Any other members?' Tweed enquired.

'Perhaps one more. They have code-named him *Oiseau . . .*'

'Bird?' Paula interjected. 'A curious code name.'

'We believe he comes and goes, that he is not only providing de Forge with funds to finance his campaign – but also secretly transporting to him advanced weapons not in his official armoury. Perhaps even lethal nerve gas.'

'Any idea who Bird could be?' Tweed pressed.

'None at all. Incidentally, do not mention any of our conversation to anyone – including a Cabinet Minister or a member of my staff. De Forge has spies everywhere.'

Tweed was stunned. He'd never heard the DST chief talk like this before. Paula reacted crisply.

'So, de Forge has a bandwagon rolling and a lot of people are climbing aboard?'

'You express it well,' Lasalle agreed. 'Let us hope it is not already too late.'

'On the other hand,' Paula suggested, 'I expect you also have your informants well placed. Otherwise how would you know so much about what is happening inside de Forge's camp?'

'I do have informants,' Lasalle replied cautiously. 'But it is not only the situation here which worries me. Strange developments are taking place inside Germany. An extreme right-wing group, *Siegfried*, is operating underground across the Rhine. This helps de Forge to portray the new Germany as a threat.'

'Is there no one – apart from the President – high up you can trust?' Tweed enquired.

'One strong man. Pierre Navarre, Minister of the Interior, and ultimately my boss. He detests de Forge. His attitude has one disadvantage. The President, I know, feels all will be well so long as Navarre is in the Cabinet to counter Louis Janin, who tells the President there is no danger of a coup.'

'So inertia rules?'

'Exactly. Before I come to a delicate subject, is there anything else you wish to know?'

'Yes,' Paula said promptly. 'Can you give us data on de Forge's personal life? That could be his weak point.'

Lasalle stood up, opened a wooden cupboard behind him attached to the wall, revealed a safe. Turning the combination dial from a code he carried in his head, he swung open the metal door, took out a thick green dossier, placed it on his desk.

'You've been busy,' Tweed observed as Lasalle opened the dossier.

'De Forge is becoming an obsession with me,' Lasalle admitted.

Paula glanced round the office on the first floor as the Frenchman searched the file. The furniture was ancient – a cheap wooden desk, the surface well-worn; all the cupboards were also shabby wood; the windows could do with a clean; the curtains hadn't seen a laundry for a long time. Yet when they had entered the old building she'd glimpsed through an open door on the ground floor a room full of computers, fax machines, shimmering green screens. DST was an odd mix of the old and advanced technology.

Lasalle addressed himself to Paula as he began speaking. 'De Forge has been married for ten years to Josette, a Parisienne society woman. She has an apartment in Bordeaux, another here in Passy. She was left a fortune by her father, who was Minister of Defence when de Forge married her. Her picture . . .'

Paula studied the photograph of an elegant brunette, seated on a sofa, wearing a short skirt with her superb legs crossed. A lady who knew how to display her assets.

'Attractive, intelligent, knows what she wants,' she hazarded.

'An excellent character analysis,' Lasalle replied, impressed. 'And she wishes to be the wife of the President of France, her husband.'

'Is he faithful to her?'

'My God! No! De Forge has an insatiable appetite for the good things of life. At the head of the list he places women. He has an English mistress, as I mentioned before lunch. She spends time at the Villa Forban, near Third Corps GHQ. May I introduce you to Jean Burgoyne . . .'

Paula studied the photo he had extracted from the dossier. She recognized the glamorous girl with long blonde hair. Seated in a canvas chair on a lawn with a backdrop of dense evergreens, Jean Burgoyne wore a tight-fitting blue sweater which revealed her enticing figure and her wide mouth was smiling, a smile of wicked amusement.

106

'The picture is a bit blurred,' Paula commented.

'Taken secretly with a telescopic lens.'

'And I suppose Josette doesn't know she exists?' Paula remarked, phrasing her point carefully.

'You believe that!' Lasalle gave a mocking laugh, relaxing briefly for the first time since they'd met. 'I have proof Josette is well aware of de Forge's many little peccadilloes. Is that the word?'

'That's the word, René,' Paula said and chuckled. 'She puts up with them?'

'She ignores them. I told you – she wishes to remain the wife of the man who will become President of France. A most ambitious woman. She also has her affairs – and always with men who could be useful to de Forge.'

'Quite a lady, if that's the word,' Paula commented.

Lasalle extracted a fresh photo. 'And this is Major Jules Lamy, Chief of Intelligence to de Forge. Some say he is de Forge's *éminence grise*, his evil genius. Lamy is a keep fit fanatic. They say he runs ten miles every day, no matter what the weather.'

Tweed leaned towards Paula to look at the picture. A foxy-faced man, strong features, staring eyes. Paula grimaced, handed back the photo.

'Don't like the look of him at all. Wouldn't like to bump into him on a dark night.'

'Finally, this is Sergeant Rey. I have two copies – take one. If the formidable Robert Newman is thinking of returning to Bordeaux, best he knows about Rey.'

'What is his function?' Tweed asked as Paula leaned to look at the photo.

Rey wore the uniform and emblems of a sergeant. He had a gnome-like face, was of uncertain age, but his eyes were cunning and cruel. Again the picture was slightly blurred.

'He is officially de Forge's batman,' Lasalle said, his tone grim. 'The important thing to remember is that he is a genius at constructing booby-traps. Inventive as the devil.'

'De Forge sounds to specialize in devils,' Tweed commented half-humorously to lighten the atmosphere.

He handed the photo to Paula who tucked it carefully inside a compartment in her shoulder bag. Lasalle slowly drummed his fingers on the desk, staring at Tweed.

'Now I come to the delicate subject. I know how much you value and look after your agents. Henri Bayle who was murdered in Bordeaux. He was taken from a place he worked at called the Bar Miami by two fake DST officers. The autopsy report has come through by fax. A detailed report.'

'What does it tell us?' Tweed asked quietly.

'That he was strangled. The aspect I find intriguing about the report . . .' He paused, glanced at Paula. 'I hope I don't sound cold-blooded?'

'Not in the least,' Paula said briskly. 'We need all the data we can get.'

'The pathologist,' Lasalle continued, 'records in his report that the strangler was a professional. An odd word to use but he goes on to explain. The act of strangulation was swift and very efficient. Thumbs were pressed against Bayle's wind-pipe and held there until he expired. After death – and this is curious – the murderer savagely bruised the neck. Sounds like a sadist, even a psychopath.'

'More likely an attempt to cover his professional expertise,' Tweed responded.

'It is rumoured – no more – that the killer was a man we have heard of. Kalmar.'

'Where did the rumours come from?'

'We think Kalmar himself advertises his existence – to increase his reputation, and therefore his fees, for such assignments.'

'Origins?'

'Shrouded in mystery.' Lasalle waved his hands again. 'Some say he is a Mittel-European. Others that he has come from the East – the Balkans. Like Interpol, we have no description, no clue as to his nationality – but he is alleged to be fluent in several languages. Again, which ones we don't know.'

'In other words, René,' Tweed smiled, 'we know damn-all about Kalmar so far.'

'He will make a mistake sooner or later.'

'After creating more corpses,' Paula suggested.

Tweed glanced at his watch, reached for his overcoat.

'We have a flight to catch. Back to London. For your help, for the information, many thanks, René. We must keep in close touch. We shall be working on this day and night. It is just possible the solution to what is going on lies in England . . .'

11

On a stormy November night all roads led to Aldeburgh, the strange old town on the Suffolk coast of Britain.

Tweed and Paula had landed at London Airport, hurried to their flats for a change of clothes, had met up again at Park Crescent. From his office Tweed made a series of quick phone calls, told Monica to hold the fort, then left the building with Paula, each carrying a suitcase. Getting into his Ford Escort, he drove them out of the city, across the flatlands of Essex in the dark and on into Suffolk. They arrived at the Brudenell Hotel on the front to find the place almost deserted of guests at that time of the year.

Paula had found it a weird experience to return to the scene of her terrifying experience with her dead friend, Karin Rosewater. Tweed had been so active she had kept quiet until he invited her to his large room on the first floor. He had summoned what he called a 'council of war' and they drank coffee while they waited for the others to arrive.

Newman had been phoned, back from Bordeaux and Paris for only a few hours. Marler was on the way, bringing with him in their own cars two more SIS men – Harry Butler and Pete Nield, who often worked in tandem. Paula asked the question as they waited.

'Why did you tell Lasalle the solution might lie here in England?'

'One interesting and deadly – literally – fact. Your friend, Karin, was strangled by someone the Suffolk pathologist described as a professional. Remember what the autopsy report said?'

'How can I ever forget it?'

'Sorry, I put that too bluntly. Then in Paris René Lasalle gives us the gist of the Bordeaux pathologist's comments on how Francis Carey was murdered at the Gare St Jean. He used the same word – professional. He even went on to give almost precisely the same description of how Carey's murder was enacted.'

'I did actually notice,' Paula admitted, 'but I thought it must be a coincidence. You're not suggesting that . . .'

'The strangler in Suffolk is the same strangler in Bordeaux? I'm suggesting just that.'

Tweed reached into his breast pocket. He brought out a current British Airways timetable, opened it at a page with the corner turned down.

'I collected this before we left Park Crescent. The murder of Karin Rosewater took place in the evening. In the evening of the *following* day Francis Carey was murdered in exactly the same way in Bordeaux. This timetable shows a BA flight leaving Heathrow at 10.55, arriving Bordeaux 12.25. There's also another direct flight via Air France – leaves a little later but gets to Bordeaux mid-afternoon.'

'Aren't you letting your imagination run away with you?'

'The facts I've given have nothing to do with imagination – allied to two different pathologists' identical descriptions of the murder technique used.'

'Kalmar?' she ventured.

'A top assassin can move fast. Operating in Europe he'll know all the routes, flight times. It's part of his stock-in-trade.'

'Kalmar,' she repeated. 'A strange name.'

'Chosen deliberately – to conceal his real identity, his real nationality. One fact common to both pathologists' reports – the strangler has large hands.'

He broke off as the phone rang. Paula answered it, said come up now, put down the receiver.

'Newman has arrived. And so have Marler, Butler, and Nield. Good job you asked for extra chairs . . .'

The spacious bedroom had a wide bay window overlooking the North Sea. The curtains were drawn against the night but Paula could hear beyond the windows the insidious surge of the sea, the thump of waves hitting the beach with the incoming tide. When the four men had entered the room, found themselves seats, she poured coffee. Characteristically, Marler refused a chair, leaning against a wall while he lit a king-size cigarette.

Tweed wasted no time. He sketched in briefly what was happening in France and Germany, gave them the data supplied by Lasalle and Kuhlmann.

'We have to take action urgently,' he went on. 'I had a quick call from Lasalle after I'd arrived back at Park Crescent. More details of the Lyons riots had reached him. He said events were assuming the character of an insurrection. I suspect de Forge is only waiting for the trigger – some new event which will give him the excuse to move on Paris. Now, Bob, you learned something while you were in Bordeaux?'

111

'I learned a lot – all of which confirms what you've just said . . .'

Tersely, he described the hazards of his experience of his stay in Bordeaux. His interview with de Forge, the punishment well, his narrow escape when pursued by the Berliet truck. And Isabelle's ordeals.

'That's it,' he concluded.

'This Isabelle,' Paula asked, curious about the way he had described her, 'she's attractive?'

'I suppose she is,' Newman replied and said no more.

He fancies her, Paula thought. She sounds to be quite a girl. And she probably likes Bob, too.

'That riot you witnessed in Bordeaux,' Tweed said in a business-like tone. 'You conjured up a picture of a disciplined force – not a mob of hotheads. The way they out-manoeuvred the CRS, a skilled paramilitary force. Almost sounds as though they were well-trained troops under those damned Balaclavas.'

'Which was exactly the impression I got, watching from that upstairs bar,' Newman confirmed. 'I was about to make the same comment.'

'Anything else?'

'Some of the smaller rioters are probably members of *Pour France* – farmers, peasants, shopkeepers. But the big stuff, I'm convinced – after what I saw in Bordeaux – are de Forge's men disguised with those Balaclavas.'

'Then the situation is more than dangerous, it is explosive. And we have very little time left.'

Marler spoke for the first time, in his off-hand drawl. 'Then why, may I ask, are we all assembled here out in the backwoods of England?'

'Because this is where it all started – the murder of Karin Rosewater, the attempt to kill both women. Why? Because they had been caught exploring underwater off Dunwich. Something is going on up there.'

'Might be able to give you a start point,' Marler

112

continued. 'While you were all gallivanting abroad I drove around up here – as far as Dunwich and then up a bit further north to Southold. Visiting pubs. The people who frequent local pubs know things.'

'So what did you discover?'

'That the man financing the new underwater exploration of that sunken village, Dunwich, is a certain Lord Dane Dawlish.'

'A millionaire several times over,' Tweed mused after digesting Marler's information. 'And someone must be financing de Forge – Lasalle made that point. He'll need money to pay his men extra for creating the riots, to smooth palms liberally high up in Paris. It's a long shot – we need a link between Aldeburgh and Bordeaux. And we haven't got one – except for the similarity between the two murders. We need far more.'

'So it's probably helpful,' Marler remarked, 'that I wangled an invitation to a shooting party on Dawlish's estate at Grenville Grange.'

'How did you work that one?' Tweed asked.

'I was having a quick lunch at the Cross Keys – a very good pub further along the front from here. Behind the Moot Hall. At the next table was a bunch of tough-looking individuals, smartly dressed. Gabbing about a clay pigeon shoot at Dawlish's place. I got talking to them, put on an act, told them I was a stockbroker on holiday, that I could shoot clay pigeons out of the sky. They took the bait – a heavy type called Brand laid a bet with me. Five hundred quid, as he put it.'

'What do you do to win?' Newman asked. 'And maybe I could join the party.'

'I have to blast all my clay pigeons out of the sky. I'm going to lose. No point in letting them know about my marksmanship. You can come – if you insist. Brand said

113

bring friends if I wanted to. Dawlish, I gather, is very sociable. Likes big parties.'

'When?' Newman asked.

'Tomorrow. Turning up at Grenville Grange about eleven in the morning. They think I'm Peter Wood. I've a stockbroker pal in the City of that name. I phoned, asked him to cover for me. If they check, his secretary will confirm her boss, Wood, is away in Suffolk.'

Tweed leaned forward. 'Why such careful precautions?'

'Something phoney about them. Except for Brand, they don't look comfortable in their fancy country gear. An athletic gang, in their late twenties, early thirties.'

Tweed took from his breast pocket the well-filled wallet he always carried. Extracting ten fifty-pound notes he handed them to Marler.

'Your lost bet. I think you're wise to conceal your markmanship. It's another long shot – Dawlish. But there is a link there. Dawlish involved in underwater exploration at Dunwich. And those scuba divers who tried to kill both Paula and Karin.'

'And I'll join you,' Newman decided. 'Under my own name.'

'If you must,' Marler agreed, shrugging his shoulders.

'That's what I like.' Newman grinned. 'Enthusiasm.'

'I'd like to come, too,' Paula suggested. 'The editor of *Woman's Eye* is a friend of mine. And they'd like an interview for their feature *Men of Distinction*.'

'That would be overdoing it,' Newman objected.

'And,' Tweed warned her, 'supposing some of the thugs who pursued you from Dunwich in dinghies turned out to be among the group of characters Marler met at the Cross Keys? You could be recognized.'

'Don't agree,' Paula insisted. 'They only saw us under murky water with our masks on. Impossible to recognize anyone wearing one of those.'

'But while you were changing out of your wet-suits on

the beach,' Tweed recalled, 'you said those killers in the dinghies were approaching the shore.'

'Too far away to recognize me. It was dusk, too. I'd turn up quite on my own,' she informed Newman. 'So I won't know either of you. And,' she pounded on, 'you are getting there at eleven. I'll phone Dawlish and make an appointment for midday.'

'If you can . . .'

'Men are vain. Successful men are very vain, love to get their names in quality magazines. Bet I pull it off.'

'Under those circumstances,' Tweed decided reluctantly, 'I suppose it might be a good idea. We're so short of time the sooner we cross Dawlish off the list of suspects the better.'

'I'd say he fits like a glove,' Marler observed. 'You quoted Lasalle a few minutes ago as saying someone was secretly supplying nice General de Forge with arms. Dawlish has armaments factories. One of them could be in the woods between Snape Maltings and Orford.'

'How do you know that?' Tweed asked sharply.

'Because, as I told you, I drove round up here. On my way to Orford I passed a track leading up into the woods off a lonely road. The area was fenced off with an eight-foot high wire fence, electrified. Plates attached to the fence with a friendly warning. "Keep Out! Danger!" Plus skull and crossbones. The lot.'

'That's a long way from France – especially Bordeaux.'

Tweed blinked, gazed into the distance. Something he had heard Paula say on another occasion. What was it? Maybe it would come back to him.

'You're looking for a French link?' Newman enquired. 'Could be one downstairs inside this hotel. When I was approaching the elevator a youngish chap stubbed his toe on a step. I distinctly heard him mutter *Merde!* under his breath. He then asked me the way to the lounge in perfect English.'

115

'Describe him.'

'Late twenties, early thirties. Clean shaven. Walks very erect. Struck me as a military type. Wearing dark glasses – Lord knows why at this time of the year.' He glanced at Paula with a dry smile. 'Some women would describe him as handsome.'

'I must visit the bar,' Paula said promptly. 'Bet he finds his way there. After I call *Woman's Eye* for tomorrow.'

'I suppose we could have come to the right place,' Tweed thought aloud.

'You don't know how right you are,' Marler needled him. 'Chief Inspector Buchanan and Sergeant Warden are staying here. I had a brief encounter with Buchanan yesterday.'

'Why are they still here?'

'The Chief Constable has asked Buchanan to continue his investigations into Karin Rosewater's murder. The whole of Aldeburgh knows about him.'

'We can't let him get in the way.' Tweed stood up. 'The exact nature of de Forge's threat to Germany is vague – so even more menacing. We can't do much this evening. All of you have rooms I reserved for you from London. I want action tomorrow.'

'Where do we fit in?' asked the heavily-built Butler.

As usual, he had remained silent with his partner, Pete Nield. But both men had memorized every single word said.

'I was coming to you,' Tweed replied. 'Are you armed as I suggested?'

'Nice to know he can't tell,' the more extrovert Nield remarked, fingering his moustache.

Both men were clad in clean denims and windcheaters. Butler nodded, produced from his hip holster under his windcheater a 7.65mm Walther automatic. Nield showed his own Walther.

'Good,' Tweed approved. 'Because tomorrow I want

you to follow Newman and Marler discreetly to this Grenville Grange place. You are to act as guards, back-up in
case of trouble.'

'We expect trouble from a man like Dawlish?' queried
Marler sceptically.

'Monica drew up a dossier on him while we were away. I
skipped through it before I drove out with Paula. He built
up his empire from nothing – and used some dubious
methods on the way. Exercise the utmost caution. Paula,
see if you can find out who Newman's Frenchman is. It is
the first whiff of the French we've had in Suffolk.'

Paula, wearing a Chanel-style blue suit with a white blouse
and a pussy bow, walked into the bar as a tall slim girl with
a mane of blonde hair turned, a glass of champagne in her
hand, and collided with her.

Paula jumped aside and the spilt champagne just missed
her suit. Jean Burgoyne stared at the suit with horror.
Paula smiled reassuringly.

'It's all right. It went on the floor.'

'My God! I'm so sorry. How simply dreadfully clumsy of
me. Are you sure it isn't spoilt? That's Chanel, isn't it? You
look stunning.'

'You don't look so bad yourself. And this isn't an
original, I'm sorry to say. I made it myself.'

Jean Burgoyne did look stunning in a light green form-
fitting sheath dress which displayed her excellent figure to
full advantage. Two slim straps supported it over her bare,
well-shaped shoulders. Her greenish eyes studied Paula,
her wide mouth smiled.

'I'm Jean Burgoyne . . .'

'I'm Paula Grey, a freelance journalist on *Woman's
Eye* . . .'

Thinking quickly, Paula had decided it was best to stick
to the same story. In a small place like Aldeburgh you

117

never knew who knew who. She had instantly recognized the glamorous blonde and hoped she was on her own.

'I buy every issue,' Jean told her. 'The least I can do is get you a glass of champagne. That is, if like me, you're on your own.'

'As it happens, I am. I wasn't looking forward to a solitary evening . . .'

Paula took Jean Burgoyne's glass to a quiet corner table. She was puzzled. What was Burgoyne doing in this part of the world? Another French link: de Forge's mistress in Aldeburgh. And she was quite a girl, Paula thought. She moved gracefully and every man in the bar was watching her.

As she brought more champagne to the table Paula spotted the Frenchman with tinted glasses Newman had identified. He ordered a drink and sat alone, erect in his chair. He looked briefly at Burgoyne and then turned away. Burgoyne had sat next to Paula, raised her glass.

'Cheers! Paula! May I call you Paula? I'm Jean.'

'Please do. I'm ready for this.'

'Join the club.' She drank half the contents. 'I'm just back from France. Bordeaux, actually. I have a friend there. My uncle, who brought me up, lives in one of the houses at the back of Aldeburgh – he likes the seclusion of the place . . .' She went on talking in her low husky voice, used a hand to throw her mane back over her shoulder. 'My parents were killed in a road smash when I was six. He took over. He's eighty now. My father – Uncle's brother – would have been eighty-two. I was born late. All hell is breaking loose in France. I was telling my uncle about it. He's still got all his marbles. Used to be a Brigadier. In Military Intelligence.' She smiled roguishly. 'Sorry, I'm rattling on about myself. You will be thinking I'm trying to manoeuvre you into interviewing me.'

'Honestly, the thought hadn't crossed my mind. But you'd be a perfect subject.'

'Not me, Paula.' The roguish smile again. 'When I came down from Oxford I trained to be a barrister, then never practised at the Bar. A perfect subject? Not for *Woman's Eye*. I like men too much – I think you'd find my life a bit too spicy.'

'I do have a commission,' Paula explained. 'Tomorrow I interview Lord Dane Dawlish. I phoned him a few minutes ago. He sounded enthusiastic.'

Jean gave Paula an odd appraising look, drank out of her half-empty glass, put it down with equal care. Paula kept silent: she felt sure she'd by chance pressed a button.

'I was at a party at Grenville Grange when I met my French friend,' Jean said slowly. 'You'll have to watch Dawlish. You're attractive. He'll make a pass at you.'

'That was your experience?'

'You can say that again. Talk about having to fight off a wolf. Good luck. Put on plenty of clothes.'

Paula was trying to keep her face expressionless while she watched a tall handsome man enter the bar. It was Victor Rosewater.

All roads led to Aldeburgh . . .

12

Grenville Grange was perched on a peninsula projecting into the river Alde several miles inland from Aldeburgh. Near Iken Church, all the lights were on that evening as Lord Dane Dawlish sat in his study behind a Queen Anne desk talking to Joseph Brand.

Dawlish was of medium height, a powerfully built man

in his late fifties. He had a bull neck and a squarish head. Thick grey sideburns curled beside his ears and he was clean shaven. His nose and jowly jaw were pugnacious. His brown eyes had a challenging expression. He radiated physical energy and his manner was aggressive.

'I didn't get where I have by being polite to people who stood in my way,' was one of his favourite maxims.

'You checked out this Peter Wood who's joining us for the shoot tomorrow?' he demanded.

'Phoned his London office. His secretary said her chief wasn't available, was away in Suffolk.'

'So he could be pukka.'

Brand pursed his thick lips. A small man, wide-shouldered, weighing sixteen stone, he regarded everyone as a potential enemy. One of his large hands drummed silently on his knee below the desk as he sat facing his boss. In his late forties, he had a pear-shaped head, terminating in a full chin below a wide thin mouth.

'How much more information do we need?' Brand asked.

'As much as we can get. He's a stranger who struck up an acquaintance with you in that pub. I like to know who's prowling under my roof. And a five hundred bet is throwing money around. His entrance fee?'

'Stockbrokers make a lot of money,' Brand protested. 'Christ! I should know. They live off commissions.'

'And off suckers like you who play the markets which I don't.'

Caught on the raw, Brand forgot his position. The words were out of his mouth even as he knew he'd blundered.

'At least I don't waste money on women right, left, and centre . . .'

Dawlish drummed the hairy knuckles of his right hand on the desk slowly. He smiled, not a pleasant smile. His eyes stared straight at Brand's.

'You've overlooked something. I get a lot back for my

money. And I think you've overlooked who you're talking to. You can easily be replaced, Brand. Your sort come ten a penny.'

'I'm tired, sir. I've been working since five in the morning . . .'

'And what have you got to show for it?' Dawlish demanded brutally.

'My informant at the Brudenell reports a lot of new arrivals today. And this is November. One of them is Robert Newman, the foreign correspondent . . .'

'Who this Peter Wood phoned me about. On the excuse of thanking me in advance for having him at my shoot. What he really called about was to ask if he could bring Newman. As I told you earlier . . .'

'Which is someone else I checked on for you,' Brand said hastily.

'Don't bloody well interrupt me. A lot of people seem to be taking a sudden interest in me – and this is a critical time. In case you've forgotten.'

'Could be a coincidence . . .'

'I've survived by not believing in coincidences. On top of those people, a Paula Grey is coming to interview me. She sounded sexy on the phone. Could be a bonus for me there,' Dawlish added and grinned coarsely. 'Is the weapons consignment nearly ready?'

'Half the delivery is ready. The balance will be at the collection point soon.'

'And you're keeping a close eye on the met forecasts for the Bay of Biscay? The voyage to Arcachon can be a real bastard.'

'I record them hourly,' Brand assured his boss, relieved that he seemed in a more amiable mood.

'And the Cat will have completed its overhaul?'

'I checked with the skipper today. The Cat will be in good shape.'

'It had better be.'

121

Dawlish stood up, walked to the large window behind his desk. He stood with his back gazing out across the lawn sloping to the landing stage at the edge of the Alde. A moonlit night showed storm clouds scudding in from the east, from the North Sea.

Silhouetted against the light from the room Dawlish stood so still on his thick legs he looked like a Buddha. Brand had never met another man who could remain motionless for long periods. Dawlish had no fear of hostile action from the grounds. For one thing they were patrolled by wolfhounds. For another the windows were made of bullet-proof glass. Brand risked disturbing his thoughts, wanting to demonstrate his thoroughness.

'Another arrival in Aldeburgh – seen in the bar of the Brudenell – is Jean Burgoyne.'

Dawlish's reaction was different from what Brand had expected. He swung round, his eyes glowing, his manner explosive.

'What the bloody hell is she doing back here? All this happening when we're approaching what I told you was a critical time. The biggest delivery yet. Plus a wad of money for our friends in France.'

'Burgoyne has an uncle in Aldeburgh,' Brand pointed out in a conciliatory tone. 'She does visit him occasionally . . .'

'Bloody hell, have you lost the few marbles you've got left? Jean Burgoyne's uncle Brigadier was Military Intelligence. Goddamnit! Another coincidence – and with this other lot arriving . . .'

Dawlish strode swiftly to the luxurious cocktail cabinet concealed behind a floor-to-ceiling bookcase, pressed a button which operated a sliding case, exposing the cabinet. He poured a large Scotch, drank the whole glass, and didn't offer anything to Brand.

'The uncle is eighty . . .' Brand ventured.

'And a perfect conduit back to the Ministry of Defence.

I'm getting the feeling I'm being crowded. Always before that feeling has meant trouble.' He handed the glass to Brand. 'Get me another. A large one. We're going to have to take precautions tomorrow. Arrange to have men ready to take up the chopper. Both men to be armed. I may want someone followed, maybe dealt with.'

'That could be dangerous,' Brand warned, handing back the refilled glass. 'Another death after what happened to Karin Rosewater.'

'To succeed in this world you have to take risks.'

'One other thing I found out today. Someone else is staying at the Brudenell . . .'

'Don't play with me, Brand. Who?'

'Chief Inspector Buchanan of the CID and his sidekick, Sergeant Warden.'

'So, if we sense danger there may be a fatal accident during the shooting party. With the blame manipulated to one of the guests,' Dawlish concluded and drank the rest of his Scotch.

13

In the bar at the Brudenell Jean Burgoyne had said she'd better get home. She gave Paula her address and a phone number before she left.

'I've found our conversation frantically relaxing,' she said warmly. 'Please promise that we'll meet for another chat soon. There may be some problems I'd like to talk over with you. That's if you don't find me a crashing bore,' she added hastily.

'Anything but,' Paula responded. 'I'm not sure how

long I'll be here but I'll call you. We'll meet.'

'I'm simply *not* after an interview,' Jean stressed anxiously. 'Please don't think that.'

'I know. We'll meet,' Paula repeated.

As soon as Jean had gone Victor Rosewater walked over to Paula. Again she thought he was a handsome-looking man and he was smartly dressed in a check sports jacket and well-creased grey slacks. But his face was drawn, his smile forced as she invited him to sit beside her. He put a glass of orange juice on the table.

'I said I would come here,' he began, 'but the last person I expected to be lucky enough to meet was you.'

'Why didn't you phone me? You've got some leave?'

'I was going to call you from here. It was a rush catching the flight from Europe. And as I told you in Basle, I've a roving commission. I came here because this is where Karin died.'

'You think that's a good idea?' she asked quietly.

'No power on earth can stop me finding out who murdered her. The solution must be here. Why? How? Who?'

His expression and tone were grim and determined. He smiled again, drank some orange juice as the wind hammered the windows as though trying to break through the glass. Rosewater put down his tumbler.

'It must have been a night like this when her life was ended.'

'Something like this,' she said, wondering what he was thinking.

'Do you mind walking in the dark with this wind blowing?'

He was gazing into the distance, staring past her, not aware of the other customers drinking and chattering. Revenge was the most potent of all driving forces, she thought as she watched him.

'What do you want to do?' she asked eventually.

'Please say no if you don't like the idea. But I want to go

124

and see where it happened, under the conditions it happened. There may be something the police have overlooked. No one knew Karin like I did. She could have left a clue.'

She was about to say there were clever men from Scotland Yard who had been all over the ground, when Newman walked in. He paused when he saw Paula was not alone. She beckoned him over.

'Bob, this is Victor Rosewater.' She gave him a warning look. 'He was Karin's husband. Tweed and I met him in Basle, as you know. Victor, this is Robert Newman.'

'The foreign correspondent . . .'

Rosewater stood up, shook hands. Newman's arrival seemed to help him. He had recovered his normal poise. Newman joined them, looked at Rosewater's glass, asked if he was drinking orange juice.

'As a matter of fact, I am.'

'You're teetotal?'

'Good God, no!'

'Then maybe something a little stronger would help on a cold night like this. How about a Scotch?'

'Thank you, but no.' Rosewater looked embarrassed. 'I just don't think alcohol is a good idea, feeling as I do at the moment.'

'Victor wanted to be shown where the tragedy happened,' Paula told Newman. 'He thinks he might just find something the police overlooked.'

'You mean now?' Newman queried, a hint of surprise in his tone.

'Yes,' Paula continued. 'Under the same conditions of weather there were that night. And I think the storm has blown itself out. I can't hear the wind.'

'And it would be about this time, wouldn't it?' Rosewater asked, checking his watch.

'Yes, it would,' Paula agreed. 'Within an hour or so, anyway.' She looked at Newman. 'I'm quite prepared to go

125

out for a walk after I've wrapped up well.'

'Then I'll come with you,' Newman decided.

'That would be a great relief to me,' Rosewater said. 'The two of you coming with me – if it's not a great imposition, which I suppose it is.'

'Nonsense.' Newman stood up. 'Let's get on with it. I'll get my things. Meet you both in the lobby a few minutes from now . . .'

Aldeburgh was dead. The streets were deserted as Paula, Newman and Rosewater left the Brudenell by the entrance away from the front. They left the town behind when they entered the public car park. The wind had dropped as quickly as it had risen. Paula had a creepy feeling as her feet crunched the pebbled ground of the car park.

It was moonlit and she could remember the exact spot where she'd parked her car when she'd arrived with Karin. The car Butler had later driven back to London for her after Newman had taken her home in his Mercedes. They walked out of the car park on the gravel road leading to Slaughden Sailing Club in the distance. As they passed the old barn-like structure with a sign reading *Boat Storage* a cloud blotted out the moon and it was pitch dark.

'Which way now?' asked Rosewater, walking alongside Paula.

'A bit further along this awful road and then we turn down a footpath leading across the marshes.'

She had switched on her flashlight at the same moment as Rosewater turned on a more powerful beam. Behind them Newman walked slowly, glancing all round, his own flashlight switched on. Paula turned off the road, led the way down the steep bank and followed the footpath over the marshes below the gravel road. Rosewater caught her up, slowed down when he realized his long legs were making it difficult for her to keep pace.

126

'How long to get there?' he asked.

'About ten minutes from here . . .'

Despite the lack of wind it was very cold. Paula was muffled in a fur-lined coat, its hood pulled over her head. On her feet she wore gumboots. The two men were also clad in gumboots as they squelched over the soggy ground.

They came to the point where the footpath forked – one fork leading back up to the road, the other up to the dyke. Paula slipped on a patch of mud, nearly fell. Rosewater grabbed her waist, kept her erect, hauled her up on the dyke. Behind them Newman paused: his acute hearing had caught the sound of the engine of a distant vehicle which seemed to be growing louder although still some distance away. Sound carried a long way in the menacing silence which hung over the marshes. He could still hear the surge of the sea.

Rosewater trod along the narrow path atop the dyke, the marshes below him on the right, the anchorage beyond a mess of grassy creeks to his left. Paula was following close behind him and Newman brought up the rear, wishing he'd brought a weapon. He could still hear the sound of the vehicle approaching across the marshes.

Paula was trembling – and not with the cold. The nearer she approached the location where Karin had been found the worse she felt. The dark didn't help. She couldn't even see the distant copse of firs where she had sheltered while Karin was being strangled.

'Stop, Victor,' she called out.

She stood still, made herself play the flashlight down the side of the dyke, along a small creek filled with stagnant water. She froze. By the light of her beam she saw the small craft, rotting, the staves showing like the bowed ribs of a disturbed skeleton. It was just as she had seen it with Karin's corpse laid out inside it. She gritted her teeth, forcing herself to speak.

'She was found inside that wreck of a boat . . .'

Rosewater flashed his own beam on the craft, ran, slithered down the grassy bank. Crouching down, he examined its interior. Then, laying the lighted flash on a grassy tuft, he grasped hold of the craft, heaved it over upside down with manic energy, hauling it on to the grassy tufts. Paula slipped a hand over her mouth to stop crying out. Newman's hand gently held her arm.

'Let him get it out of his system,' he whispered.

Rosewater had picked up the flashlight again, was now feverishly searching the grass, the muddy clefts, feeling the ground with his free hand. The moving hand stopped suddenly. Paula stiffened. Rosewater moved the beam very slowly over a patch of grass. Moments earlier he had been acting like a man in a frenzy. Now he was moving his hand slowly and systematically. The hand stopped again, the fingers closed over something. He opened his palm, shone his flashlight on an object, tucked the torch under his arm and used his gloved hand to rub it, to clean it.

He scrambled back up the bank, his bare hand clenched tightly. Facing Paula, he opened the hand, shone the beam on it. She stared at the gold ring which bore an insignia. Picking it off his palm, she showed it to Newman who glanced at it, then at Rosewater.

'Karin's?'

'No. Look at the size of the diameter. Karin had a small hand, slim fingers. Recognize the symbol on the signet?'

'The Cross of Lorraine. French. De Gaulle's symbol for the Free French during World War II.'

'And because of the size,' Rosewater pointed out, 'it was probably dropped by the murderer. Find the owner and we've found the strangler . . .'

'Put it in your pocket! Quickly!' Newman ordered.

The sound of the engine was suddenly much louder as a vehicle approached rapidly across the marshes. Newman was about to urge them both down the far side of the bank away from the marshes when a blinding glare of light silhouetted the three figures perched on the dyke.

'Stay exactly where you are,' commanded a familiar voice. 'There is nowhere to run. I repeat, stay on the dyke . . .'

Newman threw up a hand to shield his eyes against the fierce glare. He shone his torch down on to the track below the dyke bordering the marshes. The vehicle was a buggy with enormous tyres – the only type of vehicle which could have crossed the treacherous ground.

'Turn off that damned light, Buchanan,' Newman shouted back. 'We've as much right out here as you have. You hear, Buchanan?'

'*Chief Inspector* Buchanan, if you please,' Warden shouted back from behind the vehicle's wheel.

'Don't be ridiculous, Warden,' Buchanan whispered.

It was the first time Newman had heard the stolid Warden give voice to speech. He turned to Paula and Rosewater, commenting at the top of his voice.

'Miracles happen. It can actually speak!'

'All right, that's enough, Newman,' Buchanan called out. 'I'm coming up there.'

'Then tell that driver to douse his bloody light.'

The searchlight, mounted on top of the buggy, went out. Buchanan climbed agilely up the bank, produced his own torch, shone it on the upturned craft.

'That could come under the offence of tampering with evidence,' he said mildly.

'Come off it,' Newman snapped. 'You've had the markers and tapes which undoubtedly cordoned it off removed. So anyone could have played about with that boat.'

'I still need to talk to all of you. Would you prefer the police station or the Brudenell where I'm staying?'

'You can't take us to the police station,' Newman continued, keeping up his aggressive attitude. 'And you know it. But yes to the Brudenell. Provided you give us a lift back in that buggy . . .'

14

'So,' Buchanan continued, addressing Rosewater, 'you came here to see where your wife was strangled?'

They were assembled in Buchanan's bedroom which over-looked the street, on the opposite side to Tweed's much more spacious room on the floor below. It was cramped with so many people – Newman, Paula, and Warden – in addition to the Chief Inspector and Rose-water. Newman had a grim look, disliking Buchanan's brutal approach.

'That's right,' Rosewater replied. 'A rather natural reaction, wouldn't you say?'

'And you're a captain in Military Intelligence?'

'With the BAOR – British Army of the Rhine.'

'You're on leave then? Compassionate?'

'No.' As tall as Buchanan, Rosewater stared straight back at his interrogator. 'I can go where I like, when I like.'

'Unusual for a British officer. What permits you such freedom of movement?'

'My job. I told you. Military Intelligence.'

'Care to enlighten me a little further?' Buchanan suggested.

'No. Security. You have no authority to ask such a question.'

Buchanan sighed. 'May I remind you, Captain Rose-water, this is a murder investigation I'm engaged on?'

'No reminder necessary,' Rosewater told him tersely. 'May I remind you it was my wife who was murdered?'

'Did you find anything interesting when you were

messing around with that boat?' Buchanan persisted.

'Not a thing,' Rosewater lied promptly.

'Haven't you pushed this interrogation far enough?' Newman interjected.

He was seated on the bed alongside Paula. Rosewater and Warden occupied the only chairs. Buchanan kept strolling round the room, jingling change in his pocket. He stopped in front of Paula, looked down at her.

'And why were you out on the marshes, Miss Grey?'

'To guide Captain Rosewater to where it happened.'

'Really?' In one word Buchanan expressed his scepticism. 'How did you happen to meet this officer stationed in Germany?'

'Purely by chance. I knew Karin. So once I met her husband while I was on holiday over there. In Germany, to be precise,' she added acidly.

'And Newman, you're here by chance?'

'No. On purpose. Occasionally I still interview prominent people. Just to keep my hand in.'

'Even though that book you wrote, *Kruger: The Computer That Failed*, became an international bestseller, made you financially independent for life?'

'Your memory is slipping. I just told you – to keep my hand in. I don't enjoy hanging about doing nothing all the time.'

'From my previous experience of you that's something you rarely do.'

'If you say so.'

Buchanan glanced at Rosewater, at Paula, at Newman, his expression cynical. He looked at his watch, put both hands back in his trouser pockets.

'You can all go now. And while I remember, thank you for your close co-operation . . .'

'Sarcastic bastard, that Buchanan!' Paula burst out to Newman as they walked along the corridor and down the staircase to the next floor.

'Oh, he's just doing his job.' Newman glanced back at the man behind them. 'And he's good at it. I must say you handled him well. Just answered his questions, adding nothing.'

Rosewater, following them down, smiled. 'It wasn't too difficult. I've been on the other end often enough – interrogating suspects. Care to join me in the bar? I think maybe I could do with that Scotch now. Freezing out on the marshes. I hope you didn't catch a chill, Paula.'

'No, I was well wrapped up.'

Paula paused as they reached the lower floor. 'Bob, I want to go and see someone. Why don't you and Victor have a chat on your own?'

'We'll do that. See you for dinner.'

'But we will miss your company,' Rosewater assured her.

Paula waited, fiddling with the folded coat she'd worn for the trek to the dyke. As Rosewater passed her he handed her something. When they were gone she opened her hand.

It was holding the ring Rosewater had dug out of the mud. She hurried to report to Tweed in his room.

Earlier, Lieutenant André Berthier of Third Corps had waited patiently while Jean Burgoyne sat chatting with the attractive raven-haired girl. Two beauties – one brunette, one blonde. He wouldn't mind a more intimate acquaintance with either. Both would be even better. He dreamed a little to pass the time, but never for a moment did his alertness desert him. Reminding himself of the role he was playing as an Englishman, he ordered another gin and tonic because it was such a British drink. Sipping it, his mind went back to the orders he'd been given in France . . .

Outside the car which de Forge had been travelling in – leaving the Villa Forban – the instructions had been

132

explicit. Major Lamy was not noted for wasting words.

'You follow the Burgoyne woman wherever she goes. I want a detailed report on where she does go. Above all, who she meets. Names, addresses. Here is some money to finance the trip. She's flying back home to Britain. Take that motor-cycle, drive like hell to GHQ, change into civilian clothes – your English ones. Be back at the Villa Forban in half an hour . . .'

Berthier had used the same forged passport and driving licence he'd used on previous trips to Britain. Following Burgoyne aboard her flight to Paris, then her flight to London Airport, he'd collected the Ford Sierra ordered by phone during his wait at Charles de Gaulle Airport for the London flight.

For some reason he couldn't fathom Burgoyne had driven in a car waiting for her straight to the Brudenell Hotel in Aldeburgh. He had registered in the name of James Sanders, wearing his tinted glasses and a trilby hat to conceal his fair hair. If anyone joshed him about wearing dark glasses in November he had his explanation ready.

'I've weak eyes. Strong light hurts them . . .'

Lamy had trained his protégé well. Immediately he'd arrived in his room Berthier had locked the door. Moving as swiftly as he could, he'd taken the bottle of hair colourant from his case, had gone into the bathroom and applied the liquid carefully. He used a drier attached to the wall, checked his appearance in the mirror, hurried downstairs.

His fear that Burgoyne would have gone mounted when he couldn't see her in the lounge. He strolled into the bar and she was standing at the counter, collecting glasses of champagne, taking them to the table where the attractive raven-haired girl sat. Berthier had ordered his first gin and tonic, sat at a corner table. The two women chatted a while like old friends.

Berthier was confident Burgoyne wouldn't recognize him. Despite the fact he had stood in her room at the Villa

133

Forban while he'd waited to escort de Forge to his car.

The colourant transformed his appearance. The tinted glasses completed the masquerade. Besides, Burgoyne had seen him in uniform before. Wearing civilian gear could make the same man unrecognizable. He had just finished his fresh gin and tonic when Burgoyne put on her coat and walked out of the bar.

Berthier followed her as she left by the steps leading to the back entrance on to the street behind the hotel. Her car, a Jaguar, was parked further up the street. He ran to the Ford Sierra, slotted in next to the entrance. As she drove off Berthier was a discreet distance behind her.

No other traffic was about as she turned left in the cold night down a narrow side street, then right into the equally deserted High Street for a very short distance before turning left again and climbing a curving hill. Here it was all gloom with high walls and the odd glimpse of lights in a large house down a drive. The part of Aldeburgh where the well-off lived.

Berthier slowed, driving only with his sidelights on. The Jaguar abruptly swung left off the road, vanished. On this side of the road Berthier saw there was a wide grass verge with here and there occasional trees. He swung his Ford on to the verge, switched off his sidelights, the engine, got out of the car.

The bitter cold of the November night hit him. As he walked slowly to where the Jaguar had disappeared he turned up the collar of his English sports jacket, shoved his hands inside his pockets. On either side of the gap she had driven through stood stone pillars, topped with lead decorations of old sailing ships. The imposing residence was called Admiralty House.

Berthier peered round a pillar up the gravel drive and saw a small Georgian mansion. The lights were on behind the uncurtained windows of a room to the right of the front door. Berthier saw an elderly man with wisps of white hair pouring something from a bottle, standing very erect. The Burgoyne woman appeared, closed the curtains. Just before she shut out the view Berthier saw the lights from a chandelier gleaming on her mane of blonde hair.

He went back to his car, treading on damp turf. Seated behind the wheel, he tried to puzzle it out. Lamy had obviously expected she would go to meet a lover. Berthier doubted whether the old boy fitted that category.

He sat clasping his strong hands, began squeezing the middle finger of his left hand, massaging the knuckle absent-mindedly. When, after half an hour, it seemed obvious she wasn't going anywhere else that night, he drove back to the Brudenell, descending from the highest point in Aldeburgh.

Paula described tersely the visit to the scene of the crime before producing the ring. Taking out a handkerchief, she unwrapped it carefully and presented the ring to Tweed.

They were alone in his bedroom. He had had coffee and sandwiches sent up and sipped from his cup as he held the ring in the palm of his hand. Putting the cup down, he slipped the signet ring on his middle finger. It slithered off.

'You see,' Paula repeated, 'it links up with what the pathologist said. The strangler has large hands. That ring can only fit a man with large hands.'

'The Cross of Lorraine. Interesting,' Tweed commented, using a paper napkin to clean off more mud. 'It could be significant. On the other hand . . .'

'A link with France,' Paula insisted. 'So why do you sound sceptical? I've told you where it was found and how.'

'At this stage I'm keeping an open mind. We have a lot of data, quite a few pieces of the jigsaw, but some are still missing.'

'Well, what have we got so far?' Paula demanded.

'Briefly, Lasalle's belief that an insurrection is imminent

135

in France. Organized by the infamous *Cercle Noir*, with the driving force possibly General de Forge. That theory may be backed up by Newman's riot experience in Bordeaux.'

'You still sound very sceptical,' she repeated.

'Too early to interpret the data positively. I could be wrong. Then we have Kuhlmann warning us about the *Siegfried* underground movement in Germany. That *could* be linked with events in France. And don't forget the mysterious Kalmar, possibly the strangler of Karin and Francis Carey. I have the strongest feeling he is the key. Locate, identify Kalmar, and we'd know what was really going on.' He switched topics, his mind moving swiftly. 'I'll take this signet ring. You realize it must be handed over to Buchanan soon? We can't hide evidence in a murder case.'

'I could give it to Buchanan now . . .'

'No. I want the Engine Room at Park Crescent to make a perfect copy. Then it must be given to Buchanan. Does he know I'm here?'

'I'm sure he doesn't.'

'We'll keep it that way. I'll stay in my room tonight. Then leave early in the morning. I'll drive back to London in my own car. I must get back to Park Crescent. But first I'd better talk to Victor Rosewater, warn him that I'll be giving this ring to the CID. He'll have time to prepare his story.'

'I'd better go and fetch him now. Before he goes in to dinner with Bob.'

'I agree. In a minute.' Tweed studied the signet ring again. 'I have the oddest feeling I've seen this somewhere recently. No idea where. It may come back to me. And, Paula, exercise the greatest care when you interview Lord Dane Dawlish tomorrow.'

'Newman and Marler will be there, too – at the shoot.'

'You must still take great care,' he repeated. 'Monica has now completed her dossier on Dawlish.'

'Why?'

'Because he's armaments. Because he lives in the area where Karin was murdered. Probably he's nothing to do with what we're after. Just checking. One more thing I'd like you to do.' He gazed at the wall. 'And again proceed with caution.'

'Understood. What is it?'

'There's that Frenchman here – if Newman heard what he muttered under his breath when he stubbed his toe. So don't forget to meet him if you can. Find out what he is doing here. Now, wheel up Captain Victor Rosewater. Tell him I'm security chief with an insurance outfit.'

'So the best thing, I'm sure, is for me to tell Chief Inspector Buchanan I discovered the signet ring,' Rosewater said firmly.

He had just listened to Tweed's suggestion and reacted positively. Tweed studied Rosewater, remembering Paula had remarked he'd make excellent material as a new member of the SIS. Certainly he was very quick in grasping a situation, Tweed thought, as Rosewater continued.

'I'll tell him neither Paula nor Newman knew I'd found it. I shoved it straight into my pocket so I could study it later. After all, it was my wife who was murdered. I have an obvious interest in identifying the man who killed poor Karin.'

'Buchanan will give you hell,' Tweed warned. 'Suppressing evidence and all that.'

'I can handle him. Remember, I've had some experience at interrogation. You're giving me the ring now?'

'It's locked away in a safe place. And I think it would be better if we let a few days elapse before Buchanan confronts you. I may decide to be present myself.'

Rosewater settled himself more comfortably in his chair. He watched Tweed for a whole minute before he put the question.

'Paula said you were with an insurance outfit. Security doesn't seem to go with that, if you don't mind my saying so.'

'Not at all.' Tweed smiled cryptically. 'We specialize in insuring wealthy targets against kidnapping,' he lied easily. 'That's confidential. On occasions we have to negotiate with kidnappers who have snatched a client – a tricky operation.'

'So I can imagine.'

'Our territory is the whole of Western Europe. The active areas are France and Germany. So I travel a lot. Certain German industrialists are especially nervous about this mysterious *Siegfried* organization which has sprung up.'

'You mean they might try to get funds that way?'

'Exactly. Again, very confidential. Even more so as you travel a lot.'

'My job teaches me to keep my mouth shut. Going back to that signet ring, will I get warning when the police are going to be informed?'

Tweed produced his calling card showing him as Chief Claims Investigator, General & Cumbria Assurance, with only the telephone number. Tweed watched him as he slid the card into a wallet.

'You'll be staying here for the next few days I assume?' Tweed enquired. 'So I know I can reach you?'

Rosewater grinned for the first time. 'I'll be available. I plan to mosey round this strange old town a bit. Now I'd better get downstairs for dinner with Bob Newman.'

When Paula left Tweed she paid a brief visit to her room to check on her appearance. Downstairs she found the youngish man with tinted glasses Newman had described in the bar. He occupied a corner table by himself, a glass in front of him. It was then Paula remembered he'd been

138

sitting at the same table when she'd been talking to Jean Burgoyne.

She wandered in, looked round as though unsure where to perch, then chose an empty table near Tinted Glasses. Sitting down facing him, she crossed her shapely legs. Tinted Glasses noticed her immediately. He hardly hesitated. Getting up, he walked slowly across to her, the glass in his hand.

'Excuse me. If I'm intruding I'll go away at once. I am on my own and I wondered if we could chat. That is, unless you're expecting someone.'

She smiled. 'I'm expecting no one. And we are fellow guests. Do sit down.'

'After I've got you a drink.' He put his glass down. 'What do you fancy?'

'Would a glass of champers be in order? I prefer to stay with the same drink . . .'

She had listened carefully and caught no trace of accent. He brought the glass of champagne back, sat next to her, raised his own glass.

'Cheers! Here's to a memorable evening.'

'Cheers!' Paula responded. 'I'm afraid I don't have the whole evening though. I spent too much time talking to Jean Burgoyne a little while ago. In this bar.'

'Really? Who is Jean Burgoyne?'

'She's a well-known society girl. Gets her picture in the top magazines a lot. And sometimes in the gossip columns in the newspapers. She's just returned from France. Do you know France at all?'

'Excuse me. My manners must be slipping. I'm James Sanders . . .'

'Paula Grey. You don't know France, then?'

Berthier adjusted his glasses, pushed them up the bridge of his strong aquiline nose. He turned to face her. It bothered her that she couldn't see his eyes clearly.

'As a matter of fact, I've just returned from Paris . . .'

Always stick as close to the truth as you can, Lamy had trained him. 'A waste of time,' he went on. 'Business at this time of the year is dead.'

'What business is that? I'm sorry, that was rather personal.'

'Selling marine equipment. Wholesale and retail to private buyers. Boaty people. Which is why I'm here. Loads of boaty types in Aldeburgh.'

She nodded. Was he piling on the English colloquialisms a little too heavily? She couldn't be sure.

'Isn't business pretty dead here. At this time of year?'

He swallowed half his drink. 'I hope to make contacts for the spring. My business is seasonal. Out of season you can often meet a lot of chaps who'll be interested when winter is just a bad memory.' He still faced her, the tinted lens like soulless eyes.

'*Vous en voulez un autre?*' Paula asked suddenly.

She spoke very rapidly the way a Frenchwoman would, enquiring whether he'd like another drink. He moved, as though about to get up, then shifted his position, settling himself more comfortably. For a second she could have sworn his face froze.

'I'm sorry,' she went on, 'I assumed you'd speak French. Seeing as you have to do business in France.'

He grinned, waving his strong hands. 'I know I should but I don't. Usual British attitude – damned foreigners are expected to speak English. As a matter of fact, they do – the few people I deal with in Paris. And mostly I'm showing them marine spare parts in a catalogue. So it's easy. What did you say, actually?'

'I asked if you'd like another drink.'

'I'm the host,' he replied. 'How about another glass of champers?'

'I've had enough. But I was suggesting I bought you one this time.'

'I think I've had enough too.' He adjusted his glasses

again. 'You're sure you can't join me for dinner?'

'I'd love to. But I've already arranged to have dinner with two friends.' She looked at her watch. 'And if you don't mind, Mr Sanders . . .'

'James . . .'

'If you don't mind I'm expected in the dining room. It's been nice talking to you. Good luck with making useful contacts.'

She stood up and he stood with her, pulling his chair out of the way. He cleared his throat as though unsure whether to say more. Then he came out with the invitation she was expecting.

'Maybe tomorrow I could take you out for a drive round the countryside? We should be able to find somewhere up-market for lunch.'

She smiled. 'That's nice of you. But tomorrow's out of the question. I have an appointment. Maybe some other day. If we're still both here . . .'

He was walking back towards the bar counter when she left. A couple were walking out of the elevator and she dived inside, pressed the button for the first floor. Tapping on Tweed's door in a certain way, she waited until the door was opened.

Tweed was dabbing his mouth with a napkin and he had a visitor. Marler, immaculately clad in a sports jacket and well-pressed slacks, wearing hand-made shoes which gleamed like glass, gave her a mock salute.

'I suspect the clever lady has been busy,' he drawled as Tweed re-locked the door.

'Another helping of sandwiches?' Paula asked, eyeing the plate on the table alongside a pot of coffee.

'You know I'm always hungry when I've reached the stage of deploying forces.' Tweed sat down at the table. 'I've just been giving Marler some very special instructions.' He indicated sheets of papers with names scrawled, some listed in groups encircled with loops. Dotted lines

141

joined certain groups together. Tweed looked at Paula.

'Any luck with Newman's pseudo-Englishman? If he is.'

'Name, James Sanders. So he said.' She wrinkled her brows. 'The devil of it is I can't be sure. He almost talks like a foreigner with an excellent command of English, but peppers his conversation with colloquialisms in a way I'm not certain a genuine Englishman would. I threw a question at him in French – would he like another drink? He seemed to start getting out of his chair, but the movement was so slight again I couldn't swear he was French. Verdict? Not proven. Now I must get down to join Bob and Rosewater for dinner, leaving you two to plot.'

'Tomorrow ...' Tweed's expression was grave. 'Be extremely cautious at Grenville Grange. I have a sixth sense there could be danger inside that place.'

15

A Gothic horror.

Paula had stopped her car – borrowed from Nield – in front of the closed wrought-iron gates which guarded Grenville Grange. At the end of a long curving drive she saw the grotesque mansion. Victorian architecture at its most hideous: a grey, three-storey pile with a projecting wing at either end; small turrets foresting from the roof; huge gargoyles silhouetted against the clear wintry sky.

She had driven out of Aldeburgh, turning left, speeding along the A1094 past the golf course on her right. The rolling green had been covered with heavy frost the colour of *crème de menthe*. Turning left near Snape, she had driven on past the famous Maltings, turning left once more along a narrow country road to Iken. Frequently she checked the road map open on the seat beside her. One more left turn and she was out in the wilds with a view down to a wide loop of the river Alde which looked like a sheet of blue ice. Now this . . .

She pressed her horn several times, a large figure dressed like a countryman appeared, holding a savage-looking wolfhound on a leash which leapt towards her, snarling. Welcome to Grenville Grange.

'What do you want?' the big man asked. 'Private property.'

'Pretty obvious,' Paula called back. 'Paula Grey. I have an appointment with Lord Dane Dawlish. At noon.'

'Show some identification.'

'Come out and damn well look for yourself,' she shouted back. 'And keep that silly pup away from me. Or, alternatively, call up his Lordship and tell him you have stopped me driving in . . .'

Glaring, the guard unlocked the gates, opened one, shortened the leash, walked towards her. Paula noticed all his clothes looked brand new. Not what she would have expected from a guard.

She showed him the press card, one of several cards produced for her in the Engine Room basement at Park Crescent. She hung on to a corner while he examined it.

'You'd better drive in,' he said grudgingly.

'So you did know I was coming?'

She smiled at his flushed face as he went back, pushed open the other gate, then jumped back as she rammed her foot down, scattering gravel over the wolfhound as she raced up to the house. A wide semicircle gave a plenty of parking space below a wide balustraded terrace with steps leading to the entrance.

She switched off the engine and immediately heard the *cr-a-a-ck* of shot-guns firing. The shoot was in progress somewhere behind the looming pile. She noted Newman's

Mercedes 280E was parked at the edge of two rows of cars. About twenty vehicles with a number of BMWs, a Ferrari and a Lamborghini. Dawlish liked money at his shooting parties. She checked the time. 11.50 a.m. Ten minutes early. She liked to throw strangers she was visiting off balance. Sometimes you found out something they wished to conceal.

Locking the car, she avoided the steps up to the entrance, wandered round the left-hand side of the mansion. At the rear a vast lawn bordered on two sides by walls of firs ran down to a large landing-stage projecting into the Alde.

She counted about thirty guns, men of different ages, all smartly – even foppishly – dressed. It was still barely above freezing point and she wore a knee-length suede coat and a silk scarf. The shooters were ignoring the black pottery shards raining down on the lawn as the shot-gun-wielding men spaced round the edge of the lawn took it in turn with their twelve-bores. She saw Marler take aim as five more targets flew above the lawn. He missed three out of the five and in a brief silence she heard his drawling voice.

'Can't hit the damned things . . .'

Like hell, you can't, she thought. If you wanted to you'd shoot the lot out of the sky.

She looked up as she heard a chopper flying low. Skimming the treetops, it hovered, then flew on over the roof of the mansion out of sight. Paula, thinking for a moment it might be a Coastguard machine, tried to catch its identification markings. As far as she could see, it didn't have any. Staring straight up the side of the house, she saw a satyr-like gargoyle leering down at her.

'Chap up there on the roof seems quite keen on you,' an upper-crust voice suggested.

She swung round and a young chinless wonder was eyeing her with open interest. He had his shot-gun perched over his shoulder at an affected angle.

'You must be one of his Lordship's harem of fillies,' he continued. 'He's over there . . .' He jerked his head. 'Waiting for you, I'm sure – all eager beaver and able.'

Paula stared straight back. 'I've got another suggestion,' she said coldly. 'Why don't you drop dead?'

'Be like that.'

The young fop strolled off and Paula looked in the direction he'd indicated. Newman was talking to a heavily built man of medium height clad in riding gear. Dawlish was listening with a grim look and suddenly there was a hush among the crowd spread round the lawn, sensing that something dramatic was happening. Marler stood behind Newman, lighting a king-size cigarette. Paula heard the exchange clearly.

'What was that question you asked?' Dawlish rumbled.

'I hear you have an armaments factory not far from here. I gather that's one of your main sources of income. The end of the Cold War will have to make you find customers for weapons elsewhere. Or maybe you're glad we just may have peace on earth – even if it eliminates profits from wars?'

'You were invited here as a guest at my shooting party,' Dawlish rasped, one hand tucked in the pocket of his jodhpurs. 'Now you're trying to get an interview out of me, Newman. For *Der Spiegel*, you said . . .'

'Don't you want publicity for some reason?' Newman went on amiably. 'As one of the leading industrialists in the Western world? They say you can sell guns to peoples and places no one else can. You must have contacts at the very top . . .'

'The exit is that way,' Dawlish broke in, jerked a thumb towards the car park. 'If you're not off the property in two minutes I can have you escorted.'

'Save your manpower,' Newman suggested jocularly. 'Your hired thugs probably have other dirty work to do . . .'

145

'Thugs?'

Dawlish took one pace closer to Newman. He looked choleric. High blood pressure? Paula wondered.

'Your so-called gamekeepers and beaters,' Newman continued, 'in their fancy new gear. Dressed up to look like countrymen. Professional security guards would be my guess. Kicked out of respectable security firms?'

'*Two minutes . . .*'

Dawlish turned away, looked round, beckoned to a heavily-built man with dark hair, who came running. Paula realized Dawlish didn't miss much: he was heading straight for her as the other man joined him. She caught the first part of Dawlish's instructions.

'Radio the chopper. Tell them to follow Newman. He has an old blue Merc. Big job. If necessary, they teach him a lesson. I've been warned about Newman . . .'

He lowered his voice and even though they were coming closer to her she couldn't catch the rest of what Dawlish said. She saw Newman hand his gun to a guard, Marler hand his weapon to the same man and the two of them wandered towards the car park without a glance in her direction. She was worried: on her way to Grenville Grange she'd seen no sign of Butler and Nield, recalling that Tweed had told them to act as protectors. Then it struck her that wherever Butler and Nield were waiting she'd never have seen them: they were professionals.

'Get on with it now, Brand. They're leaving . . .'

She heard Dawlish's last order to the heavy-set man who hurried away as the owner of Grenville Grange approached her with a broad grin. He whipped off his hard hat.

'Paula Grey? You're early . . .'

'I like to be prompt.'

Brown eyes like bullets swept over her. A strong hand gripped her right arm as he guided her up steps, across the rear steps, opened a French window, ushered her inside, locked the door, adjusted the heavy net curtains.

'Let me take your coat, my dear . . .'

As he helped her off with the coat his fingers lingered a few seconds too long on her well-shaped shoulders. He gestured towards a large deep couch with cushions as he took her coat, opened a cupboard, slipped it on a hanger and left it on a hook.

Paula looked round for a single armchair but Dawlish had organized the room well for her reception. Each armchair was occupied with a pile of leather-bound tomes. Which left no alternative but to set herself on the couch at one end. Dawlish offered her Scotch or wine but she chose coffee. He pressed a button in the wall. A manservant clad in black opened a door in the rear of the large room.

'Coffee for my guest, Walters. A large Scotch for me. And next time knock before you come in. Get on with it . . .'

Which seemed to be his favourite phrase Paula thought as she glanced round the room while extracting her notebook from her shoulder bag. Except for the windows overlooking the lawn, the other three walls were oak-panelled from floor to ceiling with bookcases inset at intervals. In the wall facing her a log fire crackled inside a deep-arched alcove. The atmosphere was over-poweringly warm as Dawlish stripped off his riding boots, dumped them in the hearth, slipped his large feet into a pair of handmade brogues.

'Mind if I strip off my jacket?'

He was doing so while his eyes roamed over her coatless figure. He sat on the couch close to her, laid a hand on the right knee of her crossed legs, squeezed it.

'Where do we start?' he asked with a broad smile.

Dawlish emanated an aura of great physical energy and, despite his bulk, his movements were swift. Like sitting next to a sexual powerhouse, Paula thought before she replied.

147

'We start by your removing your hand off my person.'

'But such an alluring person . . .'

The nails of her right hand hovered over the hand. She had very tough nails. They dug gently into the back of his hairy hand when he didn't move.

'I'm quite capable of drawing blood, scratching so you will be scarred for weeks. Then I'll leave at once – in other words, go to hell.'

'Spirited. I like that.'

But he took his hand away from her knee. Leaning back against the cushions, he fingered the sideburn closest to her, studying her as though seeing her for the first time.

'I'm at your service,' he said eventually.

'I understand you're interested in conservation. Also underwater exploration. I hear you're financing the new expedition to explore the sunken village of Dunwich.'

'The Cat is a dream for that job.'

'The cat?'

Paula, puzzled, stared at Dawlish as there was a knock on the door. Dawlish, looking pleased with the effect he'd created, bawled out, 'Come on in . . .' They waited while Walters put down a silver tray, poured coffee for Paula, handed Dawlish a cut-glass tumbler of neat Scotch and left the room.

'Down the hatch!' Dawlish said, swallowed half the drink.

'I'm all at sea,' Paula commented after sipping coffee.

'*All at sea!*'

Dawlish repeated her words, roared a deep belly laugh. Before she knew what was happening he looped an arm round her slim waist, hoisted her to her feet, led her across the room to a section of wall to the right of the huge fireplace. He pressed another button.

There was a whirring sound of unseen machinery operating. A large section of panelling slid upwards, revealed what looked to Paula like one of the dioramas she'd seen in military museums. She was gazing at a huge sheet of plate-glass shaped like a porthole. Beyond, a strange model of a vessel perched on a stretch of blue sea. Dawlish pressed the button again. The weird vessel sailed through waves which suddenly rose up ahead of its prow.

Paula was still carrying her notebook and pen. For a moment her expression froze. Dawlish watched her with amusement, mistaking her fear for astonishment. Paula was gazing at a model replica of the weird vessel which she'd seen with Karin when they'd surfaced off Dunwich, clambered aboard their dinghy, had fled for their lives from the scuba divers with knives between their teeth. To cover her reaction she scribbled indecipherable shorthand in her book.

'The Cat,' Dawlish said with an expression of overweening pride. 'Short for a great marine technological advance. The twin-hulled catamaran. Instead of bouncing over waves – like previous vessels – it *pierces* waves, cuts through them. Top speed forty-two knots. I call mine *Steel Vulture*. The for'ard view – aft or port – seen from another vessel, looks like a vulture slicing the waves.'

Paula watched, trembling inside, as Dawlish pressed a different button. The model reversed back to its previous position on the left. Dawlish set it moving again. More waves heaved on the 'sea'. The *Steel Vulture* sailed across to the right.

'Its beam is very wide,' she remarked quietly.

'It can carry over one hundred people,' Dawlish rambled on proudly. 'Plus a number of heavy vehicles. It's like a car ferry. They have a bigger one in operation on the ferry run from Portsmouth to Cherbourg. But the *Vulture*, built in Norway, has more advanced refinements.'

Almost hypnotized, Paula watched the twin wakes slushing from the stern. She forced herself to go on talking.

'Where do you berth such a vessel?'

'Down at Harwich when she's not at sea.'

149

'And you said you use it for the Dunwich exploration?'

'Frequently. She's the mother ship for the divers who go down to map the town beneath the sea. Maybe you'd like a trip aboard my latest toy?'

'Yes, I think I could use that in my article,' Paula agreed automatically. 'You could get me by calling the editor of *Women's Eye*. I rove around a lot.'

'So you'll make my underwater exploration the theme of your piece? The last time Dunwich was investigated under the sea was by some aqua clubs in 1979. I'm doing the job on a much larger scale. I can afford the equipment . . .'

As he rattled on enthusiastically Dawlish pressed the buttons, returned the model to its original start point, closed down the sliding panelling which concealed the mobile diorama. Paula walked back to the couch, sat down, said something which transformed the previous friendly atmosphere.

'Apart from the underwater thing, which *costs* you a lot of money, I'm sure, I gather you *make* a fortune out of your armaments factories. Does that ever bother you? Being a merchant of death?'

He strode across the room, dropped his weight next to her, grasped her wrist with one hand in a grip which felt like a steel handcuff. His expression was ugly.

'What the hell made you ask that question?'

Paula wondered where Newman and Marler were, wished to God they hadn't left so early.

16

Newman had driven away from the Iken peninsula at speed. Beside him sat Marler as they drove along a hedge-lined road with fields beyond still crusted with a white coating of frost. The sun was a blurred disc and white mist like a slow-moving curtain drifted among the trees.

'Care to take a shufti at Dawlish's armaments set-up in the forest on the way to Orford?' Marler drawled.

'How do you know it is armaments?'

'What would be your guess? Out in the wilds. Closed off with a high wire fence – electrified. Guards with dogs patrolling behind the wire. Think he's running a marshmallow factory, chum?'

'If you're that keen, why not?' Newman agreed. 'Guide me.'

'Left at the top here, then later left again when you hit the main road to Snape Maltings. Then a country road to Orford.'

'We're being followed.'

'I know. Saw it in the wing mirror. Ford Sierra – I didn't even see where Butler and Nield sneaked out after us.'

'So they're pros. How do you think the party went – and you're one lousy shot when you want to be.'

'I wanted to be,' Marler commented. 'And you lit some fuse under Dawlish. Did you have to stir him up quite so much?'

'That was the general idea. When a man gets uptight he sometimes gives away more than he intends.'

'Far as I could see, the only thing he gave away was us. Push off or be escorted.'

'I achieved my objective. I rattled him. To prepare the way for Paula. You saw her arrive, of course. And after Dawlish told us to get to hell out of it he eager-beavered his way towards her. He'll run into a wildcat if he tries pawing her.'

'But you could have queered her pitch,' Marler protested. 'He'd be in a bad mood.'

'Which she'll spot and play on skilfully. Bet she gets back with some intriguing data.'

'Just so long as she does get back . . .'

Five minutes later Newman had negotiated an awkward turn left and they were driving through even lonelier country towards distant Orford. It was incredibly silent and still when Newman paused, parked for a minute, switching off his engine. On both sides forests of evergreens – firs and pines – spread away across rolling heathland. They had already passed one sandy track leading off the road into the wilderness, the track vanishing round a curve. Marler lit a cigarette.

'The entrance to skull-and-crossbones is just beyond two more bends,' he remarked.

'And how do you know this place is anything to do with Dawlish?'

'Because I'd make a good detective.' Marler smiled cynically. 'At the bottom of one of the warning plates attached to the fence there's printing in small letters. *Dawlish Conservation Ltd.* Some kind of conservation project with all the defences I've told you about.'

'I heard the sound of an engine in the sky just now.'

'Sounded like a chopper floating around. Unlikely to be Traffic Patrol out here. Could be a Coastguard machine.'

'Could be something else.' Newman started up his engine. 'Let's get moving and see what happens.'

152

'Out here? I'd say nothing ever happens out here in broad daylight.'

Newman was suddenly very conscious of the fact that they carried no weapons to defend themselves. Was it the atmosphere of brooding menace which seemed to hang over the wilderness? The utter solitude of this part of the world? They hadn't seen a vehicle since leaving Iken.

He found himself crawling along the winding road, glancing at the undergrowth bordering the road on both sides. Newman had a hemmed-in feeling. They rounded the first bend and another stretch of deserted road opened up, disappearing round another bend a hundred yards away.

'Might as well get out and walk,' commented Marler who seemed oblivious to any danger.

'Who is behind the wheel?' Newman snapped. 'And we're pretty close now, aren't we?'

'One more bend and Dawlish's private little world is on our left . . .'

Newman continued to let the Merc crawl. He frowned, pressed the switch which slid back the roof above their heads. Marler tapped ash from his cigarette into the ash tray.

'Want us to freeze? It's damn cold in these woods . . .'

'Shut up! Listen!'

Newman could hear the sound distinctly now. The chug-chug of the helicopter coming back from a different direction. They drove round the second bend. The road now stretched straight as a ruler for some distance and the forest had retreated on either side with a band of open heath beyond the low hedges. To their left a high wire fence appeared with metal plates attached to it at shoulder height.

The fence was about two hundred yards long and in the middle was a double gate, also constructed of wire. Beyond the gate a wide gravel track ran away towards copses of trees. Just visible were single-storey buildings constructed of concrete and without windows. Newman found it sinister that there was no sign of the guards, the dogs, Marler had described earlier when he had driven past this outlandish place.

He parked opposite the closed gates, leaving his engine running. Marler jumped out, walked up to the gate, then paced methodically back the way they had come until he'd reached a concrete post. He strolled back to the car. Above the open roof Newman could hear the chopper much closer. It sounded to be circling the area out of view.

'What the devil were you playing at?' he asked as Marler sank back into his seat.

'Checking the place to fuse the electrified fence with a wooden-handled screw-driver in the dark.'

'Why, if I may ask?'

'You just did, old boy. Answer, in case I decide to come back and take a closer look at that establishment by night.'

'I wouldn't advise it. Not on your own . . .'

Newman was staring up the track. Its surface was rutted where heavy vehicles with wide tyres had driven over it. He still didn't like the lack of any sign of human life. It was as though someone had sent an order for all the guards to withdraw out of sight. And he couldn't rid himself of the feeling that unseen eyes were observing them.

'Finding it all a bit creepy?' Marler enquired.

'Well, it's not the place I'd choose for a picnic.'

'Ever thought Dawlish could have taken away the guards to reinforce Grenville Grange? There was quite a pack of visitors there this morning.'

'I don't think that's the explanation,' Newman said slowly, looking everywhere. 'Dawlish is a millionaire. He has the funds to employ as many security men as he wishes . . .'

He broke off as the silence was murdered by the onset of a deafening roar. For a minute or so the chug-chug of the helicopter had faded. Now it sounded to be on top of them. Newman pressed the switch which closed the roof, released the brake, sped forward. At that moment men with shot-guns rose out of the gullies which had concealed them behind the wire. A hail of buckshot peppered the road in front of, behind, the Mercedes. Newman noticed nothing hit the car. They were being encouraged to move forward along the straight stretch of road.

'Ahead of us . . .' Marler warned.

Something darted across the road twenty yards in front of the car. A fox, startled by the roar, was taking cover. Beyond it the grey chopper suddenly appeared, skimming the treetops. The pilot changed course, flew towards them, immediately above the road. As it hurtled forward something dropped from the machine, landed on the road. There was a brilliant burst of blinding light. Newman screwed up his eyes, swung the wheel, just avoided the blaze. The machine swept over them.

'Magnesium flare,' Newman said tersely. 'One of those hits us, or I drive over it, and the petrol tank goes up.'

'He'll be back,' Marler replied, twisting round in his seat.

'And next time could be bull's-eye . . .'

Newman pressed his foot down further, wishing to heaven now that the road was winding. The endless straight stretch made them a perfect target, the pilot able to calculate their likely position in advance.

'It's gone,' Marler reported.

'Ready for another run,' Newman foresaw.

He had hardly finished speaking when they saw the chopper appear again well ahead of them, flying along the avenue of death towards the Mercedes. That was when Newman saw in his rear-view mirror the Ford Sierra racing up behind them full tilt.

Nield was behind the wheel in the Ford. Beside him Butler had wound down his window, unfastened his seat

155

belt. Now he was leaning out of the window, back pressed against his seat, both hands gripping his Walther. The road surface was good which helped him hold the gun steady.

The chopper was approaching Newman's vehicle ahead of the Ford. This time there was no magnesium flare. Instead smoke, turgid black smoke, began to streak from the rear of the machine. The smoke drifted down swiftly, heavily. The helicopter was still about three hundred yards away from Newman's Merc. Like a crop sprayer, it jetted the smoke along the road surface. Newman's mouth tightened. He slowed down, reduced speed more and more.

'What the hell are you playing at?' Marler demanded.

In the Ford Butler aimed his Walther for the pilot's cabin. It would be a chance in a million if he scored a direct hit but it was the only chance he had. Pressing the trigger, he emptied the magazine, his knuckles white with the strain of holding the weapon on target.

A different kind of smoke began to drift out of the helicopter. Whereas previously it had held an arrow-like course the machine began to quiver, wobbling. Suddenly it veered away from the road, flame flared, it vanished over the treetops. The shockwave of a distant *boom!* shuddered both cars. A column of oily smoke climbed above the forest, then there was silence as Newman stopped his car short of the eddying smoke. Behind him Nield slowed, stopped close to the Mercedes. Another fox darted out, started to run through the fringe of the smoke. Abruptly it stopped running, reared up almost vertically, flopped on to the road and lay still.

'And that,' said Newman, 'was why I slowed . . .'

He got out of his car, followed by Marler and Butler, who had reloaded. Newman approached the animal slowly, waited for the smoke to dissipate. Only then did he go close to the animal. The fox sprawled on its side, its long brush tail flat and still as the body. Its eyes were starting out of its head, its jaws wide open. Newman touched it with his

156

foot. It was like touching a rock: the corpse was stiff, unyielding.

'I want to take this back in the boot for expert examination.'

'What on earth for?' Marler enquired.

'Because that was no ordinary smoke that chopper sprayed – tried to spray us with. It contained some element which, as you see, was lethal . . .'

He went back to his car, explained briefly to Butler, and took a roll of hessian cloth from the boot. Then he put on a pair of old sheepskin gloves. They walked back to where the dead fox lay.

Butler, who was wearing gloves, helped him to place the fox on the cloth they had spread across the road, to roll up the corpse and carry it back to the car. When it was safely stacked in the boot Newman stripped off his gloves, tossed them on top of the bundle.

'I'd advise you to do the same,' he told Butler.

He shut the boot when both pairs of gloves had been dropped inside. Then he clapped a hand briefly on Butler's shoulder.

'Thanks for saving us, Harry. We'd be like that fox now but for you.'

'Part of the job,' Butler replied typically. 'Where to now?'

'Back to the Brudenell. Tweed left early this morning so we'll probably settle our bills, get back to London.' He looked at Marler who was standing close by. 'Well, it worked.'

'What did?'

'My stirring up Lord Dane Dawlish. That chopper attack was a blunder, a major giveaway. Tweed will be interested.'

17

During his morning drive back to Park Crescent in the Ford Escort Tweed was worried. Too many people were descending on Lord Dawlish for his shooting party. And besides Newman and Marler, Paula had chosen the same morning for her interview with the millionaire.

His anxiety grew as he drove into London. By the time he parked close to his HQ he'd decided what to do. Hurrying up the stairs to his office, he opened the door and spoke to Monica before even taking off his coat.

'Urgent.' He checked his watch. 12.30 p.m. And Paula's appointment had been for noon. 'Very urgent. Look up the number of Lord Dane Dawlish at Grenville Grange near Aldeburgh. Write it down and give it to me quickly.'

He opened a file after taking off his coat and sitting behind his desk. He hardly saw the papers he was looking at. Monica was having trouble obtaining the unlisted number. After speaking to the operator she broke the connection, called a friend of Tweed's in Special Branch.

A few minutes later she slammed the phone down, scribbled on a sheet of paper, tore it off the notepad, and took it to Tweed.

'Sorry it took so long . . .'

'I've got it. That's the main thing. I'll dial the number myself. I may have to crash through a screen of underlings . . .'

*　　*　　*

Paula had shown cool outrage when Dawlish grabbed her by the wrist.

'If you don't let go of me I'll walk out on you now. And you won't like the article. Headline? *Lord Dawlish Man-handles Women*. Won't do your image a power of good, I'd have thought.'

Dawlish released his grip. Still red-faced he repeated his question more quietly.

'Who the hell put you up to asking that question about armaments? Someone else threw me the same sidewinder not ten minutes ago.'

'I'm not someone else. For your information I happen to operate independently. And it was rather an obvious subject to bring up – you do control armament factories. I do my homework before I interview anyone. Or would you prefer to dodge the issue?'

'No issue to dodge, as you put it. I also control whole chains of supermarket stores in North America. Which is my main source of income.' He leaned towards her. 'I feed people. Armaments is a sideline. I suppose, like all reporters you're looking for a sensational angle,' he sneered.

'A balanced report is what I aim at. You have a really wide spread of activities. That's the way the article will read. Supermarkets, financing underwater exploration of a sunken village. I think I'll concentrate on the latter. It's unusual.'

'Do I have your word on that?' Dawlish barked.

'Look, are you deaf? I've already told you once what I'm going to do.'

'I like a girl with guts.' Dawlish became amiable. 'I spend half my time pushing thickheads into carrying out my instructions correctly. Only way I've got where I have. You're very intelligent. Shouldn't have lost my temper. There was an incident outside just before I met you. My apologies.' He grinned. 'Why not join me in a glass of wine to show no hard feelings? Then later I can show you round the house. Some interesting pictures upstairs.'

Upstairs? Bedrooms. Here we go again, Paula thought as she shook her head. 'If you don't mind I'll stay with coffee.'

'Coffee can be served upstairs,' Dawlish persisted. 'I have a Rubens up there. That would be something for your article.'

'Don't like Rubens.'

'What were your sources for discovering one of my minor activities is armaments?' Dawlish suddenly shot at her.

Paula paused. She sensed the situation could turn ugly. Dawlish was not a man accustomed to being turned down by females. His attitude and expression had become aggressive. The phone rang. Dawlish pursed his thick lips with annoyance, picked up the instrument off a table.

'What the devil is it? Who did you say was calling? I see. Hell, you'd better put him on.'

'Dawlish here . . .'

'Chief Inspector Buchanan speaking,' a voice interrupted him. 'I know you have a Paula Grey visiting you,' Tweed continued. 'I want her to drive back at once to the Brudenell Hotel for questioning. When I say at once I mean now.'

'It's not convenient just at this moment . . .'

'Make it convenient, I'm investigating a murder case – that takes priority over everyone's convenience. Put her on the line, Dawlish. *Now!*'

Dawlish looked grim. He put his hand over the mouthpiece. He decided to try once more to delay his guest's departure.

'She could leave within about an hour . . .'

'And I could send a patrol car over there to fetch her. I'm beginning to wonder about your reluctance to co-operate,' Tweed continued.

'Just a moment.'

160

Dawlish shoved the phone at Paula. His tone was brittle. He raised his voice so it would carry along the line.

'Chief Inspector Plod insists on speaking to you. He'll give you his own message.'

'Miss Grey?' Tweed went on speaking quickly. 'This is Chief Inspector Buchanan. Would you kindly drive back to the Brudenell Hotel immediately. I have further information I need from you . . .' Tweed dropped to a whisper, using his normal voice. 'Get out of there at once. I don't like the sound of Dawlish's mood.'

Paula managed to keep her expression blank. Earlier it had sounded exactly like Buchanan.

'Very well, Chief Inspector. I can't imagine how I can help, but as you insist I'm leaving now. I should be with you inside half an hour. Goodbye.'

Handing back the receiver, she put her notebook and pen inside her shoulder bag. Standing up, she walked swiftly to the wall cupboard, slipped on her coat before Dawlish could reach her, turned round.

'I'm sure I have enough for my *Woman's Eye* piece. I would like to thank you for your courtesy in agreeing to see me.'

Dawlish shoved a hand into the pocket of his jodhpurs. He looked grim and highly unsatisfied. He stood like a wooden statue as he asked the question.

'What was all that about? Are you in trouble?'

'I discovered the body of a girl who was strangled on the marshes near Aldeburgh not so long ago.'

'I read about it. Karin . . .' He snapped the thick fingers of his other hand. 'Somebody-or-Other.'

'Rosewater.' She watched his eyes, which were like bullets again. 'She was German with an English husband. No one can work out why she was murdered.'

'Some psychopath probably. You'd better go and meet Mr Flatfoot. I just wonder how he knew you were here.'

'He knows I'm staying at the Brudenell. He only had to

make enquiries – I asked some of the staff how to get to Grenville Grange.' Paula lied easily.

'Don't forget my invitation to join me for a trip aboard the Cat,' Dawlish reminded her as he escorted her to the spacious entrance hall and the front door. 'Here is my card with my ex-directory number. Don't print that, for God's sake.'

'I promise,' Paula said, taking the gold-edged embossed card.

'Just call me when you're available,' Dawlish urged her affably, one hand on her arm. 'I'll give you several dates.'

Paula turned her head suddenly as he opened one of the double doors. Leading into the hall was a single door to her right and it had been open about a foot. In the gap she caught a glimpse of a man watching her and then it closed.

'Drive carefully,' Dawlish advised jovially as she left, running down the terrace steps and across to her car.

She sank into the seat behind the wheel, sighing with relief. Dawlish had an overwhelming personality and she'd exhausted herself fighting him off. She switched on the ignition and spoke to herself as she drove down the gravel drive towards the gates which were opening automatically.

'Thank God for Tweed . . .'

Inside Grenville Grange Dawlish walked to the door in the right-hand wall, opened it and glared at the man waiting inside.

'I just hope to hell she didn't see you, idiot. Now follow me and report, Lieutenant Berthier.'

At Park Crescent Monica gazed in astonishment at Tweed. He had just completed his call to Grenville Grange.

'In all the years I've known you,' Monica began, 'I'd no idea you were such a good mimic. You really sounded just like Chief Inspector Buchanan.'

'Oh, I have hidden talents.' Tweed smiled wrily and

162

polished his glasses with his handkerchief. 'Now, we must move fast. Get me René Lasalle . . .

'I'm on scrambler, René,' Tweed warned when the call came through.

'So am I. The situation here is grim . . .'

'I'm working on it,' Tweed assured him. 'So is most of my team. Round the clock. I need certain items urgently . . .'

'Which are?'

'When Paula and I met you in Paris you showed us some photos from a certain gentleman's dossier. Can you send me quickly copies of photos of the following – Josette. You know who I mean?'

'Yes. Who else?'

'Major Lamy, de Forge, and Jean Burgoyne.'

'I'll make copies from the negatives myself, send them to you by personal courier. Code-name Versailles. I will also send you one of someone else. A Lieutenant André Berthier. On Lamy's staff. Could be a key liaison officer – and something else. That's it?'

'For the moment. Keep in touch . . .'

'Who is Josette?' Monica enquired.

'General de Forge's wife. When Newman goes back into France he'll need to be able to identify the main players.'

'Won't that be dangerous – after what happened when he was there recently?'

'Very dangerous, but knowing Bob he'll insist on going back. He was worried about that girl, Isabelle, who is hiding away in Arcachon. And something else intriguing cropped up in my conversation with Lasalle . . .'

He repeated Lasalle's comment about Lieutenant Berthier, telling her a photograph was on the way.

'That was a cryptic remark,' Monica commented. 'What do you think he meant?'

'No idea,' Tweed said quickly, too quickly. 'Talking about Newman going back to France reminds me.'

Unlocking a drawer, he took out the photograph of Sergeant Rey handed to him by Lasalle in Paris. 'Come and look at this specimen.'

'Don't like the look of him one little bit,' Monica decided after studying the photograph.

'Sergeant Rey. I think his rank is deceptive, maybe a cover. He's de Forge's expert on boobytraps. Have the Engine Room make six copies. Newman must have one – and I may send him back-up when the time comes. Anyone who goes near Third Corps – or Bordeaux, for that matter – needs a copy of that reptile.'

'I'll get it done now . . .'

'No. First, get me Chief Inspector Kuhlmann on the line. Let's hope he's at his Wiesbaden HQ.'

'You really are moving,' Monica remarked as she went back to her desk and began dialling the number from memory.

'I don't think we have much time left . . .'

'Kuhlmann here,' a familiar growly voice introduced himself on the phone. 'On scrambler. And you'd damn well better be.'

'I am, Otto. Something has happened from your tone of voice.'

'I'm on the track of this *Siegfried* movement. Imported terrorists planning to create all hell over here.'

'Any leads?' Tweed asked quietly.

'Yes. I got a tip-off. From an Englishman. We raided an address in Freiburg, found a small cache of arms and explosives. To be precise, six Kalashnikov rifles, five pounds of Semtex explosive, timers, and other devices for making half a dozen bombs.'

'And how many *Siegfried* terrorists?'

'None. The birds had flown. Not even a fingerprint in the apartment. They'd cleaned up so well I think they must have had a woman with them. Any luck at your end?'

'We're trying. I may have news soon. Patience, Otto. Is

that friend of yours, Stahl, still at the same address you gave me?'

'Affirmative.'

'Incidentally, that tip-off from an Englishman. Would it have anything to do with *The Name of the Rose*?' Tweed asked, quoting the title of a famous novel.

'Yes, it would. Let's leave it at that. And I may fly to London soon. Even scramblers can be intercepted . . .'

Tweed put down the phone, disturbed. The same sinister atmosphere seemed to prevail in Wiesbaden as in Paris. A diabolical air of nervousness and mistrust among men at the top about their staffs. First Lasalle, now Kuhlmann.

'Who is Stahl?' Monica asked.

'Give me one of the top secret cards. Thanks. Stahl is an agent of Kuhlmann's operating under cover inside Bordeaux . . .' He was writing on the card as he spoke. 'This gives the address, phone number – and the French name he's using. I want an envelope for Newman kept in the safe.' He handed back the card. 'That goes in Newman's envelope. Add to it the copy of the photo of the evil gnome-like Sergeant Rey when you've got it from the Engine Room.'

'Will do. What was that business about *The Name of The Rose*?'

'Kuhlmann had a tip-off about one of the safe houses used by *Siegfried*. The tip-off came from Captain Victor Rosewater. I told you about our meeting him with Paula in Basle. Paula thinks he'd make good material for us.'

'Sounds as though Paula could be right.'

At Grenville Grange Dawlish had taken a long phone call from New York as soon as he entered the living room with Lieutenant Berthier. The Frenchman stood staring down the lawn to the landing stage. Beyond, in the wide loop of the river Alde, a luxurious yacht was moored to a buoy. He

165

watched as a motorboat left the yacht with three men aboard. They headed the craft for the landing stage, jumped ashore, ran up the edge of the lawn and disappeared round the side of the mansion. They were a tough-looking crew: well-built men in their thirties, who moved with athletic strides.

'All right, Berthier,' Dawlish called out. 'Get to it. What news do you bring?'

Berthier, erect, swung round on his heel, felt for his tinted glasses, pressed them deeper into his top pocket. Dawlish's manner was abrupt, his tone brusque.

'I was ordered to ask you when the next consignment would arrive.'

'Consignment of what?'

Dawlish watched Berthier's reaction closely. His visitor's eyes were blank, unblinking.

'I have no idea, sir. The message was exactly as I have phrased it.'

'But you could make a guess?' Dawlish persisted.

'I could not, sir. My orders were to transmit certain questions to you. Then I take the answers back to my superiors.'

'What unit are you attached to, Lieutenant? You are just a lieutenant? Or maybe that covers a higher rank?'

'Just a lieutenant, sir. And I'm attached to the engineers. Bridge-building. That sort of work.'

'I see.'

Dawlish was careful not to show it but he was impressed. Security was as tight as a closed hatch.

'The next consignment will be delivered within roughly three weeks from now. That answers your question?'

'It does. Thank you, sir.'

'Relax, man.' Dawlish became amiable. 'You're not on duty. Pour yourself a drink. You press the button in that bookcase – next to the volume of *Pilgrim's Progress*.'

'I never drink when on duty, sir.'

'Then bloody well pour me one. A large Scotch.'

Dawlish fumed at the Frenchman's pedantic adherence to duty. He had never been able to break down the cold mask Berthier habitually displayed. Give him an order and he'd do anything. Dawlish found it disconcerting that he couldn't penetrate the armour Berthier seemed to surround himself with. Frightened of few men, Dawlish had always found Berthier's presence unsettling. He took the glass of Scotch without a word, drank half the contents.

'There is another question I was asked to transmit,' Berthier continued. 'Where will the consignment be landed?'

'Arcachon . . .'

Dawlish nearly added, 'as on previous occasions,' but stopped himself just in time. Possibly Berthier did know as little about the operation as appeared to be the case.

'And a signal confirming the exact arrival date and time will be sent by the usual route twenty-four hours earlier?'

'Yes.'

Dawlish left it at that. Again he studied Berthier. Six feet tall, strong face, good build, large hands hanging close to his sides. Almost as though standing to attention. On parade. The eyes were blue and ice-cold. The prototype of a well-trained machine.

'You're leaving when?' Dawlish demanded.

'I have been ordered to stay for a short time to explore for certain information. I am staying locally.'

Dawlish would like to have asked where 'locally' was but doubted whether he'd be told. Rather than risk a rebuff from a man whose reactions he was unsure of, Dawlish simply nodded. He drank the rest of his Scotch, stood up.

'Walters will show you out . . .'

He paced the room when Berthier had gone. People left an atmosphere behind them when they had intruded and gone. Dawlish felt that Death had just paid a visit to Grenville Grange.

18

Still furious with the way Dawlish had tried to paw her, Paula was very glad to see the man walking down the steps of the Brudenell as she left her parked car. Victor Rosewater, clad in a British warm, came forward to greet her, gave her a strong bear hug.

'You look strained,' he commented. 'Had a bad experience?'

'Actually, it was a trifle unpleasant . . .'

She was surprised and pleased at how perceptive he was. And he made no attempt to question her at that moment – instead he said just the right thing.

'I was on my way for a walk through Aldeburgh. That can wait. I suspect you could do with a drink. I'll wait in the bar while you divest yourself of your coat . . .'

In her room, Paula took a couple of minutes to check her make-up. She chose her favourite brooch to pin to the lapel of her suit, combed, brushed her raven-black hair and sprayed it.

'Champers?' Rosewater suggested when she perched by the counter.

'Lovely. I need it.'

'Let's go sit in a quiet corner,' Rosewater suggested as he carried two glasses of champagne.

Again she appreciated his consideration. Intuitively he had guessed she might want to talk where no one could overhear them. As she faced him she looked at his gear. A smart small-check sports jacket, corduroy trousers to ward off the cold outside, a cream shirt and a pale blue tie. He looked very fit. He raised his glass.

'Cheers! Do you want to talk about your experience or shall we avoid the subject?'

'I'd like to get it out of my system.' She felt a little odd getting on such warm terms with the man who had been Karin's husband. But Rosewater was not only good-looking: more important, he had an easy manner with women. He sat patient and attentive as Paula went on.

'I do a bit of journalism on the side,' she said, shading the truth. 'I've just come back from interviewing Lord Dane Dawlish for *Woman's Eye*. It turned out to be an ordeal. He couldn't keep his hands off me.'

'Nothing serious – really serious – happened?' he asked quietly.

'No. I fended him off. I should have scratched his face.'

'Probably just as well you didn't. Dawlish has a reputation for playing rough with women who don't accommodate him.'

'How do you know that?' she asked, curious.

'It's part of my job to know all about the main players in the international game.'

'Game, Victor?'

'Wrong word. British understatement. It's anything but a game – a deadly struggle for power, for money. You don't become a Lord Dane Dawlish abiding by the Queensberry Rules.'

'My research showed up that Dawlish is heavily involved in the armaments trade.'

'You mentioned that to him?' Rosewater asked casually.

'Yes I did. And he got very uptight.'

'Probably because he's running down that side of his business. End of the Cold War, and all that. He's still got plenty of other golden eggs in his basket.'

'Like his underwater exploration of the sunken village up at Dunwich?' Paula suggested.

Rosewater sipped at his champagne, took his time over

169

reacting to her sudden change of subject. He put down his glass, fingered the stem. Then he shook his head and smiled as he looked at her, his eyes moving up from her slim waist to her eyes.

'He's losing money on that, I'm sure. It helps his image as a man mad keen on conservation. Who knows, perhaps he is just that. Must make a change from business and the wheeling and dealing he's devoted his career to.'

'I suppose you're right.' Paula checked her watch. 'After a quick lunch I have to get back to town. Are you staying on – still trying to find out who murdered poor Karin?'

'I'll be coming to London myself in a few days. Tell Tweed he can get me at Brown's Hotel if he needs me. Prior to that, here at the Brudenell. Now, before you go and leave me all alone maybe we could have a quick lunch together.'

'There's a very good pub up the High Street called the Cross Keys.'

'Let's eat here. I need something substantial to keep me going. Must be the cold weather . . .'

As he escorted her to the dining room Paula had the odd feeling Rosewater had given her a clue. She was damned if she could recall at the moment what it had been.

Newman and Marler had a ploughman's lunch at the Cross Keys when they drove back from the forest where the chopper had attacked them. Butler and Nield followed them in, took another table as though they were on their own. Their normal procedure when they were guarding someone.

'We have company,' Newman whispered after he'd ordered. 'Large table on our right. Five of them. The ugly-looking customer who seems to be the boss is Brand. I heard Dawlish call him that after he left us.'

'Oh, I've made the acquaintance of Mr Brand already,'

Marler replied, talking in a normal tone. 'He's the chappie who bet me I couldn't shoot clay pigeons out of the sky.'

The burly man who sat with his back to them, his shaggy hair touching his collar, turned slowly round, his chair scraping the floor. Under thick eyebrows he stared at Marler and grinned unpleasantly.

'And took five hundred nicker off you, you lousy shot.'

'Didn't quite score a hundred per cent, did I?' Marler agreed, quite unruffled by Brand's aggressive manner.

'A hundred per cent?' Brand swept a large hand to draw his four rough-looking companions into the argument. 'This ponce couldn't hit a barn door from six feet away.'

Newman caught on to the situation. Marler had first encountered this tribe of thugs at the Cross Keys. They had undoubtedly heard of the fiasco with the chopper, had come here on the off-chance they'd see Marler again. They wanted revenge. Time to intervene.

'One thing, Brand, I could hit you from a distance of six feet, which is about the distance between us now.'

'Is that so, creep?'

Brand shoved his chair back, stood up slowly. There was movement among his companions who started to get out of their chairs. Butler stood up, hoisted the rubber cosh he kept in a special pocket in his raincoat. Walking to the table, he tapped one thug on the shoulder with the cosh.

'Anyone here who wants his skull cracked? All he has to do is try and stand up. Better stay sat down, gentlemen. Leave it between the two of them. Fair's fair. Don't you agree?'

There was something menacing in the way Butler stood, six feet tall, well built, slapping the cosh into the palm of his left hand. He was smiling as he kept looking round the table. Movement ceased. Brand edged towards Newman.

Newman remained seated, elbows on the table, hands clasped under his chin. Brand's right hand whipped forward, grabbed his plate of half-eaten food, tipped it on to the floor. He grinned unpleasantly again.

'Now you'll have to eat off the floor. Expect you're used to it. Most dogs are.'

'That remark is a trifle provocative,' Marler commented.

Brand's right hand clenched, he aimed a piledriver blow at Newman's jaw. There was a blur of movement. Newman was standing, his chair thrown back on the floor. Brand's fist had missed its target. Newman's stiffened left hand hammered down on the bridge of Brand's prominent nose. He staggered back, eyes filled with tears of pain.

Newman followed him, slammed his right fist into the exposed jaw. Brand hurtled backwards, hit the counter, collapsed in a heap below it, motionless. The man sitting to the right of Brand's empty chair started to get up. Newman's hand pressed his shoulder, forced him back into his seat.

'If you want trouble you can have it. But I'm ex-SAS. I'll try not to kill you, but accidents happen . . .'

Which was true, Marler thought. Newman had survived an SAS course when writing an article on the unit. The thug subsided, muttered something but remained seated. At the far side of Brand's table another man started to get up. Nield shoved him down, hauled the chair from under him. As the thug toppled backwards Butler's right forearm struck him in the face, increasing the momentum. The back of the man's head hit the floor and he lay still. Nield checked his neck pulse.

'Still breathing. He may have a headache when he wakes up . . .'

A waitress came rushing out, horrified. Newman took a banknote from his wallet, handed it to her.

'As you saw, they started it. Here's something to cover any damage. Sorry about the food on the floor. A decent tip out of that should make you feel a bit better.'

'Thank you,' the waitress said, glancing at the size of the

banknote. 'They're regulars. I'd never have believed it.'

'I should ban them in future,' Newman advised. 'Their table manners leave something to be desired . . .'

Accompanied by Marler, he walked out of the rear door across a small garden to where they had parked his car. Beyond the promenade a nor'easter was blowing up. The grey sea heaved and rolled with huge waves working themselves up into turbulence. Butler and Nield had melted out of sight through the front door.

Newman pulled up the collar of his trenchcoat, stared along the deserted front. Aldeburgh was strange and quaint. To his right old houses joined together lined the front, rooftops stepping up and down. At the crest of the shingle beach were several winches – used to haul in the few fishing boats which still operated out of Aldeburgh. No harbour.

'You chose the Cross Keys hoping for a roughhouse?' Marler suggested.

'Not really,' Newman replied as they settled themselves in the front of the Mercedes. 'But I was curious to see whether Brand and his henchmen did turn up – since you'd told me that was where you first met the ugly ape.'

'They did turn up.'

'Which is significant. Dawlish has just made his second blunder. First, when he sent the chopper to attack us in the forest. Second when he sent them to beat the hell out of us back there – to discourage us from coming back.'

'I think I can guess the significance.'

'The fact that we were seen outside that armaments factory hidden away in the forest. Something secret and weird is going on there. Dawlish has shown his hand.'

'So I check out the place again – at closer quarters – on another occasion.'

'*We* check out the place later.' Newman was driving away from the front, turning into the High Street, heading out of town. 'Right now we're returning to London.'

173

'I prefer operating on my own,' Marler insisted.

'We'll let Tweed decide. The next priority is to talk to him, report in detail what has happened. He might fit some of it into other data he's keeping inside that brainbox head. And don't forget the fox we have in the boot. It won't last for ever and I want an expert analysis of what killed it . . .'

Isabelle Thomas was thinking of Newman as she drove her Deux Chevaux through Bordeaux in the early afternoon of the same day. She slowed down as she approached the apartment of her mother, looking everywhere at all the parked cars. She was looking for a vehicle with a man – or men – sitting in it.

Now she had disobeyed Newman's firm warning to keep out of Bordeaux she kept seeing the Englishman in her mind. She thought he'd be furious at what would seem a trivial reason for taking this risk. But she'd remembered the brooch she had left behind in the apartment, the precious brooch given to her by Joseph, her dead fiancé.

Poor Joseph. He had committed suicide, jumping into the river Gironde with weights attached to his ankles, and all because he thought he was deformed, a cripple with horribly stretched thumbs after hanging in de Forge's punishment well.

I'd like to kill de Forge, she thought. Slowly . . . agonizingly.

She knew Joseph had saved up about half a year's pay to buy her that brooch. Her only memory of the man she had expected to spend the rest of her life with. Taking one last look round, she swung into the alley and parked her car out of sight round the corner at the end in the small yard. Just as Bob Newman had done. He'd give her hell if he knew about her trip back into the city.

She unlocked the back door, slipped quietly inside, shut and locked it. The building seemed horribly quiet as she

174

slipped up the stairs, paused outside the apartment door. Before inserting the key she pressed her ear to the solid panel, listening. Could they be waiting for her inside?

Taking out a pencil flash from her handbag, she shielded it with the palm of her other hand, switched it on and examined the lock. No sign that anyone had tampered with the lock. I'm paranoid, she thought. Inserting the key she opened the well-oiled door silently, closed it with care, slipped on the security chain. Now she was safe.

To ease the tension she leaned against the door, pushed her mane of titian hair back over the knee-length green coat she was wearing against the bitter cold. The apartment felt like a morgue. Not a happy analogy, she told herself. Show some guts.

Without switching on any lights she moved across the gloomy room to the tall windows overlooking the street one floor down. Mid-afternoon and it was almost dark outside. The sky was a sheet of lead pressing down on the shabby city. Bloody November.

Isabelle studied the street. She watched the doorway where the two DST men had hidden when she had last been here with Newman. No sign of anyone. The temperature outside was close to freezing. A woman shopper hurried along the street, stoop-shouldered, huddled against the cold, carrying two plastic bags. No one else. Yes, she had got away with it.

She walked back across the living room to her bedroom, switched on the light after drawing the curtains. It took her only a minute to burrow under a drawer of her under-clothes, to find the precious brooch. Wrapping it in a slip, she noticed the door to the living room was ajar a foot, so the light would be shining through into the uncurtained living room. Pushing the brooch inside her coat pocket, she ran across the room, closed the door, switched off the light.

She stood with her back leant against it, waiting for her eyes to become accustomed to the gloom. Really she

175

should have brought some kind of weapon to defend herself. She waited a little longer, opened the door and made her way into the bathroom. Taking a canister of hair spray off the glass ledge, she removed the cap, slipped it into her pocket, glad she was leaving. In her ears rang Newman's warning.

She was approaching the door out of the apartment when someone knocked on the door. She froze. Her mother had nothing to do with the neighbours, didn't speak to anyone else in the building. The knocking was repeated more vigorously, urgently. She stiffened herself, took a deep breath.

'Who is it?' she called out.

'Plumber. One of your radiators is leaking, flooding the apartment below.'

'Not from this one,' she called back, giving herself time to think.

'Oh yes, it is,' the voice insisted. 'A plumber can trace the source of a leak. It's in your apartment. Water is pouring down the walls below.'

It had happened once before, a long time ago. When she was a little girl. She remembered watching the plumber working. And she couldn't go round to check. That would mean switching on all the lights. Which would be a give away to anyone watching the apartment from outside.

She inserted the key very quietly, turned the lock. She hesitated before removing the chain, then decided to get it over with. She stood back a short distance from the door, the flashlight in her left hand, forced herself to call out.

'The door's unlocked . . .'

It opened slowly until it was wide open. She switched on her flashlight. Two men in trench coats stood framed in the doorway. The two DST men who had taken Henri away from the Bar Miami. The two fake DST men – as Newman had warned her – who had been involved in Henri's murder at the Gare St Jean. She went ice-cold with hate. The taller

176

man held up a hand to shield his eyes from the flashlight and grinned.

'We thought you'd be back. You're coming with us. We are DST . . .'

She aimed the spray she was holding in her right hand, pressed the button, moved it in a swift arc, spraying both of them in the eyes. The taller one swore foully, clawed at his eyes. Isabelle lowered her head, jumped forward, butted him in the chest with all her strength. He staggered backwards as she kept on charging him like a bull. His back broke the banister rail. The impetus of her enraged charge toppled him over. He screamed as he fell down the drop two floors to the concrete basement.

Isabelle swung round. The other smaller man still had his hands over his eyes. She grabbed a handful of his hair, pulled his head forward. Instinctively he jerked backwards a fraction, which was what she was expecting. She changed her tactics, pushed with all her force, smashing his skull against the hard edge of the door frame. The sound of bone meeting wood was loud. He slumped to the floor. She thrust the canister and her flashlight into her pockets, stood, took hold of his inert heels, dragged him to the gap in the banister, heaved his legs over the edge, levered his body after them. He made no sound as he followed his companion. She heard a distant thud.

Locking the door, she left the building by the rear staircase. Settling herself behind the wheel of her car, she sucked in deep breaths. She must drive normally. Near the Gare St Jean she saw an empty parking slot, a public phone booth near by. She drove into the slot, locked the car, walked quickly to the booth. Inside she used her flashlight to check the number of the Prefecture in Bordeaux. When the police operator answered she spoke forcefully.

'I have to report a very serious crime – attempted

murder. It has just taken place. Put me through to the Prefect at once. I will speak to no one else. If you keep me waiting I'll ring off. It concerns the DST . . .'

In his first-floor office in the old grey stone building with two wings flanking a central courtyard, only a short walk from the Mériadeck Centre Commercial, the Prefect frowned at the mention of the DST, told the operator to put the caller through. Using his foot, he slammed his office door shut.

In the phone booth Isabelle had covered the mouthpiece with the end of her silk scarf to muffle her voice.

'This is the Prefect. Who is calling?'

'Take this address down immediately . . . You've got it? Good. On the staircase you'll find two fake DST men if you send a patrol car now. *Now!* There was a struggle. On the staircase. Both men are unconscious – and they were involved in the murder of Henri Bayle . . .'

'Who is this?' the Prefect demanded.

But the phone had gone dead. A short stocky man in a grey business suit, the Prefect had been chosen for his ability to take quick decisions. Fake DST? But the name which really alerted him was Henri Bayle – the man murdered recently at the Gare St Jean.

He locked his office door. Picking up the phone he asked the operator to give him an outside line. And he warned the man that if he listened in he'd be dismissed instantly. Then he dialled the number of René Lasalle, Chief of the DST in Paris. He got straight through.

'Prefect of Bordeaux here. We have spoken before, as you'll recall. I've just had an anonymous call about two fake DST men at a Bordeaux address. The caller, who I think was a woman – voice blurred – said they were involved in the murder of Henri Bayle . . .'

He kept the call brief. Breaking the connection, he picked up the phone again, ordered two patrol cars to the address.

'Urgently. Break into the building if necessary. And the men should be armed with automatic weapons . . .'

Isabelle drove at speed through the night along the N650, the same route Newman had driven her on their way to Arcachon. Close to the sea she pulled in by the side of the highway in the middle of open country outside the village of Facture. Across the fields she saw an old barn, half-burnt out, the rafters exposed like human ribs.

Reaction set in. She shuddered uncontrollably as though she had a bad chill. She felt frozen. Nerves. Gradually she regained control, taking deep breaths of the icy air coming in through the window she had opened.

It was only a short distance to Arcachon now. She would stay there from now on. And in the morning she would call Bob Newman and tell him what had happened. Maybe it was important.

19

The following day at Park Crescent Tweed spent a lot of time listening to verbal reports of what had happened at Aldeburgh, later questioning all the people assembled in his crowded office closely.

Crowded into the room were Paula, Newman, Marler, Butler, and Nield. Monica occupied her desk, quietly taking notes. They had just finished their reports when Newman spoke again.

'I've just remembered something I'd completely forgotten to tell you. It concerns Isabelle . . .'

'The beautiful titian-haired Isabelle,' Paula teased him.

'I merely described her,' Newman rapped back, irked.

'It was the way you described her.' Paula purred.

'I'd now like to say something important without interruption. It was your description, Paula, of Lord Dawlish's catamaran, *Steel Vulture*. A while ago, when you told us about your grim experience when Karin Rosewater was killed, you said when you both surfaced off Dunwich there was a strange ship, its prow cut in two . . .'

'That's right.' Paula leaned forward, serious again.

'Well, when I was walking along the Arcachon front with Isabelle she described a strange vessel which sails in there – a ship "with its prow cut in two". Something very close to that. It sounds exactly like the *Steel Vulture*.'

'That is interesting,' Tweed interjected. 'Maybe now we have a link between Suffolk and France.'

'And,' Newman went on, 'she also told me a Lord Dane Dawlish turned up at some party and made a heavy pass at her, which she rebuffed.'

'That's dear Dawlish,' Paula commented. 'And surely we now have another connection between Aldeburgh and France?'

'We have what may be a vital one,' Tweed agreed. 'Between Aldeburgh and Arcachon – which is close to Bordeaux. And Dawlish is armaments. And Lasalle told me some unknown organization was supplying General de Forge with arms and money. It could be fiendishly clever.'

'What could be?' asked Paula.

'Landing arms at Arcachon instead of direct to the port of Bordeaux where the watch on incoming cargoes will be stricter. Bless Isabelle – and you, Paula.'

'But at what a price,' Paula said nostalgically. 'The price of Karin's life.'

'Victor Rosewater is available then if we need him?' Tweed asked, changing the subject.

'Yes. He may even track Karin's murderer. He's a tough character.'

'Describe again to me, Bob, how this signet ring came to be found.' Tweed leant back in his swivel chair and watched Newman. 'Start from the beginning. Every minute detail . . .'

He unlocked a drawer half-way through Newman's recall of what had happened on that dark night on the marshes with Paula and Rosewater. Tweed took a large silk handkerchief from the drawer, screwed up into a ball, laid it on his desk.

When Newman had finished, ending with their trip in the marsh buggy with Buchanan and Warden to the Brudenell, he congratulated him on his total recall. Opening the handkerchief he took out two signet rings, pushed them across the desk to Paula.

'Which one is the ring Rosewater found under the boat?'

Paula examined them carefully. She slipped both separately on her middle finger. Both were far too large to stay on. Puzzled, she looked at them again, shook her head, stared at Tweed.

'I don't understand. They're identical.'

'Not quite. There's a tiny scratch on the inside of one ring. That's the original. The Engine Room worked for thirty-six hours – including through the night – creating the twin. You see, I have to hand the original to Chief Inspector Buchanan – but I wanted a copy. Find the finger that wore it and we may have found our murderer.'

'Why *may*?' Newman asked aggressively.

'Because nothing is conclusive. Just as we can't assume yet that Dawlish is linked to de Forge. We need more solid evidence – and urgently. Which is why, Marler, I think you should get moving on that special mission in France I described to you.' He held up a hand, looked round his

181

audience. 'No, only Marler and I know about it.'

'First things first,' Marler entered the conversation for the first time. 'I have to explore that factory in the forest on the road to Orford . . .'

'And I go with him,' Newman said firmly.

'Nothing doing,' Marler said emphatically.

'Hold it, both of you,' said Tweed. 'You both just survived your previous trip into that area. No argument. You explore that factory together. Armed. Then, Bob, we'll turn our attention to France, launch a major expedition to find out what de Forge is really up to – and what this *Siegfried* business is about in Germany. It will be dangerous.'

'What about my fox?' Newman asked.

'Collected for immediate delivery to the top veterinary pathologist in the country, Robles. Hours ago. And I gave them the keys to your car because Robles wanted to examine the boot too. Now, I think we ought to go to lunch in small groups. Maybe there will have been developments even by the time we get back . . .'

Tweed realized Monica was excited as soon as he returned to his office with Paula, Newman, and Marler. She waited until he had taken off his coat and settled himself behind his desk. Outside there was a cold November drizzle, a raw biting wind.

'The courier arrived from Lasalle with the photos you asked for. He left them and went straight back to Heathrow to board a flight for Paris.'

'And?'

Newman sat in the armchair close to his desk and Paula perched herself on one arm. Marler adopted his usual stance, leaning against a wall. Monica brought over an envelope, placed it in front of Tweed with a smile of smug satisfaction.

'You're going to be interested.'

'Sounds as though I'd better be.'

Tweed extracted the glossy prints. He laid them out across his desk. There were three copies of each print. On their backs Lasalle had written names in his own neat writing. Josette de Forge. De Forge himself. Major Lamy. Lieutenant Berthier. Jean Burgoyne.

Tweed handed a set of copies to Paula, another set to Newman. He began examining them himself. Glancing up at Monica, now behind her own desk, he saw her watching him with anticipation. He went on looking at the pictures, then stopped and reached for his magnifying glass. He looked up at the others.

'I thought I'd seen that signet ring before.'

He held up the photograph he had been studying. In Paris he had spotted the ring without the aid of a glass. He was holding up a photo of de Forge's Chief of Intelligence, Major Lamy.

'So,' Newman said after an interval of silence, 'we've found Kalmar, the assassin. Nice work.'

'Not necessarily,' Tweed warned.

'But it's conclusive,' Newman protested. 'His ring was found under the boat where Karin was strangled.'

'And how do you think a man like Major Lamy flew here, stayed somewhere, and was available for murdering her? Bearing in mind his job, the danger of being recognized in England. Also does anyone know he speaks English fluently?'

'He might. He might be able to slip over here, back again without being spotted.'

'"Might" isn't good enough,' Tweed rapped back. 'It remains a possibility – no more at this stage.'

'He looked like a nasty piece of work when I met him,' Newman said and relapsed into silence.

'You're forgetting earlier events,' Tweed said cryptically. He picked up a sheet of paper with Monica's handwritten notes. 'But this is conclusive, may well interest both you and Marler. We know how your fox died. Ready?'

'Very.'

'Robles phoned a preliminary report to Monica while we were out at lunch. He suspects the fox was killed by some type of nerve gas mixed with the smoke that helicopter ejected.'

'Nerve gas?' Marler was startled out of his normal coolness. 'So if Newman and I had breathed in any of that smoke . . .'

'You'd be as dead as the fox,' Tweed completed his sentence. 'Nerve gas. That really is sinister.'

'And,' Monica interjected, 'my researches turned up the fact that Dawlish Chemicals has a high security laboratory in the factory complex on the road to Orford.'

'Robles,' Tweed went on, 'is taking the carcase in a refrigerated truck to a friend of his who works at Porton Down, the chemical warfare establishment. Then he'll be able to tell us the precise type of nerve gas used.'

'We'd better get back to Suffolk fast – Marler and myself. Time we took a closer look at Dawlish's conservation activities,' Newman suggested.

'Agreed,' said Tweed. 'The sooner the better – Marler has to go to France. But take great care.'

'We do know now we're not dealing with pussycats,' Newman retorted. He left the room with Marler.

The phone rang. Tweed waited while Monica took the call. She asked someone to wait just one moment, nodded to Tweed's phone.

'It's Lasalle in Paris. Wants to talk to you urgently.'

'More problems, René?' Tweed enquired. 'Yes, I'm on scrambler . . .'

'I've had a call from the Prefect of Bordeaux, a man I can

rely on,' Lasalle stressed. 'He had an anonymous phone call – thinks it was from a girl – who gave him the address of an apartment block here in Bordeaux. Told him he'd find the two fake DST men who were involved in the murder of Henri Bayle. Your agent found at the Gare St Jean. He went to the address himself. Incidentally, the girl said he'd find the two men unconscious. He found them all right. Dead. Both of them.'

'How did they die?'

'Hard to say, apparently. Both had fallen two floors. His men found traces of blood on the door frame of the apartment occupied by Isabelle Thomas and her mother. Both women have disappeared. But their descriptions fit what witnesses at the Bar Miami said about the two men who took Bayle away – after a little arm-twisting. I'm flying to Bordeaux to interview General de Forge. With this I can shake him, rattle his cage. He's had it all his own way too long . . .'

'Take care,' Tweed warned. 'You're not going down there alone?'

'Yes, I am.' He paused. 'Maybe with a little back-up.'

'One more thing before you go. Do you know if Major Lamy is fluent in English?'

'Speaks your language like a native. An English native.'

In his cramped office Lasalle put down the phone, checked the time. He had an appointment with Navarre, Minister of the Interior. Throwing on his coat and hat – it was sleeting outside – he left the building, walked into the rue du Faubourg St Honoré, turning to the right away from the Elysée Palace.

Normally mild-mannered but tenacious, Lasalle strode along briskly with a grim expression. Reaching the entrance to the Ministry in the Place Beauveau, he expected the guards, who knew him well, to usher him

185

straight past the gates. A guard barred his way.

'Identification, sir.'

'You know me by now . . .'

'Orders, sir. Identification, please.'

Lasalle produced his special identity pass, handed it to the guard. After examining it, the guard returned the pass, waved him on with a salute. So Navarre had stepped up security, Lasalle thought, hurrying across the spacious yard in front of the ministry building: that's good.

The minister's office is on the first floor, overlooks the front courtyard. Its occupant rose from behind his desk as Lasalle was ushered inside. Pierre Navarre was a short stocky individual with dark hair, thick brows and impatient eyes. Like General de Forge, he came from Lorraine. He shook hands with the DST chief, told him to sit down and, holding a document in one hand, hauled a chair close to Lasalle's. He handed him the document which Lasalle read quickly. Scrawled at the bottom of the letter was Navarre's strong, swift signature.

'That should do it, Minister,' Lasalle said.

'Time we put pressure on that bastard,' Navarre remarked savagely. 'When do you fly to Bordeaux?'

'Within the hour . . .'

'Report to me what happens. I will be working here a little late . . .'

A little late. The phrase echoed in Lasalle's mind as he hurried back to his office. Navarre was noted for the hours he kept – often eighteen hours a day. In his office he phoned a Bordeaux number, gave certain orders, slammed down the phone and ran to the car waiting in the courtyard to take him to the airport.

Arriving at Bordeaux Airport late in the afternoon under a murky sky he was met by a DST officer who led him to a bullet-proof Citroën. Lasalle jumped inside, followed by the officer. The driver, who had the engine running, raced away from the airport.

'What about the reserves?' Lasalle asked the officer beside him in the rear.

'Assembled and hidden in a field near Third Corps HQ. General de Forge expects you to come alone?'

'Yes. He's not the only tactician in France . . .'

Out in the country well away from Bordeaux the driver slowed, pulled up alongside a gated field. A man in a blue raincoat opened the gate, lifted his arm in a signal, then waved Lasalle's vehicle on. Lasalle glanced back through the rear window as they raced along a straight stretch of road. Behind followed a convoy of eight cars, filled with armed DST men. Behind them followed CRS motorcyclists, clad in black leather coats, automatic weapons slung over shoulders. The huge convoy pulled up in front of the entrance to Third Corps.

A uniformed lieutenant approached the Citroën, frowning. As Lasalle pressed the button which lowered the window he peered inside. Lasalle wasted no time.

'Open the damn gate.' He flashed his identity card. 'Lasalle of DST, Paris. General de Forge is expecting me. I phoned Major Lamy early this morning.'

'You were expected alone . . .'

'Don't argue with me. Open the gate.'

'I'll have to fetch Major Lamy . . .'

'He has two minutes to get here. I said *two minutes*. Move, man. Things seem sloppy round here . . .'

Within a minute a car drove up behind the gate. Major Lamy emerged, walked through the pedestrian gate. He stared along the road at the endless convoy.

'What is that white vehicle?'

'An ambulance. Now, General de Forge is expecting me, so open the gates or we'll drive through them.'

Lamy looked at the four CRS outriders who had drawn up alongside Lasalle's Citroën. Wearing black crash helmets, the CRS riders stared back at him through their sinister goggles.

'If you insist,' Lamy decided. 'But this is a military establishment . . .'

'I didn't think it was a holiday camp,' Lasalle interrupted him. 'The gates . . .'

'Only your vehicle can enter . . .'

'Then the rest will smash down the gates and follow me. Give the order . . .'

Lasalle pressed the button again and the window shut in Lamy's face. He turned, nodded, the gates opened, and Lamy had to run to dive into his car which led the way to General de Forge's quarters. Behind them the convoy streamed through the entrance, nose to tail. They proceeded down a long concrete avenue lined with single-storey military buildings. Lasalle noticed that at the beginning of each side road a large tank was stationed, each huge gun barrel aimed at a low angle, its tank commander standing in the turret. De Forge was emphasizing his power.

Lamy's car eventually stopped outside a building indistinguishable from the others. Lasalle jumped out of his own car, clutching the brief case he had held on to since leaving Paris. Lamy escorted him into a large room with a wood-block floor gleaming like glass. At the far end General de Forge waited, seated behind a large desk.

Lamy marched forward while Lasalle strolled, taking his time, glancing curiously round the room. Hanging from the right-hand wall was a huge banner carrying the symbol of the Cross of Lorraine, de Gaulle's symbol when he formed the Free French during World War II.

'Welcome to Third Corps GHQ,' de Forge said in a stiff voice as he remained seated.

Lasalle sat in the hard-backed chair on the far side of the desk, facing the General across the acre or so of desk. No papers. Three phones of differing colours. A blotter framed in leather.

'Does he have to remain?' Lasalle enquired, nodding his

head towards Lamy as though he were the Army's mascot.

Lamy, standing erect, hands clasped behind his back, stiffened even more. He looked at his master.

'It is the custom,' de Forge informed him, 'for Major Lamy to be present, even for meetings of minor importance.'

Lasalle nodded, ignoring the insult. Unfastening his brief case, he extracted a folded sheet of paper and laid it in his lap. He stared straight at de Forge, his expression giving no clue as to his mood. But his tone of voice was like a whiplash.

'This is a serious matter which brings me here. May I remind you that under the Constitution the military is entirely subordinate to – the servant of – the civil power? I represent that civil power. Let us be very clear on that before I proceed.'

'Proceed, then,' de Forge ordered, his face bleak.

'We have had several cases – even numerous instances – of unauthorized personnel impersonating DST officers. I don't have to remind you that is a grave offence, I take it.'

'I have no idea what the hell you are talking about.'

'Give me just a minute more and all will be clear. I have outside two examples of men who impersonated DST officers.' Lasalle stood up. 'Could you please accompany me.'

'Why should I?'

'Because I am ordering you to, General.'

'You have no power to order me to do anything!' de Forge roared in his parade ground voice.

Lasalle made no reply. He leaned over the desk, handed the folded sheet to de Forge. The General glanced at Lamy, looked back at Lasalle, who remained staring back coldly. De Forge slowly opened the sheet. His eyes saw the printed logo at the top, realized it was a sheet of the personal stationery of the Minister of the Interior. He read the instruction. *You will co-operate with my emissary, René*

189

Lasalle, Chief of the Direction de la Surveillance du Territoire. You will accede to any request he may make. He has plenipotentiary powers.

'Now perhaps you will come outside with me,' Lasalle said quietly.

Lasalle walked more briskly back down the long room than his pace on entering. Half-way to the door, he paused, looked back. De Forge was following, his riding boots as brilliantly polished as the floor. Lamy remained by the desk.

'Major Lamy,' Lasalle called out, taking command, 'you will come too.'

He resumed his brisk trot to the door, opened it, looked outside. His orders had been obeyed. Escort cars had moved to the far side along with his own vehicle. The ambulance stood backed up to the entrance, doors still shut, two men in white coats standing by the step. Lasalle stood aside, watched.

General de Forge emerged from his office, stood stock still, taking in the long convoy at a glance. His thin lips tightened.

'This is an invasion.'

'You could call it that,' Lasalle agreed. 'DST officers, real ones, all armed. Also CRS, again armed, as you can see.'

'This is an outrage . . .'

'I call it a precaution,' Lasalle replied mildly.

'What impertinence have you called me out here for?' He saw some soldiers standing, gazing at the spectacle. He turned to Lamy. 'Major, send all those men immediately for a run over the obstacle course in full battle order.'

'That can wait,' Lasalle said firmly. 'Major Lamy may also be interested to see this.'

He nodded to the two white-coated men, descended the steps to join them, followed by de Forge and Lamy. Opening the rear doors, the two men stood on the step. A blast of icy air rushed out of the interior. De Forge and Lamy stared at the interior. Large metal drawers were stacked inside. A drawer at floor level was opened. The white-coated men stood back, Lasalle waved a hand.

'I told you I had brought two men who impersonated DST officers in Bordeaux.'

The white-coated couple opened another drawer. In each drawer a half-clothed corpse was stretched out, its head perched on a wooden block. Icy air from the refrigerated mobile morgue continued to flow out.

'Those men are dead,' Lamy burst out.

'You are most observant,' Lasalle commented. 'They are soldiers – presumably from the Third Corps since they were found in Bordeaux.'

'How on earth do you know that?' de Forge asked contemptuously.

'Oh, they carried no identification except the fake DST credentials. They were dressed in civilian clothes – but one point was overlooked. Those underclothes are Army issue. That point is certain.'

De Forge looked at Lamy. The Chief of Intelligence went closer to the corpses. He swung on his heel, addressing the General.

'I recognize both men now, sir. They are deserters – disappeared from their unit weeks ago.'

Lamy could think fast. Lasalle privately paid him that compliment. But he did not let go so easily.

'Posted officially as deserters?'

'Major Lamy,' de Forge intervened, catching on, 'go and fetch the records so we can show the gentleman from Paris.'

He walked back into the building as Lamy ran round the corner of the building and disappeared. Lasalle nodded before following de Forge. The white-coated men closed the drawers with their grisly contents: both bodies were badly damaged round the skulls. He followed de Forge back into the building.

'Both men were involved in a brutal murder,' Lasalle informed de Forge as they waited for Lamy: de Forge seated at his desk while Lasalle wandered back and forth in front of it. His restlessness irked de Forge but the General sat immobile as a statue.

'Deserters are scum,' de Forge eventually responded.

'If they were deserters.' Lasalle phrased his comment carefully. 'Someone clever was giving them orders . . .'

He broke off as Major Lamy marched towards the desk, a file under his arm, ignoring Lasalle. He placed the file in front of the General.

'Privates Gillet and Ferron,' he reported. 'Deserted five weeks ago. Not seen since.'

'There you are.'

De Forge waved towards the two sheets he had glanced at. He made no move to hand them to Lasalle. The DST chief reached across the desk swiftly, grabbed the sheets, looked at them.

'Those copies are our property,' de Forge warned.

Lasalle was holding the sheets up to the light. He turned each sheet in turn to different angles. Then he slipped them inside his briefcase, snapped it shut.

'Must I remind you I am conducting a murder investigation? These records represent vital evidence. A spectroscope examination will prove whether these so-called records were, as I suspect, produced within the past five minutes.'

'I deeply resent your implication,' Lamy snapped.

'All part of my work. The civil power takes precedence over the military.' He stood up. 'Thank you for your co-operation. I will be back . . .'

De Forge waited until he heard the convoy moving off. He then gave Lamy the order. 'Organize really ferocious riots in Lyons. We must move fast.'

20

Newman heard the phone ringing when he opened the door of his ground-floor flat at Beresforde Road, South Ken. He ran, sure it would cease ringing just as he reached the instrument in the large living room. Grabbing the receiver, he gave his number – but omitted his name. It was Tweed.

'Bob, I thought you ought to know. Lasalle has called me from Bordeaux. The two phoney DST men who took Francis Carey from the Bar Miami before he was murdered have been found at the apartment of Isabelle Thomas's mother . . .'

'Found? What does that mean?'

'Curb your anxiety. I haven't finished. The Prefect of Bordeaux received an anonymous call – from a girl, he believes – who reported the presence of the two men. She said they were unconscious. In the basement. The police found them. Both men were dead.'

'Oh, God! How had they died?'

'Very curious. No one is certain. But they had fallen two floors, their skulls crushed. Do you think Isabelle could have done that?'

'Not deliberately. Seems unlikely she'd have coped with two of them – although she's exceptionally strong. Swims every day in a leisure club. You say Lasalle called from Bordeaux?'

'Yes. Flew there. Made an audacious move. Fixed up to see de Forge, took the bodies in a refrigerated truck, showed them to him. Identified as soldiers by their

193

Army-issue underclothes. They always forget something. He's shaken de Forge.'

'Is that good?'

'It may provoke him into a wrong move. We need the trigger to make him show his hand. Trouble is, I don't know what that trigger will be. Must go now. You're leaving soon for your return trip?'

'Just waiting for Marler. He's due in about half an hour.'

'Don't push it to the limit . . .'

Newman had hardly replaced the receiver when the phone rang again. Marler? Warning him he'd be late? He picked up the phone, again gave only the number.

'That's you, Bob, isn't it? I recognize your voice.' Isabelle. All in a rush. He told her to slow down. 'You're going to be very mad with me. I was a fool to ignore your warning . . .'

'Slow down, Isabelle,' he repeated, alarmed. 'Are you in danger? And where are you calling from?'

'It's all right, it's safe, I'm calling from my sister's apartment in Arcachon, she's not here, I'm alone . . .'

'For Pete's sake then, slow down. Now, nice and easy.'

'I went back to my mother's flat in Bordeaux, Bob . . .'

Without more interruption he listened grimly to her experience. She was talking at normal speed now, giving him a terse but detailed report of everything that had happened. She concluded by telling him about how she'd called the Prefect of Bordeaux before driving like hell back to Arcachon.

'Maybe you were followed,' he suggested.

'Not possible. I kept an eye on my rear-view mirror. There was hardly any traffic at that hour. And I stopped for a few minutes in the country outside Arcachon. No vehicle of any kind appeared.'

'Then that's all right.' Newman hesitated, decided he had to ensure she stayed in Arcachon by frightening the life out of her. 'There's one detail in what you told me you got wrong.'

'What was that?'

'You said the two fake DST men were unconscious. Both of them were – are – *dead*.'

'Are you sure? How do you know that, Bob?'

She sounded as cool as the proverbial cucumber when he'd expected hysterics. Almost a note of satisfaction.

'I assure you they're both dead as a doornail. I know, Isabelle. For a certainty. I have my contacts.'

'So the men who led poor Henri to his death are dead now themselves.'

'As dead as you can get,' he stressed.

'I didn't waste time going down to look at them. Bob, are you mad with me for going back to Bordeaux, for dis-obeying you?'

She sounded as though that possibility worried her far more than the news he'd given her.

'Will you be going back to Bordeaux again?' he asked.

'No! I promise you, I know I promised you before but this time I'll keep my word. Bob, you do believe me, don't you? Say you believe me. Please say it . . .'

Her metabolism was all revved up again. The words tumbled over each other like some river roaring down over rapids.

'I believe you,' Newman assured her. 'A lot of people will be looking for you. Are you certain no one in the city knows about your mother having a place in Arcachon?'

'I'm absolutely sure, certain, positive. I told you, she doesn't like anyone in Bordeaux, she's never let anyone know about her apartment here. So no one would dream of looking for me here. When will I see you again?'

'I'll contact you as soon as I can. Meantime read some of those books I saw in your apartment. Go out for a walk after nightfall. And push your hair up under some kind of headgear. A beret. A scarf. Anything . . .'

'I promise, Bob. I'll tie up my hair, then hide it under a scarf. And I'll wear trousers. I have a pair. I never normally wear them because I don't think they look feminine. No one even here will recognize me. I will see you soon?'

'As soon as I can make it. Someone is at the door. Must go. Chin up . . .'

Newman peered round the side bay window through the heavy net curtains which gave him a view of the entrance. It was almost dark already. November dark. Marler stood at the entrance, carrying a long hold-all. That meant he was bringing his dismantled Armalite rifle. He must be expecting trouble at the Dawlish factory on the road to Orford.

Marler's new Volvo station-wagon was parked in a slot further down the road. They'd be travelling in that, Newman thought as he went to the lobby to operate the button which opened the front door. His Mercedes 280E was still in the hands of the veterinary pathologist.

'You'll need some insulation,' Marler said as he entered the apartment. 'It's cold enough out there to freeze the whatnots off a monkey.'

Marler was wearing his sheepskin, collar turned up. Newman thought the intense cold – met forecast had said it would be below freezing point – might help them. Guards didn't like patrolling too thoroughly on cold nights. At least he hoped he was right in his assumption.

In his Park Crescent office Tweed knew Paula was excited about something as soon as she entered. She put down the cardboard-backed envelope she had been carrying on her desk, took off her suede coat, one of her few extravagances. Taking one of Lasalle's photos from the envelope, she laid it on her desk. As she asked the question she covered the print with one hand.

'Is it all right if I play around with this print with my felt

196

tip pen? It's one of the photos Lasalle sent us.'

'Go ahead. The Engine Room made up a large number of copies of all the photos.'

Tweed showed no curiosity, writing out a list of names on his pad. Monica, in contrast, surreptitiously was watching Paula as she used her felt tip pen. Paula put down the pen, lifted up the photo, held it at a distance.

'It's him,' she announced. 'I thought it was when I was looking at the photos in my flat.'

'Who?' Tweed enquired.

'Lieutenant Berthier, on the staff of Major Lamy, is here in this country. To be precise he's probably still staying at the Brudenell Hotel in Aldeburgh.'

She took the photo to Tweed, placed it in front of him. She had used the pen to sketch in a pair of tinted glasses over the eyes, to darken his hair. Tweed looked at what she had sketched, then at her.

'Clever,' he said. 'You are right. I saw this man leaving the bar at the Brudenell when I was on my way out for a night walk over the marshes.'

'He's the man Newman thought he heard swear in French when he stubbed his toe, as you'll recall. He's the man,' Paula continued, 'you asked me to chat up, which I did, as you know. I spoke to him suddenly in French, asked him if he'd like another drink. Remember? He started to get up from his chair to fetch more drinks himself, then stopped in time and pretended to be settling himself more comfortably in his chair. I *thought* he knew what I'd said. Now I know I'm right.'

'So,' Tweed remarked, 'we have another French link between Suffolk and France. Berthier. There is something very serious going on near Aldeburgh. This is one coincidence too many.'

'He told me his name was James Sanders,' Paula recalled thoughtfully, 'that he was a salesman dealing in marine spare parts, that he'd just returned from Paris.'

'Another possible link,' Tweed said immediately. 'An officer on Lamy's staff, posing as a salesman of marine parts, would have a legitimate reason for contacting Dawlish. Because of the Cat, the *Steel Vulture*. More pieces of the jigsaw are coming to light, fitting into an insidious pattern.'

'I think I'll return to Aldeburgh,' Paula suggested. 'I could use the excuse of visiting Jean Burgoyne.'

'Except we know Burgoyne is de Forge's mistress. Tricky. We don't know at this stage who we can trust – if anyone.'

'I still think I should go back, especially as we know Berthier is there. He might let something slip if I play up to him.'

'I don't like the idea,' Tweed told her. 'I have in front of me a list of names – any of which could be the highly professional assassin, Kalmar.'

'Can we see the list?' Monica interjected.

'No. Not yet. I want to be more sure of my ground – I still need more data . . .'

'Which I might obtain if I go to Aldeburgh,' Paula insisted. 'And both Newman and Marler are on their way there. Newman is bound to phone you – you could tell him I'll be at the Brudenell.'

'You can go only if you wait at the hotel until Newman has contacted you. That's an order.'

'I'm on my way.' Paula jumped up before Tweed could change his mind. 'I'll pick up my ready-packed case at my flat, then drive up to Suffolk . . .'

'Do you think that was wise?' Monica queried when they were alone. 'She's going back to where one murder has been committed. The murderer could still be in the area.'

'What baffles me,' said Tweed, his mind elsewhere, 'is *if*, by a longshot, it's Dawlish who is supplying arms to the Third Corps secretly how does he transport them there?'

'Aboard that catamaran,' Monica said promptly. 'Dawlish himself told Paula the size of the vessel – that it can carry over a hundred people and a number of heavy vehicles. And Newman's friend, Isabelle, told him she'd seen a vessel which fits the *Steel Vulture*'s description dock frequently in Arcachon.'

'You don't get my point. Dawlish also said the vessel is berthed at Harwich. I happen to know they've tightened security at Harwich. They found a large drug consignment aboard a ship bound for Rotterdam – a reverse ploy of the drug traffickers. Drugs brought in here by some other route are then sent *out* to the continent. With that kind of security would Dawlish risk a search? I think not.'

'Then what's the solution?'

'No idea. He may not be involved at all. But that has stimulated a different line of investigation. I'm calling Heathcoate, Harbour Master at Harwich. He owes me.'

Tweed unlocked a drawer, checked through an address book, found the number, dialled it himself, gave his name, asked to be put through to the Harbour Master.

'Is that you, Heathcoate? How are you? Yes, I want a favour. A ship called the *Steel Vulture*, a twin-hulled catamaran . . .'

'Owned by millionaire Lord Dawlish. A very advanced design, the ship of the future. He berths it here. It is moored here now. What about it?'

'Ever search it? The drugs business.'

Heathcoate chuckled. 'You think millionaires are outside the law? Because they're not. Answer, yes. We searched it twice over the past six months. Clean as a whistle. You think we missed something?' Heathcoate enquired. 'That we should keep an eye on that ship?'

'Waste of time. And it's not drugs I was thinking of. Don't ask me what. Top secret.'

'You expect me to talk and then you clam up,' Heathcoate grumbled with mock seriousness.

'Buy you a Scotch next time we meet. Thanks anyway . . .'

'No good,' Tweed told Monica. 'Heathcoate searched the catamaran twice in six months. Nothing. Dawlish is too smart to risk being caught. Looks like a dead end. But someone told me something which might be the loophole and I'm damned if I can recall it.'

'You didn't hear a word I said a few minutes ago,' Monica chided him. 'I said one murder has already been committed where Paula is going back to. The murderer could still be in the area.'

'I don't think that's at all likely.'

It was a remark Tweed was to regret in the near future.

The *Cercle Noir* was holding an emergency meeting at the Villa Forban near Third Corps GHQ. It had been called by General de Forge during Jean Burgoyne's absence from the villa. He sat at the head of a table in the living room with the curtains closed. Outside it was dark.

Seated round the table were Louis Janin, Minister of Defence; General Masson, Chief of the Army Staff; General Lapointe, commander of the atomic *force de frappe*; Emile Dubois, leader of the new political party, *Pour France*; and the man known as *Oiseau* – Bird.

Janin was a short, heavily built man with slicked-back dark hair who wore rimless spectacles. He had the air of an intellectual. Nominally de Forge's superior, he was awed by the General's charismatic personality. General Lapointe was made of sterner stuff: a small lean-faced man, he believed only Charles de Forge could save France from domination by an all-powerful Germany now unification had taken place. Emile Dubois was squat and a natural orator. Given to waving his arms to stress a point, he hoped one day to become Premier under the Presidency of de Forge. General Masson was a second-rate soldier, greatly conscious of the dignity of his post.

'We have reached a crossroads in history,' de Forge began. 'Now there is a growing state of turbulence in this country there can be no turning back. There will be new and more terrible riots in Lyons. Then the target is Paris itself.'

'Are we moving too fast?' Janin queried.

De Forge held intellectuals in contempt. 'We must move ahead faster now the momentum has built up. Caution is the reaction of faint-hearts and cowards.'

'Navarre has the ear of the President more and more,' Janin warned, nettled by the implication.

'Navarre may have to go,' de Forge informed him.

'Surely you do not mean Kalmar?' Janin protested.

'The General made no suggestion at all in that direction,' Lapointe said severely.

'My members are travelling *en masse* to Lyons,' Dubois assured de Forge. 'We shall be there to play our part.'

'I had a visit from a lackey of Navarre,' de Forge reported. 'Lasalle of the DST. He is trying to build up a case against us. He will fail, of course. But when we take power he will be the first to be hurled into the street. We need men of strong patriotic fibre in all key positions. I need your agreement that in Lyons we light a furnace, ignite a beacon which will be seen in Paris. And we must send advance contingents inside the capital secretly.' He hammered a clenched fist on the table. 'From this second on the momentum must be accelerated non-stop. All agreed, hammer their fists on this table . . .'

Five fists hammered the table with varying degrees of conviction. Janin's, de Forge noted, was the feeblest response. And now the Minister of Defence raised the objections which were worrying him.

'As before, I still do not like the fact that one member of the *Cercle* remains unknown to us.'

Oiseau sat at the far end of the oblong table, facing de

Forge, his head concealed beneath a Balaclava mask. He was the one man who never spoke a word at the secret meetings. Now he turned and gazed at Janin without saying a word. De Forge exploded.

'I have told you before, Janin, time and again, *Oiseau* supplies us with the extra arms we need. More important still, he supplies us with finance from his own funds – finance which is untraceable back to its source. Without that finance *Pour France*, our vital civil arm, could never have been built up. His identity is of no concern to you. And I noticed his fist hammered the table with much greater force than yours.'

'I feel it is dangerous to make a major move until we know the reaction of the President,' Janin persisted.

'So we don't make a major move until we see how he reacts to the new Lyons riots.' De Forge's mood became mocking. 'You like discussion, Janin. It is decision that worries you. Just keep me informed about the Elysée . . .'

The meeting continued for another quarter of an hour. Most of it was occupied by de Forge reinforcing morale, working up a sensation of enthusiasm, a conviction that victory lay just round the next corner.

As always, the members of the *Cercle Noir* left the Villa Forban one by one, with a five-minute interval between each departure. *Oiseau* was the first to depart. He bowed briefly to de Forge, collected his coat himself from the cupboard in the hall, walked out into the bitter night where a limousine waited to whisk him to the executive jet at Bordeaux Airport. Only when the driver, Brand, dressed in a chauffeur's uniform, drove out between the villa gates did his passenger, *Oiseau*, remove his Balaclava helmet.

Inside the villa de Forge waited until the other members had left. Then he opened the door into the next room and closed it. Seated in the study Major Lamy was working on papers at a desk while a cassette played Stravinsky's *Rites of Spring* softly. Lamy switched off the machine and looked up.

'Are there any notepads I could use? I've checked the desk – except the deep bottom drawer I can't open. I see it has a special lock.'

'That is the drawer where Jean keeps her jewellery,' de Forge told him. 'She has the only key. God save me from some of those cretins who have just left.'

'Anyone in particular?'

'Janin. I suggest Navarre might have to be removed – so Janin mentions Kalmar. Can't he remember Lapointe thinks Kalmar is merely a thug who roughs up people causing us trouble?'

'Lapointe would not approve of Kalmar's real talent.'

'Of course not. He'd leave the *Cercle* immediately.'

'Janin is a weak sister,' Lamy agreed. 'But there is nothing to worry about – he's clever at playing up to the President. Flattering him.'

'The President is the main stumbling block to our plan. I can't forecast which way he will jump. We'd better leave now. Back to Third Corps . . .'

'I shall be away for about thirty-six hours from now on,' Lamy informed his chief while they sat in the rear of the limousine moving off down the drive.

'So long – to organize Lyons?' de Forge, ever suspicious, queried.

'You ordered that Lyons should be turned into an inferno. I must check our contingent is in place, we cannot rely on that Dubois with his amateurs. Also, our contact inside Lasalle's HQ has reported a Paula Grey has met and talked to Lasalle recently. My contact thinks she is a British agent. He is providing me with a photograph he took of her secretly.'

Lamy was staring out of the window away from de Forge as he spoke.

203

'A job for Kalmar? The decision is yours. And you know,' de Forge went on cynically, 'I think we can cope, however long you are away.'

21

At Park Crescent, Tweed was checking through sheets of data prior to arranging for teams to leave for France. Most of it was in his head but, meticulous, he relied on written records in case he missed one detail. He looked up at Monica. It was late at night.

'This man, Brand, seen by Newman and Paula at Grenville Grange. Later involved with Newman in that brawl at the Aldeburgh pub. Find out everything you can about him fast. I think he's Dawlish's right-hand man.'

'Needed yesterday, of course,' Monica commented.

'Or the day before that . . .'

Marler parked his Volvo station-wagon beyond a bend in the country road before he reached the entrance to Dawlish's factory. As a precaution for a quick getaway he had executed a three-point turn so the Volvo faced the way they had come.

'At least the moon has gone behind clouds,' Newman remarked as he followed Marler out of the car. 'Let's hope it doesn't reappear at the wrong moment . . .'

Both men were armed. Newman carried a .38 Smith & Wesson in a hip holster. Marler was relying on his Armalite rifle. Both men carried duvets folded over their left arms as, in rubber-soled shoes, they walked slowly along the road. They paused at the bend, listening, watching what they could see of the fence which guarded the establishment. No sounds, no sign of guards patrolling with dogs.

'They won't expect us to try anything twice,' Newman whispered.

'You hope,' Marler said drily.

They approached the fence and again paused, to listen, to look. There was no wind. The silence of the forest in the night was oppressive, nerve-rattling. Newman took the decision.

'Let's get on with it,' he whispered. 'Your move.'

Marler took a wooden-handled screwdriver from his pocket, walked to the gate, turned, paced out the same distance he had estimated on their previous visit. Reaching up, he pressed the metal end against wires protruding from a white plastic tube. There was a brief flash.

'Electrified wire fused,' he said to Newman, standing behind him. 'Let's hope it doesn't set off an alarm.'

'We'll soon know. Don't give them time to react . . .'

Inside the folded duvets each of them also carried an extending metal ladder, attached to the duvet over a plastic hook. Newman unhooked his ladder, extended it to its full length, perched the top rubber-covered rung half-way up the wire. Marler mounted the ladder, flung his duvet higher up over the wire. Still carrying his own duvet, he swung over the duvet-covered wire, dropped to the ground inside.

Swiftly he erected his own ladder, perched it against the inside for an easy retreat later, climbed back up, swung his own duvet over Newman's. The reporter was heavier than the slim Marler. Within seconds Newman was standing beside him. They were both inside enemy territory.

'Watch where you tread,' Newman warned. 'I'll lead. I have a funny feeling about this place. The lack of guards isn't natural . . .'

205

Part of his mind was going back to a memory over the years. When he had trained with the SAS to write an authorized article on that legendary élite of soldiers. Somehow he had survived the course. He heard the voice of the SAS trainer he only knew as Sarge. *Approaching any security area never forget the ground your feet are treading on may be the greatest danger . . .*

Newman shone his pencil flashlight, shielded with the palm of his hand, downwards where he would tread next. Behind him Marler, notorious for going his own way, was carefully placing his feet where Newman had just placed his own. Damp mushy ground with here and there a rock half-embedded. The slow trudge uphill continued. Marler wanted to call out 'For Christ's sake get a move on.' He kept his mouth shut, deterred by Newman's slow, methodical progress.

Frequently Marler glanced up, skimmed his gaze round the deserted wilderness – deserted except for one of the single-storey concrete blockhouse-like buildings. All in darkness. No sign of movement, no sound. The sheer silence was uncanny, disturbing. They were within thirty feet of one of the morgue-like buildings and this one had windows facing them like black slit-eyes. Were they being watched? Would the first indication that they had walked into a trap be a hail of bullets?

Newman held up his other hand. Marler, eyes accustomed to the dark, saw the gesture, halted. Newman was crouching down, flashlight in one hand, his other hand, also gloveless – you couldn't fire a weapon wearing gloves – feeling something on the ground. His fingers were frozen to the bone but he continued his probing as Marler crouched behind him.

'Trouble?' Marler whispered.

'Could be lethal,' Newman responded calmly.

'What is it?'

Newman padded the ground to his right gently, poked at

the clumps of heather. He gestured for Marler to come forward to that piece of ground. Now they crouched alongside each other. Marler glanced at Newman, saw his expression was grim.

'Look at these,' Newman whispered.

He moved his flashlight slowly. In the beam Marler saw metal prongs protruding from tufts of grass. As the beam continued moving he counted seven prongs, protruding no more than half an inch. The metal was new. It gleamed in the glow of the flashlight.

'Anti-personnel mines,' Newman said tersely. 'Tread on one and if they're explosive you lose a leg. Maybe both legs. It's too dangerous to move any closer. We are dealing with right bastards.'

'So?'

'We go back exactly the same way we came. Again, let me lead.'

'Can we wait for thirty seconds? Before I left London the Engine Room boffins gave me a new camera. Infra-red lens and zoom. Miniaturized. I want to photograph the windows in that building . . .'

'What are you waiting for? Thirty seconds. And I'll be counting . . .'

Marler took a small oblong plastic box from his pocket, aimed the lens at the windows of the building one by one, taking six shots of each. They'd said the thing adjusted itself to light conditions – even pitch dark. Just aim, press the button. He did so.

'Finish as soon as you can,' Newman warned. 'The clicks are loud. They could have installed sensors. This lot is capable of any devilry . . .'

'Ready, Commander.'

Marler gave a mock salute after he'd slipped the camera back into his pocket. The way back seemed even more of an ordeal than their way in. Newman again checked with his flashlight – with even more care now he'd seen those

207

sinister prongs. Marler suppressed a sigh of relief as they arrived at the fence. Newman went over first. As he followed Marler paused, stomach looped over the duvet, reached down the inner side of the fence, grabbed hold of the metal ladder. As he landed on the road side Newman, the taller, stretched up an arm, hauled down the duvets. Carrying both ladders, they walked through the silence of the night back to where the Volvo was parked.

'We didn't achieve much,' Newman mused. 'Can't win them all.'

'We won't know that until the boffins in the Engine Room have developed this film,' Marler pointed out.

They had stowed everything in the rear, were sitting in the front. Newman, who liked driving, had asked Marler if he could take over the wheel.

'Be my guest . . .'

'Listen!'

Somewhere close behind them they heard a vehicle rumbling over rough ground. The sound came from inside the fenced off area: had it been driving along the road behind them it wouldn't be making such heavy weather as they listened to its slow progress.

'We *were* spotted,' Marler remarked.

'I don't think so. We checked the car thoroughly before we got into it. No sign of someone fooling around with the engine, no bombs attached underneath. And they'd have come after us inside the wire. I'm driving off now to find a place we can hide. That vehicle will be coming this way.'

'Not the other?'

'Which leads only to Orford, a dead end? I think not . . .'

With headlights undimmed he drove on round two bends, the beams sweeping over motionless trees. Then he swung off the road to the right up a track into the forest, made a U-turn, parked behind several trees with a view of the road between them, switched off, waited.

A heavy truck, lights undimmed, drove past the

entrance to the track, heading for Snape Maltings. New-man drove after it without any headlights at all, keeping his distance without losing sight of the red tail-lights. He turned effortlessly round a bend. Marler grunted.

'Without even side lights you'll end up in the ditch.'

'No I won't. You're forgetting – I drove the Merc on this very road not long ago. I can remember.'

Marler was partially reassured. He remembered New-man had only to drive along a strange route once to be able to return along the same route without missing his way once. With the Armalite perched across his lap, he settled more comfortably.

The truck turned right along the deserted road at Tunstall, still heading for the Maltings. Beyond the collection of ancient warehouses which stages Benjamin Britten concerts in summer the truck continued through the lonely countryside towards Snape village.

'Marler, I think there's only the driver with that vehicle. I'm going to overtake, then stop him. You get out, pretend you're some kind of authority, search his truck.'

'If you say so.'

Newman switched on his headlights full, pressed down his foot, raced past the truck for a short distance. Then he slowed down, swung the wheel, positioned the Volvo across the road as a barrier, his headlights blazing. He told Marler to leave his door open so the courtesy light added to the illumination. Marler nodded, climbed out, walked back, stood on the grass verge.

The truck came on, moving at a fairish speed. Its own headlights showed up the obstacle. The truck slowed, stopped close to the Volvo. The driver was opening the door of his cab when Marler jerked it open further. He caught the driver who was falling out. Shock tactics often worked.

'Bloody 'ell! What the 'ell do you think you're up to?'

He was a runt of a man, weatherbeaten face, aged

209

between forty and sixty, eyes bloodshot. He wore a padded windcheater, brand new. Dawlish seemed to be a stickler for his staff being well-fitted out. Marler smelt alcohol on his breath. Cognac? He waved his General & Cumbria Assurance identity card quickly in the runt's face.

'Ipswich CID. I want to look in the back of this truck. You can refuse – but then I'll report you for driving under the influence. My colleague already has your registration number.'

Marler saw a look of fear in the bloodshot eyes. Dawlish must come down heavy on staff who needed disciplining. The driver led the way to the rear. As he walked behind him Marler noticed the legend painted along the vehicle. *Dawlish Conservation.*

He further noticed as the driver took out a bunch of keys that the rear doors were fastened with two new padlocks. He waited as the driver had trouble unlocking them, then opened one door, stood back.

'You won't find no drugs if that's what you're after.'

'Just wait here. Don't try and lock me in – my colleague will make mincemeat of you . . .'

Switching on his flashlight he swept it over the contents. Stack upon stack of neatly piled canvas sacks. Each one tied up with a simple metal clasp. He removed one, shone his torch inside. It was full of Balaclava helmets. Not what he'd expected. He examined a number of other sacks at random. All full of Balaclavas. Odd. Most odd.

'What are the Balaclavas for?' he asked as he jumped to the road.

'Big fancy dress party at Christmas . . .'

Marler grabbed him by the shirt collar exposed under the windcheater. 'Don't fool with me. You could find yourself occupying a cell at Ipswich police HQ.'

'It's Gawd's truth, mate. Christmas is coming. Didn't you know? We deliver early. A big order. A palais do would be my guess. Don't know who you're dancin' with

210

until the great moment comes. Midnight. Everyone takes off 'is or 'er mask.'

He was talking too much, giving too much detail. Marler waved a hand, waited while the driver attended to the padlocks.

'And your destination is?'

'. . . Lowestoft.'

There had been a brief hesitation before this question was answered. First, he talked too much, then he only uttered one word. As he walked back with the driver to his cab Marler slapped him on the rump. As he expected his hand hit something hard in the driver's rear trouser pocket. A flask of cognac.

'Just watch your driving,' he warned. 'And switch off those damned lights. They're blinding my colleague . . .'

Newman manoeuvred the car swiftly once Marler slipped into the passenger seat. He moved off before the truck driver could turn on his lights again. Marler lit a king-size.

'That was smart,' Newman commented. 'Getting him to switch off his lights. That way he didn't get our registration number.'

'Which was the idea, chum. Care to guess what he is transporting at this hour?'

'Don't like guessing games.'

'You'd lose, anyway. Loads of sacks crammed with Balaclava helmets. Just that. From the middle to the cab they were piled up to the ceiling. I estimated there were hundreds, could be thousands. Told me a cock-and-bull story – they're for a Christmas bash. And he lied about his destination. Said it was Lowestoft. Maybe we should find out just where he *is* going?'

'For once I agree with you. The next turn-off is the crossroads at Snape. A tenner to a fiver he takes the right turning along the A1094 to Aldeburgh.'

'No takers.' Marler looked thoughtful. 'Yes, the number

of Balaclavas aboard that truck must run into thousands. Some fancy dress party . . .'

Well ahead of the truck, at the lonely crossroads Newman swung the Volvo on to a wide area of grass, drew in by a hedge, switched off lights, engine, waited. Marler put out his cigarette, lowered his window a fraction so he could hear.

In the silence of the dark which seemed to press down on them they heard the truck coming a long way off. Marler checked his watch by the illuminated hands. It was 1.30 a.m. A funny time to be making a delivery.

They sat very still as the truck came closer. Reaching the crossroads, headlights dipped, the driver didn't hesitate. He turned on to the A1094. But he had turned *left* – away from Aldeburgh. Newman switched on lights, started the engine, followed, his lights dimmed.

'I should have agreed that bet,' Marler said.

Once through the small village of Snape, Newman drove with only his sidelights on. The red lights of the truck were sufficient guide, and their short wait at the crossroads had brought back his night vision. The truck turned right on the A12, increased speed, proceeding north. There was no other traffic at all on the road.

'Looks as though maybe Drunky was telling the truth when he said Lowestoft,' Marler observed. 'But I'd have sworn he was lying.'

'And with things like that you have been known to be right.'

'Thanks for the unreserved vote of confidence.'

Marler found the steady drive along the main highway hypnotic as Newman drove on and on. The occasional car was appearing now, two blazing eyes rushing towards them. Newman felt it safer to switch on his own headlights, dimmed. The cars rushing past them had no such consideration. Several times Newman reacted.

'Dip your headlights, you swine . . .'

212

The truck was moving at high speed, eating up the miles. Newman pressed his own foot down to keep up, but maintained a decent distance between the two vehicles so the truck driver wouldn't suspect he was being followed. Marler checked his watch again.

'Lord knows what time we'll arrive at the Brudenell – or whether they'll let us in at this hour.'

'I coaxed a front door key out of the girl when I registered before we set out for the factory.'

'I'm surprised *you* were able to charm her to that extent.'

'We'd stayed there recently. She now regards us as trustworthy types.'

'Oh, very trustworthy. Breaking into private property.'

He was about to light another king-size when he paused. The truck was slowing down. Still a good distance from Lowestoft. And in the middle of nowhere. Newman also reduced speed. The truck's right-hand indicator light was flashing, warning it was about to turn off the highway. Newman slowed even more, glanced in his rear-view mirror. Nothing behind him for miles. The truck turned down a side road leading east towards the sea.

Newman pulled in to the side. His face was like stone as he leaned forward, staring at the signpost pointing to the truck's destination. Just one word.

Dunwich.

22

The following day at the Brudenell, Paula was restless and impatient. She felt she had to keep her word to Tweed – not to stray until she had contacted Newman. Easier said than done. The receptionist had told her they were staying at the hotel, had discreetly given her their room numbers. After all, she had seen them together during their recent visit: Newman and Marler.

Paula took the elevator to both rooms. And met the same message hanging from the door handles of both rooms. *Please Do Not Disturb*. Frustrated, she went to her own room, put on her suede coat and a cashmere scarf. It was a raw, bitter day outside but she felt trapped indoors. The first person she encountered when she stepped out of the elevator on the ground floor was Lieutenant Berthier, masquerading as James Sanders, dark-haired and complete with tinted glasses. He wore a windcheater, heavy grey slacks, and a polo-necked sweater. His feet were shod in trainers.

'Hello, Mr Sanders,' she said quickly. 'Making any contacts you might sell marine parts to?'

'The weather doesn't help – most people are keeping their heads down. You're going for a walk? I'm after a bite of fresh air myself. Along the promenade?'

'That will be bracing.'

She stepped out of the door he opened for her leading direct to the promenade. Berthier might let something slip and it was something to do until Newman decided to rise and shine. She almost made a reference to his use of the word 'bite', certain he had meant 'bit', but the first word was perfect for the weather. She decided not to say anything – he might think she'd spotted an error in his English.

'Later I could drive you somewhere nice for lunch,' he suggested.

'That's generous of you, but I have to stay near the hotel for a phone message,' she lied easily.

Berthier walked on the seaward side, protecting her from the storm which was blowing up. Mountainous waves heaved their bulk against the front, splashing spume on to

the promenade. Paula noticed several of the ancient terrace houses had shutters closed over their basement windows. In some cases the windows had been blocked up.
When the North Sea really raged it must inundate the
promenade, lapping against the basements. She walked
leaning into the force of the wind. Berthier took her arm.

'Don't want you blown over.'

'Why don't you try to contact Lord Dane Dawlish?'

She felt his grip on her arm tighten for a second when
she'd asked the question. He relaxed his hold quickly.

'Why should I get in touch with him?' he asked.

'I'd have thought your research would have turned up
the fact he's a likely prospect. He has a huge catamaran
called the *Steel Vulture*. He might be a good customer.'

'I'll think about it.'

'Do more than that,' she pressed him. 'He lives not far
away. At Iken.'

'Where's that?'

All the wrong answers, she thought. In his role as a
salesman she felt sure his research would be meticulous.
He'd hardly have missed Dawlish.

'Up the River Alde on the way to Snape Maltings. You
know the strange course the river follows,' she prodded.

'I'm a Yellow Pages man myself. Let's call in at the Cross
Keys for some coffee. It's the nicest pub in the town.'

'Good idea.'

She answered automatically. Once she had liked Aldeburgh as a comfortable refuge away from the world. Now
her main image of the place was a night of horror when
masked men with rifles, hardly human, had pursued Karin
and herself like a pack of wolves hunting their prey. She
recalled what they – one of them – had done to Karin. *Stop
it!* she told herself.

'We're nearly there.'

Berthier checked his watch as he led her away from the
promenade into the garden leading to the rear entrance.

Paula was relieved to get away from the front. She had been lucky: no ruinous salt water had splashed on her precious suede coat.

'This table suit you?' Berthier suggested. 'It's near the serving counter. Just coffee?'

He ushered her to a chair, went over to the counter to give his order. It was less cold in the Cross Keys but Paula kept her coat on. She had just noticed who was sitting at the large table close to hers.

Five tough-looking men wearing pea-jackets. Half-facing her was the wide-shouldered heavy-set Brand. She looked away, saw the waitress behind the counter staring at him. Brand turned, stared back at the girl. She took a deep breath, spoke sharply.

'I thought I told you not to come back.'

'It's all right, he's with me . . .'

Lord Dawlish appeared round a corner from the room at the front. Hatless, he was clad in a British warm, the collar turned up. He joined the five men, sitting in a chair which Paula guessed had been kept for him. She was beginning to worry: the atmosphere had become menacing.

No one was speaking at the table occupied by Dawlish. The seamen-types were watching her. She tilted her chin defiantly, looked up at the low oak-beamed ceiling, which seemed to press down on her. Dark oak. The tables, uncovered, were made of the same dark oak. She remembered the pub on a previous trip as a comfortable welcoming place. It was the occupants who had changed the atmosphere.

Berthier returned to her table, the waitress served the coffee. She looked at Berthier who sat facing her. He was gazing straight at her, saying nothing, eyes invisible behind the tinted lenses. He wasn't helping at all, she thought as she sipped the excellent coffee. He just kept looking at her, damn him.

Then she remembered he'd checked his watch before

they'd entered the place. Was this a prearranged rendez-vous? Before going up to her room at the Brudenell to fetch her coat she'd called out to the receptionist that she was going for a walk. Berthier could have been within earshot.

'Not the weather for a trip on the Cat,' Dawlish called out to her. 'You haven't forgotten my offer, my dear?'

One of the men at his table sniggered. She placed her cup carefully back in the saucer, her expression frozen. She stared at Dawlish.

'I may have the time, I may not,' she said abruptly.

Dawlish tossed back half the double Scotch he'd ordered. He held on to the glass as he spoke in a mocking tone.

'It would be a unique experience. A day – and a night – aboard the Cat.'

One of the men gave a braying laugh, cut it short when Dawlish glanced at him. Paula was convinced she was being subjected to calculated pressure. To run her out of Aldeburgh? Berthier, immobile as a statue, continued to stare at her from behind his bloody glasses. A man walked slowly into the pub from the rear entrance.

Tall, so tall his hatless head almost touched the beams, he wore a trench coat, which showed damp patches. He must have walked along the promenade from the Brudenell. He wore no gloves on his large hands.

Victor Rosewater paused, looked at Paula, Berthier, and then at the nearby table, his strong face showing no particular expression. But now there was complete silence as he remained standing there.

'Paula, you look as though you've had enough of this place. Care to come for a stroll?'

'Who asked you to interfere . . .' Brand began.

Rosewater turned his gaze on the heavy-set man. He said nothing and Brand subsided in mid-sentence. No one seemed anxious to argue any more, to mix it with the newcomer.

'Yes, Victor,' Paula said quickly, standing up. 'I have had enough of it. I'd welcome a stroll.' She looked at Berthier. 'Thank you for the coffee . . .'

Rosewater escorted her through the pub to the front exit on to the street away from the front. They began walking back along narrow streets parallel to the front and lined with quaint houses.

'This way,' Rosewater remarked, 'you won't get that lovely suede coat splashed by salt water. As you can see from my trench coat the waves are now crashing over on to the prom.'

'Thank you.'

And he was showing consideration which never entered the head of Berthier, she thought. She looked up at him curiously.

'How did you know I just wanted to get to hell out of that place?'

He smiled. 'I'm a bit sensitive to atmospheres. Seemed you were uncomfortable. That the reason could have been the people in the place. A rum bunch, I thought. And the chap you were with didn't seem to be helping all that much.'

'He says that he's a salesman of marine spare parts – that his name is James Sanders.'

She felt it might be important to put Rosewater on his guard against Berthier. She'd thought about it for a split second before saying anything. Rosewater was on to it instantly.

'*Says?* You sound as though you don't believe his name or his way of earning a living.'

Rosewater had slowed down. Paula had long legs but he had much longer: he had realized she was hurrying to keep up. Not only did he seem to have all his marbles: he was considerate in little ways.

218

'I don't,' she replied. 'I suspect he's some kind of con man. I could be completely wrong.'

Despite the rapport between them, Paula had no intention of revealing information which Tweed would regard as highly confidential. They walked in silence for a minute and neither seemed to feel compelled to talk. Rosewater took hold of her elbow, guided her down a narrow thoroughfare into the High Street.

'Where are we going?' she asked.

'You can get quite a good lunch at a place called the Captain's Table. It's quiet – at this time of the year – the service is good, the food quite edible.'

'Sounds a marvellous idea . . .'

Anything to get away from the atmosphere which had hung like a dark cloud over the Cross Keys. Somehow she equated it with the dreadful night when Karin had died. Why? She wasn't sure.

The Captain's Table was a small restaurant, an oblong room with just a few tables beautifully laid for lunch. Paula thought it was more like a room in someone's home than a restaurant. A distinguished-looking man welcomed them, escorted them to a window table overlooking the High Street, handed them menus and left them alone.

'That man in a British warm,' Rosewater began, 'isn't he Lord Dawlish? I've seen his pictures in the magazines.'

'Yes. Lord Dane Dawlish. Millionaire. Supermarket and armaments king.'

'He was talking to you when I came in. Said something about a cat. You know him?'

'Yes . . .' She explained how she had interviewed Dawlish, how he had shown her the extraordinary diorama, that the Cat was a catamaran, a big job. She left out any reference to the presence of Newman and Marler at the shoot, to the fact the Dawlish had come on strong with her.

'And those men with him,' Rosewater went on as he

closed the menu, 'a bunch of roughnecks if ever I saw one. Who are they?'

'I recognized two of them from my visit to Grenville Grange. They're members of Dawlish's staff.'

'Crewmen from the *Steel Vulture*?' Rosewater suggested. 'Incidentally, I'm having the roast lamb. I had it the other day and it was good.'

'I'm having the same.' She paused, smiled. 'How come you turned up at the Cross Keys at just the right moment?'

'I followed you and that chap from the hotel,' he said frankly. 'I didn't too much like the look of him. I'd seen him the night before in the bar. Why does he wear those dark glasses all the time?'

'He says he has weak eyes, that daylight hurts them. I think that was very sweet of you – to act as my protector. And your mind must still be full of Karin,' she said gently. 'Is that why you're still here? In the hope of finding a clue as to who did it?'

'Something like that,' he said in his reserved manner. He gave Paula the impression of a man under iron self-control. Almost superhuman endurance. Like a blood-hound, she thought, following the scent.

'These interviews you do for women's magazines,' he said after their meal had been served. 'Is it a sideline? Is your main work with Tweed's company?'

'Yes, Tweed is my boss. I'm his personal assistant – I do a lot of the confidential research for insurance cases,' she chattered on blithely. 'That's my main line of work. It's confidential, so I can't talk about it much.'

After a satisfying meal washed down with a bottle of Chablis – Rosewater found out she didn't like red wine – he escorted her back to the hotel. There was no rain but an army of low clouds like grey smoke was scudding inland, seeming to skim the rooftops. The wind had increased in force, hurtling down the High Street like air through a wind tunnel. Paula felt she might be swept off her feet. As though guessing her state of anxiety, Rosewater slipped a firm arm round her waist.

'We don't want you blown out to sea,' he joked. 'And the met forecast is for worse to come. Gales up to eighty miles an hour tonight . . .'

He still had his arm round her waist as they went inside the hotel, climbed the stairs, ran smack into Newman and Marler in the hall. Rosewater released her, said he'd enjoyed her company, and vanished inside the elevator.

'So you haven't been lonely,' Newman observed, his expression grim.

'You object?' Paula flared up, mistaking the reason for his expression.

'No. We have something to tell you. *Dunwich* . . .'

Major Lamy left the British Airways aircraft which had flown him from Charles de Gaulle Airport in Paris to Heathrow.

He had checked that the troops were in place in Lyons. From there he had flown to Paris by Air Inter. Waiting for his flight to London, he had phoned an obscure British car hire firm, ordered a Rover in the name of William Prendergast. The forged passport in the same name was the one he presented to Passport Control. With a strong following tail wind the flight had taken only forty-five minutes.

Carrying the small case he had taken aboard the plane, Lamy left Passport Control behind and walked towards the Customs exit. He wore a British business suit under a Burberry raincoat and his shoes were also British. He was the archetype of an Englishman back from abroad.

Lamy didn't notice in the crowd of passengers a tall, fair-haired man standing watching the flight arrivals. Bill Corcoran, a friend of Tweed's and Chief Security Officer, checked one of the small photos rushed to him from Park

Crescent by motor-cycle courier. He looked at the back of the photo. Major Jules Lamy.

Corcoran followed Lamy, keeping a certain distance behind him. He noticed Lamy bypassed the carousels where passengers were already waiting resignedly for their suitcases to appear one day. He followed Lamy through the *Nothing To Declare* Customs aisle.

Lamy increased his pace as he left the Customs area. Several drivers stood behind a barrier holding up cards with names. *William Prendergast.* Lamy went up to the girl holding up that name. Corcoran could have stopped him immediately, charged him with travelling on a false passport – unless he'd used his real name at Passport Control. But the request made by Tweed's assistant, Monica, had been specific.

Corcoran followed Lamy and the girl to the short-term car park. Up the ramp, across the bridge, inside the park. He took out his own car keys, twirling them as he followed the couple. The car Lamy climbed inside was a Rover – after he had paid the girl with a sheaf of banknotes and dealt with the formalities. Corcoran memorized the registration number, tried to follow the girl, who wasn't wearing a uniform, but she vanished.

When the Rover had driven off Corcoran ran back to his office. Locking the door, he dialled Monica's number, hoping to speak to Tweed.

'He's not here, Jim,' Monica said quickly. 'He had to dash off somewhere. Have you any news?'

'Sounds like Tweed – dashing off. Yes, one of your subjects in the photos just arrived aboard a BA flight from Paris. Travelling under the name William Prendergast in a hired Rover, registration . . . Major Lamy.'

Monica thanked him, broke the connection, was working non-stop for the next hour. She phoned a contact at Vehicle Registration, Swansea, gave him the number and the code confirming she was SIS. Vehicle Registration reacted with almost unique speed, phoning her back in ten minutes, giving her the name and address of the car hire firm in London. She didn't make the mistake of calling the company direct. Instead she phoned another contact at Special Branch, gave him the data, stressed how urgent it was. Inside three-quarters of an hour Special Branch called her back.

'A William Prendergast hired the Rover, phoned early this afternoon. He had to give the destination he was taking it to.'

'Go on, don't tease me, Martin,' Monica pleaded.

'Aldeburgh, Suffolk . . .'

'Look, Brand, you've got to handle this job right. No slip-ups,' Dawlish snapped.

'Have I slipped up yet?' growled Brand, stirring his bulk in the carver chair in the living room of Grenville Grange. 'I am your right-hand man, remember?'

'At the moment,' Dawlish rapped back. 'But there's always a first time for a slip-up. Make sure this isn't it.'

'The job will be handled professionally,' Brand told him curtly.

'Make sure it is. Tonight.'

Approaching Aldeburgh, Major Lamy slowed down. He had lost count of the number of times he had checked to make sure he was not being followed. In mid-afternoon the traffic had been light once he had left London behind, which had helped.

He had kept within all the speed limits: he couldn't afford the risk of being stopped by a police patrol car. Once again he checked in his rear-view mirror. Nothing. Shortly afterwards he drove into the courtyard of a hotel on the outskirts of Aldeburgh.

Carrying his small case, he entered the hotel, registered as William Prendergast with a fictitious London address. He had also phoned the hotel from Paris to make the reservation with no reference to where he was calling from.

He sneezed several times behind the scarf pulled up over his face. He wore a deerstalker hat pulled down across his forehead.

'Your room is ready, Mr Prendergast,' the receptionist informed him. 'One night, I think you said?'

'Yes. I'll pay in advance now for the room and breakfast,' Lamy said. 'I may have to leave early tomorrow morning,' he continued, in English.

He paid in cash and she handed him the receipted bill. He sneezed again as he stooped to pick up his case.

'You seem to have a bad cold, sir,' she sympathized.

Inside his bedroom he whipped off the scarf, no longer bothering to fake a sneeze. He checked his watch. He was a careful organizer. Plenty of time to do a recce of the area. He took from his breast pocket an envelope, extracted from it the photograph he had been handed at Charles de Gaulle Airport. The envelope had been passed to him by his informant inside Lasalle's Paris HQ in rue des Saussaies. It was a photo of Paula Grey.

23

Kalmar sat in the car in the public car park close to the Brudenell Hotel. No other vehicle was in sight. It was supposed to be daylight but the low storm clouds sweeping across the sky made it seem more like night.

He could hear the *thump!* of giant waves against the high rampart extending south along the coast beyond the hotel. No work was going on but huge cranes and Portacabins showed the artificial sea defences were being strengthened. He clasped his gloved hands as he saw spray rising like mist above the rampart, carried over to the marshes by the fury of the gale.

He flexed his strong fingers. You just couldn't afford to leave a witness alive. And there had been one witness to the strangling of Karin Rosewater. He thought about the witness, about her walking, talking, remembering. Then *talking* . . .

The grip of his fingers tightened. He imagined grasping her by the throat, carefully pressing his thumbs into her windpipe. Her eyes starting out of her head as he was the last person she'd ever see in this world.

He had decided. At the earliest opportunity. Tonight. He wouldn't be paid a Swiss franc on top of the fat fee he'd already collected for the Karin job. But you just couldn't afford to leave a witness alive.

Paula sat in her room with Newman and Marler. Newman had been giving her a terse account of the trip to the armaments factory in the middle of the night. He went on to describe how they had followed the truck after Marler had discovered its contents. She made her first comment.

'Who would need thousands of Balaclavas?'

'You heard what I told you about my Bordeaux trip,' he snapped. Perched on her bed she stared at him, hurt by his brusque rejoinder. He seemed edgy. 'Remember that riot I watched,' Newman went on. 'It was pretty savage stuff. And the mob was pretty well organized. *And* I didn't see one without a Balaclava mask to avoid identification. Now there's been a much bigger riot in Lyons. Haven't you seen the pictures in the papers? Every man taking part in that orgy of violence is wearing a Balaclava. My bet is to hide the fact they're troops from de Forge's Corps.'

'I still don't follow this Dunwich puzzle,' she protested. 'Just supposing they are de Forge's men, he could obtain Balaclavas in France . . .'

'And be sure the supplier – or one of his workers – wouldn't report the delivery to the DST? The police?'

'Oh, you mean . . .'

'I mean,' he overrode her, 'that with the mobs growing larger they may need a lot more Balaclavas. It would be more secure if they brought them in from abroad in secrecy. Hence that truck on the way to Dunwich. You saw the *Steel Vulture* off Dunwich the day you and Karin went scuba diving.'

'So the *Vulture* could be the means of transporting the Balaclavas to de Forge – via Arcachon?'

Newman grinned. 'Now you're catching on.'

'Why didn't the two of you follow the truck all the way to Dunwich, see where it stopped?'

'Because,' Newman explained, 'we hadn't alerted their driver up to that point. You know the side road to Dunwich is a narrow country road. I didn't want us to risk being spotted. So we came back here.'

'I see.' Paula put her hands on her hips, stretched. 'Bob, you seem irked with me, irritable. Why?'

'Because you're back here again. Where Karin was murdered. I don't like it. Someone might think of you as a witness. The killer could still be hanging around in the vicinity.'

'I doubt that's at all feasible. He'll be long gone.'

Newman shrugged. 'Please yourself.'

'I usually do – like you. Listen to who's talking.'

Marler, sensing the start of verbal warfare, broke in for the first time. He had been leaning against a wall, watching and listening.

'If I could get a word in edgeways, I think I'd like to

leave, get back to Park Crescent. I'm anxious for the little men in the Engine Room to develop that film I took of the laboratory at Dawlish's factory in the forest. You don't mind if I drive my own Volvo back, do you, Newman?'

'And how am I supposed to get back tomorrow? Swim? In case you didn't know, the trains stopped coming here quite a few years ago.'

'You can drive me back, Bob,' Paula said quickly. 'I came in Tweed's Escort.'

She was beginning to feel contrite. Newman had been brusque only because he was worried about her. Marler waved a hand – as much as to say, 'You've got transport, chum,' and left the room.

'I think I'm going for a walk,' Newman said when they were alone. 'You're right, I am edgy. Maybe it's the storm they predicted for tonight. Want to come with me?'

'I'd love to, but I'm feeling bushed. Mind if I cry off and have a bath instead?'

'I could stay and scrub your back for you, but maybe I'll take that walk instead. Wallow . . .'

Left on her own, Paula went into the bathroom, turned on the taps. Her excuse had been a bit of a white lie. Earlier she had phoned Jean Burgoyne and they'd agreed to have drinks together that evening at the home of Jean's uncle, Admiralty House. Jean had proved her efficiency: while Paula was enduring the unpleasantness at the Cross Keys she had left an envelope at reception with a local map marking the position of the house perched on the hill behind the main part of the town.

Paula had liked Jean when they'd chatted in the bar at the Brudenell during her previous visit. During that short conversation a friendship had sprung up between the two women.

But that wasn't Paula's real motive in contacting her. She had not forgotten that Burgoyne was General de Forge's mistress. She hoped to guide the subject round to

227

that delicate subject in the hope of extracting information for Tweed.

She followed Newman's advice and wallowed in her bath, gradually feeling the tension drain out of her body. In her mind she played with the problem of what to wear for the occasion. Eventually she decided on a fine wool print dress with a mandarin collar and a wide belt. She favoured wide belts: they emphasized her slim waist.

'So that's settled,' she said to herself as she stood up and towelled herself vigorously. 'And combined with my suede coat I should be warm.'

The temperature was dropping outside rapidly according to the weather forecast. A good job it was only a short drive. Jean had offered to collect her but she'd evaded the offer. Paula, independent, liked to have her own transport.

Dressed for the occasion, she went down in the elevator to see the receptionist.

'I'll be going out about six,' she told her. 'I expect to be back about eight. Could you let the dining room know? I'll be as hungry as a horse when I return. The weather . . .'

'And it's going to get worse,' a man's voice said behind her. She recognized Berthier's husky tone. 'Winds up to eighty miles an hour.'

'Sounds lovely,' she replied. 'Excuse me, I'm expecting a phone call.'

She slipped into the elevator, pressed the button, sighed with relief as it moved upwards. She'd had enough of Berthier for one day. Damn it, she reminded herself, I must get into the mental habit of thinking of him as *James Sanders*. Otherwise I'm going to put my foot in it.

She locked her bedroom door, kicked off her high-heeled shoes, reminded herself of something else – to wear sensible shoes when she was driving to Admiralty House. She was expecting no phone call and she sat in a

228

chair, picked up her paperback of Tolstoy's *War and Peace*, determined to finish the huge tome. She had about half an hour before it would be time to leave to visit Jean.

In the bar on the ground floor Brand glanced at his watch. He was drinking Scotch with water – he needed a clear head tonight. From where he sat he had seen Paula enter the elevator. He guessed from her dress that she could be going out somewhere for the evening.

Of course she could be dining in the hotel, but Brand didn't think so. Despite his coarse manner Brand was surprisingly sensitive to social nuances. He'd have bet a month's fat salary that within the hour she'd leave the hotel.

Unlike his working clothes worn during the morning at the Cross Keys, he was now dressed in a smart, heavy grey suit tailored to allow his thick arms easy movement. On a chair next to his he'd placed his motoring gloves. The last thing he needed tonight was company at this moment.

Tweed was moving at high speed across Suffolk behind the wheel of Newman's Mercedes 280E, headlights sweeping in the night over hedges lining the road. The wind battered the side of the one and a half tons of car, threatening to blow it off the road.

Tweed kept a firm grip on the wheel, indifferent to the grim weather conditions, driving automatically, his mind full of anxiety. He was heading for Aldeburgh, Monica had phoned the Brudenell to book him a room, and he was determined to get there as fast as possible.

He had Paula on his mind. His instinct that she was in danger was strong. He couldn't have explained why his earlier doubts had surfaced into fear – but he did know that when he'd had this instinctive feeling of trouble before it had always proved to be right.

He had tried to reach her on the phone at lunchtime but the receptionist at the Brudenell had told him she was out somewhere. He had decided against leaving a message: he might be alarming her for nothing.

Then Newman's car had been returned by one of Robles' staff. The veterinary pathologist had phoned him the report from Porton Down – and that had not made reassuring news. The worst possible case, had been the verdict.

It was the return of Newman's car which had made Tweed take one of his lightning decisions – that he would drive it to Aldeburgh himself. Before leaving London Newman had phoned from his flat, had told Tweed he'd be staying at the Brudenell for two days and nights.

There was another reason for Tweed's urgent flight from London. He wanted to see for himself the scene of the crime where Karin Rosewater had been murdered. You could listen to other people's detailed accounts of the landscape, but there was nothing like checking it for yourself. He looked at the clock on the dashboard, calculated he'd arrive in time to explore the marshes at about the same hour when the murder had been committed. After making sure Paula was all right . . .

Paula, wearing her suede coat, her silk scarf wrapped round her head against the wind, stepped out of the elevator, handed her key to the receptionist, told her she was driving to see a friend in Aldeburgh.

It was black as pitch outside the front entrance. She walked quickly to the Ford Escort, parked in a slot up against the hotel wall. Climbing behind the wheel, she slipped her key into the ignition, turned it. Nothing happened. Just a discouraging grunt. She tried again and again to start the engine. Nothing. She looked up as a shadowy figure appeared beyond her side window. Lieutenant Berth . . . No, *James Sanders*.

'Won't she behave?' he asked. 'Let me try.'

She hesitated, thought: I'm just outside the hotel. Getting out, she stood while he slipped behind the wheel and fiddled with the ignition. He tried six times and shook his head.

'Probably the battery is dead. You were going for a long drive?'

'No, only local. To an address in Aldeburgh.'

She wished she hadn't reacted so quickly as he climbed out. He'd wound up the window and now he closed the door.

'That's my Saab parked next to your car. I'll drive you wherever you want to go. Nothing else to do.'

Again she hesitated. She had tapped on Newman's door before coming down. No reply. Obviously he was still out walking: he could walk for miles when in the mood. And Marler had gone back to London. Paula made a virtue of punctuality and it was only a short drive.

'I have a map showing where I'm going. Admiralty House is the name. It's marked with a cross . . .'

Berthier took the map as he sat behind the wheel, left his door open, pretended to study the map. He knew damn well where he was going. Only recently he'd been outside Admiralty House when he'd followed Jean Burgoyne.

Paula again hesitated before getting into the front passenger seat. I can cope with him if I have to, she thought, and slipped into the seat. Berthier handed back the map.

'I've got the route. As you said, it's very local . . .'

She fastened her seat belt and he drove off. She adjusted her shoulder bag, wished she was carrying her .32 Browning automatic, but she wasn't. Relax, for Pete's sake.

He drove along the deserted High Street, turned left up the curving hill past houses which seemed to have no lights. Paula was surprised as they ascended how dark the back road was. Expensive houses at the end of long drives but not the sort of place she'd want to live.

231

Close to the entrance to Admiralty House, where the road levelled out at the summit, Berthier swung the car on to the grass verge. He switched off the engine, turned to her.

'I've admired you ever since we met,' he began. 'You're a very attractive woman.'

'Thank you . . .'

She unfastened her seat belt quickly. His strong left hand wrapped itself round her neck, his right hand slipped under her coat, felt the dress, slipped under that. He'd released his own safety belt and was leaning over to kiss her, pulling her towards him. She raised her right hand, free of the glove she'd slipped off, reached for his face with her hard nails.

'Leave me alone or I'll mark you for life . . .'

'Gutsy? I like that in a girl.'

His grip increased on the back of her neck. Her nails dug into his face without drawing blood. Suddenly her hand left his face, she rammed the point of her elbow against his Adam's apple. He spluttered, released the grip on her neck, his other hand sliding out from under her coat. Her left hand opened the door, her right grabbed the loose glove, she jumped out on to the mushy grass. She spoke quickly before slamming the door shut, her tone contemptuous.

'Thank you so much for the lift, Mr Sanders. I won't be needing transport back . . .'

Hurrying along the verge, she turned into the entrance to Admiralty House. Walking along the drive she saw the curtains were pulled back from an inviting living room well illuminated. Jean Burgoyne saw her coming, met her at the door.

'Welcome to the Brigadier's den . . .'

Paula went inside. She'd already decided not to say anything about the episode with Berthier. Later she would walk home. It wasn't all that far.

24

Tweed found two car slots available up against the wall of
the Brudenell when he arrived. Plenty of space to park
Newman's large Mercedes. He collected his small case off
the front passenger seat, the special walking stick devised
for him by the Engine Room, got out into the icy night,
locked the car, walked into the hotel.

'Yes, Mr Tweed, we have a room reserved for you. The
same room you occupied recently,' the receptionist
assured him. 'And a number for you to phone urgently as
soon as you arrive.'

'Thank you. I'll make the call from my room . . .'

Inside the large room with windows overlooking the
front he threw his Burberry on to the bed. The North Sea
was making more noise than it had last time. The windows
were closed but he could hear the crash of countless tons of
water against the promenade.

Dumping his case on the floor, propping the stick by the
wall, he opened the folded slip. Monica's number. Something had happened. He picked up the phone, dialled.

'Tweed here, Monica. I am speaking from my hotel
room,' he said rapidly, warning her.

'I understand.' A brief pause. 'The *brand* product was
originally used in diving operations – from a North Sea oil
rig. It was found to be defective – its use was discontinued
under a cloud. Later it was used by bodyguards employed
by two security firms. Again it was thought to be defective
– nothing proved. It was then taken up by a firm of
qualified accountants. Latest development, held in high

regard by a firm at Dawlish Warren in Devon. End story.'

'Thank you for doing such a good job.'

'Don't go. There's more. Rather sensitive, could be urgent.'

'Something affecting my business trip here . . .?' Tweed was talking rapidly. He raised his voice suddenly. 'Operator! This is a bad line. Can you do something about it?' He listened for the click telling him someone was listening in. No click. His acute hearing waited for a sharp intake of breath. Nothing. No one was listening in. 'Go ahead, Monica.'

'Lasalle called. He's worried.'

'About what?'

'His informant at Third Corps tells him Sergeant Rey has disappeared. Lasalle thinks it might be an ominous development.'

'Lasalle is right.'

'There's more. Corcoran phoned from Heathrow. Major Lamy flew in a few hours ago – just after you left. No doubt about it. Travelling as William Prendergast. You won't believe this.'

'Try me.'

'He left Heathrow in a hired car he drove himself, a Rover. On his way to Aldeburgh. I tracked him myself. That's all.'

'It's enough,' Tweed said grimly. 'Thanks again. Don't hesitate to call me with any more news. Get some rest . . .'

Tweed put down the phone, began pacing the room. Brand, Dawlish's right-hand man, had originally been a diver for an oil rig. It sounded as though he'd been mixed up in something shady. Sabotage? Later he'd been a bodyguard for two separate firms – and dismissed from both. Had he already become a spy for Dawlish? And Monica's reference to the tiny coastal resort of Dawlish Warren had been clever. She was telling him he'd moved from the two security firms straight into Dawlish's employ.

The reference to qualified accountant was strange – it sounded as though Brand had been one, which meant he was far more than just a thug running other thugs. Tweed continued pacing, thinking about the Lasalle data.

Sergeant Rey, de Forge's boobytrap specialist, had vanished from Third Corps GHQ. Where could Rey be? What mission might he be engaged on? Of course, he could be on leave. But Tweed didn't think so. De Forge wouldn't be sending anyone on leave now the momentum of his campaign was building up.

Even more intriguing – possibly more ominous – Lamy was secretly visiting Aldeburgh. That *was* another positive link between Suffolk and France. One Tweed didn't like at all.

He decided he must find Paula at once. Throwing on his Burberry, picking up his walking stick, he left the room, avoided the elevator, ran down the staircase, went to Reception.

'I'm looking for my friend, Paula Grey,' he told the girl behind the desk.

'Oh, she drove off a little while ago. She is visiting someone in Aldeburgh.'

'Go by herself?'

'Yes . . .'

'Do you know where she went? I have to get in touch with her urgently – because of that phone message,' he improvised.

'I'm sorry, I have no idea . . .'

'Are Newman and Marler in the hotel?'

'No.' The girl was surprised by the bombardment, by the sense of urgency Tweed generated. 'Mr Marler left to go back to London. Mr Newman is out for a walk.'

'Thank you.'

Tweed decided he'd do the job he'd come to do – to take his mind off his anxiety. He walked out of the back entrance, passed Newman's Merc, hurried across the car

235

park on to the gravel road. He carried the stick in his right hand, a flashlight in his left hand. It was so dark he needed the beam to find his way.

Tweed had total recall of important conversations. He was able to remember exactly the route Paula, Newman, and Rosewater had followed when the latter had unearthed the signet ring. Major Lamy's? Apparently.

Passing an old shed set back from the gravel road he noted the sign. *Boat Storage*. He was close to where the path led down off the road on to the marshes. The powerful beam focused on a narrow footpath leading away from the road, down on to the marshes. This was it. He slithered agilely down it on to level, soggy ground. The wind blew his hair all over the place but he didn't notice: he was totally concentrating on following the same route.

The beam showed him the footpath running parallel to the gravel road above. He walked rapidly, holding the stick as a soldier might hold a rifle midway along its length. He switched off the flashlight and stood still, waiting for his night vision to return. Ahead he saw the dark silhouette of a high bank. The dyke which ran alongside the harbour.

Switching on the flashlight again he came to the point where the footpath forked – one fork leading back up to the road, the other up to the dyke. He paused. Easy to go wrong here. He climbed the path to the ridge of the dyke, saw where the footpath followed the crest of the dyke east. The harbour below it on his left, the marshes below him on his right. This was correct.

He moved rapidly along the tricky path. Stopping for a moment, he swivelled his beam across the harbour, saw boats swathed in blue plastic covers like huge blue eggs. Their masts rocked wildly, then moved more slowly. The wind had dropped suddenly. He heard a strange noise. He changed his grip on the stick so he held it by the handle.

236

The walking stick was a weapon. The tip was weighted. One blow could crack a man's skull. But there was more to it. Under the handle was a button. Press the button and a two-inch steel spike projected. It was *not* a sword stick, but one jab and an attacker would be injured. It was not Tweed's habit to carry weapons but Aldeburgh was becoming a dangerous place – the marshes possibly even more dangerous. To retract the spike he only had to press the button a second time. Now he recognized the weird sound. The twanging of metal wires against the metal masts of boats. He walked on.

He was aiming his flashlight down the slope to his left now. He must be near the place where the trio had discovered the relic of the craft where Karin Rosewater had died. The beam swept over a creek of stagnant water, swept back a fraction.

The craft, staves showing like ribs of some animal, was lying upside down at the edge of the creek. This was where the signet ring had been discovered. Tweed made his way down the awkward slope, keeping his balance easily. He stood on a firm tuft of grass encircled with ooze, slowly played his torch over the area inch by inch. For a minute he crouched down, examining carefully the messy terrain. His gloved hand poked at the grass, felt its sogginess give way under his pressure.

He sighed, stood up, scrambled back to the summit of the dyke. It had all been as he expected to find it – down to the last detail.

Stooping against the wind which blew up suddenly with greater force he hurried back along the dyke, followed the same route back to the Brudenell. Inside, he made himself speak casually to the receptionist.

'Has Miss Grey returned yet?'

'Not yet.'

Tweed returned to his room, full of foreboding.

*   *   *

Jean Burgoyne was a lively hostess. Dressed in a form-fitting green dress, she also wore a wide belt round her slim waist. Her dress stopped just above her knees, revealing her shapely legs clad in dark green tights. Her long thick mane of golden hair glistened under the lights of the chandeliers in the living room. Quite a girl, Paula thought.

She was seated in a comfortable armchair close to a blazing log fire. Jean sat in a hard-backed chair next to her, legs crossed, one high heel dangling. Both women were holding glasses of champagne.

'Paula, this is my uncle, Brigadier Burgoyne,' she introduced as a man entered the room.

The Brigadier was small, well-padded under his velvet smoking-jacket. His head was egg-shaped, bald on top with strands of white hair brushed carefully on either side. He had a ruddy complexion and looked more like a man in his mid-sixties than eighty.

'Pleased to meet you, Miss Grey,' he said formally, bending to shake her hand. 'Jean has told me quite a lot about you. But I can see with my own eyes you're a woman of resource. Like that . . .'

He had walked briskly to a sideboard, was pouring himself a glass of port from a decanter, when Paula asked the question. For a fraction of a second he stopped pouring – so briefly only Paula's sharp eyes caught it.

'I understand, Brigadier, you were with Military Intelligence.'

'Oh, all that's long behind me . . .' He glanced swiftly at Jean, switched his gaze to Paula, raised his glass. 'Your good health.' He sipped the port, remained standing by the sideboard.

'You must miss that work,' Paula continued, determined to stay with the subject. 'Especially as there is so much scope for it now. France is a good example. We need to know exactly what is going on over there – at the Third Corps particularly.'

238

The Brigadier stood quite still. His eyes blinked once. Like an owl. He looked rather like an owl, Paula was thinking.

'I'm rather out of touch these days.' Burgoyne was looking vague, which he hadn't before. 'I wonder if you'd think me very rude if I went to my study upstairs? I've work on some legal papers which need my attention. Just came down to say how do you do. Hope you'll come back to see us again. Don't mind my absence. Jean stays up all hours . . .'

He shuffled out of the room. A very different movement from the quick tread when he'd entered. You're acting, you sly old thing, Paula thought.

'He tires quickly,' Jean explained. 'He liked you – I could tell.'

'But *you* know Third Corps, don't you?'

Jean drank the rest of her champagne quickly, offered more to Paula, who refused, then filled her own glass again. She pushed a wave of blonde hair back over her shoulder, watched Paula over the rim of her glass as she spoke.

'You seem to be very well informed.'

'Don't mind me, I'm a journalist. It's my job. And I promised – no interview.'

'I do know General de Forge,' Jean said slowly after drinking more champagne. Her sleeve touched the ice bucket standing by her side. She jerked it away. 'It is cold.' She chuckled, a pleasant lilting sound. 'I regard him as a friend. Very dynamic, very stimulating. One of the most important men in Western Europe. Holds strong views, which is refreshing.'

'On deporting all foreigners from France? Especially Algerians and Negroes?'

'He has a lot of support for his views. Support which is growing by the hour.' Jean drank more champagne, re-filled her glass. She was certainly knocking it back, Paula noted. 'Some people think de Forge is a second General de Gaulle,' Jean went on. Her tone was neutral.

'Do you?' Paula asked.

'De Gaulle was a great statesman. De Forge is only a soldier. How could he ever become a statesman?'

'Maybe the first stage would be to create chaos.'

Jean had long fair lashes. She studied Paula through them, her eyes half-closed. Reaching for a silver box, she raised the lid, took out a cigarette, lit it with a gold lighter she also took from the box. Paula hadn't seen her smoke before during their short acquaintance. Jean blew a smoke ring, spoke as she watched it float to the ceiling.

'You really are a professional newshound to your finger-tips,' she commented dreamily.

There was no criticism, no irritation in her manner. It was a statement of fact. She stroked her cheekbone with the index finger of her left hand. Her bone structure was perfect. She really was a beautiful woman, Paula was thinking. The kind of woman who would drive a lot of men mad with desire.

'I'm just interested in what is going on in the world,' Paula fenced.

'You're right, of course. A lot is going on in France.' Jean seemed to be speaking in a trance. 'And no one can predict where it will all end.'

'Where do you think it will end?'

'At the gates of hell . . .'

She chuckled again, but this time there was a bitter note. She switched the conversation to Aldeburgh.

'Aldeburgh is rather unreal. Haven't you noticed? It's inhabited mostly by retired people – diplomats, soldiers like my uncle. They were brought here as children for their holidays by their parents. When they came home from abroad for good this was the only place they knew. There's nothing much in the way of jobs for youngsters. Except as shop assistants. Most of the work is in Ipswich, which is quite a distance. The other residents are second-homers. They've bought some of the houses on the front for summer visits . . .'

They chatted for quite a while longer. At one stage Jean left Paula alone for a few minutes to go to the bathroom. Paula lifted the lid of the cigarette box, took out the gold lighter. Engraved on it was the same symbol which was engraved on the signet ring Victor Rosewater had discovered on the marshes. The Cross of Lorraine . . .

'I'd better get back to the Brudenell,' Paula decided a little later. 'Thank you so much for such a relaxing evening.'

'I'd like it to go on all night long. If you're ever near Bordeaux, phone this number. It's the Villa Forban. I'll come and collect you in the car.'

She handed the sheet she'd scribbled on to Paula, escorted her to the front door. Opening it, Jean peered out.

'It's a foul night. You have transport? If not I'll drive you . . .'

'I have transport,' Paula lied.

She wanted to walk back, to absorb impressions she'd stored up of the Brigadier, of her conversation with Jean. Muffled against the raw cold inside her suede coat, her head protected with her scarf, she walked down the drive, waved to Jean who stood in the doorway, turned to the right to walk back down the hill.

She was treading her away across the damp grass verge when she heard something. She was about to look back when a thick brown paper bag was shoved over her head, *rammed* down hard. A pair of large hands grasped her round the neck, swung her through a hundred and eighty degrees, so she faced her attacker. Strong thumbs pressed against her windpipe. She couldn't breathe.

She might have panicked but her first reaction was that this was the bastard who had strangled Karin. She resisted the instinct to claw futilely at the lethal hands. She jerked her hands up to the bag, to roughly the point where it covered her mouth. Her hard nails tore furiously at the material. For a moment she thought it was too tough to penetrate. Then, as the hands tightened their grip, her finger nails ripped open a large slit. She clenched her fist, hit with all her force, as low down the body of the invisible man as she could, hoping for the kidneys. She heard a grunt. For a few seconds the hands loosened their grip. She opened her mouth, pressed to the hole, let out an ear-splitting scream.

'*A-a-a-a-a-a-a-a-r-r-g-h . . .!*'

25

Paula was hurled backwards as she heard what sounded like the firing of a high-powered hand-gun four times in rapid succession. Fortunately she was still on the grass verge, but she lay there winded. She heard a fresh sound. A car's engine starting up. She made the effort, pulled the bag off her head, forced herself up on her elbows – in time to see the red tail-lights of a car retreating in the opposite direction she'd travelled when driven there by Berthier.

Jean Burgoyne came rushing out of the entrance to Admiralty House. She stopped, gazing up and down the deserted road.

'Over here,' Paula called out feebly.

She was clambering to her feet, staggering, when Jean had reached her. She flicked at her coat with her hands to brush off rubbish.

'My best coat – suede . . .'

A sudden gust of wind funnelled down the road, nearly

blew her off her feet again. Jean grabbed her by the arm, led her back slowly to the drive, along it, into the house. Only then did Paula see she was carrying a large revolver.

'My uncle's Service revolver,' Jean said, seeing her looking at the weapon. 'What on earth happened out there? Are you all right? Would you like a drink? More champagne, coffee, tea? Something with brandy in it?'

'Nothing. Really. Thank you . . .'

She took off her coat, examined it, standing in the living room. She decided it had survived without serious damage.

'It will have to go to the cleaners.' She felt dazed. 'Did you fire that revolver?'

'You bet I did. Into the air. I heard you screaming – sounded like a banshee going full throttle. Feel like telling me what happened?'

Paula did so, tersely, pausing to give her throat a rest, to drink some lime juice. She was careful to give an edited version, pretending she'd been subjected to an attempted sexual assault.

When she'd finished she agreed that Jean should drive her back to the Brudenell, but first she insisted on a brief search outside with a flashlight Jean produced for the paper bag which had been thrust over her head. It might be important evidence.

They searched fruitlessly along the verge, in the road, for five minutes, and then Jean insisted that they got into her car and drove straight back to the hotel. Paula was still holding up well, worried she might say too much to Jean. She was also worried about Newman. When he had heard what happened he would give her hell.

They arrived outside and as she stepped out of the car Paula checked the other vehicles. Berthier's Saab was parked next to Newman's Mercedes. What the devil was the Merc doing here? Jean accompanied her inside and they ran into Newman pacing up and down the lobby.

Jean introduced herself, not realizing it was unnecessary

243

– Newman recognized her immediately from the photo Lasalle had sent by courier to Park Crescent. Paula thanked Jean effusively, said she wouldn't forget her invitation if she ever found herself in Bordeaux. Something made her call out as Jean was leaving.

'And, please, be very careful to take care of yourself. It's a dangerous world we're living in . . .'

'As you have good reason to know. Bye.'

'Tweed is here,' Newman told her as they rode up alone in the elevator. 'We'll go to his room, if that's all right. You look all shook up. White as a sheet. Has something happened?'

'Better tell you while Tweed can listen too . . .'

Settled in an armchair in Tweed's room, sipping frequently at a cup of the sweetened tea she'd asked for, she told them about her experience. Tweed sat in another armchair, close to her, leaning forward, hands clasped.

He was in two minds whether to let her go on as she had insisted on doing. Her request for sweetened tea, when normally she never touched sugar, suggested to him she was in a state of shock. He'd voiced the suspicion but she had denied it. Tweed was still wondering whether he ought to pack her off to bed. On the other hand, if she *was* up to describing what had happened now she was more likely to recall small details, any of which might be important.

Paula had the thirst of the devil. She paused again to sip the tea. The truth was she was in shock, but concealing it by asserting her strong willpower. As she went on speaking she kept herself under control by moving two fingers slowly up and down the shoulder strap of her bag. She had come to the point when Jean said she would drive her back and they got into her car. Newman spoke for the first time.

'Didn't anyone think of calling the police?'

'Oh, yes. Jean was very determined to do just that but I

dissuaded her.' She looked at Tweed. 'You've had enough trouble with Buchanan and I suspected it would get back to him. He might have asked awkward questions you don't want raised at this moment.'

'You could be right,' Tweed agreed. 'Good thinking.'

'I don't agree!' Newman burst out. 'If they'd put out an all-points bulletin they might have stopped the car.'

'What car?' Paula asked him. 'All I saw were two red tail-lights disappearing. No idea of the make – even of the size of the car.'

'They might have set up roadblocks,' Newman persisted.

'Probably no point,' Tweed objected. 'Supposing the man who attacked Paula is staying in Aldeburgh? Which I suspect is likely. His car will be parked in a garage.'

'And that occurred to me,' Paula agreed. 'I studied a map of the town – the road where Jean Burgoyne's uncle lives is a kind of horseshoe. He could have driven back into the High Street from the opposite direction to the way Berthier brought me. He might have his car parked outside this hotel. I did notice Berthier's Saab was parked back in the same slot we took it from.'

'Did you feel the radiator to see if the engine was still warm?' Newman asked.

'Oddly enough,' she flared up, 'I didn't think of it. After you've just escaped being strangled it's easy to forget something.'

'In any case,' Tweed pointed out, 'on a night like this an engine would cool quickly.' He looked at Paula. 'You have slight bruising on your neck . . .'

'Which I noticed in the mirror when I slipped into my own room for a wash before Bob brought me along here.' She felt her throat. 'It's very slight – probably my scarf saved me a worse bruising.'

'I was going to say,' Tweed continued, 'maybe we ought to get a doctor to examine it.'

245

'No doctor,' Paula said as she stood up, stifling a yawn. 'If you don't mind I think I'd like to get some sleep. I was going to have a bath . . .'

'Don't,' Newman warned. 'You could fall asleep in it.' He grinned. 'Unless you'd like me to come and help you into the bath.'

She smiled gratefully, realizing he was introducing an element of humour to soothe her nerves, shook her head. When she reached the door she paused, her mind racing as she turned to speak to them before leaving.

'I told you every word that was said at Admiralty House. There's something odd about Brigadier Burgoyne. He was spry as a five-year-old when I arrived – physically and mentally. When I started talking about Third Corps in France he dried up.'

Tweed leaned forward, a gleam in his eye. 'How do you mean?' he asked quickly.

'Prior to that he had all his marbles. He suddenly went vague on me. I had the distinct feeling he was acting out his old man routine. He even shuffled out of the room. When he entered you'd have thought he wasn't a day over sixty.'

'Interesting,' said Tweed, gazing into the distance.

'And there's something strange about Jean Burgoyne,' Paula went on.

'Strange?' Tweed probed. 'In what way?'

'I don't know. Yet. She invited me to the Villa Forban if I was ever in the Bordeaux area. I think I'd like to go there if ever the opportunity crops up.'

'No point in thinking about that now. Get to bed as soon as you can,' Tweed urged her.

Paula seemed reluctant to go. 'Do you think that the murderer could be a woman?' she asked suddenly.

'Why do you think that?' Tweed, surprised, queried.

'I don't know that either, yet. Sleep well, both of you . . .'

*   *   *

246

'Kalmar is somewhere here in Aldeburgh,' Tweed said as soon as they were alone. 'I'm convinced of it. I was careful not to say that while Paula was here. She's gone through enough for one day. Kalmar's identity is the key to this whole European riddle – to what is happening in France, in Germany.'

'And there are plenty of candidates for the role of assassin here in Aldeburgh at the moment,' Newman commented. He had been told by Tweed of the conversation with Monica as they had waited for Paula's return. 'Major Lamy, Sergeant Rey, Lieutenant Berthier – and Brand.'

'So your first priority in the morning is to drive Paula back to London in your Merc. That's an order.'

'Which I'm happy to carry out . . .'

'She mustn't linger here a moment longer,' Tweed stressed. 'You must remove her from the zone of danger – Aldeburgh.'

'And then, I suppose,' Newman said cynically, 'she'll want to move into a zone of even greater danger when she hears where I'm going. France.'

26

SECOND LYONS RIOT. FRENCH SITUATION WORSENS.

In his Park Crescent office next day Tweed read the text below the alarming headline. Monica had obtained the copy of the leading Paris newspaper, *Le Monde*, during his absence.

Over 2,000 casualties . . . more than 400 killed . . . Lyons

in a state of chaos . . . The President may visit city . . .
martial law considered . . .

He skip-read the account in French quickly, glanced at Paula who sat behind her desk. She was looking more normal. A good night's sleep in Aldeburgh before Newman had driven her back had done her a world of good. Earlier, Newman had repaired Tweed's Escort.

'I read it,' she said. 'Could it be General de Forge stepping up the pressure?'

'Someone is,' Tweed replied cautiously. 'I'm flying to Paris later today to consult with Lasalle. He doesn't seem to trust the phone. That's after I've seen Chief Inspector Kuhlmann.'

'Here? He's flying to London?'

'Yes, expected any moment. Monica took the call before I arrived back. Someone else who doesn't trust phones. It worries me – the atmosphere of intrigue at the very top. While in Paris, I'm meeting Pierre Navarre, Minister of the Interior – the only strong man in the government.'

'We've come back from a troubled time in Aldeburgh to an inferno.'

'I suspect the inferno is still to come.' He noted her understatement – 'a troubled time' – which covered a near-successful attempt to strangle her. Paula was very resilient. 'On top of all this,' he told her, 'we have Chief Inspector Buchanan descending on us later. At my request, admittedly, and Victor Rosewater will join us. I must give Buchanan that signet ring and both of us – Rosewater and myself – will have to take a few salvoes from our friend, Buchanan. I expect we'll survive . . .'

As he was speaking the phone rang, Monica answered it, said could he wait just a minute. She put her hand over the mouthpiece.

'It's started. Otto Kuhlmann is downstairs.'

'Wheel him up . . .'

The German walked in, wearing a dark business suit, an

248

unlit cigar clamped tightly between his teeth. He looked grim but went over to Paula, put his arm round her shoulders, gave her a hug. He stared at the scarf tucked in above her form-fitting powder blue sweater. The scarf had slipped. Kuhlmann's sharp eyes missed nothing.

'Your throat,' he rasped. 'You've been in the wars?'

'You could say that,' Tweed intervened as Paula adjusted the scarf. 'Tell you about it in a minute. Sit down. Welcome to London. Coffee?'

'Please. Black as sin.'

Kuhlmann sat in an armchair, shifted his bulk, staring again at Paula. He twiddled his cigar as he watched her.

'Do light your cigar,' Paula urged. 'I like the aroma of a Havana.'

Monica had hurried from the room to make coffee. Kuhlmann lit his cigar, looked at Tweed, waved the cigar towards Paula.

'Her throat,' he persisted.

Tweed gave a terse account of their trip to Aldeburgh, expressed his certainty that Kalmar had been in the area. He gave the German a list of his suspects, told him he'd not reached the stage where the finger pointed at one man.

'Any idea where he comes from, his nationality?' Kuhlmann asked. 'I also have been trying to get a grip on him. All I hear from my contacts is he's from somewhere in the East. That covers quite a lot of territory. Not a hint of his age, his description.'

'The shadow of a shadow,' Tweed remarked. 'Rather curious. Possibly even significant. But that isn't why you flew to see me, Otto.'

He waited while Monica poured a large cup of black, steaming coffee. Kuhlmann thanked her, drank half the cup in one steady stream.

'Siegfried,' he began. 'Rosewater rang me again from somewhere. I didn't ask him from where. He is Military Intelligence. Gave me another address he'd just obtained from an informant. An apartment in Munich. We raided it, found another arms cache. Twelve Kalashnikov rifles, spare mags, six grenades, and two kilos of Semtex.'

Tweed leaned forward. 'And terrorists?'

Kuhlmann waved his hands like a swimmer. 'I think the local police fumbled it. Patrol cars approached with sirens screaming. No terrorists. No one in the apartment. And again, not one single fingerprint. Another woman at work, I'm sure. A man would have missed something.'

'So *Siegfried* is in place,' Tweed commented.

'Our own informants in the criminal underground say they are – and they know what's going on. Upwards of a hundred trained saboteurs and assassins. Likely targets: leading members of the government, including the Chancellor himself. Apparently they're waiting for a signal from abroad. Then they start to destabilize Germany. What I'm really worried about is the growing campaign in certain parts of the French press against Germany.'

'All of which is orchestrated. Every responsible person knows Germany is the most peace-loving nation on the continent,' Tweed continued. 'Certain elements in France are whipping up anti-German feeling for their own sinister ambitions. To cover up the fact that all they're interested in is seizing power in Paris. The *Cercle Noir*.'

'The Black Circle.' Kuhlmann waved his cigar. 'And we've heard rumours about them. They're anti-Semitic, anti-American, anti-British. The trouble is we don't know who they are. But they wield a hell of a lot of clout. And if I can't smoke out the *Siegfried* terrorists before they break loose they'll justify what the yellow Paris press is saying about us.'

'Which is the whole idea, the core of the plan.'

'On top of this the criminal underworld reports they expect huge reinforcements to arrive soon. From where? If it's from the East – like Kalmar – they'll get through.'

'You have any good men at Wiesbaden who speak French?' Tweed asked.

'Yes, why?'

'Send them undercover into Geneva. Spread the word they are trying to contact Kalmar for a big job. Fee – three million marks. No, make that Swiss francs.'

'If you say so . . .'

'And send more undercover men, German-speaking, into Basle. Same message.'

'You know something?'

Kuhlmann watched Tweed through blue cigar smoke. Then he drank the rest of his coffee and Monica refilled his cup.

'Just do it. What about Stahl, your agent posing as a Frenchman in Bordeaux? Any news?'

Kuhlmann hesitated. 'Hell! You've been frank with me. He's still there. The trouble is you warned me that he shouldn't use his transmitter. His last signal said he had a load of information – that he'd bring it out as soon as he could. A very brief signal. You're operating in France?'

Kuhlmann looked at the ceiling as he asked the question casually.

'On a large scale.'

'That's really why I came. It's difficult for German agents to operate inside France. The Chancellor has put a veto on the idea.'

'Why?'

'As you know, he has a good relationship with the President of France. If the Paris press could get hold of a story that we have agents inside French territory they'd have a field day.'

'What about Stahl then?'

Kuhlmann looked up at the ceiling again. Paula knew he was working out his answer.

'That's my secret,' Kuhlmann said eventually. 'And if

251

the fact ever came to light, I sent in Stahl before the Chancellor said there was a veto. And now it could be difficult for Stahl to get out quickly. That Black Circle may have done just that – put a circle round Bordeaux.'

'They have.' Tweed recalled Newman's evading action when he'd slipped past the watchers at Bordeaux Airport. 'The airport is a trap,' he warned. 'And my guess is they're also watching the rail stations, maybe even have check-points outside the city for motorists.'

'So Stahl is trapped.'

'We might be able to reach him. No guarantees. So, we are on your side, Otto. All you can do is to go back, hope, and pray . . .'

Tweed checked his watch when Kuhlmann had said good-bye, had left for Heathrow. Monica guessed what was on his mind.

'Yes, Victor Rosewater is due very shortly . . .' She picked up the phone which had started ringing. As she listened her expression changed. 'You mean all three of them have arrived together? That they're here now?'

Her expression was a mixture of puzzlement and annoyance. She looked at Tweed.

'I don't think you're going to like this. The idea was Rosewater arrived for a half hour's quiet chat with you before Buchanan grilled him.'

'What's gone wrong?'

'They're all waiting downstairs. Rosewater, Buchanan, and his sidekick, Sergeant Warden.'

'Very odd. Oh, now I get it.' He raised his eyebrows at Paula. 'Send them all up, Monica . . .'

Rosewater entered the room first. Wearing a trench-coat, hands thrust in his pockets, he looked at Paula, winked. His manner was cool and poised as always. Behind him a wooden-faced Chief Inspector Buchanan followed with Warden, also wooden faced, as always, bringing up the rear.

'Coats off, gentlemen,' Tweed said breezily. He looked at Buchanan. 'And you're half an hour early.'

'I like to be in good time,' Buchanan said as he handed his coat to Monica. 'We bumped into Mr Rosewater as we were walking up and down outside. It seemed a good idea to get on with it.'

Tweed had already caught on to Buchanan's tactics. With Warden he had deliberately turned up very early, hoping to see Rosewater arrive. That way there would be no time for Tweed to prime the Intelligence officer.

With his guests seated, Tweed wasted no time. Leaning into the back of his chair he explained how Rosewater, Newman, and Paula had found the signet ring on the marshes. He unlocked a drawer, took out the copy of the original ring, handed it to Buchanan.

'This comes under the heading of suppressing evidence in a murder . . .' Buchanan began, staring at Rosewater.

Tweed's clenched fist crashed down on his desk. 'Now you listen to me – and don't forget where you are. You have been given the ring. Voluntarily. In case you've forgotten, you're at the headquarters of the SIS. And, in case you've overlooked it, Captain Rosewater is a member of Military Intelligence. I happen to know that he is involved in a matter of the utmost importance to national security. There will be no questions asked, no accusations made, without my agreement. I will not have you adopting an overbearing manncr in my office.'

He sank back in his chair, his expression furious and his mouth tight-lipped. Paula was staring at him.

'So that's the way you're going to play it,' Buchanan observed calmly, stretching out his legs, crossing his ankles.

'I'm not *playing*, as you put it!' Tweed leaned forward again. 'Men have died outside this room. One of them my

253

agent. Abroad. Where you have no jurisdiction. I can and do operate abroad,' he snapped. 'If you want information which may help you in *your* invesigation, then you will cease and desist. Now!'

'My main concern is who murdered this gentleman's wife, strangled her in cold blood on those marshes where this ring was found.'

Buchanan's manner was still mild. He might have been conducting a friendly conversation in a pub. In contrast Tweed still appeared to be in a controlled rage.

'You've got the ring. You've heard the circumstances under which it was found.' His voice rose. 'But I am concerned with the cauldron boiling up in Europe, a situation which is worsening by the hour. In case you don't know what I'm talking about, read the papers.'

'I realize you have grave responsibilities. Perhaps it would be better if we came back when you are less fraught. And I would like to ask Captain Rosewater a question . . .'

'No!' Tweed stood up. 'Captain Rosewater is directly involved in what is happening in Europe. I know you will not think me impolite if I say I do not have the time to prolong this discussion. I'm under pressure. A major conflagration is building up in Europe.'

'I think I have what I came for.' Buchanan stood up, the signet ring held in his hand covered with a surgical glove he had slipped on before accepting it. He dropped it inside a plastic bag Sergeant Warden held out. 'But I may need to see Captain Rosewater at the Yard . . .'

'Sorry, Chief Inspector,' Rosewater interjected, 'but I expect my job to take me back to Germany today. Where I'm based.'

'But you'll have time to come and make a statement.'

'I'm afraid not. Tweed has described what happened very precisely. I'll be on the first available flight.'

254

'*Bon voyage*,' Buchanan replied ironically and left the room.

'You saved me a tough inquisition,' Rosewater said as soon as they were on their own. 'That Chief Inspector is one bright cookie.'

'I didn't want him trying to penetrate your role in France and Germany. You'll be based in Freiburg if I need to contact you?'

'Mostly.' He looked at Paula. 'If you can coax your boss into being generous, maybe you'd come and visit me. I gave you the address.'

'I may be waiting on your doorstep,' Paula joked.

Rosewater stood up. 'I meant what I said to Buchanan. I'm leaving for the continent now. If you can't get me in Freiburg, contact Kuhlmann. He may be able to reach me. We're keeping in close touch.'

'Take care,' Tweed warned, watching him, '*Siegfried* is deadly. I gather you're having trouble tracking them.'

'They've organized themselves into independent cells, each with a mission when the balloon goes up in Germany. Sabotage and assassination on a large scale. That much I have learned. Strictly between these walls I'm trying to infiltrate agents inside *Siegfried*. It's a race against time – before their controller gives the signal. He could be Kalmar . . .'

'Why,' asked Paula when Rosewater had gone, 'haven't you told Buchanan about Major Lamy and Lieutenant Berthier? Both were in Aldeburgh. Even Sergeant Rey?'

'Because,' Tweed explained, 'I'm letting them run on a loose rein, giving them plenty of rope. Meantime you and I are leaving for Paris. You have your usual case packed here for emergency take-offs? Good. Monica has booked three seats on the Paris flight today.'

'Three?'

255

'I'm expecting Newman to arrive here any moment. He's going in via Paris. The Bordeaux Airport is closely watched. And you'd better ask Lasalle for a weapon – we're moving into the cauldron.'

27

Major Lamy, wearing his normal French civilian clothes, disembarked from the Air Inter flight at Bordeaux Airport. He did not know it but later that same day Tweed would fly to Paris. Lamy was met by a chauffeur in a civilian uniform, escorted to the waiting Citroën.

Half an hour later he entered the large room where General de Forge was studying the newspaper accounts of the devastation caused by the fresh Lyons riots. De Forge neatly folded the paper he was reading, added it to the pile, waved to Lamy to sit opposite him.

'Did you get *Oiseau* to agree?' he demanded.

'Mission accomplished.' Lamy sat erect, aware this was a formal interview. '*Oiseau* agreed to supply double the original number of missiles with nerve gas warheads.'

'*When?*' De Forge fired back at him.

'He said he would send a signal from the transmitter aboard the *Steel Vulture* giving the delivery date. I had the impression it would be soon.'

'*Soon? Oiseau* wants to learn military precision. We may need those weapons within one week from now. Have you heard the President is thinking of travelling to Lyons to inspect the damage? Because he dislikes flying he'll go there aboard the TGV?'

Lamy's expression showed no sign of his surprise, that

he hadn't known: de Forge expected you to know everything that was going on. The TGV – the *Train de Grande Vitesse* – famous for its bullet-like speed of up to 150 m.p.h.

'That concerns us?' he enquired.

'I will give you orders soon. Urgent orders. This may be our opportunity. Have you also heard the Prefect of Paris – the man who might have got in our way when we focus on Paris – has been assassinated?'

Lamy nodded. 'Kalmar has delivered again . . .'

'Kalmar! Are you sure you know it was him? I had a phone call on my private number from a man calling himself by the code-name *Manteau*.'

He watched Lamy closely as the Intelligence chief stared back, sitting more erect. Lamy found himself still thinking in English, a mental habit he'd easily slipped into during his trip to Aldeburgh. *Manteau* meant *Cloak*.

'What did this *Manteau* say?' Lamy asked.

He hardly had the words out of his mouth before de Forge exploded.

'He said *he* had shot the Prefect. He gave me a detailed description of how and where and when – which has not appeared in the press yet. I ordered Berthier to phone our contact inside Lasalle's DST. He gave exactly the same details of the assassination. *Manteau* has asked for a fee of half a million Swiss francs. He said that if I refused that was all right, but he would expect my next commission.'

'How the devil could he know we wanted the Prefect eliminated?' wondered Lamy.

'Because there has to be a leak inside my own GHQ,' de Forge shouted back. 'You had better discover that leak fast. Whoever it is must be shot in the Landes. His body disposed of in the usual way.'

De Forge was gazing closely at Lamy as he spoke. Aware of the scrutiny, Lamy gazed back without blinking. Then he changed the subject quickly, opening the briefcase in his lap.

257

'I will carry out the investigation myself.' He took a large fat envelope out of the case. '*Oiseau* has supplied the funds requested. Three million Swiss francs. He gave them to me without hesitation.' He placed the envelope on the desk.'

'Why aren't you already conducting that investigation?' de Forge stormed.

Lamy was hurrying out of the long room to change into his uniform when de Forge called out for him to wait a moment. His voice was dangerously quiet. Lamy was well accustomed to his chief's unpredictable changes of mood, knew he was treading on tricky ground. He turned.

'Yes, my General?'

'Did you organize that Ku-Klux-Klan-style attack on the Jews in the south before leaving for England?'

'Yes. It was to take place last night. I'm sure you'll hear news of it today. And a reporter with a gun in his back and a camera in his hand will have recorded it.'

Tweed, Paula, and Newman met a grim Lasalle when they had arrived at rue des Saussaies in Paris. The Frenchman grected them courteously, ordered an aide to bring coffee, waited until the four of them were alone.

'What's happened now, René?' Tweed asked quietly as he sat down, sensing his host's disquiet.

'This newspaper has just been flown to me by courier from Bordeaux by the chief of my team in the city. It is the most hideous atrocity.'

He spread the newspaper over his desk facing them, said nothing, knowing they could all read French. The front page carried a huge picture, one of the most sinister Paula had ever seen. The headline screamed:

'ANTI-SEMITES GO BERSERK AT TARBES. TWENTY JEWS BURN.

The photograph was weird, macabre. Figures clad in what appeared to be white sheets from head to toe carried

258

blazing torches. The sheets were shaped so they rose to the point of a triangle above the invisible heads with slits for the eyes. Each figure carried a flaming torch in one hand, a long knife in the other. The group of roughly forty men was formed into a triangular formation. At the apex – in front of the white-sheeted figures – the leader carried the Cross of Lorraine blazing with fire.

It was not the only thing blazing. Men, mostly bare headed in the night, were running as flames enveloped them. One desperate fugitive wore a skull cap. Tweed turned to the next page which was covered with photos. Corpses burnt to a cinder littered the ground. Paula swallowed, stiffened herself.

'This happened last night?' Tweed asked.

'Yes,' Lasalle explained. 'Apparently there is some old castle where a Jewish group gathered to discuss the scriptures. I gather it was some kind of club – that they attended meetings regularly. So the fiends who did this knew when their victims would be there.'

'It's horrific,' Paula whispered. 'Why?'

'Obvious, I'd have thought,' Newman commented. 'We all know there's anti-Semitism below the surface in many countries. Someone in France is working up the population – that part of it which is anti-Jewish.'

'But this is a massacre,' Paula protested.

'Exactly,' said Newman. 'A vicious atrocity to work up more chaos. The man behind this is a monster.'

'Dubois, I'm sure,' Lasalle said. 'His speeches are vitriolic against all foreign elements, as he terms them. Especially the Jews.'

'What about the reporter?' Newman probed.

'My DST chief who is in charge in Bordeaux says he was kidnapped at gunpoint. Then he was forced to take these foul pictures. The President is appalled. The trouble is he's just about to leave on the TGV for Lyons.'

'Today, you mean?' Tweed queried.

259

'Yes. And he's taking the Prime Minister with him. The security problem is a nightmare. Still, that's simply something else to pigeonhole in my mind. As Churchill once said, my mental culvert is almost overflowing – something like that. What I'm about to tell you now is top secret.'

'Understood,' said Newman, knowing he was the visitor Lasalle was bothered about.

'The Prefect of Paris was assassinated last night.'

'Oh, my God!' Paula burst out. 'He was one of the few strong men you could rely on in an emergency.'

'Which was why he was a target. Now, listen, we have decided to keep it quiet, away from the public and the press.'

'How on earth can you do that?' Newman protested.

'By saying he has gone on holiday. He was due for some leave. I'd cancelled it but no one knows that. There was a witness to the killing. The disturbing thing is I had a phone call from a Frenchman calling himself *Manteau*. He claimed he had shot the Prefect. We have been hearing rumours about this new professional assassin, *Manteau*. A professional. So now we have two to cope with – Kalmar and *Manteau*.'

'Unless,' Tweed said quietly, '*Manteau* is Kalmar. He could be cleverly confusing the search for him.'

Lasalle stared at Tweed. 'I had never thought of that. It fits in with the pattern of mounting chaos. I've kept the witness downstairs. You might like to question her. With your skill at interrogation you might extract something I've missed . . .'

He spoke into his intercom. Paula watched the door, curious to see who was the witness. Tweed accepted Lasalle's offer to sit in the chair behind his desk, sat with his hands clasped. The door opened and a DST officer ushered inside the last type of witness Paula had expected.

A short overweight bag lady shuffled into the office. She clutched a large bundle held together with a piece of soiled

260

cloth. Glaring at the DST officer she spoke to Tweed, assuming he was the boss, that Lasalle must be an underling.

'They tried to take my bundle. All my possessions in the world are inside it. Never let it out of my sight. I sleep under one of the Seine bridges. The *flics* keep moving me on. Say I'm not nice for the tourists. Who gives a monkey's cuss for the tourists?'

'Please sit down, Madame,' Tweed said in French. 'And I will personally ensure no one touches your possessions.'

'You'd better if you want to ask me questions. And I'd like more money first.'

Lasalle, standing to one side, brought out his hands from behind his back. He riffled through the wad of banknotes he was holding.

'You get these later. But only if my chief is satisfied with your answers.'

'I've already told *you*,' she went on grumbling. 'Why don't you tell him?'

'Because,' Tweed intervened in a sympathetic tone, 'it's important I hear what happened to the Prefect from you. You strike me as a woman who keeps her eyes open.'

'Don't miss much, I can tell you,' the bag lady replied, mollified by Tweed's manner.

'So tell me, please, what you saw.'

'I was crossing the Île de la Cité on my way to doss down. It was one o'clock in the morning. I know that because I'd looked at a clock. The Prefecture is on the Île de la Cité. But you know that. I know the Prefect by sight. I should do. In the past he's given me a few francs. More than any *flic* would do.'

'So tell me what you saw last night.'

Paula was studying the bag lady's clothing. She was wrapped in a khaki-coloured army blanket, fastened at

261

the neck with a huge safety-pin. Round her head she wore a large scarf, the colours faded, wisps of grey hair protruding. Newspaper projected from the worn pair of man's shoes encasing her large feet. But her bare red hands looked strong and her jaw jutted as she began, staring at Tweed.

'I was a distance away from the entrance to the Prefect's building. A car was parked on the opposite side of the street, the side I was on. A man was crouched behind the car, seemed to be doing up his shoe lace. I recognized the Prefect as soon as he came down the steps towards his car . . .'

Her previous rasping tone had sunk to a monotone, like a woman reciting by rote. Of course, Paula thought, she's told this same story before to Lasalle.

'The man crouched behind the car stood up. He was holding what looked like a rifle. He steadied it on the roof of his car, took aim, fired. The Prefect stopped half-way down the steps, then collapsed.'

'And the assassin?' Tweed coaxed.

'Jumped into his car, didn't he, and drove off like hell. Don't ask me the make of the car. I don't know them. Never owned a car.'

'What did the assassin look like? Height? Weight? Was he bare-headed? What colour of hair if he was . . .'

'Stop! Stop! For God's sake . . .'

'Sorry. Take your time.' Tweed spoke very slowly. 'I expect you noticed how he was dressed?'

'Wore a cloak, didn't he? A dark cloak. Dark like his hat. Don't see them much these days. Cloaks. Except sometimes when the toffs are going into the Opéra.' Her mouth clamped shut.

'You probably noticed something else about – the Cloak.'

'That's it. All happened so quickly. I wouldn't know him if I saw him again. Then the police came running out of the

262

building, waving their guns. Too late, as usual. That's it. Except they grabbed me. What about my money?'

Tweed nodded. Lasalle held out the wad of banknotes, then withdrew it as she reached out. His voice was harsh.

'You remember the conditions. You don't talk about this to the press, the radio, to anyone on God's earth. If you do you lose the bigger sum I'll give you later.'

'Bigger? How much?' Quick as a flash.

'That you'll find out when I decide you've earned it. I'm having you watched twenty-four hours a day.'

He gave her the banknotes. Without checking the amount she stuffed them somewhere under her blanket, glared at Tweed, stood, picked up her bundle, refusing help from Lasalle who opened the door. The DST officer was waiting in the corridor, escorted her away. Lasalle closed the door and looked at his three visitors with raised eyebrows.

'I know that *Manteau* isn't Kalmar,' Newman said flatly.

They all stared at him. Newman shrugged, rubbed one eye and spoke again.

'I didn't phrase that well. I was up half the night. I don't believe *Manteau* is Kalmar.'

'Why not?' Lasalle enquired, his tone soft.

'The *modus operandi*. Kalmar strangles his victims. Carey in Bordeaux at the Gare St Jean. Karin Rosewater in Aldeburgh. *Manteau* shot the Prefect.'

'The assassin would have had trouble getting close enough to the Prefect to strangle him,' Tweed pointed out. 'As you learned from your SAS training, Bob, there's more than one way of killing – and men skilled with different techniques.'

Lasalle waved an impatient hand. 'There was also a witness to that hideous massacre of the Jews near Tarbes. He's waiting downstairs. I think you ought to meet him. The head of the discussion group. Moshe Stein . . .

* * *

263

Moshe Stein was a heavily built man of medium height with a tough face and a gentle smile. Above his beaky nose, dark alert eyes took in everyone in the room. His thick black hair was neatly brushed back from a high forehead. He wore a well-pressed dark blue business suit and above the firm mouth was a bushy moustache. Lasalle introduced his other guests as 'members of a top-security organization'. He spoke in English and as Stein responded in the same language he smiled warmly.

'Moshe Stein,' Lasalle explained, 'is the sole survivor of the Tarbes massacre.'

'I am afraid I am a coward,' Stein said to Paula, settling in his chair. 'I saw this horrific attack from our HQ, the chateau. Very old but very small. I realized I couldn't help – there were too many of the killers. I felt someone should live to tell the authorities. So I hid in a secret cellar. When they had gone I walked to the local station, took a train to where I could board the Paris Express. I feel ashamed and guilty.'

'Nonsense,' Paula said robustly. 'You did the sensible thing. You may even end up avenging your friends . . .'

Stein talked in his quiet voice, recalling the arrival of the assault force. He thought they'd imitated the American Ku-Klux-Klan which, he understood, had revived in a small way in the deep South of the States. He looked at Newman.

'I'm going back to my small villa in the Landes. That is a beautiful area of France. Great forests of firs and pines spread a great distance until the Atlantic stops them. Even the beach is beautiful – great sand dunes rear up, concealing the endless cold blue water beyond.'

Paula thought Stein was rather poetic: as he spoke a dreamy look came over his weatherbeaten face. Again he looked at Newman.

'There is something mysterious going on in the Landes. You are a newspaper reporter. I thought we'd travel together. That is, if you think there may be a story.'

'I agree,' Newman said at once. 'Providing we can leave today. Also, providing we can call in at Arcachon.'

'We take the Paris–Bordeaux Express,' Stein suggested.

'Yes. But we must leave it at an intermediate station before Bordeaux. I have a reason. Trust me.'

'I do. I have been watching you. We could leave the express at Angoulême, hire a car, drive the rest of the way. First to Arcachon, then on to the Landes.'

Newman took out a map of France he'd brought with him, located Angoulême and agreed. He didn't say it was far enough north of Bordeaux not to have watchers.

'That was quick,' Lasalle said when the two men had left his office. 'Newman is decisive, Tweed.'

'Newman is pretty good at assessing character. Clearly he liked what he saw. We meet Navarre now? Good.'

'And I've decided I'm going to visit Jean Burgoyne at the Villa Forban,' Paula announced. 'She told me she was going back there before she drove me to the Brudenell from Admiralty House.'

'Wait here in Paris,' Tweed ordered. 'Phone Monica when you've got a hotel room, give her the name and address and phone number. If I decide to let you go you'll be accompanied – by Butler and Nield.'

'If you insist. Don't look so worried.'

'I am.' Tweed stood up as Lasalle checked his watch. They were due at the Ministry of the Interior. 'I am worried,' Tweed stressed. 'I'm convinced General de Forge is waiting for a trigger to set Europe ablaze. I just don't know what that trigger will be.'

PART TWO

Trigger of Death

28

The President of France walked down the six steps which lead from the entrance to the Elysée Palace to the waiting motorcade in the courtyard.

He stepped into the rear of his Citroën as his *chef de cabinet* held open the door. Closing the door the *chef* ran round the rear of the vehicle to join the President. The chauffeur and armed guard in civilian clothes waited until both rear doors were closed, then slipped into the front.

There were eight Citroëns comprising the motorcade drawn up in the courtyard behind the grille gates fronting on the rue du Faubourg St Honoré. The Prime Minister got quickly into the car behind the President's. Staff members and armed guards climbed into the other vehicles.

Uniformed armed guards carrying automatic weapons patrolled the street immediately outside the Elysée. Traffic had been diverted. In the distance curious crowds were held well back by uniformed police. At a signal the gates were opened, the President's limousine was driven out, proceeded at speed towards the Gare de Lyon with the rest of the motorcade streaming close behind.

Armed motor-cycle outriders kept pace with the vehicles. Four more outriders formed a group ahead of the President's limousine. A further group of outriders brought up the rear behind the last vehicle.

The President held himself erect, knowing that despite the speed, residents of Paris were lining the pavements, gazing with excitement as the motorcade raced past them.

Only when they were close to the Gare de Lyon did the President's driver slow down. He turned into the station, pulled up precisely alongside a red carpet leading to the presidential coach.

Stepping out of his car, the President inspected the guard of honour drawn up, uniforms immaculate. He nodded his approval to their commander, boarded the train. A white-coated steward, spotless, bowed, led the way to his armchair seat in the luxurious coach. Aware now that the permitted TV cameras were focused on him, the President, small and stocky, sat with his profile tilted at the correct angle. He took a leather folder handed to him by an aide and pretended to be reading a file.

The presidential coach was immediately behind the huge locomotive which would transport him to Lyons. The *Train de Grande Vitesse*, the pride of French Railways, sat in the Gare like a long sleek polished bullet.

When it had left Paris behind it would move like a bullet, travelling at speeds up to 150 m.p.h. There was a pause while the rest of the President's entourage boarded the express. The Prime Minister's coach was behind the President's and he also had a large entourage.

The rear coaches were reserved for the press, radio, and TV personnel. They would record the President's tour of devastated Lyons. His political aim was to show France how much he cared for the victims of the outrage.

There was no signal to warn of the TGV's departure. One moment it was standing in the Gare de Lyons, the next moment the magnificent train was gliding out into the cold sunlight of a bitter November day.

For the first time the President spoke to his *chef de cabinet*.

'Is everything arranged for my arrival at Lyons? I need a car for the first part of the tour.'

'A bullet-proof limousine will be waiting at the station.'

'Later, I shall leave the car at an appropriate moment

when the crowds are massed. I will walk and mingle with them, express sympathy, shake many hands . . .'

'The chief of security was worried that might be what you intended. Lasalle has warned there is a professional assassin, Kalmar, operating. He has already killed at least two people. He would prefer you to remain in your car.'

'Lasalle fusses. The President of the French Republic must show himself to the people in their hour of need. That is what you will tell security . . .'

The President busied himself with state papers, rarely looking out of the window. The amount of paperwork which crossed his desk at the Elysée was formidable. He was paying close attention to detailed reports of the unrest in the south. He really had no idea how to placate the disturbing growth of terror.

In the open countryside farmers and workers heard the express coming. They paused to watch as it passed them in the distance. A blur of movement – incredible movement for a train. In the large cab of the locomotive an engineer checked his watch, looked at a colleague.

'We shall be there soon. Keep up maximum speed. The President will expect it . . .'

South of Roanne the line crossed a high viaduct spanning a river far below. The TGV was approaching at top speed as it neared the viaduct. This was normal procedure. The Chief Engineer peered through a window, saw the viaduct rushing towards him. He tucked a Gauloise between his thick lips, decided not to light it yet.

The locomotive reached the viaduct, began crossing it, hauling the coaches behind as though they were made of plastic. In the distance, not more than half a mile away, a large village was perched on a hill. France spread away . . .

The whole length of the TGV train was crossing the viaduct when the explosion occurred ahead of it near the end of the viaduct. A large stretch of track was hurled skywards. The TGV thundered forward, the wheels encountered the gap. The locomotive swept sideways, rammed the stone wall as though it were constructed of paper. The TGV continued its onward rush – into space. It shot forward like a torpedo, dragging the coaches with it. Then it curved downwards, plunging at hellish speed into the ravine. The locomotive swivelled in mid-air. The Chief Engineer bit clean through his unlit Gauloise. They found his decapitated head later, half the cigarette inside his mouth.

The locomotive hit the bottom of the ravine like a bomb detonating. A tumble of coaches smashed down on top of it, behind it, in front. No one survived in the President's coach. No one survived in the Prime Minister's coach. Many died instantly in the other coaches, some were terribly injured.

At the edge of the village a middle-aged man in tattered clothes had been waiting for the express, staring through a pair of old binoculars. He focused on the viaduct. The gap in the wall reminded him of a gap in a man's teeth.

29

General de Forge's limousine pulled up outside the Villa Forban. He didn't wait for the chauffeur, he opened the door and dived out as soon as the car had stopped. He had the keys to the two locks on the front door in his hand, inserted them one by one, pushed open the heavy door, walked inside, slammed it behind him, and stopped.

'What are you doing here?'

Jean Burgoyne, wearing a green form-fitting sweater and a mini-skirt, pushed a wave of blond hair over her shoulder. She waved her shapely hands in a gesture of surprise.

'Aren't you glad to see me, Charles?'

'You didn't inform me you were coming back so soon,' he responded stiffly.

'You think I am your serf? That I should report all my movements to you?'

Her voice was soft and husky, showed no sign of annoyance. She took a gold cigarette case from her handbag, selected a cigarette, placed it between her lips, lit it with her gold lighter. The one engraved with the Cross of Lorraine.

De Forge strode up to her, snatched the cigarette out of her mouth, threw it on the polished wood-block floor.

'That will burn the nice flooring,' she remarked.

'So pick it up.'

'No, darling, you put it there, you pick it up.'

His lips tightened. He moved a few paces, crushed the burning cigarette under the heel of his riding boot. Jean was intrigued by his rage. She walked to one of the bullet-proof windows flanking the door, peered out. Only the chauffeur stood by the limousine.

'Where is your friend, Major Lamy? And your guard, Lieutenant Berthier? They always come with you.'

'I've told you before. Don't ask questions about military affairs.'

She made a moue. 'I'm only thinking of your protection. You do have enemies. Would you like some coffee?'

'Might as well . . .'

When she had disappeared he walked into the living room, paced restlessly. She had touched a raw nerve mentioning the two officers.

Much earlier Lamy had contacted Kalmar through the cut-out telephone the assassin used. A woman's voice had told Lamy which public phone box to go to, the time Kalmar would call the phone box number. So Lamy had reported, confirming that he'd passed on de Forge's new request. All this after Lamy had phoned their informant inside Lasalle's HQ at rue des Saussaies. Lamy had then driven to Bordeaux where he'd caught an early Air Inter flight to Lyons.

Berthier, as instructed, had been flown to Lyons aboard a Third Corps helicopter. Neither man knew of the other's movements. He continued pacing, checking his watch. He should get news by lunchtime.

Another thing which irked de Forge was finding Jean at the Villa Forban. In her assumed absence he had come there to search her possessions, to go through the place with a fine-tooth comb. He checked his watch again. Would it work – his masterstroke?

In his large office overlooking the courtyard and the Place Beauveau beyond, Pierre Navarre, Minister of the Interior, got down to business without any formality. Tweed was impressed by the drive and determination of the lean-faced dark-haired Frenchman. *Formidable* – as the French said.

'Your plan is working, Tweed,' Navarre began. 'As I imagine you already know.'

Navarre looked at Lasalle, raised his dark brows, and Lasalle nodded agreement. Three people sat in chairs arranged in a crescent round the Minister's desk. Paula sat to one side, Tweed faced Navarre across the desk, Lasalle occupied a chair on Tweed's right. Paula risked a question.

'Minister, why is France so suddenly in a ferment? I have always regarded your country as stable. Now we have riots, this horrible eruption of the Ku-Klux-Klan mob attacking the Jews.'

274

'A good question.' Navarre leaned forward in his chair behind the Louis-Quinze desk, his piercing dark eyes fixed on hers. 'Under the surface France is desperate to become itself again. Certain elements hanker for the time of de Gaulle – when France bestrode Europe like a colossus. The unification of Germany has increased this hankering. De Forge is exploiting this nostalgia to the full, putting himself forward as a new de Gaulle. It is naked ambition.'

'Surely he can't get away with it,' Paula persisted.

Navarre made a Gallic gesture, spreading his hands.

'I don't think he can. But he is cleverly appealing to this unspoken desire on the part of certain Frenchmen – for France to make a great *impact* on Europe, on the whole world later.'

'I'm still not sure,' Tweed intervened, 'why you've asked for my support.'

'Simple!' Navarre made the same gesture. 'We are submerged in the situation. So perhaps we do not see it as clearly as we should. You are insular – no criticism intended, rather the reverse. But you therefore see the crisis through detached eyes. What you have already suggested may confuse the enemy. General Charles de Forge.'

'I am fearful,' Tweed responded. 'I sense de Forge is just waiting for what I call the trigger. An event which will give him an excuse to act.'

'The President of France stands between de Forge and chaos,' Navarre replied in his rapid French. 'He may hesitate. He listens too closely to that poodle of de Forge's – Janin, the Minister of Defence. But the second riot in Lyons has, I know, stiffened the President's determination. And soon I expect another visitor who will give us the German point of view. Chief Inspector Otto Kuhlmann is flying here at my request. With the full authority of the Chancellor of Germany . . .'

*   *   *

General de Forge, an expert tactician, a man not liking to waste time, had decided he might as well take advantage of his visit to the Villa Forban he could no longer search. He went to the bathroom as Jean Burgoyne, clad only in a short slip, perched on the rumpled bed and slid on her tights.

She was again fully dressed when de Forge emerged, buttoning up his uniform. It seemed a good moment to chat to him as she brushed her mane of golden hair.

'Who is really behind all these terrible riots, Charles?'

'How would I know?'

'Major Lamy should have been able to tell you. That is what Chiefs of Intelligence are for.'

'The French people are getting fed up with the foreigners who infest France, who take their jobs, who pollute the streets by their very presence.'

'And yet I saw a report in *Le Monde* that the so-called mobs operate with military precision. And if they were ordinary people why wear these Balaclavas? It seems to be very important not a single person is identified.'

'I suppose they're worried the police might be able to pick them up if they knew who they were.'

De Forge spoke in an off-hand manner as he studied his appearance in a wall mirror. Jean knew that manner, that tone of voice: he was covering up. He'd just enjoyed himself so maybe he'd talk.

'You haven't convinced me, Charles. And what about that horrible massacre of the Jews near Tarbes? The killers wore Ku-Klux-Klan robes. Again, masked men – and again the reporter they temporarily kidnapped to witness the horror used the phrase "an assault carried out with military precision".'

De Forge adjusted his képi, turned slowly to face her. His hands were on his hips as he stared at her with his hypnotic eyes. She stared back. His voice was quiet, menacing.

'What are you suggesting, Jean?'

'I'm not suggesting anything. But I am waiting for you to suggest an explanation for strange, sinister events.'

'The people are rising up to express their fury – their fear – at the emergence of an all-powerful Germany.'

'I see.' She sounded quite unconvinced, switched to a different topic. 'Is your wife, Josette, still indifferent to our friendship?'

'Josette remains loyal to me – to my position as the leading soldier in France,' de Forge said cynically. 'She has gone back to our apartment at Passy in Paris. She feels the time has come to hold some more of her famous salons. A lot of influential people attend them.'

'I also get the impression,' Jean remarked, 'that you are waiting for some important news. I felt that while we were in bed.'

De Forge shrugged, another giveaway gesture. 'You have too lively an imagination.'

All de Forge's instincts of danger close to him surfaced.

He was careful not to look at Jean. She had a way of inveigling herself into his mind. Had he told her too much? She was very curious about his activities, his future plans, had recently asked some dangerous questions.

'I must go.'

He hugged her tightly. Out of her line of sight his eyes were ice-cold. Had the time come to take precautions? Perhaps she was another assignment for Kalmar?

Or for *Manteau*?

The phone began ringing insistently.

The Paris–Bordeaux Express had stopped at Angoulême, well north of Bordeaux. Newman and Moshe Stein had alighted, were moving fast. While Stein went to collect the hired car Newman found a public phone, called Lasalle's office in rue de Saussaies.

He was told Lasalle was not available. Newman used all his powers of persuasion to convince the man at the other end that Lasalle was expecting his call. He was asked to give his number, to wait . . .

Moshe Stein drove up in a Renault, parked on the opposite side of the street, pretended not to see Newman. It was late afternoon, the sky was a storm of low dark clouds. It would soon be night and they still had a long drive to Stein's villa in the Landes. After they had visited Arcachon *en route*.

Before leaving Paris Newman had purchased a complete outfit of new clothes. He wore a beret, a French windcheater, French trousers and shoes. He fretted as he waited. Would anyone ever call him back? The phone began ringing . . .

Lasalle, still in Navarre's office with the three English visitors, answered, grasped that Newman was in a call box, put Tweed on the line.

'We've reached Angoulême,' Newman reported, speaking fast. 'I'm running out of coins. Arcachon next stop. Then on to the Landes with Moshe.' He was careful not to use the name Stein. 'In an emergency you can leave a message with Isabelle. I forgot to give you her number. It is —. Moshe has told me things which make me suspect we may be a target. Strange things happen in the Landes. Nearest small place to his villa is St Girons. He gave us a false address in Paris. Villa is close to the sea. St Girons is on the D42 – which cuts off west from the N10. Phone number . . .'

'Got it,' Tweed replied. 'Paula is coming south – may need a bolt-hole. Have you one more minute? I'll put her on the line . . .'

'Do it.'

'Bob . . .' Paula spoke clearly, quickly. 'Don't say

too much. Could Isabelle be my bolt-hole?'

'Yes. I'll warn her you're coming. "Gruyère cheese" is your password . . .'

'Thanks, Bob. That's all.'

'Paula! Don't come. Moshe has told me things during our trip so far. Down here is a greater danger zone than round the Brudenell.'

'Then take care. Won't hold you.'

The connection was broken before he could protest any further. He stood in the box for a minute longer, thinking. God! There was mistrust, danger everywhere. Moshe had given a false address inside the DST! A second before Lasalle had answered Newman had heard a girl operator say 'Ministry of the Interior . . .' Even in that stronghold of French security Tweed had listened, had said very little. Paula had said *Don't say too much.* She had used Isabelle's first name but not her surname. And his call had passed through the Ministry's switchboard.

Had he said anything directly linking Isabelle with Arcachon? He recalled his conversation. No, he hadn't. It all amounted to something quite terrifying – treason, treachery, paid informants in the highest places.

He left the box as it began to drizzle, a cold, raw drizzle of rain like a mist. Walking swiftly across the street he got into the passenger seat beside Stein. His suitcase was in the back. Stein, who knew the way, was behind the wheel.

'Let's move, Moshe . . .'

A long way south Newman saw in the night, in open country in the middle of nowhere, a petrol station illuminated like a glowing torch. He asked Moshe to stop for petrol.

'We're still well-tanked.'

'Stop for petrol,' Newman insisted.

He got out with Moshe and wandered round the inside of the cabin-like shop attached while Moshe had the

Renault filled to the brim. Newman had seen plenty of Second World War photos and on a shelf he recognized an old German jerrican with a capacity for many litres.

The old boy who ran the station stared as Newman strolled out, holding the jerrican. Newman grinned.

'Wartime souvenir?'

'I have several,' the old boy responded as he held the nozzle from the pump. 'A truck driver threw them out when he was fleeing back to Germany.'

'Mind filling it up? So we have a spare supply? I'll pay whatever you want for the souvenir.'

The old boy, having filled up the car's tank, carefully filled the jerrican, Newman handed over the agreed price, placed it carefully in the back of the car under a rug after making sure the cap was well screwed down.

'We need that?' Moshe enquired as he drove off.

'We might. Keep moving at high speed, but just inside the limit. And avoid Bordeaux like the plague. Straight to Arcachon.'

Earlier in Navarre's office in Paris the phone had rung again soon after Paula had spoken to Newman. She was just about to leave but waited on a gesture from Tweed.

Navarre took the call, spoke briefly, handed the phone to Lasalle. The DST chief listened, asked a couple of questions, again held out the instrument to Tweed.

'It's for you. Your butler is calling,' he said with a blank expression.

'Tweed here . . .'

'Thank God!' It was clearly Harry Butler's unmistakable voice. 'We flew in about an hour ago as you'd asked. I've had a helluva job at rue de Saussaies to persuade them to put me through to you. Had to show my card, describe what you looked like. Pete is with me, again as requested. What now?'

'Go to the Swiss Restaurant in the street leading off rue St Honoré direct up to Place de la Madeleine. It's on the first floor.'

'I remember. We met there once before. Then?'

'Both of you wait for someone to turn up. Stick to that someone like glue. Take instructions from the person you're guarding.'

'Got it. We need ironmongery?'

He meant weapons – hand-guns with plenty of spare ammo. Tweed assured him that they would be supplied. He put down the phone, looked at Paula who was lingering near the door. She had plenty of time to catch her Air Inter flight to Bordeaux.

'When you've been back to rue de Saussaies,' he told her, 'you walk straight to that Swiss restaurant – I'm sure you heard what I said on the phone. First floor.' He switched his gaze to Lasalle. 'Can you help again? I'd like Paula to go back with you now to rue de Saussaies. She needs two 7.65mm Walther automatics and plenty of spare mags.'

'And also,' Paula added, 'I need a .32 Browning – with extra mags . . .'

Navarre stood up when they had gone and he was alone in the large office with Tweed. He paced slowly, hands behind his back.

'What is the ultimate objective of this devious plan you have set moving?'

'De Forge is trying to destabilize France,' Tweed replied. 'I am going to destabilize de Forge. Apart from the fact that he was responsible for the murder of one of my agents – something I won't forget – it is essential we have a stable Europe to face whatever might confront us from the East . . .'

He stopped talking as Navarre answered the buzzing of his intercom. The dark-haired, agile Frenchman listened to the message Tweed couldn't catch, told them

281

to send him up, switched off, and faced Tweed.

'Otto Kuhlmann has arrived. He will be with us in a moment. We are keeping in close touch with Germany . . .'

The door opened, Kuhlmann entered, his expression grim. He shook hands with Navarre, with Tweed, settled his bulk into a chair, studied his unlit cigar and then began speaking.

'I've come to hear whether there have been any further developments. The German press is full of the riots in Lyons, the anti-American and anti-German slogans which were shouted.'

'Don't worry,' Navarre reassured him. 'We are all working together. Tweed has a plan. I can't reveal the details. Tell us the present situation in Germany.'

'Germany is very uneasy, uncertain of itself. Suddenly we are the most powerful country in Europe with unification. It worries thoughtful men and women. Gorbachev took the lid off Russia – but I'm not sure he realized he was also taking the lid off Germany. He may have opened the gate to dark forces. To *Siegfried*. What scares me is *Siegfried* could be the weapon of the extreme Right. I just hope to God the members of *Siegfried* are imported terrorists. If so, our dragnet must locate them sooner or later . . .'

Kuhlmann talked on while Tweed sat thinking of Newman and Paula. Each of them by now well on their way to the south, to the Bordeaux region – de Forge's territory. He was still pondering the future when the phone rang once more.

Navarre ran behind his desk, picked up the phone, listened. It was a long call with the caller doing most of the talking. Watching him both Tweed and Kuhlmann were aware of a rising sense of tension. Navarre sat up straighter, leaned forward, his facial muscles taut. He put down the phone slowly, looked at his visitors.

'A catastrophe has occurred. That call was from Lyons – from the DST chief there.' He took a deep breath before continuing. 'The President of France is dead. The Prime Minister is dead. A saboteur blew up the track ahead of the TGV they were aboard. The whole train plunged into a deep ravine. Huge casualties.'

'The trigger,' said Tweed. 'The trigger General Charles de Forge was waiting for. France is about to erupt like a volcano.'

30

As they approached Arcachon at reduced speed Newman watched Moshe's headlights sweeping over the fringes of the *bassin* – the almost land-locked harbour. In the beams he saw beyond the country road a marsh-like area, small creeks of stagnant water with an oily gleam. In the near distance the lights of Arcachon came closer in the dark.

'I have to visit someone,' Newman said. 'Probably for no more than an hour, maybe longer. Do you mind staying at a small hotel until I come for you?'

'Of course not, my friend. I know a small hotel near the station. Why don't we drive there first, then you can take over the car?'

'It would be a help,' Newman admitted.

He felt a sense of relief. He was tired and the idea of walking to Isabelle's apartment did not appeal. Earlier, from a public call box in a village he had called her to warn he was coming. She had sounded wild with excitement, which worried him.

Moshe pulled up in front of a small hotel, got out with

his case, wished Newman luck and ran inside. The cold was intense as a bitter wind scoured the resort. Ten minutes later Newman was inside Isabelle's apartment. Dressed in a warm two-piece blue suit she flung her arms round him.

'Oh, my God! You have no idea how glad I am to see you. Have you heard the news, Bob? It's terrible . . .' Again the words came tumbling out. 'The President is dead, has been assassinated. The TGV he was aboard on his way to Lyons was blown up. And, Bob, the Prime Minister is also dead. He was aboard the same express . . .'

'Slow down, slow down, Isabelle.'

'I'll make you some nice hot coffee. You feel cold. You must be in this weather. Milk but no sugar. You see, I remember . . . Come and make yourself comfortable in the living room. There is a log fire. Then we can talk . . .'

Newman welcomed the log fire crackling away as he sat by himself on a couch in the cosy room. Not only for the warmth after the arctic conditions outside – but also it helped him to marshal his thoughts.

The President of France dead – and the Prime Minister. When interviewing de Forge he'd sensed the General straining at the leash – the partial straitjacket of Presidential authority which had restrained him – to some extent. Now de Forge was free to act in any way he wished. There would be confusion – chaos – in Paris.

And all this, he thought grimly, meant that Moshe Stein and himself, too, would be in far greater danger in the Landes. What Moshe had told him had previously alerted him to the risks they were taking. Now those risks were tripled.

'Coffee . . .' Isabelle placed a tray on a small table and poured. 'Isn't the news frightful? It's so good to have you here. With me. The two of us alone again.'

She had splayed her long legs like a cat underneath her

284

as she sat on the floor, leaning against his knees, sipping her coffee. He asked the question bothering him.

'Where is your sister? Any risk of her coming back?'

'No.' A cat-like smile. 'After your phone call Lucille called me from Stockholm at her boy friend's place. She is staying there longer. She's very understanding about us.'

'Is she now? She knows my name?'

'Of course not!' Her back stiffened. 'I'm careful about your safety, even though I trust Lucille. But you know – pillow talk with her boy friend. All she can tell him is a friend is with me. You look very French in your gear.'

'That's the idea.' Newman had removed his beret and raincoat. He made the effort before the warmth – and Isabelle – overcame him. 'I'll have to leave soon.' Her hand gently fondled his knee. Much more of this and he'd be spending the night with her.

'Bob, were you furious with me when I told you on the phone about my trip back to my mother's apartment in Bordeaux?'

'No, just concerned. And relieved that you escaped from those two phoney DST thugs. They'd have murdered you – like they did Henri at the Gare St Jean.'

'Instead I murdered them.'

'You defended yourself with great courage and ingenuity. It was an accident they deserved.'

'I have another confession to make . . .'

'I'm not a priest.'

'I know that.' She smiled wickedly. 'Anyone less like a priest I can't imagine.' Her hand moved up to his thigh, rested there. He clamped his own hand on top of hers, squeezed it to encourage her. And to prevent her hand wandering too much.

'Henri kept a notebook. He had filled it up and was going to record things in a fresh one. He gave me the old notebook to keep, said I should guard it. I promised not to look inside – he said that would be dangerous – and I kept my promise. I hid it among my underclothes in the Bordeaux apartment. It's still there.'

'Why didn't you give it to me?' Newman asked quietly.

'I forgot. I know it sounds crazy but so many things – awful things – happened. Henri's murder. Then when we were at the apartment we spotted those men watching. I was concentrating on doing what you told me so we could get away safely.'

'And during your second visit – to get Henri's brooch?'

'For God's sake!' she flared up. 'Those men knocked on the door. You know what happened afterwards. I forgot the notebook again. Can you wonder I did?'

So Henri Bayle – alias Francis Carey, Tweed's agent – had left some kind of record of what he'd discovered in the Bordeaux region. Maybe he hadn't died in vain – an outcome Newman knew Tweed would live with for the rest of his time on earth unless Carey's mission had produced something vital. And maybe there was vital data in that hidden notebook. It could be even more important now France was sliding into anarchy after the brutal removal of the President and his Prime Minister.

'Isabelle, you have a key to the apartment in Bordeaux?' he asked casually.

'Of course. It's in the drawer of that escritoire.'

'Mind if I borrow it for a few hours?'

'*Why?*' Her eyes blazed with anxiety. 'What are you up to now?'

'Fetch me the key and I'll tell you.'

'I'm coming with you.'

She threw the remark over her shoulder as she jumped up and ran to the drawer. Newman was thinking it was fortunate he'd warned Moshe Stein he might be a while before he picked him up at the hotel – even more fortunate that Moshe had loaned him the hired Renault. Isabelle came back, holding the key in her hand behind her back. She knelt in front of Newman.

'You can't have the key until you tell me why you need it.'

'To get hold of Henri's notebook. We need to know where to look before we go.'

She took his statement as agreement that she could come with him. She explained exactly which drawer in the bedroom contained the notebook, buried deep among her underclothes. Newman nodded, leaned forward, pulled her towards him. She came willingly as he hugged her, reaching one hand behind her shapely back. She kissed him greedily, felt to be devouring his mouth. His right hand grasped hers, forced the fingers apart, felt metal, took the key.

She wrenched herself free, a flaming fury. Standing up she looked down at him.

'You tricked me! Damn you! You're going by yourself.'

'Supposing we went together,' Newman said calmly, pocketing the key. 'The apartment may still be watched. You come with me. Half my attention is concentrated on protecting you, making sure no harm comes to you. When all my attention should be concentrated on guarding myself. Taking care of you, we could both get killed. My chance of survival is enormously increased if I'm on my own.'

She stood with her arms folded. Her flash of rage had subsided. Newman was counting on her intelligence to grasp the sense of his argument. She smiled suddenly.

'I do understand, Bob. I liked your use of the word "protecting". You realize that is the back door key?'

'I was going to ask you that. Much easier to slip in and out that way.'

'And you'll be coming back here afterwards?'

'Your mother has a key to the Bordeaux apartment?'

'Yes . . .' The word was out of her mouth before she realized the implications of what he'd said. 'You mean you won't be coming back here? Then how will I know you are safe? I *must* know that, Bob.'

'I'll phone you when I can. Can't promise when that will be, but I can promise I'll phone.' He hesitated, knowing the next topic could be sensitive. 'Isabelle, an important girl who works for another man may come to see you . . .'

'Important to you?' Her eyes gleamed.

'I've just told you, she works for someone else – a man who is a close ally of mine. Her name is Paula. She'll identify herself by using the phrase Gruyère cheese.'

'I will look after her,' Isabelle promised, mollified to some extent.

Newman wondered what would happen if the strong-minded Paula did meet the equally strong-willed Isabelle. Maybe it hadn't been too good an idea giving Paula the French girl's address and phone number back in London. Too late now. He stood up.

'Would you by any chance have a few empty bottles? Wine, whatever?'

'It just happens that I was about to throw out a whole collection of empty mineral water bottles. I drink a lot of mineral water.' She looped her arm through his. 'I'm a thirsty soul – and not only for you. They're in the kitchen.'

They walked through a swing door and Newman noted everything was spotless, well organized, in the kitchen, which had a pleasant light blue colour scheme for the cupboards and working surfaces. Isabelle opened a cupboard, dragged out a strong plastic bag.

'There are twenty inside here – empty but with the caps on. I know, I counted as I dumped them. I do things like that. What are you looking at?'

On a shelf were stacked a series of aluminium funnels. Newman picked up a funnel, dived into the bag as she

288

held it open for him, took out a bottle, removed the cap, inserted the end of the funnel. It fitted inside the neck of the bottle perfectly.

'Could I have this too? Unless it's your favourite?' he asked.

'Funny man.' She smiled. 'Drop it inside the bag. You are most welcome . . .'

He hugged her before he left, had trouble disentangling himself from her octopus-like embrace, walked through the deserted streets to where he'd parked the Renault, hid the plastic sack under a travelling rug in the back. He was driving slowly through Arcachon when he thought he recognized a lone French officer in uniform. The beams played over him for only seconds, then the solitary man merged with the shadows. Despite the uniform, the kepi pulled well down over the forehead, Newman could have sworn he'd just seen Lieutenant Berthier.

Something about the way he held himself, moved. Newman recalled his encounter in the lobby of the Brudenell – when the man posing as James Sanders, salesman of marine spare parts, had stubbed his toe and muttered *Merde!* It was an added worry as he drove out of Arcachon along the N650 to Bordeaux.

The first thing Newman noticed on entering the centre of the city was that there were far more troops in uniform walking in groups. Even at this late hour. He had decided to drive to the Bar Miami where Henri Bayle had been kidnapped by the phoney DST men before being murdered.

He knew the address from something Isabelle had told him on his previous visit. Doubtful whether the bar would still be open at this time of night, he parked close to it, walked the rest of the way.

Newman was confident that in his French clothes, his

beret worn at a jaunty angle, he would pass unnoticed among the few couples hurrying to get out of the cold. The Bar Miami was still open.

He walked inside slowly, staring round to check whether there were any French officers among the patrons. They appeared to be mostly civilians – the hardened drinkers still clustered at a few tables. The head barman, described by Isabelle, was polishing the counter.

'Pernod,' Newman ordered.

'We'll be closing soon,' the heavy-set barman said as he took the money.

'Isabelle Thomas,' Newman whispered. 'Can't find her at her apartment. We're like that.' He showed two fingers entwined, winked. 'Any idea where she could have gone?'

The barman was about to shrug: Newman sensed the beginning of the negative gesture. Then the barman saw the two hundred-franc notes peering out from between Newman's fingers. His hand polishing the bar moved more slowly, he took a swift look round, leaned forward.

'I can't give you an exact address.'

'A location would help. Somewhere to start.'

'The other . . .' The barman stopped in mid-sentence and mentally Newman completed what he'd been on the verge of saying. *The other man said almost the same thing* . . . He couldn't take his eyes off the banknotes just out of his reach.

'Arcachon,' he whispered. 'That's the best I can do.'

'I need to know how *you* know that,' Newman persisted.

'The girl was in here some time ago – with her boy friend. The one who got mugged down at Gare St Jean. I heard him tell her he'd visit her when she was in Arcachon. That's it.'

'Somewhere to start,' Newman repeated.

With a sleight of hand he passed over the banknotes.

290

The barman began polishing furiously as though regretting his indiscretion. Newman drank his Pernod, left the bar, hurried to his car.

He sat behind the wheel with the engine running for a few minutes. The news was the worst possible. If the barman would betray Isabelle to him, a stranger, for a handful of banknotes, then he'd clearly done the same before. It looked very much as though Isabelle was being traced by de Forge's men. And he couldn't get out of his mind the instinct that it *was* Berthier he'd seen in his headlights. He'd have to warn her at the earliest possible moment.

But the next job was to try and recover Bayle's – Francis Carey's – notebook. He drove away as men began to drift out of the Bar Miami. From now on he had to be careful.

31

Newman drove slowly as he came close to the apartment building. He planned to park the Renault in a side street about a hundred yards beyond the alley where he'd parked during his visit with Isabelle. Far enough away not to arouse the suspicion of any watchers; close enough to run for it if he had to.

The street was fairly deserted. It was dark except for the glow from an illuminated shop window opposite the entrance to the apartment block and the murky glimmer of the street lights.

No one lingered outside the entrance but a group of men in heavy overcoats were crouched on the pavement outside the illuminated shop. They were playing some game with dice. In this bitter cold? As he cruised past them he glanced at the motley gathering. Inwardly he stiffened but he maintained the same speed.

A hundred yards or so beyond them he turned left into a narrow cobbled side street, parked with two wheels on the sidewalk. Grim-faced, he sat behind the wheel, his engine still running.

One of the group of dice-players had looked up as he'd passed them. Clad in his old heavy overcoat, collar turned up, the man also wore a fur hat. For a brief second Newman had had a clear view of the face beneath the hat. A face he'd seen before in a photograph.

An evil, grinning face. Like a gnome. A dangerous gnome. Sergeant Rey of the Third Corps. De Forge's boobytrap genius. A man rumoured to carry far more clout than his rank of sergeant would suggest.

So why was he sitting crouched on the pavement opposite the apartment block in the freezing cold night? And grinning? As though in anticipation of some professional delight?

Newman adopted a slouching walk as he left the side street and moved towards the alley with the back entrance. A few couples also slouched along the street, huddled together, even pausing for an embrace.

Newman was recalling something Isabelle had told him. The staircase they had come down from her mother's first-floor apartment – the staircase down which the two fake DST men who tried to attack Isabelle had ended up dead – led only to her mother's apartment, which was peculiar. Round the back another rear staircase led to the other apartments.

So anyone investigating that staircase by picking the lock would realize the same fact. Someone like Sergeant Rey. Expert at rigging up boobytraps.

Out of the corner of his eye he was watching the group

292

of dice-players who seemed absorbed in their game. As he drew level with the alley Newman was collided into by a couple absorbed in their own company.

'*Pardon!*' said the youth automatically.

When they had moved on Newman was inside the wide alley. Parked at the end of the alley before it turned the L-shaped corner to the rear of the apartment was a battered old van. By the glow from a low-powered wall light Newman read the legend *Ramoneur*. Chimney sweep.

He walked alongside the wall of the next building beyond the apartment block, his rubber-soled shoes making no sound on the cobbles. He was watching the closed door which led to the staircase, the door to which he had the key in his pocket. It was pure fancy – maybe nerves – he told himself, but the closed door had a sinister look.

He was also watching the van as he came closer, wondering if the chimney sweep was behind the wheel, smoking a cigarette before he went home to his nagging wife. He came up to the front, peered inside. Empty. Parked for the night. Probably the sweep had the nicest wife in all Bordeaux. He looked back at the closed door.

The idea came to him suddenly. Brought on by his certainty that it was Sergeant Rey he had seen with the dice-players. He took a bunch of keys from his pocket, selected the pick-lock given to him by a small-time villain in the East End of London. It all depended on whether the sweep was using old-fashioned equipment still favoured by some housewives – especially out in the countryside, the type of brush with a long handle composed of bamboo lengths inserted into each other – as opposed to a vacuum sweep.

It took him less than a minute to fiddle open the rear door. Shielding the beam with his hand, he examined the interior with his pencil flash. Thank God! The old-fashioned type.

Newman worked quickly, assembling the long handle. When he had the handle ready he attached the brush. Leaving the van, he looked round the alley, towards the main street at the end, listened. Nothing. No sign of life anywhere.

Holding the long, supple handle, he approached the rear door to the apartment block at an angle. Extending the brush in front of himself, he crouched low, moved the brush over the door. He covered the upper half, ran it slowly round the framework, then he pressed the brush as hard as he could against the area of the lock and the door handle.

The explosion was a muffled boom. The whole door flew out, shattered into several pieces. The brush and handle were ripped out of his hands. Dust drifted from the inside of the apartment block. Had he attempted to open the door he would have been blown to pieces.

Newman ran towards the devastated entrance, ran inside. Holding his breath against the cloud of dust, he raced upstairs, pencil flash in one hand, key to the apartment door in the other.

If he moved swiftly he had no worry about the other inhabitants reacting quickly. They'd be in a state of shock, would stir themselves slowly. He opened the drawer in the bedroom, searched among Isabelle's underclothes trying not to leave a mess. The notebook was wrapped inside a slip. Francis Carey's notebook. Small, slim, and bound in blue leather. He slipped it into his pocket, ran out of the apartment, closing the door before he hurtled down the staircase. He glanced over the banister which remained intact – opposite Isabelle's apartment a large chunk had been torn away. Looking down into the well he saw a dim light on the concrete basement floor. No wonder the two DST men had ended up dead – plunging down that drop.

He peered out into the alley before leaving the building. Deserted. But sooner or later the police would arrive. He walked swiftly towards the entrance, keeping close to the wall. He had just reached the corner when a man in a heavy overcoat walked round it. Sergeant Rey.

Newman reacted instantly, reinforced by his SAS training. Rey also reacted swiftly, shoving his right hand inside his coat. Newman's stiffened edge of his right hand struck Rey a vicious blow on the side of the neck. Rey slumped to the cobbles, began moaning and wriggling. Newman had hoped to kill the bastard. No time to hang about.

He ran towards his parked car after glancing over his shoulder. The dice-playing group was still watching the front entrance. He was half-way to the side street before they saw him, began clambering to their feet.

Newman's feet hardly touched the ground as he rushed to the Renault, dived inside, started the engine, drove off in the opposite direction from the main street behind him. At the bottom he turned into another side street. A second before he turned he glanced in his rear-view mirror. No sign of the dice-players. Slow on the uptake. And they hadn't seen his make of car.

He drove out of Bordeaux just inside the speed limit, headed along the lonely road back to Arcachon.

Moshe Stein opened his bedroom door in the small hotel on the third tap from Newman. Fully dressed, he ushered him inside, pointed to the rumpled bed.

'I slept in my clothes. I'm ready to drive through the night to my villa if that suits you. But maybe *you* need sleep. And your windcheater is covered with dust. Also, I repeat, I'm happy to go there by myself.'

'Don't talk rubbish. Give me time to make one phone call. Get ready for instant departure . . .'

Newman used the bedside phone to call Isabelle. She

spoke on the second ring: Newman guessed she'd been sitting by her phone.

'It's Bob,' he said. 'Now listen, I haven't much time. The sneak of a chief barman at the Bar Miami heard Henri mention Arcachon when you were talking one night. Just one bribe and he passed on to me what I'm sure he's also passed on earlier to others less friendly . . .'

'I will be very careful, Bob. Wonderful to hear from you. Where are you speaking from?'

'A long way off,' he lied. 'Now *listen*! I think when I was driving out of Arcachon I saw a certain Lieutenant Berthier. Got the name? Good. He's one of General de Forge's inner circle of confidants. Description . . . Got it? He's in uniform but he might change into civvy clothes. Which is why I emphasized his physical appearance. Stay indoors as much as you can . . .'

'I have to go out shopping some time.'

'Go out early – as soon as the shops open. Avoid crowds. Wear a scarf round your head. Stay indoors as much as you can. I may phone you again in the not very distant future.'

'When? *When*, Bob?'

'As soon as I can. Must go.'

He put down the phone before she could protest. He had been careful not to mention her name. He trusted Moshe implicitly – but how much torture can any man resist? After what had happened in the alley in Bordeaux he was beginning to think de Forge had become a monster. It could have been Isabelle – even her mother – who had tried to open that rear door. Their bodies would have been shattered into a bloody pulp.

'I'm ready when you are,' Moshe's voice said behind him. 'That is, if you still insist on coming. They know they missed one man during the massacre at Tarbes. A list of the members of the reading group and their addresses was left behind in the visitors' book everyone signed. I'm known to be an outspoken opponent of de Forge. I – we – will be targets.'

'I'm ready now,' Newman replied.

Half an hour later they were driving well south of Arcachon through the night towards the Landes.

Paula disembarked from the Air Inter flight at Bordeaux well after dark. Behind her, but apparently on his own, Harry Butler followed, dressed in casual clothes and wearing a leather jacket. He carried his suitcase in his left hand and he glanced all round the concourse.

Only a few passengers had come off the flight but there were quite a few uniformed French soldiers strolling round, carrying automatic weapons. Behind Harry Butler, also appearing to be on his own, walked Pete Nield, clad in a smart business suit and looking like a salesman.

It was Butler who spotted the girl in the uniform of a stewardess filming the new arrivals. He hurried on past Paula, walked into the raw cold of the night and found the waiting hired car he'd phoned for before leaving Paris. The courier girl was holding a card. *Pierre Blanc*. A nice common name and the Engine Room back at Park Crescent had provided all the necessary papers in that name.

Butler shoved his bag in the back, leaving a seat vacant, paid the girl in cash. Paula, carrying her small case, was walking away from the airport. Butler got behind the wheel, took his time settling himself, drove away and caught up with her. He stopped briefly, she jumped into the back, he drove off towards Bordeaux.

Behind them Pete Nield, who spoke fluent French, had joined the taxi queue. Paula stacked her case alongside Butler's, stretched – stiff from the flight – then relaxed, gazing out at the lights of the night.

'Well, Harry, we managed that well.'

'No, we didn't. A fat little man smoking a cheroot is on

our tail in a Fiat. He saw me pick you up.'

'That's a problem.'

'Not really.' The burly Butler shrugged. 'The plan is we go first to the Pullman Hotel in the Mériadeck area, book in, pay in advance with cash, leave a few things in our rooms, then take off.'

'So? The fat little man with the cheroot?'

'We don't drive straight to Arcachon when we leave the Pullman tonight. I've studied a map of the area. First we drive south. That Fiat has a very advanced-looking radio aerial. Cheroot may make regular reports. There is a country road I'll take, again heading south. Later we double back, make for Arcachon and the delectable Isabelle. Newman's description, not mine.'

'And Cheroot?'

'Will no longer be with us . . .'

Paula had phoned Jean Burgoyne at the Villa Forban from Paris. Jean had told her tomorrow afternoon would be a good time for her visit: she would be *alone* at the villa. Paula had decided it would be a good chance to go and see Isabelle Thomas at Arcachon in the morning.

It was Harry Butler who had worked out the strategy on the assumption they were spotted by so-called 'DST' agents. They arrived at the modernistic Pullman, registered for one week, paid for two rooms in advance in cash. The hotel reminded Paula of a concrete bee-hive, especially when she looked round her room on the floor entitled *Privilège* – which meant their expensive accommodation.

The solid double-glazed window was shaped like a cell in a bee-hive, was difficult to look out from at that height. She moved quickly, lifted the lid of her case, took out a large plastic bag. Inside were a few clothes she'd been on the verge of throwing out.

298

She hung several things in the small cupboard. In the bathroom she put a half-used tube of toothpaste in a glass, tucked a worn toothbrush beside it and added one canister of talcum powder. Anyone secretly entering the room would conclude she was returning there shortly. Checking her watch, she closed her suitcase, waited exactly thirty minutes, and took the elevator back to the lobby.

Butler, having furnished his own room in a similar fashion with articles he never wanted to see again, was waiting behind the wheel of the Renault. Pete Nield sat in the back: arriving later by taxi from the airport he'd furnished his room with similar unwanted articles.

'Arcachon, here we come,' whispered Paula, sitting next to Butler.

'Not yet. Cheroot and his Fiat are parked up the road. First south out of Bordeaux into the countryside . . .'

Half an hour later they were driving along a traffic-free country road. Free except for their Renault and the head-lights of a car some distance behind them. As they drove on Paula began talking.

'I wonder what's happened to Marler? He seems to have vanished off the face of the earth.'

'He's over here somewhere,' Butler responded. 'Don't ask me where because I haven't a clue.'

'Tweed had some very special mission for him. Love to know what it is. Most mysterious.'

'Why not ask Tweed when you next see him?'

'I suppose he's still in Paris. I got the impression he intends to stay there for a while to maintain contact with Navarre. We really have arrived at a historic time. The President and the Prime Minister killed in that TGV crash.'

Paula had first heard the news from a Frenchman she'd chatted to aboard the flight to Bordeaux. The few passengers were all talking about it excitedly. She also thought she had detected signs of alarm.

299

'I suppose I could ask Tweed,' she said with a poker face.

'And get a flea in your ear.' Butler grinned. 'And I'm willing to bet Marler – wherever he is – doesn't have any idea where we are. Tweed is playing this one very close to his chest.'

He stiffened as the car crested a hill, glanced quickly in his rear-view mirror. Nothing behind except Cheroot and his Fiat. They descended a long straight slope. Nothing on the road ahead as far as they could see by moonlight. Butler slowed at the bottom of the hill, paused, manoeuvred his car so it blocked the narrow road broad-side on.

'As good a place as any,' he said in his matter-of-fact manner.

'For what?' Paula asked.

'Wait and see.'

Butler checked the Walther in his hip holster, the weapon Paula had handed to him in a briefcase in the Swiss restaurant in Paris. Lasalle had been very accom-modating and Paula was carrying a .32 Browning in her shoulder bag. Similarly, Nield was armed with another Walther. Butler took a map from the door pocket, got out of the car, leaving his headlights full on.

He walked a short distance back the way they had come and then stood in the road, holding up the gloved hand gripping the road map. The Fiat crested the hill, came rushing down towards him, slowed, crawled cautiously as Butler waved.

The Fiat stopped. Only the driver, Cheroot, behind the wheel. Butler walked confidently forward, displaying the map in the car's headlights. He came up on the side of the driver who had lowered the window, was gazing at him suspiciously. Butler began to gabble in French.

'We have lost our way. I don't even know where we are. This map is no help. Maybe you could . . .'

The fat little man, wearing a dark suit, kept the smoking cheroot clamped between his thick lips as he listened. Butler's right hand, encased in a motoring glove, struck like a snake. His clenched fist smashed into the Frenchman's jaw. There was a click as though something had been dislocated. The driver sagged behind his wheel.

Butler opened the door, felt around inside his overcoat, hauled out a .32 Browning. He hurled it over a hedge into a field, then followed it with the mag he'd first extracted.

Continuing his search, Butler found an Army identity card in his breast pocket. *Caporal Jean Millet.* He skimmed the card after the weapon into the field. A soldier who loses his identity gets into a helluva lot of trouble. Butler then noticed Millet had bitten right through his cheroot, leaving half of it presumably in his mouth – the other half lay burning on the floor. Maybe it would set the Fiat ablaze. With luck.

Butler ripped out the microphone apparatus attached to the dashboard, reached up and broke the aerial off the roof. Next he drew the key out of the ignition, hurled that into the night. His last act was to open the bonnet, feel around with his gloved hand, ripping up wires. As he walked back to the Renault he decided he could assume the Fiat had been immobilized. He got in behind the wheel.

'Trouble?' enquired Paula.

'For Corporal Jean Millet, yes. Now we can double back to Arcachon. Let's hope the natives are more friendly there.'

32

General Charles de Forge was alone in his office at GHQ, Third Corps, when the phone rang. Expecting Lamy, he lifted the receiver, announced himself in a brusque tone.

'*Manteau* speaking,' a voice said in perfect French. 'I did the job for you. Not bad. The President *and* the Prime Minister with one bomb. Which is what you wanted, I know . . .'

'Who the hell are you?'

'*Manteau*. I just said so. Wrecking the TGV should come cheap to you for two million Swiss francs. I'd advise you to pay up this time, General. You don't want me to turn my attention to Third Corps GHQ, do you?'

'I need proof . . .'

'Which you will get shortly. When you are convinced I'll tell you how to make the payment. In high-denomination banknotes. I hope the serial numbers don't run in sequence. I wouldn't like that.'

'Are you threatening me?'

'No, of course not. I never threaten. I act. Take it as a piece of life-saving advice. Goodbye . . .'

The connection was broken. Stunned by the audacity of the call, de Forge sat still. Where the hell was Lamy? A knock on the door jerked him out of his state of momentary confusion. He called out in a barrack-room tone.

'Enter!'

The door opened and Lieutenant Berthier, immaculate as always in his uniform, walked in holding a sheaf of papers in his left hand. His hair was still browner than normal: the result of the colourant he'd used before travelling to Aldeburgh. Just in time he remembered to salute.

'Well? Is it important? I'm expecting someone else.'

'Major Lamy phoned on his way here. I told him about the Reuters reports we'd just received and he said you would wish to see them at once.'

'Then put them on my desk.' De Forge prided himself on his ability to think of three things at once. 'You were sent to Arcachon to locate Isabelle Thomas, the mistress of the spy, Henri Bayle. You succeeded?'

'Not yet, General. She is not in the phone directory . . .'

'Phone directory!' De Forge's fist crashed on his desk. 'I send you there to find someone. You have her description from that barman at the Miami dive. And all you can do is to check the phone directory?'

'I did more, I assure you. I made discreet enquiries – no shop-keeper in Arcachon I was able to contact had any knowledge of her. I walked the streets in the hope of seeing her. Walked the streets all night . . .'

'Then go back and walk the streets all day. She could be dangerous. We do not know what Bayle told her. Return to Arcachon at once!'

'Yes, General . . .'

During the conversation de Forge realized the marked map of Paris was spread open on his desk. He folded it while he gave Berthier his dressing down. Alone, he began to read the reports with growing amazement. An hour later he was staring into space when there was another knock. This time it was Major Lamy.

'Where the hell have you been?' de Forge demanded. 'You have been absent for many hours.'

'I have just returned from Lyons. My return flight was delayed because of what happened. Have you read those reports?'

'I have read them.' De Forge sat very upright in his

high-backed chair. 'It says here some old man in a village near the viaduct was train-watching through binoculars. Some damned stupid hobby of his. He says he saw just a few minutes before the TGV arrived a man in a cloak on the viaduct. *Manteau!* Later, DST officers searched the village, found a grey cloak stuffed in a litter bin. I don't understand any of this. Kalmar was supposed to . . .'

'Kalmar was assigned the mission . . .'

'Don't interrupt me! While you were taking for ever to return from Lyons I had a phone call. Guess who from?'

'Kalmar?' Lamy suggested.

'No! From *Manteau*! How the devil would he get hold of my private number? *Manteau* said he had wrecked the TGV. I didn't believe him. Now I read these reports. That idiot of an old man couldn't have invented his story – no one had heard of *Manteau*. On the phone he demands two million Swiss francs for destroying the TGV. You'll have to handle him when he calls again.'

'You don't mean we pay that enormous sum?' Lamy queried.

'Tell me, Lamy, just how much have we paid out to the unknown Kalmar so far?'

'Three million Swiss francs. That is for various jobs.'

'I know that!' De Forge stared down his subordinate. 'I have handed over three million for you to pass on to the ghost man, Kalmar. *Someone* has a lot of money in their Swiss bank account. Haven't they, Major?'

'General!' Lamy protested, shaken. 'I have told you how Kalmar operates. I phone a number, a girl answers, tells me the public phone box I have to go to, its number. Or, frequently, she asks me for names – the *targets*. Then she tells me the remote phone box I must go to. I wait for Kalmar to call me at that box at the agreed time. I give him more detailed instructions about the target – or targets. He speaks to me in English but with an accent I can't identify. I leave the money in a cloth bag behind the box.

304

Every time he warns me he is watching – that if I attempt to identify him when he collects he'll kill me.'

'All very convenient,' de Forge sneered. 'Now we will turn our attention to Operation Austerlitz. The organization of panic in Paris. The sabotage units are moving into place?'

'All is going according to plan . . .'

'The famous phrase which means everything is going wrong. What is your view of Berthier?'

'One of my most trusted men,' Lamy replied emphatically.

'Those are the ones to watch,' de Forge observed cynically. 'A successful traitor is the man everyone has the utmost confidence in.' He unfolded the map of Paris which was marked with the positions of the saboteur cells moving into the capital. 'I had Berthier here an hour ago and I noticed he was studying this battle map upside down.'

'He is a member of the inner circle – the selected few who make up the top security section of Intelligence. I would expect him to be interested in all that is going on.'

'If you say so.' De Forge sounded unconvinced. 'The main thing is we must time Austerlitz carefully. It is too early to strike yet. The explosion must precede our march on Paris – to restore order when the present system is on the verge of collapse.'

'Our men will await the agreed signal.'

'See that they do. It could be soon now. Meantime step up security in the Landes. Do it now.'

'And Kalmar? When he calls?'

'Stall him. Although it is my bet this *Manteau* will call you first. Insist on finding out how he knew our next requirement.' De Forge stared grimly at Lamy. 'My main worry is still this Kalmar–*Manteau* mystery. Is it the same man or are there two of them? But that is your problem. And don't forget,' he repeated. 'I want security in the Landes tighter than a steel drum.'

*   *   *

305

In Paris the lights were burning late in the Ministry of the Interior. Navarre had ordered food and drink to be brought in for himself, Tweed, Lasalle, and Kuhlmann.

The German police chief had been frequently on the phone to his Chancellor. The news of the catastrophe of the TGV wreck had reached Germany. Navarre also spoke to the Chancellor, assuring him that the crisis was coming under control, that all anti-German and anti-US demonstrations had been banned, that they represented only a tiny fraction of fanatics, which was the truth.

'Your plan is working, Tweed?' he asked during a brief interval of peace.

'My people are in place,' Tweed replied. 'They know what they have to do. We have moved with extraordinary speed. But what are your plans now France is without a President, a Prime Minister?'

'I have called an emergency meeting of the surviving cabinet for two this morning.'

'Why that unearthly hour?'

Navarre grinned. 'I plan to take control. Someone has to. I have great stamina. I am an owl – the night hours are my friend. If necessary I will exhaust the others until they agree to my appointment as temporary Prime Minister. But I will also retain control of the Ministry of the Interior.'

'A key post,' Tweed observed.

'Exactly. I am already mobilizing large numbers of heavily armed CRS units ready to move south. I have commandeered a large fleet of helicopters. We may need them in the Landes.'

'Why the Landes?' Tweed asked.

'Because General de Forge's strength, his support, is in the south. Reports are coming in of civilians buying up carbines and ammunition. Ostensibly for hunting. But I know they fear the Algerians. Dubois of the *Pour France*, backed by de Forge, will do everything he can to add fuel to the flames. He is already making speeches saying the Muslim element must be deported before North Africa goes up in flames.'

'Going back to your taking over the Premiership,' Tweed pointed out, 'won't your appointment have to be confirmed by the National Assembly deputies?'

Navarre grinned again. 'Quite true. But there is a precedent. In 1958 de Gaulle was called back, confirmed by the Assembly to form a government. The deputies were scared witless, desperate for strong leadership, fearing a paratroop landing in Paris by French troops from Algeria. A similar situation prevails now. The deputies are again scared out of their wits, desperate for strong leadership. De Forge hopes to put himself forward – but I'm pre-empting him. Tonight. At 2 a.m.'

They were eating when a further phone call came through for Kuhlmann. He listened, said very little, asked to be kept constantly informed, put down the phone.

'My informant has located another *Siegfried* cell. This time in Hamburg. Armed police stormed the building they were holed up in.'

'They?' Tweed queried. 'You mean this time you trapped some terrorists?'

'Three men and a very small cache of explosives and arms. Early interrogation indicates the men captured are small fry from Alsace. Which makes sense since they speak both French and German in that French province near Switzerland.'

'The same informant who put you on to the other places, the one in Freiburg?' Tweed asked quietly.

'Yes. Why?'

'I just wondered. And now I am also wondering how Newman is getting on. Heading straight into the Landes.'

*　　*　　*

After bypassing the city, Moshe drove on and on along the N10 over a hundred kilometres south of Bordeaux. It was the middle of the night but Moshe seemed tireless, refusing to let Newman share the driving as he overtook long-distance truck after truck. The road surface was excellent and they were now deep in the Landes.

On both sides dense stands of black fir trees walled in the road, an endless land of trees. Newman noticed that some of the juggernauts they overtook had Spanish names. A reminder of how far south they were, that Spain was not so far away. Newman was becoming hypnotized by watching twin glaring eyes approaching from the opposite direction, speeding past. Then the traffic thinned. Moshe began talking to keep himself alert.

'One incident during the Tarbes massacre I forgot to tell you. All the other Jews were burnt to death, as you already know. Two of us decided we would escape by a rear exit. My friend went ahead of me to open the door while I searched for a weapon. When he opened the door it blew up in his face, threw his mangled body against the wall opposite.'

'I guess that would be an acquaintance of mine. Sergeant Rey. De Forge's boobytrap specialist. I met him but when I left him he had trouble with his jaw. How did you get away?'

'After seeing what happened to the door, I scrambled out of a window, dropped into a narrow gully concealed by dead ferns. I crawled to safety. There is a similar escape route from the Villa Jaune, where we are going. I will show you. I will also introduce you to an old woman who knows how de Forge uses the Landes near the sea. As a burial ground . . .'

It sounded macabre, but Moshe would tell him more when the time came. Moshe had now swung off the main highway to Biarritz on to the more countrified D42. The signpost had carried the legend ST GIRONS. With what

308

Moshe had just told him Newman was recalling Tweed's precise instructions before he left Paris.

'It is the south which is de Forge's domain. Bordeaux is the symbol of defeat in 1871 and 1940 which he is exploiting to the full. This time, victory and power for France will come from Bordeaux, or so he is saying.'

'How do you know that?' Newman had asked.

'Lasalle has planted at least one informant inside de Forge's camp. I've no idea who it is, but Lasalle receives regular reports. So that is why I'm pleased you're going south. Find out what that devil is up to. Above all, if you can, find evidence which will bring him down. We are supporting Germany as well as France in this endeavour. And when you can, maybe you'd like to contact Kuhlmann's secret agent in Bordeaux – Stahl. You have his details . . .'

Tweed, Newman remembered, had been unusually emphatic and forceful, stressing his points with chops of his hand. All indications that under his calm, detached manner Tweed was more worried than he'd ever been.

'Moshe, this Villa Jaune we're going to. Describe for me its location.'

'West of St Girons. Hidden in the forests of the Landes. But very close to the sea. At night especially you can hear the waves crashing on the nearby beach. And during the day, often, if it's a heavy sea. The dunes run for miles. It was an idyllic spot before the murders began.'

'What murders?'

'Better that you see for yourself. One demonstration, they say, is worth a thousand words. And there is someone who can show you maybe better than I can.'

'Describe the layout of the villa. Inside.'

'A single-storey old building built of wood. On the side facing the sea there is a verandah running along the front. Inside two bedrooms, one living-dining room, a kitchen, a toilet. That's it.'

309

'The entrances and exits,' Newman persisted.

'A heavy wooden front door leading to the verandah, windows at the front and on both sides. None at the back – except for one low down, almost level with the ground, which has bars. The window opens close to another deep gully similar to the one which saved my life at Tarbes. There is a rear door to one side. Also a cellar – with no way out.'

'I've got the picture,' Newman replied.

He said nothing more as they drove on through the night, passed through St Girons, which had no lights, and some distance beyond Moshe swung on to a track leading through the fir forest.

Newman checked his watch. It would be dawn in about two hours' time. Assaults were often launched at dawn.

In Arcachon, by chance, Butler chose the same small hotel Newman and Moshe Stein had used earlier as temporary accommodation for Stein. They walked in as planned during the middle of the night. Paula was hanging on to Butler's arm, pressing herself close to him.

Butler wasted no time dealing with the sneaky-looking night clerk who studied the couple and Nield bringing up the rear with the cases. In his hand Butler held folded French banknotes, asked for three rooms alongside each other speaking in French.

'That might be difficult.' The clerk peered over his half-moon glasses. 'We are almost full up.'

'In late November? Come off it. We've had a long drive from the Côte d'Azur. I said three rooms, alongside each other. Of course, if you can't manage it . . .'

The banknotes began to disappear inside his pocket. The action galvanized the clerk. He made a brief performance of studying the register.

'Pardon me. It so happens we have three such rooms on

310

the first floor. Even in the middle of the night . . .' He named an excessive price.

'You think I'm a raving lunatic?' Butler continued in French. 'Take this for all three rooms for the night.'

'I will see you are not disturbed.'

The clerk leered. He was convinced the three rooms were a ploy – that Paula would be sharing a bed with Butler. Which was exactly the impression they wished to create.

Butler carried Paula's case into the middle room, so she would be flanked by Nield and himself in the other two rooms. He was leaving the cramped room when Paula spoke.

'Thank you, Harry. For looking after me.'

'Which reminds me,' Butler responded. 'No slipping away without us.'

'I promise. In the morning I'll phone Isabelle and hope I can go see her – with my two escorts. Then in the afternoon we'll drive to the Villa Forban so I can renew my acquaintance with Jean Burgoyne. After phoning her first.'

'Should be OK. Just so long as we remember we're right in the danger zone. Anything could happen. Goodnight . . .'

In a small apartment near the rue du Bac on the left bank in Paris, Marler sat up in bed smoking a king-size. He was fully dressed in French denims and a French shirt, and his only concession to brief relaxation was his open-necked collar.

By his side was one of the most sophisticated mobile telephones in the world, engineered by the basement crew at Park Crescent. It was equipped with a powerful transmitter and a very long aerial which extended at the press of a button. He was in frequent communication with Tweed at Navarre's Ministry of Defence. But its potential range was far greater.

311

Inside a ready-packed suitcase was an assortment of items apart from a change of clothes. Marler was posing as a cosmetics salesman: inside the small case were 'samples' of his trade – certain articles of equipment disguised by the Engine Room at Park Crescent to look like cosmetics.

Inside a large hold-all under a woollen scarf was a dismantled Armalite rifle complete with sniperscope and ammo. The weapon had been delivered to him inside the hold-all by one of Lasalle's trusted couriers in a dubious Montmartre club. Marler had then travelled aboard the Metro to return to his base. The only person in the world who knew his whereabouts was Tweed.

Marler was also carrying a very large sum of money and a collection of open-booking Air Inter tickets. Some had already been used. Checking the time, Marler closed his eyes and fell asleep. He had the ability to catnap at any hour. The mobile phone was tucked on the pillow close to his ear. He'd hear the beep instantly. He was expecting fresh instructions.

33

'Here we are. My little home in the forest,' said Moshe.

Newman stared grimly at the Villa Jaune. It was large – but little more than an old wooden cabin. Located in a clearing, it was encircled by a dense palisade of firs which seemed about to advance on it in the night, to swallow it up. Where the hell the 'Jaune' – the 'Yellow' – came in was more than Newman could fathom, but he felt disinclined to ask Moshe.

He checked his watch. Well over an hour to dawn yet. As Moshe carried both cases to the verandah and opened the heavy front door, Newman gathered his own load. He took the sack containing twenty empty mineral water bottles, Isabelle's metal funnel, and the jerrican of spare petrol out of the car.

The vehicle was parked near the side of the 'villa', and was partly concealed by the bank of undergrowth Moshe had driven it into. Newman arrived on the verandah as Moshe switched on lights. Dumping his load, Newman called out: 'Moshe, I'm going to take a look round the outside. Be back in a minute.'

'A glass of wine will be waiting . . .'

A high wind was blowing spasmodically. As Newman prowled round the area he heard a sound like the surge of the sea, realized it was the wind in the treetops. The wind dropped suddenly and a similar sound continued. A crashing of breakers on the nearby shore.

Newman studied all the approaches. He went to the rear of the cabin, found the deep gully Moshe had told him about. Masked by last autumn's dead bracken, it ran a distance away from the back of the Villa Jaune. A man crawling along it would be completely concealed from anyone standing at ground level. Half-way along it ran through a culvert, then continued on the other side.

Newman found the atmosphere of the Landes claustrophobic. He felt hemmed in as he moved silently over the spongy ground, his Smith & Wesson in his hand. He felt a need to get into the open and walked towards the sea.

The forest ended abruptly. Ahead of him was the vastness of the Atlantic, huge rollers sweeping in slowly, thumping down on the shore, spreading a carpet of surf on the beach. His night vision was good and he was aware suddenly of movement on the beach.

He was perched up where he stood and between where he waited and the beach was an area of Sahara-like sand

313

dunes. Further south the dunes rose to a great height. The figure crouched by the shore, picking up something, was an old woman wrapped in a black shawl.

He moved back into the forest slowly, then walked rapidly to the cabin. Easy to find – from a distance it was a beacon of lights. Was Moshe crazy? He opened the front door and his companion was sitting in front of a large wooden table, sipping from a glass of wine. He gestured to a second glass.

'That is for you.'

'Are you mad? This place is lit up like a Christmas tree. If they are coming for you, you're making it so damned easy for them.'

'If they're coming, I am ready.'

'Well, I'm not. And there's a weird old woman fooling around on the beach. At this hour.'

'Good!' Moshe jumped up. 'Old Martine. She is the one who will tell you what has been happening here. We go to her now . . .'

'After you've switched off the bloody lights and locked the door . . .'

Together they hurried to the sea. Newman had trouble keeping his balance as he plunged after a more sure-footed Moshe down the sand dunes. Moshe called out to the old woman, then warned Newman.

'Old Martine is suspicious of strangers. She has reason to be, as you'll hear. I will introduce you as a security agent from Britain – which in a way you are. She thinks all French security personnel are in league with de Forge.'

Newman now saw what the crone had been doing. Close to where the surf carpet covered the sand she was collecting brushwood washed ashore. Her lined face with a beaky nose and a strong jaw peered out at Newman from under the shawl as Moshe made the introduction.

'I am here on an official mission,' Newman told her

frankly in French. 'To investigate the crimes of General de Forge.'

Her alert eyes studied him. 'Your French is very good for an Englishman,' she observed.

'I have been told that I can pass for a Frenchman . . .'

Newman spoke the words slowly in English, waited a moment, then reverted to French.

'You have information which would be useful to help me bring him to justice?'

The dam broke. She spoke rapidly, brandishing her sheaf of brushwood like a weapon. Her eyes glittered with hatred.

'My nephew was in the Third Corps. De Forge had him shot as a spy. Just as he had many others shot here. This is de Forge's cemetery – the Landes. Come with me. Come! I will show you. Come!'

Her free gnarled hand grasped Newman's arm. He was surprised at the strength of her grip as she hurried him back to the sand dunes, released her grasp, scrambled in front of him up the dunes with great agility. The wind had dropped and as she led them into the forest away from the surge of the Atlantic an eerie silence closed in on the small group.

She was heading towards the Villa Jaune and then turned south away from it, following a path between the trunks of the giant firs. Newman checked his watch. He hoped this wouldn't take long. He was anxious to return to the cabin. As they'd passed through sleepy St Girons he'd noticed a car parked in a side lane with two men inside. He had the strongest instinct the maximum danger hour was close to dawn.

The crone led them down a shallow slope into a clearing littered with low humps shrouded with dead undergrowth and rotting bracken. Old Martine brandished her brushwood like a wand.

'De Forge's burial ground.' She peered up at Newman. 'You have strong nerves, sir?'

315

'I've seen some grim things in my time.'

'Then use your foot to dig into one of those humps. If you like, use your gloved hands – although you may not like what you find . . .'

Newman crouched over the nearest hump, thrust aside a deep mass of matted bracken, swept soil damp from recent rain to one side. His hand encountered something hard. He dug deeper, stopped. He was staring at a skull, part of a skeleton stretched out and which, he guessed, must have lain there for at least two years.

But what fixed his gaze was the third eye in the skull. A hole which could only have been made by a bullet. No trace of clothes. Removing his gloves, he took out the small camera supplied by Park Crescent, pressed the button for night shots, took three. Putting on his gloves, he then replaced the soil, hauled the undergrowth back in roughly its original position.

'Now here!'

The crone had taken charge. She stood, erect now, her bony finger pointed at another hump which showed signs of recent disturbance. He walked over to it, crouched again, gritted his teeth, removed the covering of bracken and soil. Underneath lay the body of a French soldier in the early stages of decomposition. This time there was no doubt that he had been dispatched by a bullet fired into the forehead. Newman knew he was a French soldier because he still wore his uniform of a private.

He used his camera to take ten shots of this corpse. It was the body of a young man who had joined up to serve the Army and this was his fate. Newman then forced himself to search the corpse's pockets but all traces of identification had been removed. He looked at the man before he rebuilt the grave. The victim gave a macabre impression of being asleep.

'Now here!'

The crone again. The bony finger pointing at death, at

another hump. Newman was experiencing a feeling of nausea. He shook his head, glanced slowly round the clearing, counted twenty makeshift graves. A horrific crime.

'Why?' he asked the crone.

Martine spat on the ground. 'De Forge eliminates those who do not support him. I told you about my nephew . . .'

'Yes. Suspected of being a spy. But what about all the others? They can't all have been spies.'

'Some objected to digging the graves. They were shot.'

'How do you know that?' Newman pressed.

'I saw, heard one man throw down his shovel, protest to his officer. He was shot immediately.'

'How could you see them without their seeing you?' Newman demanded, still unconvinced.

'I sat in the undergrowth at night when I heard activity. You don't believe Old Martine? Watch.'

She moved away, dressed in black, suddenly vanished into thin air. Newman had been watching her and was disconcerted. He looked round carefully, then called out.

'Martine, where are you?'

'Over here.'

Newman, followed by Moshe, walked in the direction her voice had come from. He damned near stumbled over the huddled form crouched at the foot of a thick tree trunk. He was convinced. He told Moshe he was going down to the beach for a moment. Newman was not taking any chance of infection after messing about with corpses. He threw his gloves out to sea: the tide was receding. Bending down, he washed his hands thoroughly in the surf.

When he was making his way back to Moshe he saw Martine in the distance, moving north up the beach, gathering more brushwood.

'We must hurry back to the villa,' he told Moshe. 'You know where Martine lives?'

'In a tiny abandoned villa on the outskirts of St Girons.

317

She keeps herself warm with brushwood fires and logs from the forest. She sells the excess, uses the money to feed herself.'

'How some people live.'

'At least she is alive.' Moshe waved a hand towards the hideous burial ground. 'Troops from de Forge's army land in rubber dinghies from the sea. I sometimes heard the crackle of rifle fire. I thought it was target practice. I never dreamt I was hearing firing squads.'

'Talking about survival, we have to make certain preparations as soon as we reach the villa. This is what we will do . . .'

The attack came a little earlier than Newman had expected. They were settled inside the cabin with only lights switched on illuminating the verandah when they heard the distant chant coming closer.

'Death to all Jews! Death to all . . .!'

Since returning to Moshe's home both men had been working non-stop. Moshe had oiled the rear barred window so it slid open noiselessly. Newman had obtained cleaning cloths from Moshe, had torn them into strips. Then he attended to the mineral bottles he'd obtained from Isabelle. He divided them up – ten for himself, ten for Moshe. The bottles, caps screwed on, were distributed in the pockets of Newman's trenchcoat, tucked down inside his belt. Moshe wore a jacket with large pockets, similarly stuffed with bottles; more inside his own belt. Newman gave him his spare lighter as the chant grew in volume. They were very close now.

'I still think you should leave,' Moshe began arguing. 'If you go now you could probably escape.'

'It's my war as well as yours. My job is to help stop de Forge. Those are his men coming to get you. I'll bet ten thousand pounds on it.'

'I think you ought to leave,' Moshe persisted. 'I wish I had never agreed to let you come.'

'Don't you want vengeance? Isn't that the same chant you heard at Tarbes just before your friends were all incinerated?'

'The very same chant . . .'

'So it could be some of the same men. Don't you want revenge?' Newman repeated.

'We cannot just lie down and die again as once we did.'

'So what the hell are you grumbling about?'

'I wasn't grumbling,' Moshe protested.

Newman grinned in the dark. 'You were giving a very good imitation of it . . .'

He stopped speaking as he heard the chanting increasing in venom. They sounded to be inside the clearing which surrounded the villa now. He crept to a window as a glow of light lit up the interior of the cabin, creating sinister shadows on the walls. He sucked in his breath.

The leader of the attacking group was holding aloft a cross of fire – the Cross of Lorraine adopted by General de Gaulle during the Second World War. Newman stared at this ghastly perversion of a sacred symbol. The leader was flanked by four men spread out like a military wing on either side, advancing on the cabin. All nine men wore terrifying white sheets which came to a peak at the tops of their invisible heads. All the flankers carried flaming torches as they chanted the same dirge over and over. It was pure Ku-Klux-Klan.

'You must go now, Bob,' Moshe whispered.

'Two of us will leave here alive – or two of us will be left here dead,' Newman said calmly. 'You know the plan.'

'Yes, I can do it. Is it time?'

'Let them get a little closer. The bastards are enjoying themselves, want to make the terror last a little longer.'

'They will burn the villa to the ground.'

'That is *their* plan. Now we operate ours . . .'

319

They left the villa by the rear window, closing it behind them. Newman led the way, crawling swiftly along the gully below the level of the surrounding ground. He had already made one trip earlier to make sure they could ease their way swiftly through the culvert pipe. He emerged from the end of the stuffy gully and smelt the aroma of pines. Moshe clambered out behind him. As planned, Newman moved to the right of the villa, Moshe to the left.

Newman had a bottle in his hand, uncapped it and the pine aroma was replaced by the stench of the bottle full of petrol from the jerrican – fed inside with the aid of Isabelle's funnel. He pulled out a short length of the strip of cloth he had stuffed in the neck, came round the end of the villa to face the two outer flankers on his side. Using his lighter, he ignited the cloth, hurled the bottle. It landed between the flankers, exploded into flame. Greedily, the flame set light to the sheets of both men and they became human fireballs, screaming.

Newman lit a second fuse, threw it at the leader holding the obscene fiery cross. The bottle exploded at his feet, swept a sheet of flame over his strange clothing. The cross wobbled, fell on to the ground and the leader fell into the inferno, shrieking with terror. Newman threw a third bottle. It exploded just before it landed, firing the white sheets of two more attackers. They dropped the torches and this added to the conflagration.

Over to his left Moshe was hurling his own fire bottles. His aim was accurate. Four attackers were in flames, running a short distance as they shrieked, then collapsing. Hell that night was flames soaring into the night. The chanting was replaced with the shouts and shrieks of the men who had come to murder Moshe Stein, to burn him to death.

There was a sudden silence. The only sound was the dying crackle of fire burning itself out as an unpleasant stench began to drift through the Landes. Two men had rolled on the ground in a futile attempt to save themselves, and their action had extinguished the fire more quickly compared with the others now burnt to a cinder.

Newman walked over to these two dead men. The sheets had been destroyed but their clothes had miraculously survived as they lay motionless. Under the sheets they had been wearing French Army uniforms. Newman calmly took out his camera, recorded five photos of each corpse.

'It is horrible,' said Moshe, hurrying up behind Newman.

Hardened by his experiences a few years before behind the lines in East Germany during the days of the Cold War, Newman's hand was steady as a rock as he took his pictures. He put away the camera, emptied his pockets of unused bottles.

'It was them or us. Now I have evidence. I suggest we pack at once and drive straight back to Arcachon. I have to make contact with Paris . . .'

34

At 8.30 a.m. in Arcachon smoke-coloured clouds pressed down on the resort like a lid. It was bitingly cold as Paula stepped out of the Renault near the entrance to the apartment block where Isabelle Thomas lived.

Butler stepped out of the rear to escort her. Pete Nield remained at the wheel – to guard the car, to watch the entrance ahead of him. Both Butler and Nield carried small walkie-talkies. At any sign of danger approaching while they were inside, Nield would warn Butler.

Paula had phoned Isabelle from the hotel before they set out. The French girl had not sounded enthusiastic about the arrival of Paula, but had agreed to see her. Butler had insisted on accompanying Paula to the apartment.

Isabelle opened the door on a chain. She peered out and studied Paula.

'Yes?' she enquired.

'I'm Paula Grey. I wonder if you have any Gruyère cheese?'

'Who is the man with you?'

'My minder.' Paula smiled. 'A friend and a professional bodyguard. He has me on a tight leash.'

Isabelle released the chain, opened the door, closed and replaced the chain, locking the door when they were inside. She led them across the dining-living room to a sitting area. Butler said he wouldn't intrude, was there somewhere close by he could wait?

'You would like coffee?' Isabelle asked.

'Yes, please. Black, no sugar,' Paula responded.

Five minutes later Isabelle returned with coffee, leaving Butler in the kitchen. Again she studied Paula from tip to toe, unsmiling as she sat opposite her with the table between them. Paula sensed an underlying hostility and realized its source with Isabelle's next question.

'You are a very close friend of Bob Newman's?'

'I work for a security organization. Mr Newman helps us from time to time. He knows the world so well from his experiences as a foreign correspondent. *I* know him well but I wouldn't say he's a very close friend.'

Paula saw the relief in Isabelle's eyes she tried to conceal. So it was jealousy. She could understand Newman being attracted: Isabelle was not only an extremely good-looking girl, she was also very intelligent. It explained the enthusiasm with which Newman had described her. Paula changed the subject quickly.

322

'Do you feel safe here? You've suffered some ghastly experiences.'

'There's something I should tell you, Paula. May I call you Paula?' Her mood had changed, had become animated. 'Good. I'm Isabelle. Bob told me to do any shopping early in the morning. To keep under cover here the rest of the time. I've done exactly as he said.'

'You're wise . . .'

'Wait! I heard something. A shopkeeper told me about a rumour that the peculiar ship from Britain with its hull split in two may arrive here soon. Bob was interested in that ship. And in a lecherous man called Lord Dane Dawlish.'

'He's expected?' Paula asked sharply.

'I don't know.'

'Have you any idea where this shopkeeper heard the rumour?'

'Yes!' Isabelle looked pleased. 'He told me he heard it in the Martinique Bar near the front.'

'Could you describe to me the location of this Martinique Bar?' Paula probed.

'Yes!' Isabelle seemed eager to help now. 'I can draw you a plan showing you how to get there from here. It will be open now. It's not really a very nice place. I'll get a pad . . .'

When she had drawn her diagram Paula noticed how neat and clear it was. Like her handwriting. She drank more coffee as the French girl made sure she understood the directions. Although like a coiled spring in her intensity, Isabelle moved with great gracefulness.

'Can I ask you a question?' she asked when Paula folded the diagram.

'Ask away.'

They had conversed in English ever since Paula's arrival. A feeling of warmth was developing between the two women.

323

'Have you any idea,' Isabelle began tentatively, 'when we may expect to see Bob back in Arcachon?'

'No idea at all. Most of the time he doesn't reveal to me his movements.'

'Paula!' Isabelle was intense again. 'I almost forgot. This may be something you should know. Bob phoned me some hours after he'd left. To warn me he felt sure he had seen an officer called Lieutenant Berthier when he was driving out of Arcachon late at night. He described him. He said I should be careful of this man.'

Paula was taken aback. Her mind flashed to the incident when he'd driven her to Jean Burgoyne at Admiralty House in Aldeburgh. When he'd attempted his amorous approach. Berthier – who had posed as James Sanders, who was a key member of General de Forge's inner circle. Arcachon was no longer the safe haven they had hoped for. She worded her reply carefully.

'I have heard of this Berthier. He is a dangerous man. Please do take Bob's advice and stay under cover. And now I must go.'

'You must be careful yourself,' Isabelle urged. 'If you need a safe place to hide, come here immediately.'

'I won't hesitate to take up your offer.' Paula hid her dismay at the news of Berthier's presence. 'And I will keep in touch with you.'

Butler emerged from the kitchen. 'Thank you for the cup of excellent coffee,' he said formally.

He waited until they reached the pavement after he had peered out in both directions. They walked towards where Nield appeared to be sleeping behind the wheel of the Renault.

'Do you trust her?' Butler asked.

'The only people I trust in this situation are Tweed's team. Berthier turning up here is a shock. We'll have to keep a lookout for him where we're going.'

'And where might that be?'

'To the Martinique Bar. That's where the rumour originated that Dawlish's *Steel Vulture* may be coming here. I shudder every time I think of that ship. It takes me back to when poor Karin and I were scuba-diving off Dunwich. When we surfaced we saw that evil-looking ship. Let's hope we can find out something at the Martinique.'

It's not really a very nice place. Isabelle's description of the Martinique was pure British understatement. Paula, dressed in a trenchcoat, walked in by herself as Butler strolled in half a minute later, giving the impression Paula was on her own. This time Nield did not stay with the car: he wandered in shortly after Butler had entered.

A seaman's waterfront bar – even though not on the front. Paula walked straight up to the bar. She was aware of seamen in pea-jackets staring openly at her. One made an obscene suggestion in a loud voice. She ignored it.

'A dry Vermouth, please,' she asked the barman.

Perching herself on a stool, she chanced a tricky question when the barman, a rough-looking type with a cast in his right eye, brought her drink.

'I hear that British twin-hulled ship, the *Steel Vulture*, is due to arrive back in Arcachon soon. Is it?'

'I wouldn't know. My job is to make this place pay.' He glanced over Paula's shoulder. 'The customer you should ask is sitting at that table in the corner behind the door.'

Paula sipped her drink. It was too early in the day for any drink, but it would look funny if she just left the glass full. She looked round the bar which had pictures of nude girls in various poses on the walls. Then she had a bad shock. Sitting at the corner table was a heavily-built man with wide shoulders, dressed in a clean pea-jacket. Brand.

She had last seen Dawlish's deputy at the shooting

party held at Grenville Grange on the river Alde. The day she had interviewed Dawlish, repelled his advances. Brand was staring straight back at her. He said something to his two tough companions, stood up, made his way towards her. His large hand gripped her shoulder as he climbed on to the adjoining stool.

'Miss Paula Grey. Now what would a nice lady like you be doing in Arcachon – and in a bar like this?'

'If you want to talk to me will you kindly first remove your paw?'

'A choosy dame.' The hand left her shoulder. 'It's a small world, as they say.'

'As you just said – so what are you doing here far away from Aldeburgh?'

'Still the nosy investigative reporter. Always asking questions. One day that habit will get you into nasty trouble.'

'I happen to do the occasional interview. My main job is with an insurance company.'

Brand grinned unpleasantly. 'And you're practised at evading questions. I asked why you were here. In this bar. In Arcachon.'

Paula swivelled her stool, to face him, to make it easy to get away if necessary. She smiled icily.

'Brand, I'll make a deal with you. I'll answer you if you first answer me. Fair enough?'

'No, it isn't.' Brand's expression was ugly. 'Don't get clever-clever with me.' His hand reached out again, grasped her forearm, held it tight. Paula willed herself not to wince. He had the grip of an ape. 'The last woman who tried that is still bruised all over. I want an answer . . .'

'I can give you one.' Butler had come up behind Brand. His tone was as controlled as his expression. 'Miss Grey and I have an appointment to keep. And if you don't take your hand off her pronto I'll break your arm. Maybe both arms.'

Brand let go of Paula, dropped off his stool, swung round to face Butler who stood a good two inches higher. Brand bunched his huge fist, stared at Butler who stood quite still. Something about Butler's stance, his poker-faced expression, bothered Brand. He shrugged, turned to go.

'I could make mincemeat of you,' he growled.

'Try it,' Butler suggested.

Brand's bull-neck, his face, reddened. He turned back and measured up Butler again. His arm stiffened, ready to strike the first blow.

'You can have a brawl if you want to,' Butler went on calmly. 'Of course someone will call the police and I have plenty of witnesses as to who started this. When you're lying poleaxed on the floor.'

'You'll be late for your bloody appointment.'

Brand marched off back to the corner table where his two companions waited. One of them had started to get up when he saw what was happening. Nield, who had wandered close to the table, pressed his left hand hard on the man's shoulder. He held him down as he spoke in French, his eyes flickering to the other man.

'DST. Make any trouble and I'll crack you on the skull.' His right hand was inside his coat, gripping the Walther. 'And then I'll haul you in for questioning as a suspected terrorist . . .'

Paula and Butler passed the table where Brand had just sat down again. Dawlish's right-hand man looked away from the group as it left.

Paula reacted as she settled herself beside Butler who was behind the wheel. Nield slipped into the back of the Renault.

'Thank you, Harry. That was getting grim. Did you see the size of his hand? He was really hurting me. But he backed off from you.'

'Which is interesting,' Butler commented. 'It was the

327

mention of the police coming which scared him off. Of course, you know who he is.'

'Brand. Dawlish's close confidant, as far as we know. He got uptight when I asked him what he was doing in Arcachon. I'm wondering whether the *Steel Vulture* is expected. If that's why he's here.'

'Unless he has some other job in mind first. Where do we go now?'

'To the Villa Forban so I can meet Jean Burgoyne. She is confident de Forge won't be there today. But we'd better be careful – very careful.'

'I thought that was why Pete and I were with you,' Butler remarked drily.

He'd studied the map Lasalle had provided Paula with showing the most solitary route to the villa. He was driving along the windswept front as Paula had suggested. She wanted to check that there was no sign of the *Steel Vulture*. It was a dirty day for any fishing vessels out beyond the shelter of the *bassin*. Paula suddenly sat up very erect.

The front was almost deserted. A strip of folded canvas above the window of an ice-cream parlour was flapping furiously, trying to tear itself loose. Even inside the *bassin* waves were rolling in, high and surf-crested. In the distance the clustered masts in the port were swaying madly. One man, dressed in a trench coat, his hair flying all over the place, was striding towards them. Paula felt sure she recognized the athletic stance, the swinging stride of the tall solitary walker.

'Harry, pull in when we reach that man coming this way.'

As he came closer Paula saw that it was Victor Rosewater. The last person she'd expected to see in Arcachon. She stepped out into the wind as Butler parked the car.

'Victor! What a wonderful surprise. I certainly never expected to see you down here.'

328

Rosewater gave her a bear hug, glanced into the car and looked a question at Paula. How like him she thought – not to pry directly.

'It's all right,' she assured him. 'They're Tweed's. So you can talk freely. What are you doing?'

'Tweed told me you were in this area when I phoned Monica. Careful lady, that. I had to give her a number where Tweed could call me back.'

'And why are you here, Victor? It's good to see you.'

'My immediate purpose was to find you. Which is why I was walking along the front. Can we talk?'

'Later in the day. I'm off to see someone. See the café down that side street? Could we meet there about four this afternoon?'

'I'll be there at three-thirty. If necessary I'll wait and wait and wait . . .'

'Who was that?' Butler asked as he drove down the side street away from the front, still heading for the port.

'Victor Rosewater, a Military Intelligence officer based at Freiburg in Germany. Has a roving commission . . .'

She told him how with Tweed she'd first met Rosewater at the Drei Konige Hotel in Basle, recalled the murder of his wife, Karin, which she had almost witnessed. Butler drove back to where the road continued along the *bassin* as she talked. They arrived at the port. No sign of the *Steel Vulture*.

'We'd better go straight to the Villa Forban,' Paula said, checking her watch. 'I wish I could tell Tweed about Brand being here.'

'I noticed a public call box on the way in,' Nield called out. 'You could contact him from there . . .'

Tweed, still in Paris, had spent the night at the Ministry of the Interior. Navarre had supplied himself and Kuhlmann with camp beds. The close co-operation between Britain,

France, and Germany – between Tweed, Navarre, and Kuhlmann – was to become legendary in later years when it came to light.

Tweed was still stiff from his night on the camp bed when Paula phoned. He listened as she reported the presence of Brand in Arcachon, her meeting with Victor Rosewater.

'Yes, I told him he might find you in Arcachon,' Tweed confirmed. 'He's moving closer in to the enemy. Tell me what he says to you after you've met him later in the café. He may have obtained fresh information. I need to be kept very up to date.'

'How is Bob Newman?' she asked.

'No word from him. I expect I'll hear what he's found out soon. Now listen, Paula. This visit to the Villa Forban is fraught with danger. France has no President, but Navarre was confirmed as Prime Minister early today by a narrow majority. This may activate de Forge to make his ultimate move. He's unpredictable. You could run into something pretty dangerous at the Villa Forban.'

'The coast is clear at the moment. It's a unique chance to discover something vital. Jean is very close to her friend.'

'You will have company?' Tweed pressed.

'The whole time. They're staying closer to me than one of those sticking plasters. Stop worrying. Must go. Bye.'

Tweed put down the phone with grave misgivings. He now wished he'd forbidden her to risk the trip.

General de Forge straightened a ruler so it was precisely parallel with the edge of his desk. Lamy thought it a typical gesture: de Forge was noted for his meticulous attention to detail. Some officers called it an obsession. The General looked at his subordinate, seated opposite in the large room, who had just reported on the arrival of more sabotage units in Paris.

'So,' Lamy concluded, 'Paris can now be destabilized at

the moment you give the signal. Despite the appointment of Navarre as Prime Minister. He won't be able to control the situation.'

'I keep thinking of Jean Burgoyne,' de Forge remarked, staring into the distance. 'Whether I can trust her.'

'You'd decided not to see her today,' Lamy reminded him. 'There is a great deal requiring your attention.'

'Security is paramount,' De Forge continued as though he had not heard Lamy. 'It takes precedence over everything. Order the car.' Taking one of his instinctive decisions, he stood up and put on his képi. 'We are driving immediately to the Villa Forban. With a heavily-armed escort.'

'You are sure about this, General?' Lamy enquired.

'I am a very observant man.' De Forge's mouth tightened. 'I was at the villa recently and left my dispatch case on a table while I had a bath. Afterwards when I came to pick up the case I noticed it had been moved slightly, did not line up with the table's inlay design as I'd left it. I know we have a spy who is reporting to Lasalle. When we identify that spy he – or she – will pay the ultimate penalty. They will end up in the Landes with the others. My escort is to carry automatic weapons . . .'

35

Marler carried two hold-alls as he disembarked from the Air Inter flight which had transported him from Paris. The fact that there were no security checks on internal flights was a huge advantage.

Dressed in denims, a windcheater, and trainers, he wore his beret down over his forehead at a jaunty angle. He strolled across the concourse at an easy pace, whistling a French tune. Slim and slight in build, no one could have picked him out from the average Frenchman.

The hired Peugeot he'd phoned ahead for from Paris was waiting for him. He showed the girl his false papers in a common French name, paid her in cash, winked at her and got behind the wheel.

Driving a few yards along the kerb, he paused, took out a map of the area. Checking his recollections of the route, he drove on. The call from Tweed giving him his fresh instructions had come through to his base in the apartment near the rue du Bac.

'Step up the pressure,' had been Tweed's final order.

At the Ministry of the Interior in Paris Tweed had been given his own small office by Navarre, a room equipped with a scrambler phone. It was mid-afternoon as he sat in his shirt-sleeves, polishing his glasses on his handkerchief.

He was trying to work out how Lord Dawlish could smuggle arms aboard the *Steel Vulture* – assuming his Lordship was doing just that. After all, he was in the international armaments business. But the *Vulture* had twice been subject to search at its base port, Harwich, for drugs. So would Dawlish risk using his unique vessel for transporting arms? At any time Heathcoate, the Harbour Master, might order a third search. No, Dawlish was too shrewd to gamble on ruin, a heavy term of imprisonment. There was something at the back of Tweed's mind he couldn't bring to the fore. He dialled the number for Park Crescent, spoke to Monica.

'Paula dictated to you a statement of the events at Dunwich and Aldeburgh – on the day her friend, Karin

Rosewater, was murdered. Could you read it back to me. Detail is what I'm after . . .'

He listened as Monica rapidly read the report back to him. Occasionally he made a note on the pad in front of him.

'That's it,' Monica said eventually. 'Any help?'

'I'm not sure. Something still eludes me, but I'm certain it's there. It will come back to me – I just hope it does in time. No further developments here . . .'

Earlier Tweed had called Monica, had given her details of his new temporary base. *No further developments –* that was not strictly speaking true. Navarre had been confirmed as Prime Minister by the National Assembly – by the most narrow of margins.

The door opened and the man he was thinking about walked in. Navarre had had only two hours' sleep but was full of energy. He perched on the edge of Tweed's desk, clasped his lean wiry hands.

'Well, my friend, I now have a problem. I was about to dispatch a large contingent of heavily-armed CRS south together with a fleet of helicopters. Now Lasalle tells me a small army of saboteurs have infiltrated Paris, taking up position to start an insurrection. So do I concentrate on the north – here – or the south?' He waved a hand. 'I expect no answer. Only I can decide. But de Forge is close to making his big move, his masterstroke. The take-over of the French government.'

'What about the Chief of the Army Staff, General Masson, de Forge's superior? He could remove him.'

'I have already asked him to do so. He refused. Said if I insist he will resign. What would that do to public morale? The announcement that the Chief of the Army Staff had resigned. It would play straight into de Forge's hands. I now suspect Masson is a secret member of the *Cercle Noir*, that he is de Forge's creature.'

'You have a difficult decision – where to position the

para-military CRS units,' Tweed observed.

'A decision I have to take within hours. Oh, Kuhlmann is wanting to see you . . .'

The German police chief came in almost as soon as Navarre had left. Smoking his inevitable cigar, he looked fresh, determined, aggressive. He sat in a chair, looked directly at Tweed as he spoke.

'I've decided to handle this *Siegfried* problem in my own way. Nearly every Kriminalpolizei officer has left Wiesbaden, covering most of Germany. They're putting maximum pressure on all known underworld informants to locate the hidden *Siegfried* cells. I've told them to use any method necessary to make people talk.'

'The Chancellor knows this?'

Kuhlmann clapped a hand to his broad forehead in a mock gesture of forgetfulness. He grinned.

'You know something? With all that's going on it never crossed my mind to tell him. Now I think I'll wait for the results of this ruthless and intensive search. I'll keep you in touch . . .'

Alone again, Tweed read through Paula's report for the second time. Everything was becoming a race against time. Navarre's protection of Paris. Kuhlmann's offensive to locate *Siegfried*, and his own search for the way Dawlish might be smuggling huge reinforements to de Forge. Paula's report that Brand was in Arcachon made it all the more urgent.

It was dusk as Lord Dane Dawlish walked down the beach at Dunwich to board the large waiting rubber dinghy with a powerful outboard motor. He had substituted for his hard riding hat a peaked naval cap. He also wore a blue blazer with gold buttons and dark blue trousers.

Dawlish believed in dressing for the role he was adopting at any given moment. He was now presenting his sailor image. It went with the occasion. And emphasized his reputation as a playboy. Of course, if he happened to meet a beautiful woman so much the better: he'd live up to his playboy image with her.

The *Steel Vulture*, which had sailed from Harwich early that morning, was anchored offshore. Even in the twilight scuba divers were going over the side, exploring the depths of the sunken village.

'Is the operation completed?' he asked the First Mate who had come to escort him as the crew manoeuvred the craft closer to the weird twin-hulled giant.

'It is still being carried out, sir.'

'Should have damned well been completed by now. Butts will be kicked if we're behind schedule.'

'I'm happy to report we're exactly on schedule, sir.'

'You may be happy. I'll only join your happiness when the skipper reports the cargo is aboard . . .'

Onshore a few villagers, well wrapped against the zero temperatures, were gazing through field-glasses at the *Steel Vulture*. They were fascinated with Dawlish's persistence in locating Dunwich under the sea. And it was good for business.

The local pub had been packed with customers – divers coming ashore for a break, slaking their thirst with a roll of banknotes. Dawlish was popular, Dawlish was good for business. No one suspected that anything sinister was taking place. They watched as Dawlish climbed on to the platform suspended just above a calm sea.

When the *Steel Vulture* had raced north from Harwich early in the morning it had swung through a hundred and eighty degrees before anchoring off Dunwich. It floated about a half-mile out from the coast and the activity visible from the beach was on the starboard side.

What could not be seen by the curious sightseers was the very different and furious activity on the port side facing out to sea. A squat mobile crane was operating a long chain suspended deep down. When not in use the

335

crane was telescoped inside a huge cube of a deckhouse.

Close to the stern was an advanced seaplane. It was not only equipped with floats for landing on water: it also had a retractable undercarriage which could lower wheels below the floats, enabling it to land on the ground.

The *Vulture*, specially designed in a Norwegian shipyard, had cost Dawlish forty million dollars with its various accessories. Dawlish went straight to the bridge and his mood was aggressive as he addressed the skipper, Santos.

'I presume we can sail for Arcachon tonight?'

Santos spread apologetic hands. 'I am not sure the loading will be completed for a few hours. We may have to sail tomorrow . . .'

'A few hours!' Dawlish was outraged. His bullet-like eyes glared at the skipper. 'I should have come here earlier to crack a few skulls together. Why the hell do I have to supervise everything myself to ensure the schedule is kept? Always the same story. I have to do every bloody thing myself.'

'It is dangerous work,' Santos pleaded. 'You would not wish us to have an accident with such a cargo.'

'Report to me every half-hour. The trucks loaded the vessel during the night?'

He was referring to the trucks which had brought their consignments from the factory in the forest on the road to Orford. The factory Newman and Marler had earlier tried to search, had been frustrated by their discovery of land mines which caused them to abandon the expedition.

The villagers in Dunwich were not surprised when trucks arrived in the middle of the night. Two divers who patronized the Ship Inn had casually mentioned the trucks were bringing in food supplies for the crew and high-tech equipment for the divers who were using new techniques to explore the sunken village.

Santos wished Dawlish would leave the bridge. His nationality was Panamanian and he was paid a larger

336

salary than he'd get anywhere else in the world. Large enough for him to keep his mouth shut.

'Report to me on progress every half-hour!' Dawlish repeated, and stormed off to his luxurious cabin.

His quarters were also equipped with the latest communications technology. He had hardly closed the door, started to pour himself a large Scotch, when his private radio telephone rang.

'Hell and damnation.'

He put down the drink, sat in the armchair, picked up the phone. Brand's burring controlled voice came over the receiver from Arcachon as clear as a bell.

'There could be trouble here. Guess who I ran into in a local bar . . .'

'I don't like guessing games. Get to the point, for God's sake.'

'That cow, Paula Grey, who interviewed you. I tried to find out what she was doing here and got nowhere.'

'That is too much of a coincidence . . .'

Dawlish gave Brand precise instructions, coding them in language no one else would have understood. Aware of the British government's highly sophisticated listening system at Cheltenham, Dawlish took no risks with security. And during their conversation neither man had mentioned the other's name. As for Paula Grey, Dawlish didn't think her name would ring any bells.

Tweed had just returned from a brisk walk round Paris in the drizzle drifting down from a miserable overcast sky which blanketed the city. He had sensed a growing unease among the population.

Walking into a bar he had listened to some bargees chatting while he sipped at a cup of coffee. Their views struck him as alarming, considering they weren't among the élite of Paris society.

337

'We need General de Forge to take over,' one man had said.

'I reckon he could be a second de Gaulle,' his companion had agreed.

'A strong man to clear out these Arabs and other foreign trash,' a third bargee had said emphatically. 'I know exactly what I'd do. Round up the bastards and deport the whole tribe back to where they came from. De Forge is the man to do just that . . .'

Arriving back at the Ministry of the Interior, Tweed showed the pass Navarre had issued him with. He hurried back to his office and the phone was ringing. He grabbed for it.

'Yes? Who is this?'

'Monica. I have more news. I hope you'll understand me. First, those films Marler took when he was on a fishing expedition with Newman. Are you with me?'

She was referring to the pictures Marler had taken of the laboratory-like building during their brief raid on Dawlish's factory in the forest on the road to Orford in the Aldeburgh area.

'Yes. They've taken the devil of a time to develop them and come up with a comment.'

'It's weird. I'll jump ahead a bit. When the data came back from Porton with their scientific report the Home Secretary authorized Special Branch to investigate the place. They were accompanied by experts from Porton. I have to tell you they came up with nothing.'

'Nothing?'

Tweed was taken aback. He recalled the veterinary pathologist's report on the dead fox Newman had brought back. Nerve gas.

'I don't understand,' he replied.

'Wait, please. I said I'd jump ahead a bit. The photos taken by Marler were subjected to intensive examination at Porton – using, I gather, new magnification techniques.

338

It was the opinion of the experts that certain containers which showed up were just the type used for storing nerve gas. Hence their agreeing to travel all the way from Porton to join the Special Branch men.'

'So what the devil did they discover – or not discover – inside that laboratory?'

'The place was empty. Not a single container left. And they tested the whole place with special instruments. It was clean as a whistle. Almost too clean – that's a quote from one of the scientists. And no landmines.'

'Thank you, Monica. Keep in touch . . .'

Tweed felt depressed as he replaced the phone. He still felt certain he was missing something. He picked up the report of what Paula had said, began re-reading it again. Word by word.

Butler drove the Renault along the country road and stopped a hundred yards from the entrance to the Villa Forban. As agreed in advance, Paula stepped out and walked swiftly to the closed grille gates.

'I've got a bad feeling about this,' said Nield who sat in the rear.

'Join the club,' answered Butler. 'Which is why we are taking the precautions I thought up.'

Paula reached the gates, saw the entryphone Jean Burgoyne had told her to look for set into one of the pillars. She pressed the button, looking along the road which led to GHQ Third Corps.

'Yes? Who is it?'

Jean's distinctive voice speaking in French. Paula put her mouth close to the entryphone.

'Paula here. Are you alone?'

'Yes. Come in. I will operate . . .'

'*Don't* open the gates. We are coming in from the back of the estate. Please trust me. Leave a rear door open – I'll be there in about five minutes. OK?'

'Anything you say. Looking forward very much to seeing you . . .'

Paula ran back to the car, jumped in beside Butler. She told them Jean was alone, that it was all right. Butler nodded, said nothing as he drove off the road up a very narrow side road. He'd studied a large-scale map before they had left Arcachon, had found this road led to the back of the villa. He'd also discovered that it forked, that another narrow route led across country before it rejoined the road they'd come along.

To their right was a high stone wall. This didn't worry Butler, who had cross-questioned Paula about the location of the villa the night before in Arcachon. Early that morning he had visited a ship's chandler, had purchased a length of strong rope and an iron grapple. They'd be able to scale the wall at the back.

It was mid-afternoon and the sky was like thick grey soup. No wind, but it was arctic cold. The met forecasts, which Butler monitored when he could, had talked of a heavy sea mist coming in. And they were later than they'd expected to be, which again worried Butler. They'd taken a wrong turn.

Following the road round the back of the walled estate Butler saw the rope and grapple wouldn't be needed. He positioned the car carefully under the branches of an overhanging tree which had its trunk on the far side of the wall.

'Think you're athletic enough to shin up that branch and climb down the other side of the tree, Paula?'

She gave him a dirty look, started to open her door to get out. Butler laid a hand on her arm.

'We do this my way. We're in enemy territory.'

'General de Forge's stronghold,' Nield commented. 'We must be crazy.'

'So,' Butler continued, 'I'm coming with you. If you

340

prefer to talk to Burgoyne on your own, OK. But I want to be in the next room. And I go up the tree first.'

'What about me?' asked Nield.

'You stay with the car – and turn it in the opposite direction for a quick getaway. This won't be any pleasure trip.'

'The other way?' Nield repeated. 'That means about an eight-point turn. Thanks a lot . . .'

Butler checked his Walther, got out of the car, gripped the strong branch, swung himself over, paused to view the estate. Trees forming a screen by the rear wall – useful. Through the bare branches he saw a few acres of lawn, the back of the villa. He scrambled down the tree.

Paula, dressed in denims, a windcheater and trainers under her trench coat, followed. First she took off the coat, folded it, threw it over the wall. Agilely she scaled the tree, dropped beside Butler who helped her on with the coat. The silence inside the wall was eerie, unsettling.

'I'll go ahead, check the ground,' Butler said.

'But Jean said she was alone . . .'

'And could have been speaking with a pistol held to her skull.'

Marler settled himself comfortably in position where he had a wide range of view. The Peugeot was concealed beneath a copse of evergreens: impossible for anyone to catch sight of it.

Crouching low on the knoll behind dead undergrowth he adjusted the focus of his field-glasses. Slowly he systematically swept the lenses searching for anyone – anything – he had missed. He spotted nothing.

It was very quiet. No birdsong. No wind. Dead silence. Patiently he waited – inactivity he was long accustomed to.

36

Tweed was seated at the desk in his temporary office in the Ministry of Defence when the phone rang. He recognized Monica's voice.

'Go ahead,' he urged.

'I told you I was going to try and get information on the structure of the *Steel Vulture* which was built at a Norwegian shipyard. Our Oslo contact has reported back. He apologizes for the delay. He wanted you to have the complete picture.'

'Which is?'

'Dramatic. The yard where the ship was built was burnt to the ground soon after they'd dispatched the *Vulture* to Britain. It was a catastrophe. The workers who had built the ship were celebrating in a shed with the doors closed. The building went up in flames and no one survived. The police suspected arson, but no one was ever arrested.'

'Deliberate, ruthless, and horrific . . .'

'I haven't finished yet. Our Oslo contact went to the office of the marine architect who designed *Vulture* – to get a copy of the plans. They'd had a break-in just about the time of the shipyard fire. A lot of plans had been stolen – including those of *Vulture*.'

'Naturally . . .'

'I'm still not finished. Our contact asked where the marine architect lived. He apparently skidded in his car on an icy road in the mountains – ended up at the bottom of a deep abyss. Dead.'

'Of course. Thank you very much, Monica. And do not hesitate to phone me again . . .'

Tweed put down the phone, leant back in his chair. He was now totally convinced there was something dangerously unorthodox about the *Steel Vulture*. So vital that it had to be kept secret at all costs. Even at the price of incinerating the whole work-force of a shipyard – and faking an accidental death of the marine architect who had designed her. Brutal murder.

He sat playing back in his mind from memory the report Paula had dictated of her horrific experience off Dunwich, followed by the equally terrifying pursuit across the Aldeburgh marshes, ending in the strangulation of Karin Rosewater. He wasn't going to leave it alone until the significant fact in her account sprang at him.

At the Villa Forban, Butler found the rear door unlocked. He opened it quietly but as he pushed it slowly open it creaked. He was holding the Walther in his hand while he pressed it wide open and stepped inside an ultra-modern kitchen. He found himself staring into the muzzle of a 7.63mm Mauser.

Behind the automatic pistol a woman with long blond hair stood, gripping the butt with both hands in a most professional manner. Butler spoke in English, whispering as his eyes swept the kitchen.

'Can I write a message on that pad?'

As he spoke he carefully laid down his Walther on top of a working surface. He had noticed the pad with a pen lying beside it. The woman, who was beautiful, nodded, still aiming the weapon. Butler tore a sheet from the pad, turned it over, placed the sheet on the cardboard back, wrote a quick message. He then held up the sheet so she could read it.

Are you alone in this place? Paula Grey is waiting at the bottom of the garden. I'm her escort.

'Thank God! I'm Jean Burgoyne.' She had lowered the gun. She looked badly shaken. 'I caught a glimpse of you through the window. A strange man with a gun. I thought de Forge had sent someone to kill me. Please ask Paula to come in. I'll make coffee. Do you take milk?' She managed a wan smile. 'Isn't it ridiculous? One moment I'm scared witless, the next I'm asking if you take milk. Do you? And sugar?'

'Black for me,' Butler replied calmly. 'And for Paula. Can I take my gun? Thanks. I'll fetch Paula . . .'

He went back outside and beckoned to Paula who came running from behind a tree trunk. He stopped her before she went inside, told her briefly what had happened. Following her into the villa, Butler inwardly felt the tension draining out of his system.

First, he'd thought maybe hidden men had forced Burgoyne to confront him. Second, he'd noticed how her finger was on the trigger: one squeeze and that would have been that. He needed the coffee.

'I'll watch the front of the villa while you two talk somewhere else,' he suggested. 'Then if anyone turns up unexpectedly we'll leave by the rear door. I'd just as soon you left it unlocked.'

'Gladly.' Jean gave him a warm smile. 'I'm so sorry I startled you. You must have had an awful shock.'

'All in a day's work . . .'

Butler left the kitchen, checked the layout of the ground floor, took up a position behind a curtain in the living room where he could watch the drive leading to the grille gates.

'. . . and I'm so glad to see you,' Jean went on as she poured coffee. 'I'm a bit jittery. We can talk in the study at the back after I've taken your escort his coffee.'

She was back very quickly and led the way to the study

which overlooked the large garden at the back. Paula sat in an armchair, noticed Jean's hand shaking as she drank her coffee. This seemed a perfect moment to tackle her host on a dangerous topic, to try and get her to talk frankly.

'Jean,' she began, 'Harry told me you thought de Forge had sent someone to kill you. Why would he do that?'

Burgoyne seemed to close in on herself. Her mood became wary. She smoothed down her long thick hair. Paula kept up the barrage gently.

'You've reached the stage where you have to talk to someone about it. I sense that you've been under strain for months. And my job is actually security.'

'National security?' Jean enquired casually.

'It can impinge on that.'

Jean smiled. 'I think I told you my uncle in Aldeburgh was in Military Intelligence . . .'

'And still has contacts with the MOD?' Paula interjected.

'I didn't quite say that, did I?' Jean studied her cup. 'But after you'd been attacked and I'd driven you back to the Brudenell, what do you think he said when I got back?'

'I couldn't even guess.'

'Uncle said that girl is something to do with Intelligence. I always know, he went on.'

'So, let's suppose he wasn't a mile away from the truth. Pure supposition on my part, of course.'

'Of course.' Jean smiled her warm smile again. 'You may have guessed I've been de Forge's mistress for more months than I care to count. Not for the pleasure of it, either.'

'And what have you discovered? That man is a bloody menace to France – to the world,' Paula said vehemently.

'He plans to make himself President of France,' Jean said, staring at the wall. 'He is secretly co-operating with

345

Dubois, the fanatic who heads the *Pour France* movement. He is plotting to create so much chaos the ordinary
women and men will see him as a saviour.'

'But exactly how will he go about it?' Paula pressed.

'I don't know whether I should tell you.' Jean hesitated, but only briefly. 'He left his dispatch case here one
day for a short time on a table in the living room. While
he had a bath I went through it – there were plans for a
military coup. Details of the units to be used, the routes
to be followed for a swoop by his Third Corps on Paris.'

'What details?'

'I memorized them at the time. After he'd gone I wrote
them down. I'd give you the notes I made but it would put
your life in danger.'

'Leave here now with me and my escort. Bring the
notes with you.'

'Where are you staying?' Jean asked.

'In Arcachon.'

'It shouldn't be too difficult for me to drive there, to
hand the notes to you. Here we are too close to the Third
Corps GHQ. It's my responsibility. Where can I get in
touch with you in Arcachon?'

Paula decided it would be useless to press her further to
hand over the notes. Jean Burgoyne was a strong-willed
woman. The exchange would have to take place in
Arcachon.

'I'll be staying at a small hotel. The Atlantique. A silly
name for such a small place, hardly more than a
pension . . .'

She looked up as Butler walked swiftly into the room,
grabbed her by the arm. Something had gone wrong. He
hustled her towards the door, speaking quickly in a low
voice to Jean.

'Trouble has arrived at the front. De Forge, I think.
And a heavy escort . . .'

'See you in Arcachon,' Paula whispered.

346

They hurried to the back of the villa, out of the door which had been left unlocked. As Paula took off like a marathon runner for the rear wall Butler paused to shut the door quietly. He then tore after Paula. When he reached the wall Paula had already shinned up the tree, dropped out of sight on the far side. Butler paused again for a second astride the wall top, glanced back at the villa. No sign of life. He dropped to the ground from the overhanging branch, ran to the Renault.

Paula was already seated in the rear, Nield had the engine running. Butler dived into the front passenger seat and Nield drove off at a moderate speed: if he rammed his foot down he'd make more noise.

General de Forge had his keys ready to open the front door of the villa. He glanced over his shoulder to where Lamy waited in his limousine and the group of armed motor-cycle riders sat astride their machines, weapons looped over their shoulders.

De Forge walked swiftly through the living room, opened the connecting door to the study. Jean Burgoyne was sitting reading a book. She looked surprised, closed the book, stood up.

'I thought you weren't coming today, Charles . . .'

'Exactly!'

As he spat the word at her he shoved her roughly back into the chair, made his way into the kitchen. He looked round, turned the handle of the rear door and it opened. Security at the villa was tight. All windows were bullet-proof. The rear door had a fish-eye spy-hole. But it also had three bolts in addition to the lock. It was seeing the bolts drawn free which had attracted his attention.

Drawing his pistol, de Forge stepped outside, stared down the full length of the garden. He saw nothing but

347

he heard something – the faint sound of a car retreating in the distance.

He rushed back inside, locked the door, ran straight to the front door. Throwing it open he ran down the steps to the limousine. Lamy was outside the vehicle instantly, stood on the gravel.

'There's a road at the back of the villa leading across country, isn't there?'

'Yes. And very much a lonely country road . . .'

'Send an outrider along that road. If he overtakes a car he's to stop it – by force if necessary. Get someone on that road now.'

He walked back inside the villa as Lamy issued instructions. Alone in the study, Jean took the Mauser from a drawer. Should she shoot the bastard now? She hadn't had time to go and lock and throw the three bolts across on the rear door. She'd heard his key rattling in the front door and he might have caught her.

When de Forge walked into the study she was sitting in the same chair, staring at him with a cold look, the book closed on her lap. She'd decided against using the gun: Paula's escort had warned her de Forge was not alone. If she killed him she'd end up dead herself. She got her verbal blow in first.

'Have you gone mad? I'm not one of your slave privates you can knock about whenever the whim takes you. This time you have gone too far.'

'No!' De Forge gripped the top of her armchair, partly to regain self-control. '*You* have gone too far. The rear door was open. Who was with you? Who ran for it when I arrived unexpectedly?'

'No one,' she said quietly, laying her book on a table as she stood to face him. 'I went into the back garden for some fresh air. Then I heard your cavalcade arriving so I came quickly back because you expect me to be waiting for you. And I'm damned if I see why I have to explain all my movements. In fact, I'm not prepared to.'

De Forge had his fury under control. His brain was ice-cold and racing. He smiled, took her in his arms, kissed her. She stood there, letting him do it, without responding. He released her from his embrace.

'You're looking more beautiful than ever,' he commented. 'The fresh air did you good. I just called in *en route* – to make sure you were all right. I'll come tomorrow – in the evening. Until then . . .'

He was careful to walk quickly across the polished wood-block floor of the hall, so she would hear he was in a hurry. His expression changed as he sat in the limousine beside Major Lamy and the vehicle began moving. His voice was harsh.

'You sent an outrider to look for that car?'

'Immediately. He will stop it, identify the occupant. He will then use his radio to call me to say who it is, still detaining the car.'

'Good. There might well be an unfortunate shooting accident. A fatal one. Back to GHQ.'

'Press your foot down, Pete,' Butler ordered. 'If they did hear our car they may send someone to follow us. I want to be off this loop road, back on the main highway before anyone catches us up. Then we have no connection with the Villa Forban.'

'Hold on, Paula,' Nield warned and rammed his foot down.

The narrow winding country road was sunk in a gully which meant they were concealed from the main road they were looping round to join. Its surface was uneven and bumpy. Paula braced herself as Nield swung the wheel to the left, to the right and the car rocked at high speed.

Nield had been a racing car buff who earlier had driven

at Brand's Hatch. Few drivers could have moved at his pace and kept the vehicle on the road. Paula watched the needle climbing on the speedometer and then decided she didn't want to know how fast they were travelling.

They were within a couple of miles of the highway when Paula glanced back. The road had straightened, was stretched ahead of them like a ruler. The rocking had stopped, the road surface had improved. Paula stared through the rear window, reached for her field-glasses inside her shoulder bag. She was now able to swivel round and aim the binoculars.

Behind them a dot had appeared, a dot which grew steadily larger. She focused on it and sucked in her breath. She patted Butler on the shoulder. He twisted round.

'Trouble?'

'I think so. There's a soldier coming up behind us like a bat out of hell. A tall aerial on his motor-cycle. What looks like an automatic weapon looped over his back.'

'You could shoot him, Harry,' Nield suggested, checking his rear-view mirror.

'No,' said Butler. 'Killing one of de Forge's men with a bullet would raise all hell. As I keep reminding you, we're in enemy territory.'

'You've got a better idea?'

'I might have . . .'

Butler explained his suggested tactic – providing they had the right situation. Paula looked back again and the rider was closer, but not close enough yet to see him clearly. Butler glanced in his wing mirror for the third time. Then he gave the order to Paula.

'Get down out of sight. Huddle on the floor as far as you can. We don't want you seen.'

'Anything you say, sir.'

Paula squeezed herself as low as she could. She curled her long legs in a most uncomfortable posture. Thank God the road surface was smooth now.

Nield kept up his speed but the rider overtook them rapidly. The road was wider – wide enough for him to speed past them, then maintain the same pace ahead of the Renault. Butler saw the camouflage jacket. As the rider had flashed past he'd seen the sinister helmet, the goggles which made the rider seem eyeless, the tall aerial quivering with the speed, the automatic weapon across his back.

The rider held on to the handlebars with one hand – not a difficult feat since this stretch of road was so very straight – and used the other gloved hand to waggle it up and down. A signal. A command. *Stop your car!*

'Keep moving,' Butler ordered Nield, 'but gradually reduce your speed.'

'I don't see any chance of carrying out your tactic,' Nield commented.

'Just keep going,' Butler replied calmly. 'We could get lucky.'

'You're an optimist,' Nield chided him.

'Positive thinking, pal.'

'Anything happening?' Paula called out.

'Yes,' said Butler. 'You're to keep your head down.'

The motor-cyclist suddenly increased speed, roared on ahead, then vanished from sight. Butler grunted with satisfaction when the rider didn't reappear in the distance. There was obviously a dip in the road. The motor-cyclist was waiting for them out of sight. He looked at Nield, who nodded, reduced speed a little more. Butler twisted round to speak to Paula.

'Go on keeping your head down. There may be a little excitement in the next minute.'

Nield drove on and without warning the road sloped to a shallow dip. A hundred yards away the motor-cyclist, his machine standing on its strut beside him, stood in the middle of the road. He held his automatic weapon in his hands. As the Renault appeared he began to raise it, prepared to aim it.

Nield reacted as Butler had suggested. He rammed down his foot, shot forward at high speed, driving point blank for the soldier who had almost aimed his weapon. When he saw the projectile hurtling towards him he hesitated, which was a mistake.

At the last moment he jumped to one side. The bumper of the Renault struck him a glancing blow. The rider hit the hard road surface like a sack of cement, lay still. The Renault also hammered into the motor-cycle, toppled it on its side. Nield braked and Paula swore inwardly, but had cushioned her head with her shoulder bag. Butler looked back. The aerial on the motor-cycle was a mangled wreck. No means of communication.

'You did a nice job, Pete,' he commented.

'Flattery will get you a long way.'

Nield drove on to join the highway, to proceed at speed towards Arcachon where Paula had an appointment with Victor Rosewater.

37

General de Forge's limousine, preceded by outriders with a second group bringing up the rear, was travelling along the lonely road half-way back to GHQ. On both sides in the distance rose low hills, some topped with clumps of trees. Major Lamy sat beside him, studying a map of Paris.

The chauffeur braked suddenly. De Forge sat up more erect and stared forward. The leading outrider lay in the road, his machine sprawled beside him, the wheels still revolving slowly. Shakily, the rider clambered to his feet.

'What the hell!' de Forge snapped. 'Can't he even keep in the saddle . . .'

The crack of splintering glass stopped him. Something shot across the interior of the car. The window next to de Forge was crazed – like the window next to Lamy where the bullet had entered.

'Down!' Lamy shouted. He grabbed de Forge, forced him below window level. 'That was a bullet. Stay down and I'll investigate . . .'

'You bloody fool,' de Forge stormed. 'Tell the chauffeur to get moving. At speed . . .'

Lamy gave the order. The chauffeur drove the limousine round the fallen machine and its rider, scattering the rest of their escort. As they moved past Lamy looked out, saw the machine lying in the road. He stared at de Forge.

'They stopped us by firing a bullet into the front tyre of the lead machine. I saw it, ripped to shreds. And it must have been a special explosive bullet to penetrate the windows.'

'The bastards can't even shoot straight.'

De Forge was quoting almost exactly the words General de Gaulle had used after the abortive attempt to assassinate him on 22 August 1962. The General was fond of using similar language to that employed by the legendary de Gaulle.

To demonstrate his iron self-control, his ability to keep in mind different problems at the same moment, he switched the topic.

'I have decided Jean Burgoyne is a spy. She must be eliminated swiftly. Contact your woman agent, Yvette, at once. Tell her to drive immediately from GHQ back up this road, to take up a concealed position near the Villa Forban. If Burgoyne leaves she is to follow her and report back where she has gone to. She'll need a civilian radio car from the Transport Section.'

As the limousine drove at speed closer to GHQ, accompanied by several outriders who had caught up with them, Lamy picked up his mobile phone. He got hold of Yvette in her room immediately, repeated de Forge's instructions.

'I will leave at once, sir,' Yvette reported back.

Lamy put down the phone. He glanced at the bullet holes in the windows. Certainly a very special bullet must have been used to pierce the glass. And the bullet had passed within inches of de Forge's head. Yet the General appeared to have his mind on other things. He issued a fresh order.

'Lamy, just before I left I had a call from *Oiseau* in Britain. He told me his trusted confidant, Brand, had encountered a Paula Grey in Arcachon. She also sounds to be a spy. So Kalmar now has two targets. Inform him to act urgently . . .'

In Paris Tweed was talking from his temporary office on the phone to Pierre Loriot of Interpol, based in the same city. Loriot was replying to the question he had been asked.

'Tweed, I am afraid I have no concrete information on the assassin, Kalmar. Only unconfirmed rumours. That he has operated in Bucharest, Warsaw, and Berlin. That he comes from the East, whatever that means.'

'I'd like one solid fact,' Tweed insisted. 'Method of killing, any knowledge of explosives, a hint about what he looks like, his age. So far he's a ghost.'

'I was coming to two of those points. Only rumours, but fresh ones. That his favourite method of assassination is strangulation. That he has an expert knowledge of explosives.'

'I said one solid fact,' Tweed repeated.

'We're still searching for just that. I'll be in touch,' concluded Loriot.

Tweed was putting down the phone when Otto Kuhlmann came into the office with a bouncy tread. He waved
his cigar.

'What are you concentrating on now?'

'What about yourself?' countered Tweed.

'We're turning Germany upside down tracking *Siegfried* – and we may be getting results. The pressure is so
great their cells are beginning to move around to safer
houses. We missed one gang of three men and a woman
by one hour. In Düsseldorf. They left behind a large
cache of guns, explosives. And fingerprints. This time
they hadn't time to clean up the place.'

'And you've sent these fingerprints to Interpol?'

'Of course.' Kuhlmann made an impatient gesture. 'Do
you think it significant that Interpol, after checking its
records, reported they couldn't link them on their computers with any known terrorists?'

'Highly significant,' Tweed replied with satisfaction,
certain that it confirmed a theory he held.

'And what are you concentrating on?' Kuhlmann
repeated.

'The identity of Kalmar. I'm waiting for a few more
pieces of the jigsaw I'm building up – you might call it an
identikit of Kalmar. There's something very odd about
that killer.'

The private phone began ringing almost as soon as de
Forge had sat behind his desk in his office at GHQ. Lamy
had gone to his own quarters to arrange arm's-length
contact with Kalmar: to phone the girl who would give
him a public call box to go to.

Placing his képi carefully on his desk so the peak faced
him, de Forge picked up the receiver. Maybe Lamy was
calling to say he was on his way, driving to another
remote public phone.

'Yes? What is it?'

'The bullet which penetrated your limousine was aimed to miss you by five centimetres precisely. Which it did. Next time it will go through the side of your skull.'

'Who the blazes is this?'

'You know perfectly well. *Manteau.* You owe me two million Swiss francs. Arrange for Lamy to make the payment. I will call Lamy at his private number five minutes from now.'

'How do I know you . . .'

'You can read the papers. I presume you can read?'

'You dare to insult me?' de Forge said in a clipped tone.

'I dare to kill you if I am not paid. Others have paid. Except one. He paid too – with his life.'

'I am heavily guarded,' de Forge continued in his icy tone.

'You were this afternoon. And travelling in a bullet-proof limousine. That didn't save you. I know all your movements. If there is another job you require executing, let me know. Through Lamy. But only after you have paid up. In Swiss franc banknotes. As I said before, with the numbers out of sequence . . .'

'I must consider your proposition . . .'

De Forge realized he was talking into space. The Frenchman at the other end had broken the connection. De Forge sat quite still, then dialled Lamy's number.

'Come to my office immediately.'

'But General, I have to leave *immediately*. I have made contact.'

'My office. *Immediately.*'

De Forge slammed down the phone. It gave him brief satisfaction to do to his subordinate what *Manteau* had done to him. He aligned his notepad with the edge of his desk, his face grim. Lamy came in without knocking on the door, out of breath, and his chief ignored this breach of etiquette. He was working out how to conceal that he was in a totally irresolute mood.

'Is there an emergency, General?' asked Lamy.

'Sit down. Keep still. Concentrate while I talk. Do not interrupt . . .'

Tersely de Forge outlined the conversation he had just had with *Manteau*. As he spoke he watched his chief of Intelligence closely. There were beads of sweat on Lamy's high forehead. It could, of course, be the result of his rushing to reach his master's office.

'So that is the situation,' de Forge concluded. 'And he made a reference to reading the papers. I assume that *you* are keeping up to date with developments – that you read the newspapers?'

He took hold of a tidy stack of piled newspapers. *Liberation*, *Figaro*, *Le Monde*. He threw them across his desk into his subordinate's lap.

'Read!'

The headline in large type jumped at Lamy. He had read them but it seemed discreet to do what he was told. He arranged the headlines one under each other.

'MANTEAU' KILLED PRESIDENT, PRIME MINISTER

'MANTEAU' ASSASSINATED PARIS PREFECT

'MANTEAU' MURDERS TOP STATESMEN

'*Manteau!*' de Forge burst out. 'Nothing but this *Manteau*. So why are we paying Kalmar? Is he subcontracting the jobs to *Manteau*?'

'I doubt that very much,' Lamy ventured.

'Oh, you do! And not an hour ago *Manteau* carried out his threat. That bullet passed within centimetres of my head. And,' he continued sarcastically, 'in case you hadn't realized it, his attack was brilliantly organized. First he shoots the front tyre of the lead outrider to stop my car. He didn't shoot the outrider – although I'm damned sure he could have done just that. And *Manteau*

357

is calling you on your private number in your office in five minutes. God knows how he obtains these numbers. But you'd better be in your office when *Manteau* calls.'

'What are your instructions, General?'

Lamy had stood up quickly. De Forge threw up his hands and looked at the ceiling, as though asking the Almighty for sympathy in coping with the idiots he was surrounded with.

'You pay him, of course. Two million Swiss francs. And make sure the numbers are not in sequence.'

'But I have to go to a phone box in the wilds to take the call from Kalmar. What do I say to him?'

'Can't you work that out?' de Forge grinned sardonically. 'I always have to plan everything. You give Kalmar the two targets. Jean Burgoyne and Paula Grey in Arcachon. When he asks for payment, tell him we're expecting huge new funds shortly. Which is true.'

'And *Manteau*? I just pay him, whatever way he wants?'

'You do that.' De Forge grinned again. 'And you give the new targets. Jean Burgoyne and Paula Grey. Let's see who does the jobs for us, who earns the money. Time you rushed back to your office . . .'

Alone, de Forge walked round his office, hands clasped behind his back. He was pleased with his devious ploy. Which of the assassins would succeed? It was clean-up time, the elimination of all spies before he made his bid. For the Presidency of France.

In Paris at the Ministry of Defence Tweed had also been reading the newspaper headlines and the text beneath them. He looked up as René Lasalle came into his office.

'Has Navarre decided where to concentrate his forces?' Tweed asked. 'In the north, here round Paris – or in the south close to de Forge's GHQ?'

'He is still waiting before he decides. He expects some new development which will point the way. He has heard that Josette, de Forge's wife, has arrived in Paris and is holding what she calls "salons" – afternoon parties at the de Forges' apartment in Passy. A lot of influential people attend these salons, including the press. She seems to be preparing the ground for her husband's arrival in Paris.'

'I see.' Tweed looked out of the window. The sky was still a leaden blanket. 'René, could you give me the address of the Passy apartment?'

Lasalle tore a sheet off Tweed's notepad, wrote an address in his neat script. Folding the sheet, he handed it to Tweed.

'What are you up to now?'

'Time I went back into the field, saw for myself. This place is fraught with tension. It's becoming positively claustrophobic.'

'I have one more piece of information,' Lasalle continued. 'There is the foreign member of the notorious *Cercle Noir* who goes under the code name *Oiseau*. He is attending these conspiratorial meetings much more frequently.'

'How on earth do you obtain such information?'

'That's top secret. I have informants.'

'In the plural?' Tweed queried.

'You heard correctly. One bit of advice. If you do go to Passy, take care . . .'

By himself again, Tweed wrote the word *Oiseau* on his notepad. He added the English translation. Bird. Then he drew a vulture. It was all adding up. But who could be Lasalle's informants?

Yvette Mourlon, Lamy's woman agent, had received her orders from her chief. She was sitting in the battered Peugeot she had driven from Third Corps GHQ and was now in position to watch the Villa Forban. She had driven the vehicle with a souped-up engine into a field where she could see the grille gates but couldn't herself be seen.

Yvette was a plain-looking girl with sallow skin and poor legs. In addition she had a cruel mouth. Her loyalty to General de Forge was carried to the point of devotion. The General cleverly gave her small gifts from time to time, a compliment she'd never received from any other man. He was careful to keep her at a distance but her dedication to him was complete.

Her Peugeot had also been equipped with a high-powered transmitter which enabled her to communicate with Third Corps GHQ from long distances. Her great advantage was she was a girl no one ever looked at twice. She wore a crumpled raincoat and a pair of old, worn gloves.

She leaned forward as she saw the gates opening. Even from a distance she recognized the driver of the Rover as the car drove away to the north. Jean Burgoyne's long blond hair was unmistakable. Yvette waited, then turned on the ignition, drove out of the field and followed the Rover.

Jean Burgoyne had not been fooled by de Forge's apparent change of mood just before he left the villa. She had seen through his pretended amiability, and realized he no longer trusted her an inch.

She had always known this day would come – the day to run for her life. Packing quickly, she slipped the notes she'd made of Operation Marengo – after skip-reading the papers in de Forge's dispatch case – in a polythene bag. Using adhesive tape, she attached the bag to her body under her panties.

She had taken with her only the minimum selection of everyday clothes. Without a qualm she had left behind the mink cape, the silk underclothes de Forge had given her: she wanted to wear nothing which reminded her of their relationship. But she did slip the Mauser pistol into her handbag.

The devious country route to Arcachon was deserted as she drove through the late afternoon. She would go to the Atlantique Hotel in Arcachon, book a room, contact Paula. If Paula wasn't available soon she'd contact Paris.

The man known as Kalmar sat in his hotel room studying a photograph of Jean Burgoyne. He had no doubt the opportunity would soon present itself when he would strangle her.

He hadn't a photo of Paula Grey, but he didn't need one. After all, he'd met her. He didn't often get an assignment to eliminate two targets. He was rather looking forward to the double killing.

Lamy's instructions over the phone had been precise and simple. The odd thing was Lamy had given him no idea of the location of either target. That was most unusual. Sometimes Kalmar wondered about Major Jules Lamy. His pay as Chief of Intelligence would hardly amount to a fortune. And he was the only other man – apart from de Forge presumably – who knew the targets. Which might explain some strange events which had occurred.

Putting the photo back into an envelope, he tucked it inside his pocket. This looked like very easy money. The thought that the fee paid involved the murder of two women never crossed his mind.

Newman had slept for twenty-four hours in his bedroom at the Atlantique Hotel in Arcachon. Driving north from the Landes non-stop to Arcachon with Moshe Stein, he had arrived exhausted in the late afternoon.

And, like himself, Moshe had been flaked out, all reserves of energy used up. Both men had retired to their rooms. Newman had wanted to phone Tweed but when he lay on the bed after a quick wash he fell fast asleep.

It was a troubled sleep, crucified by nightmares. Firing squads on a lonely beach backed by the sand dunes with the forests of the Landes behind them. Stretcher parties carrying the dead victim up over the dunes into the forest, dumping a body whose face looked like his own into a hole in the ground. An old woman watching, cackling with obscene delight at the spectacle. A man wearing a Ku-Klux-Klan mask bending over him. The man removing the mask to reveal the grinning face of Major Lamy.

Eventually Newman woke, feeling his head was stuffed with cotton-wool. He forced himself out of bed, checked the time. It was almost dusk outside. Stripping to the waist, he sluiced himself with cold water, dried off. His brain was beginning to function.

He was shivering from the cold. The heating in the hotel was meagre. He threw on a few fresh clothes, the first ones he came to when throwing back the lid of his case.

Sitting on the edge of the bed, he dialled the special number at the Ministry of the Interior from memory. He had to be very forceful to get put through to someone in high authority, who turned out to be Lasalle.

'Need to speak urgently to Tweed.'

'I'm afraid he is not in the building just at the moment, Mr Newman. Can I help?'

'Only Tweed can. Thanks. Call you back,' Newman mumbled and put down the phone.

Only Tweed could be trusted with the information he had gathered. He went along the corridor to Moshe's room, knocked on the door. He had to knock several times before the door was opened on a chain. Moshe's bleary-eyed, unshaven face peered at him.

'Oh, it's you. Sorry, I was asleep.'

Moshe put the chain back on the door when Newman had entered. He ran a hand through his tousled hair.

'I feel as though the Eiffel Tower fell on me. What do we do now? I still think you should leave me here. Go north. Take the car. No reason why you should risk your life any more.'

'I'm sticking with you until you're safe in Paris. Meanwhile, I may have to go out. You have money? Good. Bribe the people here to send a decent meal to your room. Stay here until I knock on the door like this.'

Newman rapped his knuckles with a certain tattoo on the dressing table. Going back to his room, he had a quick shave, tidied himself up, put on a warm coat. It would be pretty raw outside.

First he'd enquire whether Paula was in the hotel. Accommodation in Arcachon was fairly limited in winter. He found she was registered but was out. That would give him time to visit Isabelle. Maybe she had seen someone floating round Arcachon, someone he ought to know about.

38

'I'm sorry I'm so late, Victor. I never expected you would wait.'

Rosewater grinned as Paula hurried up to him in the bar restaurant she'd earlier called a 'café'. Clad in a black leather jacket and heavy navy trousers with a razor-sharp crease, he gave her a bear hug, asked her what she would like to drink as they sat at a table.

'Vermouth, please.'

'Are you hungry?' he enquired.

'Ravenous. Haven't eaten for hours.'

'There's the menu. What do you fancy?'

'Don't need to look. A huge mushroom omelette with lots of fried potatoes. Damn watching my figure this evening.'

'I'll take pleasure watching it instead,' he assured her and summoned a waiter.

The restaurant was only half full. Butler wandered in as though on his own. He chose a small table by a window. Paula had said it was unnecessary for her two escorts to come, that she'd return to the Atlantique as soon as she'd finished her meal with Rosewater.

'You can go in on your own,' Butler had told her. 'Then I'll follow, merge with the wallpaper. But we're staying with you all the time. Tweed's strict orders.'

Outside Nield sat in the parked Renault where Butler could see him through the window. Nield was surveying his surroundings. What attracted his attention was a red Porsche, parked twenty yards or so further along the road.

Parked in the shadows, away from the nearest street lamp, it was difficult to tell whether there was anyone in the driver's seat. Nield slipped his Walther out of its holster and laid it on his lap. The Porsche bothered him.

Inside, Paula was sipping her vermouth, studying Rosewater. Even late in the day he looked as fresh as paint with his strong jaw, his handsome face, and pleasant smile. Paula liked men who smiled a lot.

'Tell me what you've been up to,' Rosewater invited.

'Oh, just visiting an old friend.'

'Man or woman?'

'Now you're prying.'

364

'I'm jealous . . .'

His gaze swivelled as a tall elegant Frenchwoman entered the restaurant. A waiter relieved her of her coat. She made a performance of the action. Slipping her arms out of the sleeves slowly, she raised her hands to smooth down her long sleek hair. The movement emphasized her well-built slim figure. Dressed in black, her breasts protruded against the tight dress. She was looking directly at Rosewater and gave a slow smile.

Paula followed Rosewater's fixed gaze. Across the room Butler chose the same moment to turn round, taking his time to lift a salt cellar from the empty table behind him. His eyes swiftly scanned the new arrival.

The waiter led her to a table by a window next to where Butler sat. He put down the salt cellar, which he had no intention of using.

'That woman . . .' Rosewater switched his gaze back to Paula. 'She's attractive so it's odd she's alone. She is just the sort of woman who could be one of de Forge's army of spies.'

'Let's forget her, enjoy our evening,' Paula suggested.

'So was it a man or a woman? I am jealous,' Rosewater repeated.

'You've increased my appetite no end. And what, may I ask, have you been occupying yourself with?'

'Driving all round the countryside, stopped at roadblocks, showing my papers. Not my real ones.'

'Roadblocks?' Paula was puzzled.

'Soldiers of the Third Army . . .'

'You mean the Third Corps.'

'No. I questioned that. They clearly said the Third Army. They seemed to be searching for someone. I tried to get them to talk but all they'd say was they were on military manoeuvres. Then they shut up like clams. You'd think it was a state of martial law.'

'Rather disturbing,' Paula probed.

365

'It's not going to disturb our meal . . .'

An hour later Paula felt her stomach. She had pigged it, but felt much better for the experience. Glancing at her watch, she grimaced.

'I'm afraid I must go now, Victor. Thank you for a wonderful evening. I've enjoyed every moment.'

'Hold on,' Rosewater protested. 'I thought we'd go for a drive. I know a club which will still be open. We could have a nightcap, maybe even a dance.'

'Sorry. I'd love to. But I'm tired. Give me a number where I can get in touch with you.'

Rosewater took out a notebook, scribbled a number. Handing over the sheet he'd torn out he put the same question to her.

'Where can I contact you?'

'You can't.' She smiled. 'I move around. My job.'

'Mysterious lady . . .'

The waiter brought her coat. Rosewater helped her on with it. His hand squeezed her shoulder affectionately. As they walked to the door Butler, who had paid his bill, strolled after them. He caught them up as they stood outside. Paula introduced him to Rosewater.

'This is my cousin, Harry.'

'Saw you in the restaurant,' Rosewater commented as they shook hands. 'You should have joined us,' he added without enthusiasm.

'I'm no gooseberry.' Butler's expression was blank.

'We're walking,' Paula explained. 'Where is your car?'

'Parked round the corner in a cul-de-sac off the front,' Rosewater replied. 'Let's keep in touch. Good night.'

He walked off towards the front. Butler touched Paula's elbow and she stayed where she was until Rosewater had disappeared round a corner. Then they walked to where Nield still sat patiently in the Renault. Paula thought of him sitting in the car while she had eaten a prince of meals. She dived into the back.

366

'Pete, when did you last eat?'

'Half an hour ago.' Nield twisted round, grinned at her, holding up something. 'Sandwiches from a cool bag. I always travel with rations. Plus a flask of coffee.'

'Get moving,' said Harry as he sat beside Nield. 'Back to the Atlantique. Drive slowly.'

'Not yet. Before we go I want to investigate that Porsche. It's been sitting there ever since we arrived. Back in a minute.'

He was out of the car before Butler could reply. Paula saw Nield was carrying his Walther in his right hand held down close to his side. Nield walked along the pavement on the opposite side of the road to where the Porsche stood like a tiger crouched to spring.

He strolled along like a local on his way home, collar turned up against the bitter night. No one else was in sight. His rubber-soled shoes made no sound as he came close to the car shrouded in the unnerving shadows.

With his left hand he pulled his collar tighter round his neck as he glanced across at the stationary vehicle. Paula felt moisture exuding from her palms as she saw Nield casually cross the road at a diagonal angle so he could see the driver's seat from the rear. Paula tensed herself for the sound of gunshots.

He circled the car from the rear, walked in front of it and back down the street. Climbing in behind the wheel of the Renault, he holstered his Walther.

'False alarm. No one there. So back to the Atlantique.'

'And drive slowly,' Butler repeated as they started to move.

'You said that before.'

'I'm hoping Jean Burgoyne will phone me,' Paula remarked. 'The sooner she gets away from that villa the better.'

'She'll have to look after herself,' Butler replied.

Nield stopped suddenly, swore, said he'd dropped his

367

wallet. He left the engine running, hurried back the way they had come. He returned fairly quickly, saying he'd been lucky as he stuffed his wallet into his pocket. Paula thought his behaviour odd: Pete never lost anything. They cruised the streets of Arcachon on their way back to the Atlantique. Mostly the streets were deserted: the late hour, the sub-zero temperature, the time of year – November about to run into December. They turned a corner and Paula called out.

'Crawl, Pete.'

Ahead of them a man walked on the pavement on their side. Despite his heavy overcoat, his astrakhan hat, Paula recognized his way of holding himself, of walking with a deliberate tread like a man pacing out a specific distance.

'That's Lieutenant Berthier again.'

'Sure?' asked Butler.

'Certain. I should know. I spent time with him during my visit to Aldeburgh when he was posing as James Sanders.'

'Move just a bit faster, Pete,' Butler advised. 'He'll be suspicious if we crawl past him.'

Paula glanced quickly out of the window just before they came alongside Berthier, then ducked out of sight. Yes, it was definitely de Forge's man. They were approaching the Atlantique when Butler made his comment.

'It's a bit odd. Berthier prowling round the town. And we encountered polite Mr Brand, also in Arcachon. You would think something was about to happen in this neck of the woods.'

'Don't!' Paula protested. 'I'm worried about Jean Burgoyne. She could have called while I was out.'

'Soon know that,' Butler replied.

Yvette Mourlon, de Forge's agent, had followed the Rover driven by Jean Burgoyne without her quarry suspecting she had been followed. Yvette's beat-up Peugeot looked like so many other French cars involved in a collision.

Arriving at the Atlantique after dark, Jean went up to the desk clerk. She phrased her enquiry carefully.

'My friend, Paula Grey, said she was staying at a hotel in Arcachon. I hope I've got the right place.'

She rested on the counter her hand holding two bank-notes. The clerk's hand straightened up the register and with the same movement he relieved her of the money.

'You've come to the right hotel. She's here.'

'Great! Could you give me her room number?'

'Wouldn't do you any good. She's out.'

'Have you any idea when she's expected back?' Jean pressed.

'None at all. She doesn't tell me her movements.' He hesitated, leaned over the counter. 'I had the impression she was going out for the evening. Had a man with her.'

'Thank you. Do you mind if I wait?' She glanced round the gloomy lobby. 'On that banquette over there?'

'Please yourself . . .'

The leather banquette had a slit in it and stuffing pro-truded. Not exactly the Ritz, Jean thought, as she settled down to wait. She sat there for quite a long time and then began to get nervous. De Forge might have returned to the villa. In which case men would already be out looking for her. She felt very visible.

Opening her bag, she extracted a well-worn local map and studied it. The trouble was she was going to have to leave it with the night clerk who was the nosy type – so she'd little doubt he'd find a way of opening a sealed envelope. The solution occurred to her and she marked three different locations on the map with crosses. Then she inserted a number inside a circle above each cross. One. Two. Three. She scribbled a note, put map and note in one of the large envelopes she always carried, wrote Paula Grey's name on it.

Taking it to the night clerk who sat reading a newspaper,

she handed the envelope to him with two more banknotes.

'I have to go out. Could you please give this to Paula Grey as soon as she returns? And I expect you'll have a room for me at this time of the year?'

'Name?'

'Lisa Mason. No. I'm in a rush. I'll fill in the register when I get back . . .'

Earlier Yvette Mourlon had watched Burgoyne enter the Atlantique. She waited for a few minutes to see if she was coming out again. Convinced she was staying for the night, she drove a short distance further down the street, parking in the shadow of a high wall. She elevated her aerial and turned her transmitter to the right point on the waveband. She gave her codename when she had made contact and began talking.

'Yvette here. Subject at Hotel Atlantique in Arcachon at moment. Appears to be there for the night. Any orders?'

'Yes, Yvette. Keep subject's hotel under surveillance. Report immediately any fresh movement of subject. Follow if necessary. Repeat – immediately.'

'Understood . . .'

Yvette slammed the microphone back inside the concealed compartment. Arrogant bitch! And she found it strange that this uppity cow of a girl took certain messages – that Major Lamy, whom she normally spoke to, was absent sometimes. Always when someone died later.

Lieutenant Berthier was walking along a side street close to the front when his mobile phone beeped. He stepped inside the alcove of a doorway, pulled out the phone from under his coat, answered, listened.

He received exactly the same message which had been transmitted to Yvette except for the reference to continue surveillance. He was also told to phone back at fifteen-minute intervals.

Berthier closed down his aerial and began hurrying to the front where he'd left his means of transport.

Brand made the phone call from a cubicle in a corner of the bar. He listened, replied briefly, replaced the receiver. Leaving the money for his drink on the counter he hurried to where he'd parked his car.

39

Paula took the envelope handed to her by the night clerk at the Atlantique. She was hurrying upstairs with Nield and Butler when the clerk called after her. His expression said worlds: all three together in one room?

'A man called to ask if you were in.'

'Leave a name?'

'Just puts down the phone on me when I say no.'

Inside her room Paula examined the envelope with Butler while Nield peered out between the curtains.

'This has been opened,' Paula decided. 'Then it has been crudely stuck down again.'

'Old Nosy behind the counter,' Butler remarked.

She opened up the envelope, took out the folded map and the note. The message was short. *A courier will come tonight with a number giving my location. 22.00 hours.*

'Jean is being very security-minded. I don't like this.'

She spread the map open on the only table in the cramped room. Number One was inscribed above a cross with 'Villa Rose' written in. Number Two had an inscription, 'Crossroads'. Number Three was inscribed 'Boathouse'. She gave the map to Butler, checked her watch, 9.45 p.m.

'Harry, you be navigator when the courier arrives with the rendezvous. I wish to God he'd hurry up. There isn't much time. The precautions she's taken – I wish I'd been here when she called in.'

'Let's just relax and see what happens,' Butler reassured her. 'From what I saw and heard at the Villa Forban she's a resourceful woman.'

'I'll go downstairs and wait for this courier,' Nield said and left the room.

He was back within a minute, his manner urgent as he rushed into the room when Butler opened the door. Nield took hold of Paula's arm.

'He insists on handing it to you. Be quick. That clerk is kicking up about him being inside the hotel . . .'

Paula ran downstairs, closely followed by Nield as Butler leaned over the banister, his Walther held behind his back. A scruffy-looking man with a day's beard on his chin was glaring at the clerk. He turned, moved towards Paula, handed her an envelope.

'I was given your description,' he said in Provençal French. 'I had to give it to you personally. No other person.'

'Thank you. Can I give you something?'

'I've been well paid.'

The down-and-out tipped his soiled hat to Paula, glared again at the clerk, left the hotel. In her room Paula ripped open the envelope. A sheet of folded paper in the same handwriting as the previous note carried the terse message. *Number Three.*

'It's the boathouse,' Paula said. 'Between Gujan and

Facture. Guide me, Harry,' she said as she was leaving the room.

'I'll drive,' Nield offered as they ran down the stairs.

'No, damnit! I'll drive,' Paula snapped as they reached the street. 'I don't like any of this one little bit.'

Jean Burgoyne stood on the verandah of the boathouse smoking a cigarette. She rarely smoked but her nerves were stretched to breaking point. She shielded the light of the cigarette with her left hand. Huddled in a sheepskin coat, she had found the interior claustrophobic. The only sound was the lapping of the water against the piles. At the end of the verandah was a creek, the shell of a small craft lying in the stagnant water.

The boathouse was perched close to the edge of the *bassin*. Abandoned, at one time a slipway had led across marshland to the water. Now only the outer struts of the slipway were left and all around was an air of decay.

The verandah had wooden steps leading up to it at either end. One flight from firm ground where Jean had mounted the verandah; the other at the far end leading down to the lonely creek. She had parked her Rover in a shallow bowl by the side of the wide track leading off the road to the boathouse. The quiet lapping of the water in the middle of the boathouse, where an inlet from the *bassin* reached it, would normally have been a soothing sound. At night, in this remote sport, it was getting on her nerves.

She had chosen this rendezvous because it was well away from any other habitation. She felt convinced that de Forge would have discovered her absence, that she was in danger. She was determined to hand to Paula the notes of Operation Marengo attached to her upper leg. It was an outrageous plan, a plot for a coup. It was vital the details reached Paris.

She heard a creak. Like a footstep on old wood. Flattening herself against the wall of the verandah, she held her cigarette cupped in the palm of her hand, listened, stared at the steps from firm ground. There was no repetition of the sound. She let out a sigh, straightened up. Old wood creaked by itself.

She had thought of waiting at the Atlantique, hoping Paula would appear at any moment. But she hadn't liked the way the leering night clerk had kept glancing at her surreptitiously. If she could bribe him so could anyone. And any search would start with the few hotels open in Arcachon. It had seemed safer to wait at an out of the way refuge.

She dropped her cigarette over the railing into the water. It fizzled, went out. She wasn't risking stubbing it out on the ancient planks beneath her feet. The last thing she wanted was for the place to go up in flames. Then she heard two other faint sounds. The noise of car engines. Probably passing on the main road. But the sounds stopped. Had she heard *two* cars? She wasn't sure: sound travelled a long distance at night. She shivered. It was horribly cold. But she was honest with herself: she had shivered with fear.

The strain of spending months at the Villa Forban had at last taken its toll. The strain of ministering to the needs of de Forge, of coaxing him into saying too much, of sending back secret reports to Paris. While it was going on the adrenalin had kept her cool and calculating. Now she'd left it behind she was suffering a reaction. God, she'd be glad to get back to Aldeburgh, to Admiralty House, to the peace and quiet of her uncle's home and his intelligent conversation – conversation she could listen to without memorizing every word.

The wood creaked again. She stiffened. The sound had been different, the creak stronger – as though under pressure from the tread of someone heavy. With her back against the wall she slithered towards the steps leading down to the creek. Then remained motionless. The slurp of the water reminded her of the movement of a shark. Absurd! Get a hold on yourself, girl. Then she saw the enormous shadow appearing above the steps from firm ground. The silhouette of a large figure. She couldn't see the face. That horrified her.

This was for real. The planks creaked ominously as the figure advanced towards her. Jean ran in the opposite direction. She reached the steps leading down to the creek. She hurried down them and heard the squelch of other feet in the soggy ground close behind her. She swung round, suddenly remembered the Mauser she'd tucked in her coat pocket. She grabbed at the butt, hauled out the weapon. She was terrified.

Her night vision was good. She saw why she hadn't seen a face. The man wore a Balaclava helmet. One large hand grasped her wrist, twisted it, nearly broke it and she dropped the Mauser. Two hands fastened themselves round her throat, two gloved hands, the thumbs pressing expertly against her windpipe. She stumbled back into the old boat and his weight pressed on top of her. Not for a second was the remorseless squeeze on her throat relaxed. Jean Burgoyne's last view of this world was the Balaclava helmet, the cold eyes staring down at her through the slits. The vision began blurring, then faded for ever.

The killer stood up, breathing heavily. He crouched to search her and heard the sound of approaching cars. He jumped up, made his way, crouched low, across the marsh, his rubber boots sinking into the mush. Later he reached the car he had parked some distance from the boathouse where an eerie silence had descended.

Yvette Mourlon had followed Jean Burgoyne when she'd left the Atlantique. When she saw her quarry making for the boathouse she'd elevated her aerial, reported the location. Then she had remained parked a good way off from the boathouse which, she suspected, was a killing ground.

Yvette had a crush on de Forge. What might occur inside the boathouse to the rich well-dressed woman concerned her not at all. Yvette loved only one thing more than de Forge. Money.

40

'There's the boathouse. Pray to God we're in time.'

Paula spoke as she drove like hell along the road with her headlights undimmed. There was no other traffic at this hour, so what the devil did it matter. She had the bit between her teeth and, beside her, Butler was careful not to speak.

'Bleak-looking bloody spot,' Nield commented in the back.

Paula slowed, searching for the track leading off to the left. Her headlights picked it up and she swung on to the track, headlights blazing. A signal to Jean that she was coming, that help was very close and she wouldn't be alone much longer.

Jamming on the brakes in the lee of the boathouse, she reached for the handle of the door. Butler's restraining hand gripped her arm.

'Better leave me to go first . . .'

'Get your bloody hand off me! I'm in a hurry.'

Wrenching the door open, she jumped out, unzipping her shoulder bag, extracting her Browning .32. Her other hand hauled out a torch from her coat pocket. As she climbed the steps Butler was close behind her, Walther in his hand.

Paula slowed down when she arrived on the verandah, swivelling her torch beam. She tried the door into the boathouse half-way along the verandah, flashed the beam over an ancient yacht, its hull falling to pieces. Was Jean unsure who had arrived?

'Paula here. Jean, it's Paula with friends. Are you in there?'

Only when there was no answering reply did she proceed further along the verandah, aiming the beam ahead in case one of the planks was rotted. She didn't want to fall through, ending up in the lapping water. She arrived at the end of the verandah where another flight of steps led down.

Nield had stayed with the car. He heard another vehicle approaching, slipped out of the vehicle on the side furthest away from the road. He crouched low as headlights illuminated his car, gripped the Walther more firmly.

Paula's flashlight had also shown up smudged footprints of mud, large footprints, too large for Jean. She paused at the top of the steps, again aiming the beam. It stopped moving suddenly. She froze. Close behind her Butler whispered.

'What is it?'

'Oh, my God! Not again! Please! Not again . . .'

She ran down the steps and over the short stretch of the marsh. Stopping afresh, she held the torch steady with sheer will-power. The body sprawled on its back inside the wreck of a craft. The blond hair splayed over the stern. The creek with its oily surface, the ooze. It was Aldeburgh all over again. She gritted her teeth as Butler pushed past her, leant over the corpse, using his own flashlight.

'Stay where you are, Paula.'

She nearly jumped out of her skin as a hand grasped her arm. It was Newman's voice. She turned to face him, the

377

last person she'd expected to meet during this horrific experience.

'Bob. Thank heaven. She's dead, isn't she?'

Even as she spoke she heard herself and thought it was a stupid question. The ugly bruisings and swellings on Jean Burgoyne's neck had been only too apparent in the beam of her torch. She turned to follow Butler and Newman stopped her.

'Wait here. Don't move an inch.'

'She was going to give me some valuable papers.'

'I told you not to move one inch. Pete is back-up at the other end of the verandah.'

Newman joined Butler, treading over the spongy grass. He bent alongside the other man. It was an ugly spectacle. Burgoyne's eyes were starting out of her head. Her throat was a brutalized mess. Mangled. But her mane of blond hair was still beautiful. Pathetic was the word which occurred to Newman.

The bottom of her sheepskin had been ripped open, a button torn away. Gently he lifted the coat higher, exposing her skirt, which had also been thrust up in her struggle for life. Something was protruding below her panties. Delicately he lifted the panties higher up her long slim leg. A polythene envelope was attached to her body with sticking plaster. You're not supposed to fiddle around with a murder victim, he thought. He pulled at the tape, released the polythene envelope, pulled down her panties.

'I think the killer heard us coming,' he called up as he approached Paula, his tone matter-of-fact. 'So he failed in his search. She may not have died in vain.'

Putting his arm round her, he led her back along the verandah. She walked like a zombie, remembered she was still holding the Browning. She slipped it back inside her shoulder bag. He kept his arm round her as she descended the steps, walked back to the car. Beyond, Newman's own Renault was parked.

'I'm all right,' she said as they reached the car.

'You're damn well not.'

'No, I'm not! Oh, Bob, it was just like Karin at Alde-burgh. She was found strangled. She was left like some unwanted child's doll in an old boat. It's exactly the same nightmare all over again. If ever we find out who did these things I'll shoot him myself. I'll empty my whole bloody gun into his guts . . .'

Then, as Newman was hoping, she broke. Sobbing, she buried her head against his chest. He clasped his arms round her, hugged her to him, stroked the back of her neck, her hair. Gradually the shuddering left her body. Butler and Nield had tactfully stayed at a distance, both with guns in their hands, both surveying their surround-ings. Paula tugged the handkerchief out of her shoulder bag, dried her eyes, looked up at Newman.

'I don't care what her relationship with de Forge was – she was a good woman. I was beginning to like her very much. I suspect she was very brave, that she had been spying on that swine.'

'You could be right.' Newman held up the envelope. 'We can look at this when we are well away from here. There could be reinforcements. And we don't want the locals in on this.'

'Legally, I suppose . . .'

'Damn the law. De Forge is the law here. This is a job for Lasalle. I'm phoning him from the hotel. And I'm getting you well clear of this area.'

Paula had recovered, was standing away from him, tidying up her coat. She shook her head.

'I'm not leaving here until Tweed orders me out. I came to do a job. Jean's dead, but I'm alive.'

'I'd like to keep it that way,' Newman told her and led her to his Renault.

∗   ∗   ∗

'How on earth did you happen to turn up when you did?' Paula asked.

They were driving back to Arcachon with Butler and Nield in the other car close behind. Newman was moving fast as he explained.

'When Moshe and I arrived from the Landes we flopped out in the Atlantique for twenty-four hours. You were out when I surfaced. I decided to visit Isabelle, which I did. I was just arriving back at the Atlantique when I saw you diving into a car and driving off like a bat out of hell. I decided to follow to see what was up.'

'You saw. I hate leaving Jean like that. Seems awful.'

'So what was the alternative? We take the body away and then what? Inform the local gendarmes and we're up to our neck in trouble. Worse still, we could be immobilized. You think Tweed would like that – just when France is exploding? Now there have been anti-American and anti-Arab riots in Marseilles. It's spreading.'

'How do you know that?'

'Isabelle has been listening to the radio, watching TV. She said there have been a lot of casualties. And our old friends, the Balaclava mob egging things on.'

'You mentioned the Landes. How did you get on there?'

'Talk about that later,' Newman said grimly. 'Now I just hope we can reach Tweed and Lasalle. De Forge's world is closing in on us.'

In Paris, Tweed had experienced a disturbing evening. The courier Monica had sent with his forged press card had arrived. Lasalle had told him Josette de Forge was holding one of her 'salons' starting at eight o'clock.

Arriving by cab in Passy, Tweed had told the driver to drop him a few doors from the address he was making for.

As he walked up to the elegant terrace house facing a small park he saw limousines pulling up, disgorging the guests. Among them he recognized Louis Janin, Minister of Defence and catspaw of General de Forge. The flunkey at the door asked him if he had an invitation.

'Press,' said Tweed. 'Tell Madame de Forge I'm from the *Daily World*. And hurry it up. It's cold out here. If you're not back in three minutes I won't be here. But I'll make a phone call to Madame tomorrow – and I doubt whether you'll be on the staff any more. My card . . .'

As he waited other guests arrived in limousines, all wearing evening dress. Some of the women sported a fortune in jewels. Tweed, in his neat business suit, felt quite at ease. Why should he dress up for this nest of vipers?

The flunkey returned, hurrying, his manner very different. He ushered Tweed inside, took his coat, led the way across the red carpeted hall into a large room crammed with guests. The room was tastefully furnished and illuminated with glittering chandeliers. There were pictures on the wall and Tweed thought one was a Gauguin.

The flunkey had to edge his way through the chattering throng, their babble punctuated by the clink of champagne glasses. Tweed noticed a full general in uniform. Masson, Army Chief of Staff. He shouldn't have attended. Then he was ushered into the presence.

Josette de Forge was a tall, slim woman clad in a black velvet dress which showed to advantage her superb figure. A commanding woman who was also chic, her long sleek black hair was tied in a chignon. The dress was low-cut, exposing her excellent shoulders and held up more by hope than by gravity. Her dark eyes surveyed Tweed as she held his card and he quickly realized she was putting herself out to charm him.

'The *Daily World*, Mr Prentice. You are most welcome to my little salon. Champagne?' She summoned a waiter and Tweed reluctantly took a glass. 'Come and sit with me so we can talk,' she continued in English. 'All these people. It really is simply too dreadful. But you ask one, you have to ask so many others. They so easily take offence if not invited . . .'

As she prattled on she led him to an elegant couch next to the wall, waved a hand for him to join her, sat down crossing her long legs which were revealed by a deep slit in the dress. Tweed made a point of noticing them: he felt sure it was expected. He replied in English, concealing the fact that he spoke fluent French.

'You have a very distinguished gathering here, including General Masson. He gives you moral support in the present crisis?'

'It really is most intriguing, Mr Prentice, that now the British press is beginning to take an interest in France. Soon Paris will once again become the capital of Europe as it was in the time of Napoleon.'

'What about Germany?'

'They respect power.' She made a dismissive gesture with her free well-shaped hand. 'And soon we shall be recognized as the superpower of Europe. After all—' she sipped at her champagne— 'we have the *force de frappe*, atomic weapons. There is General Lapointe over there, commander of the *force*.'

The eagles gather, Tweed thought, turning to look at the uniformed general she had indicated. Of medium height, slim, with a neat small black moustache, he was listening to a blonde beauty who gazed up at him with adoring eyes.

'He has divorced his wife,' Josette went on, 'so Lisette is hopeful. He may bed her but she will not become his second consort.'

'I gather Prime Minister Navarre has other ideas – that he approves close co-operation with the new Germany.'

'Navarre! *Pouf!*' She blew him into the wind. 'He will

not last long once my husband arrives in Paris.'

'You are expecting him? With an army, you mean?'

Her magnetic black eyes narrowed. She studied Tweed before she replied. Then she looked round the room and her full red lips made a moue.

'We can't talk properly in this dreadful bedlam. Come with me. They'll have to do without me for a while.'

She made it sound like a deprivation as Tweed stopped a waiter topping up his drink and followed her. Opening a side door she went through into a smaller room which was mostly furnished with *chaise longues* wide enough to take two people lying down. Locking the door, she led the way to a *chaise longue* against the wall. As she arranged herself on it she patted it.

'Come and sit close to me so we can put the world right.'

Tweed perched on the edge, turned to face her while she lounged against the head-rest. He took out a compact tape recorder from his pocket, placed it on a small coffee table, pressed the start button and there was a whirring sound.

'I hope you don't mind,' he suggested.

She reached forward, used her pink-varnished index finger to press the stop button. The whirring sound ceased. She smiled languidly, her bare arms clasped behind her swan-like neck.

'You might not want a recording of all we say to each other. In any case, I don't like those machines.'

'As you wish.' He took out a notebook and pen. 'You won't mind if I make notes? Good. Perhaps you'd say again what you told me in the other room? I couldn't catch all you did say,' he lied.

'Of course . . .' She repeated what she had said, drawing up her knees and leaning on them as she watched him. Her movement again exposed her long legs. Tweed scribbled as she spoke.

'And,' he coaxed her when she was silent, 'you said you were expecting your husband to arrive in Paris with an army.'

'You newspaper men are wicked.' She gently slapped his knee, let her hand linger. 'You asked me that question. I hadn't answered.'

'And your answer?'

'He will come to Paris, of course. At the right moment. When France is crying out for a strong man to save her. And maybe an army will come with him – he inspires great loyalty and may not be able to prevent them following him.'

Which was a pretty damned devious approach, Tweed thought as he went on scribbling. He could see now how the coup could be justified. Her revelation had already made his visit worthwhile. Immensely so. Her hand began to wander. He clamped his own hand on hers. He was finding her the most dangerously attractive woman. He decided to face her with it.

'Supposing your husband walked in and found us like this now?'

'The door is locked.'

'You know what I mean.'

'Oh, Charles finds his amusement elsewhere. He has a long-term mistress. English, as it happens. Then he has other feminine sources of relaxation. Don't you ever relax?'

She had turned over her hand under his, entwining their fingers together. She tugged gently to draw him closer. Tweed asserted his considerable will-power. He reminded himself that de Forge was probably responsible for the cold-blooded murder of his agent, Francis Carey, in Bordeaux. And was she just feeling playful – or did she see this as a golden opportunity to spread de Forge's propaganda across the Channel? He took a deep breath.

'If we don't continue this interview I could lose my job.'

384

'Fire away, Mr Prentice. Then we can relax later.'

'I have heard rumours of some kind of high-level club which is planning to take over France. Even a rumour that one of the club's members is a foreign armaments manufacturer who is secretly supplying General de Forge with new weapons.'

He had shaken her, but she was a clever woman. Her reaction was unexpected. She stretched out her exposed leg and laid it across his lap. He perched his notebook on the leg, smiled, waited for her answer.

'I can't imagine where you heard such a melodramatic idea. Of course, as you will have seen from the guests outside, very influential people attend my salons. They wish to keep up with the latest developments. Events are close to a climax.' She wiggled her leg. 'Talking about climaxes . . .'

'Your weakness,' Tweed said brusquely, 'is you haven't any political support.'

'You think not!'

She removed her leg, jumped up. He had struck a nerve. Straightening her dress, she walked over to a wall mirror to make sure she was decent. Then she beckoned to him as she unlocked the door. Tweed followed her back into the salon. Josette took his arm, used her other hand to point to a man talking non-stop to a small brunette, chopping a hand up and down to emphasize what he was saying.

'There,' Josette said, 'is your – our – political support. Emile Dubois. Leader of the *Pour France* party. Thousands flock to his banner every day.'

Tweed studied Dubois. Of medium build, running to fat, he would be in his fifties. He had a mass of shaggy hair, a straggly moustache above thick lips. With his dinner jacket he wore an ordinary white tie which looked a trifle soiled. A thoroughly unsavoury-looking character who reminded Tweed of pictures he had seen of Pierre Laval, wartime collaborator.

385

'You certainly have the big guns on your side,' Tweed remarked, wishing to leave Josette in a satisfied frame of mind.

'And the big guns always win. Why don't you come to see me tomorrow evening? I have no salon and will be alone. Let me give you my card. Phone me to say when you will arrive so I can be ready for you . . .'

Josette opened the drawer of an escritoire standing by the wall. She took out an engraved card with a red rose above the lettering. Her smile was inviting as she gave it to him.

'My personal card, my private number. Given only to a few.'

Tweed thanked her, said good-night and the flunkey brought his coat. As he left the building Tweed patted his jacket pocket to check the small tape recorder was safe. He had been careful to collect that off the table before moving back into the salon.

'There is a taxi waiting across the road, Mr Prentice,' the flunkey advised him, ever-helpful now.

Prentice. It was the cover name Monica had chosen before having the card printed, and she had told Tweed's close friend, the editor of *Daily World*, that this was the name Tweed would be using. Inside the cab Tweed took out the tape recorder, looked at it and smiled to himself.

You think not!

Josette de Forge's voice came clearly out of the recorder as Tweed stood up, switched it off, looked at Lasalle in Navarre's office at the Ministry of the Interior. Navarre, who had retained the portfolio of the ministry when he became Prime Minister, was spending time in another building. Lasalle had just listened to Josette's whole conversation with Tweed.

'How did you manage it?' he asked. 'You said that she switched off the recorder.'

'She thought she had. The Engine Room at Park Crescent are ingenious. They structured it so the stop button starts it, and the start button simply creates a whirring noise as though the tape is running – when it isn't. When the tape is really running it's completely silent.'

'But supposing she'd agreed to your using it and hadn't stopped it?'

'I'd have said it didn't sound right, fiddled with it, and operated a concealed lever which starts the tape running.'

'We could use a few of those ourselves. But the critical result of your visit is her vague reference to de Forge arriving in Paris with an army. That is vital data. You have heard that de Forge has been appointed temporary commander of the Third *Army*?'

'No. Navarre approved that?'

'Didn't get the chance. General Masson announced the appointment publicly without reference to him. Navarre's only remedy would be to dismiss both his Army Chief of Staff and General de Forge. That could provoke an uprising. He can't do it.'

At that moment Navarre himself strode into the office with a brisk step. His lean face was grim and determined. Lasalle explained about Tweed's visit and Navarre asked to listen to the recording.

He sat behind his desk, quite relaxed. He stared at the tape recorder, listening intently as it played back all Tweed's conversation with Josette. As he switched it off Tweed made his observation.

'I'm very glad you retained the portfolio of the Ministry of the Interior when you became Prime Minister.'

Navarre grinned. 'My trump card. Control of the DST, the police, above all of the CRS, our paramilitary units. The question is when to play that trump card. I need hard evidence of de Forge's treachery.'

The phone rang, Navarre listened, handed it to Tweed.

'Robert Newman for you . . .'

41

General de Forge was also up late, pacing his office at GHQ as he listened to Major Lamy reporting the success of Kalmar. Lamy found it disconcerting to have his chief prowling round, often behind him as he spoke. It was a psychological trick de Forge was fond of – to put a visitor at a disadvantage. He interrupted Lamy's flow of words.

'The bottom of your coat and your shoes are caked with mud.'

'It's muddy in the countryside.'

'Even so, before you come to see me you should clean up. You are expected to give an example of smartness at all times to any soldier who may see you.'

'My apologies. I was anxious to let you know what Kalmar confirmed over the phone. Jean Burgoyne is dead.'

'One spy eliminated. And I'm considering developing the present manoeuvres into Operation Marengo – the march on Paris. After you've activated Operation Austerlitz – to throw Paris into chaos. And the cross of fire must appear everywhere from now on.'

While talking another part of de Forge's mind considered his conviction that there was a traitor at GHQ. Paris was being fed information – the informant at the DST in the rue des Saussaies had confirmed this. It had to be a member of his inner circle. Lieutenant Berthier?

Major Lamy himself? He had to be detected quickly, liquidated. An essential condition before he ordered Austerlitz and then Marengo.

'The cross of fire was used both in the Marseilles and Toulon riots,' Lamy assured him hastily. 'The newspapers will be full of pictures tomorrow. You wish me to set in motion Austerlitz?'

'Not just yet. Timing is everything in a successful campaign. You said Berthier phoned you, that he was sure he caught a glimpse of Paula Grey inside a car with two men in Arcachon. She is Kalmar's next target. He must finish her off within the next twenty-four hours.'

'That doesn't give Kalmar much time. He's a meticulous planner.'

'Then he'll have to speed up his meticulous planning. I am equally concerned with your contact with the mysterious *Manteau*.'

'He phoned me, told me to put the two million Swiss francs in a cloth bag, to deposit the bag behind an isolated telephone box outside a village south of Bordeaux. I did so. Then drove away.'

'But what else did he say?' de Forge asked over Lamy's left shoulder.

The General was a devil, Lamy thought. How could he have guessed there was more?

'*Manteau* told me I was to drive back towards GHQ for half an hour, then I could return. That if I felt inclined to return earlier that was all right by him, but I'd be shot through the head.'

Yes, de Forge ruminated, that sounded like typical *Manteau* language. Not a bit like Kalmar.

'Anything else?' he rapped out.

'Yes. He said he'd deal with Paula Grey. And any other people you needed extinguished. The very word he used.'

Well, at least the payment should stop any further attempts on his own life, de Forge decided. He felt relieved: the bullet which had penetrated his limousine had come rather too close for comfort.

'Send a yellow signal to the Austerlitz units in Paris,' he decided suddenly. 'Immediately . . .'

When Lamy had left he checked his watch. The next and final signal would be red: the signal for the saboteur units to set Paris aflame. He must strike soon before Navarre established his hold on the government.

Navarre and Lasalle watched Tweed as he took the call from Newman but could read nothing from his expression. Tweed made brief notes, asked a question now and then, eventually told Newman to hold on. He looked at the two Frenchmen.

'He's calling from a hotel in Arcachon. Should be a safe line – he has Butler watching the clerk who operates the switchboard – but I want quick decisions.'

'Tell us the problem,' Navarre said crisply.

'Newman has photographic evidence of atrocities committed by de Forge's men . . .' Tersely he told them about the burial ground in the Landes, the attack on Moshe Stein's villa by men masked as Ku-Klux-Klan.

'Let me speak to him,' Lasalle said.

'Lasalle here. I'll be brief. You have the film? Good. Do you know the airfield just north of the Etang de Cazaux, to the west of the N652?'

'Yes. I noticed it when Moshe and I were driving up here from the Landes.'

'An Alouette chopper will land there at daybreak. Give the pilot the films. Code-name Valmy for the pilot.'

'I'll be there.'

'Tweed is gesturing, hold for a moment . . .'

Tweed had been thinking of Newman's shorthand description of the discovery of Jean Burgoyne's body by Paula. He'd decided to pull her out of the area. He told

Lasalle quickly about the murder. Lasalle clapped a hand to his head.

'My God! Jean Burgoyne was one of my agents I told you I had in the area. This is terrible. Now I only have one left . . .'

'Give me the damned phone,' Tweed snapped. 'Bob, where is Paula? With you. Put her on quickly . . . Paula, I'm sorry about Jean Burgoyne – it must have been a shock. A great shock . . . Yes. I can see how it brought Aldeburgh back to you. Now listen, I'm pulling you out. Bob knows Lasalle is sending a chopper. You're to board it, come back to Paris.'

'No. I'm staying on to try and find this killer. Up to now he's strangled two of my friends – Karin Rosewater and Jean Burgoyne.'

'Paula.' Tweed's tone was grim. 'This isn't a request, it's an order. You're to fly back in the Alouette.'

'No,' she repeated with the same firmness, 'I'm staying here. There's Bob with me – as well as Harry and Pete.'

'I don't think you heard me,' Tweed rasped. 'I am giving you an order . . .'

'Which I'm disobeying. You don't like it, you can sack me later.'

'You're an obstinate woman . . .'

'When I want to be. And I want to be now. How is everything there?'

'Put Newman back on the line. Now!'

'Tweed, I'm here,' Newman responded after taking the phone.

'Paula is being difficult, as you doubtless realize now. So I want her aboard that Alouette – even if you have to carry her into the machine physically.'

'Can't do that,' Newman said laconically. 'You're making a mistake. She'd feel she was running away. Can't say that I disagree with you in one way. But she's a fully paid up member of the team. Don't forget that.'

'If you say so.' Tweed's tone was abrupt. 'I'm hoping that evidence you're providing will give us a powerful lever to neutralize the enemy. Of course, a witness would have made all the difference.'

'There is a witness,' Newman told him, thinking of Martine, the old woman who collected brushwood by the shore. 'Getting on a bit, but still with all the marbles there. And could be very impressive on TV.'

'We want that witness.'

'It means my going back to the Landes. But I can see that it's important, could tilt the scales.'

'The Landes?' Tweed was alarmed. 'I can't ask you to do that.'

'You didn't. I've just decided myself I'm going soon as I can.'

'Bob, before you leave promise me you will let me know – or get one of the others to do it.'

'OK. Promise. Take care.'

'*You* take care.' Tweed's tone was urgent. 'I'd better warn you we have reason to believe that all hell is about to break loose. Prepare yourself . . .'

As Tweed put down the phone he reflected this was the critical point in the titanic struggle to save France. After laying out the situation, Navarre had stood as though gazing into the fog of an uncertain future while he listened to Tweed's phone call. Tweed looked at him first, caught his expression, guessed his thoughts, then studied Lasalle.

The DST chief was edgy and also unsure. Should he launch his battalions – the DST, the paramilitary CRS and other forces under his control? If so, in which direction? To the south where de Forge was organizing controlled chaos? Or should he dig in round Paris?

Only Tweed was certain what was needed. A foreigner in a foreign capital, he seemed as relaxed as if he were behind his desk at Park Crescent. He spoke decisively.

'I know what we must do, but first bring me up to date on the present situation as you see it.'

It was Navarre who answered, still forceful even at this late hour.

'As you know, Masson has bypassed me, has announced publicly the appointment of General de Forge as temporary commander of the Third Army. That army is now manoeuvring over the whole of the south of France. Pretended objective of the so-called exercise? To repel an invasion force landing at Marseilles, Toulon, and Bordeaux from the sea and the air. The fictitious enemy is a General Ali, a dictator based in North Africa – coming to the aid of his persecuted Arabs in France. Which fits in with the anti-Arab propaganda of Dubois.'

'And the real objective?' Tweed asked.

'It gives de Forge the perfect excuse to move his army over a huge area in any direction.'

'We must strike now,' Tweed insisted. 'Without pause, without mercy. These are evil forces we confront – racist, anti-Arab, anti-German, anti-American.'

He had stood up when Chief Inspector Otto Kuhlmann hurried into the room. His teeth were clamped tightly on his unlit cigar. He held a folded sheet of paper in his hand.

'I've just returned from a lightning trip to Germany,' he informed Navarre. 'May I continue?'

'By all means.'

'Tweed,' Kuhlmann began, 'early in the campaign you advised me to send undercover police to Basle and Geneva. You said that was where Kalmar passed on instructions for the next phase. In neutral Switzerland. And where he got orders.'

'So what has happened?' Tweed enquired.

'Four people we know are involved in this business visited either Basle or Geneva – or both – recently. Here is a list of their names and destinations.'

Tweed unfolded the sheet. He glanced down the list, handed it back to Kuhlmann.

'The man we know as Kalmar is on that list. I just can't prove it. Yet.'

Tweed went straight to his own office, closed the door and sat at his desk. There were urgent phone calls he wanted to make without anyone overhearing him, specific instructions for action he wanted to give.

His first call was to Marler.

His second call was to Newman and he spoke to him for some time. Then he asked to speak to Butler. His orders were brief. He asked to speak to Pete Nield. Again the orders were brief.

He asked Nield to put Paula on the line. Again it was a long conversation – far warmer than his previous call to her. He had just put down the phone when Kuhlmann came in.

'Take a seat, Otto. No, I'm not identifying Kalmar. My strategy is that the assassin should feel he's safe, unsuspected.'

'OK by me. I came to talk to you alone. While in Germany I had a brief radio signal from Stahl. Remember him?'

'Of course. The Hotel des Bergues in Geneva – seems ages ago. You told Paula and me about him. Your agent posing as a Frenchman inside Bordeaux. You gave me the assumed name, his address, his phone number.'

'I said the signal was brief. It was also encouraging – and disturbing. He has valuable information but can't get out of Bordeaux. Can you help?'

'I think so. I have people in the area. The codeword for identification was Gamelin.'

'Correct. And thank you for your help.''

'I can promise nothing, Otto,' Tweed warned, and the German left the room.

Tweed reached for the phone, dialled the number of the Atlantique Newman had given him. He was going to make it very clear to Newman that it was up to him whether he ventured into Bordeaux again to rescue Stahl. Newman had had more than his fair share of ordeals so far.

When Tweed had phoned Marler earlier the slim Englishman was perched on the edge of his bed in the apartment near the rue du Bac in Paris. Smoking a king-size, he had a large-scale map of France spread out and was studying it. When the phone rang he picked it up and was careful not to give any name.

'Yes? Who is it?'

'Tweed. Another mission. Urgent. Of course. I want to step up the pressure, screw it down tight. We're launching full-scale psychological warfare. At least, I am. Any ideas?'

'Give me a sec to think.'

Marler blew a smoke ring, watched it float up to the cobwebbed ceiling of the small scruffy room. The ring dissolved.

'I've thought of something. Pure psychological warfare. It means I'll be away from here for a while.'

'Good luck . . .'

Marler put down the mobile phone inside his small open case on a chair. He checked his open-flight Air Inter tickets. He'd used several but there were plenty left. Selecting a container of face powder with a yellow undertone, he walked over to the wall mirror and applied some.

It was an innocuous item among his samples. After all he was posing as a cosmetics salesman. The powder gave his skin the sallow tinge which is common to certain Frenchmen. He studied himself in the mirror, adjusted his beret to a jaunty angle.

He wore washed-out blue denims and a windcheater. He had days before tested out his appearance, walking into a bar, ordering a drink. He had lingered over the one drink the way Frenchmen in bars do. He had chatted to the barman, to several customers, complaining about how bad business was. They had all agreed. More important, they had all accepted him as one of them.

'Time to go out and do your thing,' he told his mirror image.

He was aware he was talking to himself. It was a habit he occasionally indulged in when on his own for long periods. He looked forward to leaving the run-down apartment on the Left Bank where the heating was nil.

At the Atlantique in Arcachon Newman also had a map spread out on his bed, but this was a large-scale map of Bordeaux. In the room with him were Paula, Butler, and Nield.

'I have to go back into the city to haul out Stahl, a German agent in hiding,' he explained. 'I'm going in tonight. Best chance after dark.'

'You're crazy,' Paula burst out. 'First, you were lucky when you went there before. And all the news reports far more security now than there was earlier. Look at the papers . . .'

They, too, were spread over Newman's bed. All showed pictures of the riots in Marseilles and Toulon. The most prominent feature of the photographs was of men in Balaclavas with the Cross of Lorraine – the crosses blazing with fire in the night. The atmosphere of insurrection was growing by the hour.

'Second,' Paula hammered away, 'you'll have no sleep if you go to Bordeaux. And you have to meet that helicopter near the *étang* at dawn tomorrow. Your reflexes won't be so good if you run into something, which you probably will.'

'Thanks for the vote of confidence,' Newman snapped back.

'I'm just thinking of your safety, you cretin.'

'Let's cool it.' Newman grinned. 'I'd grasped that and I am grateful, touched.'

'Obstinate bastard,' she chaffed him, her good humour returning with his infectious grin.

They hugged each other. Pete Nield winked behind them at Butler. There always came a moment like this during an operation. A situation of continuing danger. Too little sleep. Fatigue. Nerves frayed.

'I can't find Stahl's address on the map,' Newman admitted as he released Paula. 'The Passage Emile Zola. Before I head for Bordeaux I'll visit Isabelle. She should know.'

Paula grinned wickedly. 'Mind she doesn't keep you there all night in her apartment.'

He slapped her on the rump, looked at Butler and Nield.

'You two take good care of her while I'm away.'

'But you have to come back here before . . . you drive down to meet the Alouette,' Butler said.

He'd been on the verge of saying *before you drive down to the Landes*. But he guessed Newman had omitted to tell her about that dangerous expedition. And Newman's instruction about her had been superfluous: on the phone Tweed had told Butler and Nield separately that he held them personally responsible for Paula's safety, that she was in grave danger.

42

Victor Rosewater was a long way from Arcachon. He sat in the living room of his ultra-modern flat in the Konvikstrasse in Freiburg – on the edge of the Black Forest in Germany. He checked his watch. 4 a.m. Helmut should arrive shortly.

Rosewater had been flown by a private plane from Bordeaux Airport to Basle in the middle of the night. After paying the pilot the substantial sum agreed, Rosewater had driven his car parked near the airport across the Swiss border up the autobahn to Freiburg.

The weather was lousy. Heavy snow smothered the ancient rooftops of the University city. Rosewater got up, walked into his kitchen which had every up to date appliance. He poured himself another cup of coffee from the percolator, went back to his chair in the living room. As he sipped coffee he stared at the photograph of Paula Grey he had secretly taken. The print was propped up against an old silver jug he had bought in an antique shop. Silver was his hobby and he had quite a collection.

Paula was a very attractive girl, he thought. And, unlike so many attractive women, she had a vibrant personality. 'You've got everything going for you,' he mused.

Helmut Schneider: his mind switched to the German he had flown to Freiburg to meet. Helmut was an extraordinary man. He had a network of informants through the whole of Germany, a number of them unsavoury characters. Among the more respectable were barmen, hotel commissionaires and concierges, cab and bus drivers – all people who noticed what was going on round them, who heard unguarded conversations.

Among the less savoury were brothel-keepers, unlicensed arms merchants and dubious night club bouncers. It was a world the public had no idea existed.

Until recently Helmut had told them to inform him, for a price, about any strangers patronizing these establishments with Irish accents, their modes of transport. By using these sources Rosewater had tracked down several IRA cells before they'd had time to become active.

He had recently given Helmut a new instruction. To search for clues as to the whereabouts of *Siegfried* units. Now he waited to hear if Helmut had had any luck.

The weird thing was Helmut rarely left his cheap apartment in Frankfurt. All communication was carried out over the phone. But Helmut was a man of cunning. He took short-term leases on an apartment, rarely using the same phone number for more than two months.

He would then move on to another part of Frankfurt. This involved calling a host of informants to give them his new number. But Helmut had a strong instinct for survival. Staying in one place for long was risky, could easily be a lethal mistake.

A tapping on the knocker of the front door interrupted the mind-wanderings of Rosewater. He jumped up, hauled from his holster a 7.65mm pistol, went to the solid front door, and peered through the spyhole before drawing bolts and unlocking the door.

Outside crouched a bizarre figure. Dressed in black from head to foot, the man wore black glasses and carried the white cane of a blind man. It took Rosewater a moment to recognize Helmut Schneider.

'Shake the snow off your coat,' he ordered. 'And maybe you'd be considerate enough to remove your boots.'

The apartment had fitted carpet wall to wall. Meticulous in his dress, Rosewater kept the luxurious apartment clean as a new pin. He closed the door after Schneider had removed the soft snow from his coat, divested himself of his boots and walked into the warmth of the hall. Rosewater gestured towards the living room, took coat and boots to the kitchen, hung up the coat behind a door and dumped the worn boots in the sink. He poured another cup of coffee and handed it to Schneider, who had seated himself in an armchair, feet in socks stretched out towards a radiator, in the living room.

'Any results? About *Siegfried*?' Rosewater greeted his guest.

'A clever girl has infiltrated their High Command. Won't tell you who she is.' Schneider grinned, exposing two missing teeth. 'She has personal reasons to hate the guts of shit like that. She has brains – and she's got guts.'

Schneider had removed his dark glasses and his cunning eyes gleamed with satisfaction. Arriving at the apartment he'd looked like a down-and-out: now he was alert, erect, and watchful. Like a clever ferret.

'But actual results?' Rosewater demanded impatiently.

'Contain yourself,' Schneider reproved him, continuing in German, the language both men were speaking. 'It's warmer in here. Like bloody Siberia out there.'

'Why the elaborate disguise?' Rosewater asked, suddenly anxious. 'You weren't followed?'

'I was.'

'You mean to here? For God's sake . . .'

'Contain yourself,' Schneider repeated, pleased that he had shaken the normally cool Englishman. 'You really think I can't spot a shadow? Two of them, moving separately. I lost them in Heidelberg. Then I changed cars at a friend's place. Then I put on this gear when I'd left the second car on the outskirts of your patch.'

'Very professional.' Rosewater forced himself to mask his growing irritation. 'And the results?'

'*Siegfried* is in Hamburg, Dortmund, Berlin, Hanover,

Düsseldorf, Frankfurt, Karlsruhe, Munich, and Stuttgart. It's a big operation.'

While talking Schneider extracted an old wallet from beneath three layers of clothing: two woollen pullovers and a jacket. He unzipped a concealed compartment, took out a grubby, folded sheet of A4 paper, handed it over to Rosewater. Then he spread his feet a little closer to the radiator.

Rosewater looked down the list of detailed addresses and recognized several. He looked at Schneider who had removed his mittens, was holding the cup in both hands to warm himself.

'This is the lot?' he asked.

'By no means.' Schneider finished his coffee, placed the cup on the hearth. 'I expect to have another long list very shortly. I'll phone the number you gave me so they can contact you.'

'Good.'

Rosewater was thinking Schneider was ideal for the job. A social outcast, a man able to mingle with, to haggle with the shabby half-world which was his network. And there was no danger he'd try to pre-empt Rosewater by handing to the police this information. The police were his enemy.

Schneider, a pickpocket, had served five short sentences in German prisons. One more misdemeanour and he'd go down for a very long sentence.

'Time you left,' Rosewater suggested.

Schneider made the universal gesture asking for money – rubbing thumb against middle finger. Rosewater made it a matter of policy to wait until he asked for money: it discouraged the German from thinking there was a bottomless pit available.

Taking four five-hundred Deutschmark banknotes from his pocket he handed them over. The equivalent roughly of seven hundred pounds. But Helmut's expenses came high. The German looked dubious.

401

'Not enough to cover what I'll have to pay out. Double this might just manage it.'

'I haven't got that to spare.' The usual haggling which Schneider expected. 'You'll have to get by with this. Not a deutschmark more.'

He produced two more five-hundred Deutschmark notes, dropped them on the table. Schneider scooped them up as Rosewater went into the kitchen, collected the coat and boots. He banged the latter to get rid of the snow which hadn't melted in the warmth of the central heating. He was anxious to get Schneider out of the apartment.

The German put on his disguise before leaving. Adjusting his dark glasses, he adopted a stooped posture, tapping the white cane against the walls to accustom himself again to his role of blind man.

Rosewater was glad to see the back of him. He was anxious to drive to Basle Airport. There he would catch the first flight to Bordeaux via Geneva, driving on to Arcachon. Rosewater had overheard in the Bar Martinique a man with a distinct Irish accent. Discreet enquiries had confirmed the Irishman frequented the bar. And also he wanted to meet Paula Grey again.

Twelve hours earlier during the previous evening Newman had driven to Isabelle's apartment from the Atlantique. As he moved along the front the *bassin* was a seething mass of heaving waves, reminding him of Aldeburgh.

He was also thinking of the notes he'd extracted from the polythene envelope attached to poor Jean Burgoyne's lifeless body. Reading them alone in his room he had been startled to find he was looking at plans for an army movement on Paris. The details gave the route to be followed north by a lightning thrust of de Forge's armoured divisions. Their objective was Paris.

Could the information be genuine? Newman thought so:

Jean had given map references, used language which sounded to have been extracted from military dispatches. His dilemma was whether to entrust such vital data to an Alouette which might crash before it arrived in Paris. How else could he get the notes into the hands of Tweed?

Parking in a side street a short distance from her apartment, well away now from the front, he stepped out. Before he approached the entrance he stood banging his gloved hands round his body while he made sure he had not been followed.

He had phoned Isabelle just before leaving the Atlantique. When he pressed the bell beside her apartment door she had it thrown wide open in seconds. She was talking while she locked and bolted the door.

'It has been so long since I've seen you, Bob. You will stay the night? If you don't want to make love we'll sit and chat. Perhaps I shouldn't have said that. But I've been thinking of you. Have you been thinking of me?'

All in one breath. She snuggled up against him. Her body pressed against his. She was moaning with pleasure, hands clutching at him. I have a problem here, he thought. He grasped both her shoulders, gently pushed her to arm's length, and she stood staring at him, quivering, her eyes huge.

'Isabelle, I need your help. I have to leave almost at once. To go to Bordeaux again . . .'

'No! Not Bordeaux! You don't know what it's like now. Friends have told me. There are Army patrols in all the main streets . . .'

'I don't want a main street. I want the Passage Emile Zola. Ever heard of it?'

Releasing her, he took out his street map of the city and spread it over the living room table. She stood next to him, her hair brushing his face, a pen in her hand. She had it poised to make a mark when he stopped her.

'No. Marked maps are dangerous. You do know where it is?'

'Yes. It is very difficult to find. You can walk past it a dozen times without seeing it. But I can take you there.'

'Nothing doing. This is one trip I make on my own.'

'Really?' She pulled at strands of her hair. 'Which way will you drive in to Bordeaux? I suppose you will follow the same route we used?'

'It seems sensible, since I know it.'

'Very sensible. When the Passage Emile Zola is on this side of the city.'

She pointed to the eastern area, furthest from Arcachon and on the way to the airport. He looked at the area she had vaguely indicated and couldn't see the passage. In any case, it wasn't included in the map's index. His tone changed, became rough.

'Look, stop fooling around, Isabelle. Someone's life is at stake. Without making a mark just damn well show me where this passage is?'

'There.' She retracted her pen tip and lightly touched the map. 'And to have any chance of surviving the army patrols we'd take a roundabout route and approach it from the east. I can guide you.'

'Thanks. I won't risk you coming again.'

'Excuse me. I must turn off the coffee percolator.'

She disappeared through the swing door into the kitchen, was absent for no more than thirty seconds, then came back with a coat over her arm, a leather bag in her hand. Newman said good-night after swiftly folding the map. He went to the door, threw back the bolt, turned the key, and left the apartment.

He had unlocked the door of his car, was easing himself behind the wheel of the Renault, when the passenger door opened and Isabelle, wearing the coat, slid in beside him, closing her door. She moved like a cat. He'd not heard a footstep. Her arrival had been so sudden he'd slipped his

404

hand inside his sheepskin to grip the butt of his Smith & Wesson.

'Give me the map,' she said calmly. 'You said someone's life was at stake. That makes two of you. Without my local knowledge you'd never make it. Hadn't we better get moving?'

'*Manteau* here.'

General de Forge, alone in his GHQ office, froze. Only two words but they'd had an extraordinarily sinister ring over the phone.

'Yes, what the hell is it now? You've been paid.'

'Trickery. My God, you do take chances. Don't you want to go on living?'

'Just hold it there.' De Forge had a grip on himself now. 'I would appreciate an explanation of that cryptic remark.'

'The money, General.'

'What about it? The amount was as agreed.'

De Forge was puzzled. Lamy had delivered it as instructed – or was his Chief of Intelligence going into business for himself? Was Lamy the rotten apple of the inner circle?

'The amount was as agreed,' *Manteau* repeated. 'But three-quarters of it is counterfeit. The remaining quarter has bills in numbered sequence. That was a grave mistake, General. Maybe even suicidal.'

The voice was so deadly calm it was unnerving. As though discussing a perfectly normal business transaction. The man was like ice. And de Forge was appalled at what he had been told, hardly knew how to react.

'I'll investigate,' he said brusquely. 'I handed over the money to the emissary myself. It was as requested at that moment.'

'So you say. So you would say, of course. I'm going to have to provide one last demonstration. Incidentally, I have left the cloth bag containing what was inside behind

405

the same phone box. Have it collected. Just in case you are telling the truth. Which I very much doubt.'

'What demonstration are you talking about . . .'

De Forge realized he was talking into a dead line. Shaken, he put down the phone, thought for a moment, picked up the phone again, ordered Major Lamy to come at once. He next called Lieutenant Berthier's quarters, found the officer had just returned, told him he wanted to see him, to wait outside his office when he arrived. De Forge was standing with his back to the huge silhouette of General de Gaulle when Lamy entered. Which meant Lamy had to remain standing.

De Forge told him about the *Manteau* call. He watched Lamy closely as he spoke, his manner grim. The Chief of Intelligence was careful to wait until his commander had finished, his face devoid of expression.

'So what have you to say?' de Forge demanded.

'This is crazy,' Lamy protested. 'I delivered the money as arranged. Counterfeit? Impossible.'

'Unless someone is stashing away a nest egg for himself,' de Forge remarked coldly.

'Is that an accusation, General?'

'Rather call it a suggestion. There's one way to discover the truth. As I told you, he has left the cloth bag behind the phone box. Go and bring it back to me immediately.'

'Now? At this hour of night?'

'Have you gone deaf? I said immediately. And take with you an escort. Lieutenant Berthier will be waiting outside. Take him with you – and one other officer.'

'What about Kalmar, General? He has just phoned me and asked for his fee. For eliminating Jean Burgoyne . . .'

He stopped speaking as the phone rang. De Forge looked Lamy up and down with a chilling expression he was famous for. He lifted the receiver.

'De Forge. I'm busy. Who the hell is it now?'

'*Manteau* reporting, General. During my previous call I

omitted to tell you I have extinguished Jean Burgoyne. That will cost you one million Swiss francs. Tell Lamy he'll receive instructions how to make payment. This time in real money, if you please.'

'Listen to me . . .' Again the line went dead.

De Forge replaced the phone carefully as though it might explode in his face. He looked at Lamy again for almost a minute before he told him about this latest call. Lamy listened, his mind racing over how to respond.

'I don't know how he could possibly have known where she was. Jean Burgoyne chose a very remote rendezvous. And without Yvette following her no one would have known.'

'But someone did know,' de Forge said softly. 'You knew – or that girl who took the call here from Yvette knew. She passed the information to you over the radio and you *said* you'd phoned Kalmar at an agreed number.'

'What do you suggest?' Lamy asked stiffly.

'That you carry out my order – collect that bag with the money from behind the phone box.'

Lamy turned to go. Then he decided to risk more protest. De Forge didn't seem to realize what he was asking.

'If *Manteau* is in the area, watching that isolated phone box, he'll think it's a trap – when he sees my escort in the car with me.'

'It's a risk you'll have to take,' de Forge told him brutally. 'Send in Lieutenant Berthier and wait outside for him . . .'

Berthier stood rigidly to attention as de Forge studied him. The General was watching for any signs of nervousness, of sweat appearing on his forehead – as he had with Lamy.

'Paula Grey,' de Forge snapped. 'Any news by now?'

'Yes, General. She is staying at the Hotel Atlantique in Arcachon. The night clerk showed me her signature in the register. The problem is she's protected by two bodyguards. Professionals, by the way they behave. Never let her out of their sight.'

'Thank you, Berthier. You have done well.' De Forge had become amiable. He made it a point never to be at odds with more than one officer at a time. 'I may send you back to Arcachon. At the moment Major Lamy has a job for you and is waiting outside . . .'

Alone, de Forge sat at his desk, drawing Crosses of Lorraine on fire on a pad while he thought. Kalmar. *Manteau*. Could they be the same man? Or were both an invention of Major Lamy's?

Lamy was an expert marksman. Lamy had always been the go-between separating de Forge from the unknown killer. It was an arrangement which suited de Forge: no one could ever link him with the assassin. Lamy had suggested the idea. Lamy always took the huge sums paid to the assassin when someone had to be eliminated. The President and the Prime Minister, for example. And before transferring to Intelligence Lamy had been an explosives technician with the Engineers. Was Lamy accumulating a fortune at the expense of the Army?

De Forge was irritated and confused. He should be concentrating all his brainpower on Operations Austerlitz and Marengo. The mystery of the assassins – if there were two of them – was taking up valuable time. I should know the solution when they return with the money, he decided. And the problem of Paula Grey should also soon be solved.

43

Major Jules Lamy was a loner. He intensely disliked his escort and had sat both officers in the rear of the car. In the middle of the night his headlight beams, undimmed, swung over a bleak landscape of deserted fields with not a single habitation in sight.

He was within two miles of the small village which had the phone box on its southern outskirts. The advantage was he could search round the box for the canvas bag containing the money without risk of being seen by any villager. That was, assuming the money was there.

In the rear Berthier sat beside the other lieutenant and behind the empty front passenger seat. His Service revolver was resting in his lap, his hand holding the butt. He had removed it from his holster surreptitiously, certain that Lamy would object if he had known about the gun.

Neither of the lieutenants had spoken a word during the long drive from GHQ. Both knew Lamy wished them in hell and were careful not to break the silence. Berthier was on edge. He mistrusted this drive through the darkness without a motor-cycle outrider escort. They were a sitting target, in Berthier's opinion.

The thought had just passed through his mind when Lamy slowed as he negotiated a sharp and dangerous bend. He was crawling when their silence was broken. A shattering *crack* stunned the three occupants. Berthier was the first to realize it was a bullet.

The *crack* was followed instantly by a splattering of breaking glass. The officer next to Berthier was showered with glass splinters. Berthier saw a hole in the window on his side also. He took off his képi and the brim had disappeared.

'Move!' he shouted at Lamy. 'We're under fire. That was a bullet . . .'

At the moment he spoke Lamy pressed his foot down on the accelerator. He saw a straight stretch of road and zigzagged along it at speed. He was careful not to keep up a predictable rhythm: his zigzagging was erratic and proved Lamy was a skilled driver. He also asserted his authority as he drove.

'Anyone hurt back there?'

'Our colleague is cut about the face,' Berthier reported. 'But I think he'll live.'

Berthier had escaped any injury. The bullet had scattered shards of glass over his companion when it entered, but had blasted the glass outwards on Berthier's side. Siberian air sheered into the interior through the two holes. Descending into a deep gully beyond the straight stretch, Lamy slowed, stopped, gave the order.

'When I'm searching round the phone box you take up position – away from the car and well separated. Can you manage that, Lieutenant Chabert?'

'I think so sir . . .'

'Think isn't good enough.'

'I can, sir,' Siccard replied hastily.

Using a large handkerchief he was mopping blood off his face. As the car started up again he examined his face with his fingers but there were no shards of glass embedded in the skin. The two officers prepared to leave the car as Lamy pulled up a few yards from the phone box.

Wasting no time, Lamy jumped out, crouched low, gun in hand, peered inside the box with his pencil flash. Empty. He found the cloth bag where *Manteau* had said it would be: behind the box. The same bag – Lamy recognized a dirty mark – but the cord tying it had been unfastened and retied with a different knot. Lamy dumped it on the front passenger seat, the lieutenants dived into the rear, Lamy turned the car round and drove back towards GHQ. What they would find inside the bag was his great concern. And fear of another bullet.

After listening to Lamy's report de Forge walked out of his office into the icy night without bothering to don his greatcoat. He stood, hands on his hips, looking at the bullet-holes in the car. He gestured with his head to Lieutenants Berthier and Chabert.

'Get into the rear of the car and remember exactly how you were sitting when the bullet struck.'

Berthier, still wearing his képi minus the brim, leaned forward beyond Chabert as he had been doing, about to say something to Lamy. De Forge studied their positions, recalling his own experience when a bullet had penetrated his limousine. He waved for the two officers to get out.

'You'll have to draw a new képi from the quartermaster,' he observed to Berthier.

'He nearly got me, General.'

'No, he aimed to miss by centimetres again.' He looked at Lamy. 'We've had the demonstration we were promised. Back to your quarters,' he ordered the two lieutenants. 'Berthier, leave for Arcachon as soon as you've put on civilian clothes. Check on that girl, then report back to Major Lamy immediately . . .'

He marched back into his office with Lamy following him. The cloth bag lay on his desk. De Forge waved a hand.

'Open it up. Check the money.'

Another major from the Paymaster's Office, summoned by de Forge, entered while Lamy was examining the packages. The Paymaster officer had been a banking official before joining the Army and de Forge handed him a Swiss thousand-franc bill.

411

'Would you say that was genuine?'

De Forge wandered restlessly while the officer took out a magnifying glass. Switching on de Forge's desk lamp he examined the banknote carefully, left his glass on the desk, gave his verdict.

'It's a counterfeit. A very good one. But definitely a counterfeit.'

De Forge picked up two more of the notes Lamy was checking. He handed them to the Paymaster officer without a word. Again the process of careful examination was repeated before the officer returned them to de Forge.

'Also counterfeit. No doubt about it.'

'Would these be supplied by a bank in error?' de Forge enquired.

'Absolutely not. They are high denomination notes. No bank would be fooled. One note, possibly – although it would be most unusual. Three? Never.'

'Thank you. Major, you may go now. And not one word about this to anyone. There may be a scandal I have to investigate.'

'Well, Major Lamy?' de Forge asked softly when they were alone.

Lamy looked disturbed, puzzled. He held up a stack of notes.

'The numbers are all in sequence. They weren't when I delivered them.'

'You think our English friend, *Oiseau*, has been swindling us?'

It was a trap question. De Forge waited for an answer as Lamy considered his reply. He pursed his thin lips.

'I don't think so for a moment. He is buying friendship – yours – for future arms deals with countries France has close relations with.'

'Take the lot away and put them in the safe. Now!'

When Lamy had gone de Forge's confidence in *Manteau* had risen in direct relationship to his loss of confidence in

412

Lamy. Now he must concentrate on Operation Marengo.

About the same time, early that morning when de Forge was watching the checking of the money, Helmut Schneider sat eating breakfast at a truck drivers' café on the outskirts of Karlsruhe.

After leaving Victor Rosewater in Freiburg he had driven north along the autobahn. It was a very different Helmut in appearance. Prior to getting into his car he had discarded the dark glasses, the white cane, the disreputable overcoat and boots, stowing them into a hold-all which he hid at the back of the boot of his car.

In the café he wore a clean windcheater, his denims, and a peaked cap of the type German students used to wear. He drank his steaming coffee slowly, took his time over consuming a hamburger. Frequently he checked his watch.

As soon as the main Post Office was open he parked close to it in Karlsruhe, centre of the German judicial system. Walking the rest of the way, he entered the Post Office, glanced at the few early customers, slipped inside one of the phone booths.

Dialling a number inside Germany, he spent several minutes transmitting a coded message which, to an eavesdropper, would have sounded like a normal business conversation. Replacing the receiver, he walked back to his car and resumed his journey back to his apartment in Frankfurt.

To reach the Passage Emile Zola, Isabelle had guided Newman along a devious route round the southern fringes of Bordeaux. Her idea was they would enter the city from the east to avoid any idea they had come from Arcachon.

Newman also had had an idea before they drove off. They went back into her apartment and raided the wine store, carrying a dozen bottles of Beaujolais to the car. At Newman's suggestion Isabelle had borrowed a white scarf

413

from her sister's wardrobe. She wrapped it round her head. White – the colour of 'just married'.

The round-about route took a long time and it was early morning but still dark as they entered the city. Newman drove in from the direction of Bergerac along the N136. They had seen large numbers of mechanized vehicles manoeuvring in the distance but had encountered no trouble so far.

'We are approaching the Pont de Pierre,' Isabelle warned him. 'That is where there could be a checkpoint.'

She proved to be right. Coming up to the bridge over the river Garonne, Newman saw in his headlights troops with automatic weapons standing in the road. Behind them a wooden barrier with gates barred the way. His headlights were blurred in a mist rising off the river.

'Get ready to go into our act,' he reminded her.

With the white scarf concealing her hair and draped over her shoulders, she snuggled up close to him, holding a bottle of wine in her hand. Newman lowered his window and with her free hand she lowered hers. Newman stopped the car, left the engine running, grabbed a bottle of wine and began rolling in his seat as troops crowded in round the vehicle. In a drunken voice Newman began singing the *Marseillaise*.

'The new Beaujolais,' he shouted and tossed a bottle out of the window.

He had thrown it over the heads of the troops near the car and there was a mad scramble as one soldier caught it in mid-air. Newman was again singing and the refrain was taken up by the soldiers who a moment earlier had been shivering in the icy mist, bored to tears with the task of manning the checkpoint.

Isabelle threw her bottle. She flashed a smile at the men near her. They stared at her lecherously and then jostled to grab the bottle. She picked up another as Newman hurled a fresh one well clear of the car.

414

'The new Beaujolais!' he roared in drunken tones.

'It's a bit late in the season this year,' Isabelle whispered and giggled nervously.

Newman threw another bottle, repeating the well-known slogan and Isabelle hurled a bottle from her side. The troops were standing further back to have a chance of catching the bottles. Newman, grinning drunkenly, began honking his horn for them to remove the barrier so he could drive on.

'We're in a hurry,' he shouted good-humouredly.

'You won't be a virgin much longer,' a soldier shouted at Isabelle.

'Obscene lout,' she muttered, smiled, threw out another bottle.

Newman kept his hand on the horn, leaned out of the window, hurled a bottle at a soldier close to the gates. The soldier caught it in mid-air. Several soldiers were already drinking the wine, passing bottles round. The soldier close to the gate opened it, waved them on, bottle in his hand. Newman grinned, saluted, sped across the bridge to the far side and Isabelle guided him through side streets.

He began to recognize where he was – in the vicinity of the Mériadeck office and shopping complex. A concrete horror which was more like a fortress. He checked his rear-view mirror and saw an Army jeep with four soldiers following him. He told Isabelle. Then told her the mist had blotted it out.

'Turn right!' she said.

He swung into a narrow side street. In the murk Bordeaux looked even more dreadful. Wrecks of old buildings, with Cinzano posters on the end walls, smeared with grime and peeling at the edges. Again he had the impression of a city which had been bombed.

'Turn left quickly!'

He found himself in a narrow street with battered cars parked on both pavements. Isabelle was leaning forward

415

staring through the gloom. Newman looked in the mirror. No sign of the jeep.

'Grab that slot! We're nearly there.'

Newman swung the Renault on to the pavement, swivelled the wheel, crawling, straightened up an inch from the car parked in front. He backed a few inches, stopped, switched off the engine. Even in London no one would have regarded the space he occupied as a feasible slot.

He'd noticed the Citroën backing down the street towards him as he'd swung in so swiftly. The car stopped as he stepped out and nearly slipped on a patch of solid ice. The air on his face was cold as the Arctic. A smartly dressed woman jumped out of the Citroën, came up to him, her face distorted with fury.

'That was my slot. Didn't you see me backing? I want that slot,' she raved.

Newman reopened his door, reached in, brought out the only vintage bottle of Beaujolais. He bowed, presented it to her with a flourish.

'We've just got married. A present to celebrate our happiness. Please.'

She grabbed the bottle, turned it round, peered at the vintage. Glancing at Isabelle who stood on the pavement, she tossed her head.

'I suppose it is some compensation. God knows where I'll get another slot. The bloody troops have surrounded a building just up the street. Their jeeps have five slots. It's disgusting . . .'

Without a word of thanks she returned to her car, backed it past the Renault. The vehicle disappeared into grey mist. Newman looked at Isabelle, spread his hands in a gesture of resignation.

'I thought it best to keep her quiet.'

'She'll keep quiet, the greedy harridan. While she was telling you about the troops I saw the gleam in her eye. It was the vintage, wasn't it?'

416

'Yes. And she may have done us a favour. I don't like the sound of those troops surrounding a building. How far is it to the passage?'

'About a hundred yards further along this street.'

Newman put his arm round her and they walked slowly, more interested in each other apparently than where they were going. He thanked God he'd taken the precaution. As the mist drifted away they saw ahead the military jeeps parked either side of the street on the pavements. Two cars, which had presumably occupied slots the Army needed, lay on their sides in the middle of the street.

Newman sidled them into the deep alcove of a doorway. On both sides troops with automatic weapons were stationed. All were staring at the same building on the same side as Newman and Isabelle. A familiar figure was crouched by the entrance, packing something against the base of the door. Newman recognized the evil gnome-like Sergeant Rey.

'Could that be the building we're going to?' he asked Isabelle.

'Yes, it is. The Passage Emile Zola is just a few yards from here. It runs down the side of the building.'

'The troops are preparing to assault it. De Forge's boobytrap expert is packing what I imagine is explosive by the door to blow it open.'

'We've arrived in the nick of time.'

'Or just too late,' Newman replied, thinking of the poor devil, Stahl, holed up inside.

44

Tweed took the call from Paula in his office at the Ministry
of the Interior. His first concern was to ask whether it was a
safe line.

'Quite safe,' she assured him. 'I've taken precautions.
I've had time to think about your request for me to return
to see you.'

'I'm listening,' Tweed coaxed her when she paused.

'I've read certain documents Jean Burgoyne was carrying. I think I should bring them to you at once aboard the
chopper Lasalle is sending. Jean risked her life—' she
gulped— 'lost her life to get these to me. And they're really
important. That's one thing.'

'And the other?' Tweed enquired concealing his relief.

'I think it's awful the way Jean is lying out you know
where. Out in the cold and the damp. I know it doesn't
make any difference to her . . .'

'Stop worrying,' Tweed interjected. 'A team of DST
men was dispatched by Lasalle from Bordeaux to take her
away, fly the body back to Paris. The machine bringing her
is already in the air.'

'Thank God. There's one more thing.'

'Which is?'

'I'm only returning to Paris on the understanding I can
come back here very quickly. You know who I have to
locate.'

Kalmar, Tweed thought. He was careful not to tell her
Lasalle was very upset about the murder of Burgoyne. He
was thinking quickly about her request.

'I agree to your suggestion,' he decided.

'And the condition laid down?'

'The request you made,' Tweed corrected her.

'Of course, I'm sorry. It was a request.'

'I agree.'

'And that DST team,' she persisted. 'They did know where to find her?'

'Newman was very specific when he phoned me earlier. About the location. I repeat, she is already in mid-air. We look forward to seeing you. Now please put Butler on the line . . .'

He had put down the phone when Kuhlmann came into the office. In his hand he held a folded fax sheet. He handed it over to Tweed.

'Just came in from Wiesbaden. You were right. Damn it, you always are.'

At the Atlantique they had devised a simple system of making sure the duty clerk – who also handled the small switchboard – didn't listen in while someone was making a call. Nield had made friends with the day and night clerks.

Both smoked. The day clerk favoured Gitanes, the night man Gauloises. Nield always had a spare pack to give them, plus a generous tip for services like sending up sandwiches and coffee.

He made it a habit to stroll down and engage them in conversation whenever a call was being made. So they wouldn't suspect his intention he also stopped by for a chat when no call was being made.

When Butler had finished speaking to Tweed, Paula asked him what had been said. Butler punched her arm gently.

'If you must know everything, Pete and I have to accompany you to the dawn chopper, see you safely aboard. When you come back from Paris we're not to let you out of sight for a second. Tweed was pretty ferocious about that.'

'I have the feeling Tweed knows a lot more than he's telling us. It's almost as though I'm a target and he knows that,' Paula mused.

'Tweed knows what he's doing.' Butler checked his watch. 'You've had no sleep and you have to meet that Alouette at dawn. How about some kip?'

'You're right.' She sat perched on the edge of her bed with a worried look. 'I suppose I ought to flop out now.'

'You look bothered about something.'

'Recently I've remembered something very weird that happened in Aldeburgh. Don't ask me what – I need to think it through. And I wonder how Bob is getting on in Bordeaux?'

'There may be a rear entrance to that building in the Emile Zola passage,' Isabelle said. 'Like there is to my mother's apartment here.'

'Then I'd better risk it,' Newman decided. 'Before those troops storm the building.'

'*We* had better risk it,' Isabelle said firmly. 'Using a different version of the trick which came off at the Pont de Pierre. Don't argue. I know that passage.'

She gripped his arm, pressed herself against him after making sure her white scarf was draped over her shoulders, gazed up at him with adoring eyes. They walked slowly and when a soldier turned to look at them Isabelle pulled Newman's head down and kissed him full on the mouth. The soldier grinned, turned away as they drew level with the entrance to the passage.

They slipped inside the narrow alley unchallenged. There was a smell of rancid rubbish, Isabelle wrinkled her nose as she hurried Newman to a door near the end of the alley. He noticed that at one time there must have been an exit at the other end but the outline of an arch was blocked up. Pity. No alternative escape route. Isabelle aimed a pencil flash Newman had lent her. The light showed the name plate below the entryphone, the grille smeared and rusty.

Jean Picot. 3ème.

'That's the name Stahl is hiding under?' Isabelle whispered.

'Yes.' Newman looked round the end of the alley. No sign of any life. 'It's strange there are no troops here.'

'Don't you see? They missed this alley. You nearly walked past it yourself. I dragged you in.'

'True.' Newman was looking up the sheer wall. 'He's at the top of the building according to that name plate. So here goes.'

He pressed the button on the entryphone, pressed his ear close to the shoddy grille. Was the damned instrument still in working order? A voice spoke in French.

'Who is it? I'm just going to bed.'

'Gamelin.' Newman repeated the codeword. 'Gamelin.'

'Come up quickly.'

Isabelle pushed the door when the buzzer went. Newman pulled her back when it was open an inch or so, his foot keeping it that way. He took the pencil flash off her, swiftly ran the beam all round the door frame. No wires. No indication of a boobytrap. Was it possible that the troops didn't know about this entrance?

'Is this passage marked on any map?' he asked quickly.

'None that I've ever seen. Shouldn't we hurry?'

She nearly slipped on the ice before dashing inside as Newman aimed the flashlight ahead of her, showing an old iron-railed staircase. Despite the large cloth bag she had hung over her shoulder she ran up the stairs with great agility as Newman, annoyed at her impetuous act, followed and guided the way, shining the beam in front of her. He had pushed the door to the alley shut with his foot.

Isabelle was flying up the stairs, flight by flight, the bag

421

swaying against her hip. At any moment Newman expected to hear the muffled explosion of the front entrance being blown in. Had they walked into a trap? What kept him going was the thought of Stahl, the agent of Kuhlmann who had stayed under cover for so long. He must have a lot of guts.

Pounding up the worn bleak concrete steps, the treads worn in the middle by God knew how many thousands of footsteps which had naturally moved up the centre. The whole place had a musty smell – bleak was the word. The atmosphere of one of the many abandoned-looking buildings which infested Bordeaux. They reached the top landing.

Newman raised the beam, saw alongside the closed door a similar name plate to the one in the alley. No entryphone. Just a button to press the bell. He pushed his thumb against it, held it there. They had so little time left.

The door opened a few inches still on a chain. The face which peered out was not what Newman had expected. Round and with a bushy mop of hair and a bushy moustache. Eyes behind horn-rim glasses peered at them.

'Gamelin,' Newman repeated quickly. 'Troops are surrounding the building. We've got to get out of here fast.'

'English?'

The query was put in the same language, not French this time. Newman felt brief annoyance. Everyone else had accepted him as a Frenchman. He reverted to English.

'Yes. Do you want to escape or don't you? We've risked our own lives to . . .'

'Come in.'

The door closed for a second, the chain was released, and they were inside as Stahl closed and bolted the door with one hand. In the other he held a grenade. Newman stared at it, then at Stahl. The German was small, tubby, and exuded energy. His eyes studied Newman, then Isabelle. He moved close to Newman.

'I recognize you from pictures in the papers. Kuhlmann has talked about you. But who is this girl?' he whispered.

'Isabelle Thomas. She's proved herself.'

Isabelle's hearing was more acute than Stahl had anticipated. She glared at him.

'I have already killed two of de Forge's men. How many more would you like me to dispatch before you're happy?'

'I have to check,' the German said sharply. 'That's how I've survived so far.'

This conversation was quick-fire. But Newman was anxious to get out of the building. Just assuming that was possible.

'We have to leave here fast,' he told Stahl. 'Back down the staircase we came up and into the passage?'

'Too dangerous.' Stahl shook his head. 'Show me the soles of your shoes,' he ordered Isabelle. She perched on one leg like a steady stork, showed him the sole of her trainer studded with rubber. He nodded, turned to Newman, who swiftly performed the same action. Why was Stahl wasting valuable time? He was wearing rubber-soled shoes with the surface hardly worn. Again Stahl nodded.

'It's very dangerous – going out over the rooftops. They are covered with ice. But more dangerous to risk that staircase.' As though to confirm his opinion they heard somewhere way below them the muffled thud of an explosion.

'Rey has blown open the front door,' Newman warned. 'Have you collected information?'

He was asking the question as Stahl, clad in a leather jacket and corduroy trousers, moved quickly to a door, opened it, revealing a narrow staircase going upwards to a skylight. Stahl darted up the staircase, pulling on a pair of thick gloves. He answered as he reached the top tread and

423

raised a hand to the skylight window. Over his shoulder was slung a leather bag similar to the canvas bag Isabelle was carrying as she rushed up the staircase behind Newman after closing the door at the bottom.

'A lot of information,' Stahl replied. 'In a book in my pocket. The grenade was in case it was soldiers outside the door when you arrived. I'd have threatened to blow myself up with them. Remember, the roofs are like a skating rink. I go up first, then you. We'll haul Isabelle up after us.'

Earlier he had dropped the grenade inside his bag. While talking he had pushed back the skylight on to the roof and icy air flooded down the staircase. Agilely, Stahl hauled himself on to the roof, spread his body flat and extended a hand to Newman.

Moving cautiously, Newman emerged into the bitter air of the Siberian night. The roof had a steep pitch and he saw it was above the street where the troops were assembled for the storming of the building. They must already be on their way up. On one landing Newman had noticed when they were racing up to Stahl's apartment another staircase. At this point the troops could run straight up to Stahl's apartment.

By the light of a sputtering neon sign on the far side of the street Newman saw the sinister gleam of pack ice on the tiled roof. He was sprawled alongside Stahl, one foot dug into a hole where a tile had disappeared. He heard below a splintering crash from inside Stahl's apartment. They had already broken down the door. He was reaching down for Isabelle, had grabbed her under her left armpit when he heard the thud of Army boots coming up the staircase. He tried to haul her up, but she wouldn't budge. She stared up at him, her expression grim.

'He's got hold of my leg. Hang on to me, Bob. Don't touch my right arm . . .'

It flashed across his mind what a wide range of moods she had: excitable when he'd arrived at her apartment in

Arcachon. Now with her life at stake she was cold, calculating. Her right hand fiddled inside her canvas bag, came out holding a kitchen knife with a wide blade. Taking a firm grip on the handle, she looked down, saw the soldier staring up at her, holding her leg in an iron grip. She raised the knife, aimed for the side of his neck, plunged it in deep, still gripping the handle. He emitted a horrible gurgle, let go of her leg as blood spurted, collapsed into the staircase.

Newman hauled her on to the roof. She sprawled beside him, her left hand gripping the rim of the skylight frame, her right hand wiping the mess off the knife before she dropped it back inside her bag. Newman used his left foot to kick ice off the roof. Three tiles scuttered down with the ice, exposing rotting rafters. He jammed his foot inside the exposed hole and Isabelle rammed her left foot into the hole he'd left for her. Newman was holding on to the skylight frame as he glanced round. Stahl was perched on top of the roof, legs astride each side as he beckoned them to join him.

'We go this way,' he called out, still speaking English.

Newman was about to help Isabelle to join him when she slipped. Appalled, he watched her sliding down the icy slope to the brink. Her feet dug into the metal gutter below the roof. Her gloved hands clawed the roof for better purchase, found none. Only the gutter was saving her. Newman let go of the skylight frame, slithered towards her. His gloved hands grasped one of the exposed rafters. Holding on, he swivelled himself through one hundred and eighty degrees, let go, hoping one foot would embed itself in the same hole. Both feet slid into the hole, were held by the cross beam below the rafters. He stretched out a hand as Isabelle stretched hers and he had her round the wrist. He was on the verge of hauling her up when she jolted, the full weight of her body jerking in his hand, but he held on. The bloody gutter had given

425

way, falling into the street. Which he should have
expected. This was Bordeaux.

He hauled her slowly up over the glistening surface
and now the ice helped her body to move smoothly.
Lying alongside him, she jammed her feet into the large
hole, managed a wan smile. He looked up at the ridge of
the roof where Stahl had moved further along like someone astride a vaulting horse in a gymnasium. Stahl
beckoned again for them to join him.

'We go this way,' he called out.

Newman had one arm round Isabelle's waist as his
other hand hammered at the ice, dislodged more rotten
tiles, found purchase to haul them higher. It seemed
slow progress but the skylight was close to the ridge and
Newman had hauled both of them to the summit.
Isabelle was closer to the skylight as Stahl shouted a
warning. Glancing over her shoulder, Newman's arm
still holding her firm round the waist, she saw a soldier
gripping an automatic weapon emerging. Newman was
heaving her up to the ridge when she spoke.

'Hold my right arm,' she commanded.

Perched on the ridge, he did what she had told him to,
leaning down to grip her arm as she deliberately let her
body slide a foot or so. Drawing up her left knee, she
shot out her leg as the soldier, now on the roof, fumbled
with his weapon. Her trainer hammered into the face of
the sprawled soldier. He lost the grip his left hand had
had on the skylight frame. They watched as he began to
slide. Desperately his hands clawed at the roof as the
weapon slithered out of view. His feet dug into the ice,
loosened a large slab. The slab skated over the edge.
High up Newman could almost see to street level. The
soldier's momentum increased. He followed the ice slab
over the brink, his arms windmilling as he screamed, an
ear-splitting yell of terror, while his body plummeted
downwards. The yell stopped abruptly as his body hit the

426

iron-hard cobbles four storeys down.

Newman had hauled Isabelle on to the ridge, they were easing themselves along the ice-cold rounded tiles when the head of another soldier appeared above the fanlight opening. Stahl took a grenade out of his bag, removed the pin, tossed it carefully. The grenade disappeared down the fanlight opening. A sharp *crack!* The soldier's head disappeared. There was one further sound – the tumbling of bodies down the staircase. Then a sudden silence. Newman and Isabelle worked their way along the ridge. He was worried by the sudden disappearance of Stahl who had dropped out of sight. Literally. He was aching from the effort of straddling the ridge top when he reached the end. Looking down he saw why Stahl had vanished.

Six feet or so below the end of the ridge was a railed metal platform. Stahl stood looking up with a beaming smile. The German had nerves of steel. Newman glanced over his shoulder, saw Isabelle was close behind him and there were no signs of activity from the distant skylight. He dropped to the platform, his body loose, his knees bending to cushion the drop.

Turning round, he was just in time to grab hold of Isabelle by the waist, breaking the force of her fall. She was breathing heavily, had removed her white scarf and stuffed it inside her bag. She smoothed her hair.

'Where to now?' Newman asked.

Stahl put a finger to his lips, ushered Newman to the rear of the platform, leaned forward and pointed down. Newman leaned over and saw he was looking down into the Passage Emile Zola. It was crowded with troops who carried automatic weapons. Presumably they'd found their way down from the landing where the two staircases met inside the building. He moved away as Stahl tugged at his sleeve.

'Is there any way out?' Newman asked. 'I don't fancy any more rooftop climbing – we might not be so lucky next time.'

'How did you get here?' Stahl asked.

'By car. A hired Renault. Left it parked the other side of the entrance to the passage. About twenty yards from it. We'll never be able to reach it without being spotted.'

'I think we might,' Stahl replied. 'They won't expect us in that street. They'll be sending troops all over the rooftops. We go down this fire escape first. I suggest I lead the way with Isabelle . . .'

Newman noticed for the first time a flight of metal steps leading down the side of the building from the platform. He followed as Stahl descended, one hand on the side rail, the other round Isabelle's waist. It was a gesture she resented.

Inwardly her nerves were screaming but outwardly she was composed. They descended one flight, reached a landing, turned down a fresh flight. Stahl kept glancing into the well below them. Then both Isabelle's feet slid from under her and she'd have crashed down the flight but for Stahl's tight grip, holding her against him until she recovered her balance.

'These metal treads are coated with solid ice,' he explained. 'It really is no time to practise skating.'

She looked at him and he grinned impishly. From that moment she liked Stahl. And she felt that with these two men looking after her there was a chance they'd escape from the hell that Bordeaux had become.

On the first floor Stahl led the way across a treacherous metal bridge where the ice was solid underfoot from rail to rail. At ground level he led them through a labyrinth of alleyways on what seemed to Newman to be a circular route. They emerged into the street where the Renault was parked only fifty yards away.

The street was deserted. Stahl's prediction had come true: the troops were scaling the world of the rooftops. At Newman's suggestion the German slipped into the back, hid himself under a travelling rug. Poking out his bushy head, his moustache frosted with ice mist, he joked.

428

'I've found a bottle of Beaujolais. May I imbibe? My excuse is that if we're stopped you're taking a drunken friend home. Me!'

Isabelle guided Newman through the ice mist along a new route. The grey vapour made Bordeaux even more shabby and derelict, if possible. There was a checkpoint and a barrier on the far side of the Pont Saint Jean, but Newman was in no mood for further encounters with de Forge's troops. He had also noticed the mist was very thick by the river – more like a fog. In his undimmed headlights he saw shadowed figures drifting as though in a nightmare and beyond another of the flimsy barriers they'd seen on the Pont de Pierre.

'We're not stopping,' he warned his passengers.

Isabelle was puzzled. Approaching the western end of the bridge Newman dimmed his headlights, reduced speed to a crawl as though pulling up. Suddenly, driving on to the bridge, he pressed his thumb on the horn and kept it at a blaring howl. Switching his headlights full on, he pressed his foot down, roaring over the bridge, smashing through the barrier. The drifting shadows jumped out of his way to both sides. He increased speed, thought he heard a rifle shot, then they were way beyond the bridge.

'Turn right now!' Isabelle shouted, straining against her seat belt to see where they were.

He swung the wheel, his horn silent, the tyres screeching at the wildness of his driving. He slowed down as they came to a sharp corner in a narrow street. Isabelle guided him through a complex labyrinth which seemed to go on and on for ever. Without warning they were clear of the suburbs, free of even a hint of ice mist, driving through open country along a deserted road.

'How long to Arcachon?' Newman asked.

'We'll be there well before dawn.'

'We have to be.'

Newman was almost exhausted, flaked out with two

endless drives, the tension of rescuing Stahl. And ahead of him was a drive to meet the Alouette near the *étang*. After that a long drive south to the Landes, to pick up their witness. Martine, the crone who collected brushwood on the Atlantic shore. Could he last out? And if he ran into trouble, would his reflexes be fast enough?

45

The tension which grows in the early hours under pressure was showing itself inside the Ministry of the Interior in Paris. Tweed, unshaven, sat behind his desk as Navarre came in from an emergency Cabinet meeting. Lasalle, also short of sleep like the others, was pacing restlessly. Only Kuhlmann, seated in a leather armchair was, like Tweed, relaxed and alert.

'Any news?' Navarre demanded, looking at Lasalle as he perched his buttocks on Tweed's desk.

'A whole fleet of CRS trucks is speeding down to Bordeaux, may already have reached the city. They're being parked round the Prefecture.'

'More psychological warfare,' Tweed said quietly.

'Psychological warfare?' Navarre queried.

'The Berliet trucks have no CRS inside them,' Lasalle explained. 'Only a driver and one other man in the cab. Their arrival will be reported within minutes to de Forge. With luck they'll have to wake him to tell him – ruin his night's sleep. Tweed wants to wear him down.'

'But how will you transport the huge number of CRS when it comes to the final confrontation?' Navarre asked brusquely.

'I have secretly assembled a whole armada of helicopters at airfields on the outskirts of Paris. When we strike we do it from the air.'

'I like the idea,' Navarre decided. 'I have recorded a TV address to the nation. I hammer home the point that the civil power takes precedence over the military in democracy.'

'The Cabinet was told this?' Lasalle, alarmed, enquired.

Navarre smiled grimly. 'No, Louis Janin, our so-loyal Minister of Defence, would have informed de Forge at once. I have a feeling we are close to that final confrontation.' He took a cassette from his jacket pocket, handed it to Lasalle. 'That is the recording of my address to the nation. Lock it in your personal safe at rue des Saussaies. Please remain available there or here. It's only a short walk to your HQ.'

'When do you expect de Forge to make his move?' Kuhlmann asked.

'I suspect it has already begun. This dangerous exercise General Masson has sanctioned – with the so-called assumption that they're repelling a North African invasion by the fictitious General Ali. I have just heard that some of de Forge's advanced motor-cycle patrols have reached Angoulême.'

'A long way north of Bordeaux and closer to Paris,' Tweed observed.

'Exactly,' Navarre agreed. 'And now, gentleman, I must snatch a few hours' sleep.'

The others agreed it was a sound idea and Tweed was left alone. Opening a map he studied the position of Angoulême, shook his head. He was folding the map when the phone rang. It was Monica at Park Crescent, still at her desk in the early hours.

'Howard has returned from his extended trip to the States,' she told him. 'He wants to see you over here for consultation at the earliest moment. He's just come from a visit to the PM.'

431

'Tell him I'll catch the first available scheduled flight this morning. Also tell him I'm flying back to Paris before the evening.'

'I don't think that's quite what he had in mind,' Monica warned.

'Then I'll put it in his mind when I get there. All you need to confirm is that I'm coming. And I may want to drive to Aldeburgh while I'm in Britain. Again a quick trip. Back in town in time to catch a Paris flight.'

'Should I have your car ready?'

'The Ford Escort,' Tweed replied. 'Very reliable but not too noticeable. Also check on the present whereabouts of Lord Dane Dawlish and his catamaran, the *Steel Vulture*. Heathcoate, the Harwich Harbour Master, might help.'

'I'd already thought of him. Look forward to seeing you.'

Tweed frowned as he put down the receiver. Howard was the Director, his only superior in the SIS. What on earth was this urgent summons all about? And what had passed between Howard and the new PM, a man of very decided views? He'd interviewed Tweed before the journey to Paris, listened to what Tweed had to say, had agreed his mission was vital.

He picked up the phone after checking his watch, dialled the number of the Atlantique in Arcachon. When the duty clerk answered he phrased his request carefully. No name.

'I wish to speak to Mr Harry Butler who is staying with you. Tell him it's a friend – he's expecting my call . . .'

'Butler here. I'm glad you called. Please hang on just a sec . . .'

Butler put his hand over the mouthpiece, called out to Nield who was catnapping on the bed with his clothes on.

'Pete, a call's come through.'

'I'll get down fast.'

Nield slipped on his shoes, checked his jacket pocket as he ran to the door to make sure he had a packet of the Gauloises favoured by the night clerk. When he reached the lobby the clerk hastily put down his phone as Nield asked for a cup of coffee, explaining he couldn't sleep.

'Go ahead,' Butler said in the bedroom.

'I have to leave for London by the first flight. I'll be back late this evening. Warn Paula. That's it.'

'Will do.'

In Paris Tweed picked up the phone again to call the airport – to ask them to hold a return ticket to London for him. He had no inkling of the consequences which would follow his call to Arcachon.

At the Atlantique in her bedroom Paula was wakened by the alarm clock she'd set for 4 a.m. She wanted to be ready in good time to board the Alouette.

She showered, dressed quickly, applied make-up in three minutes. She snapped shut the lid of the case she had packed the night before and at that moment she heard the agreed tattoo tapping on her locked door. Even so, she took the Browning automatic from her shoulder bag before opening the door on the chain. It was Butler.

'Come in, Harry. I'm ready for the trip. Is Bob back?' she asked anxiously.

'Not yet. Not to worry. It was one hell of a round-about route they were taking.'

'I hope nothing's gone wrong,' she said as she closed and locked the door. 'I didn't like the idea of his going back to Bordeaux again one little bit.'

There was a note of concern verging on affection in her tone, Butler noticed. He smiled reassuringly.

'Bob can look after himself. What I came to tell you is I've decided we ought to move out of here. It's dangerous to stay in one place for long.'

433

'But where to?'

'I can't find another suitable hotel. I'm going to ask Bob whether we could move for a few days to Isabelle's apartment. Difficult for anyone to trace us there.'

'Isabelle?' Paula sounded doubtful. 'I can get on with her but I'm not so sure it would work the other way.'

'Bob will fix that . . .'

He looked at the door where the correct tattoo rapping had been repeated. Extracting the Walther he opened the door on the chain, saw Newman standing outside with a bushy-haired stranger. He let them inside and Newman introduced them by first names only to Stahl. Paula took an immediate liking to the amiable German who looked her straight in the eye as they shook hands. Newman was determined to check the bona fides of Egon Stahl.

'Egon wants to put through a call to Kuhlmann,' he said. 'I'll get the number.' He looked at Butler. 'I see Nield is still downstairs, playing poker with the night clerk . . .'

Butler nodded. In fact Nield had been unable to sleep, so he had gone down into the lobby to play cards. An expert card sharp, Nield was just about to deal when he saw Butler peer over the banister very soon after Newman had returned with the jolly bushy-moustached man. Butler was signalling they were about to make a call. Nield shuffled the pack again, dealt the clerk a winning Royal Flush. That should keep his mind on the game while the call was being made.

In Paula's room Newman dialled the Ministry of the Interior, gave the code word Tweed had suggested, asked to speak to him. After a pause Lasalle, sounding fogged with sleep, came on the line. He listened to Newman before telling him his boss had just left for the airport.

'Actually we want to speak to Otto Kuhlmann,' Newman explained.

A far more alert Kuhlmann came to the phone quickly and Newman handed the instrument to Stahl. He had concealed from the German that he spoke his language as fluently as he spoke French.

Listening to Stahl he heard a reference to *Kapitan* Fischer. The emphasis on *Kapitan* told him this was Stahl's identification word. Stahl reported that he had obtained vital data, that he would keep it until he met Kuhlmann. From the rest of the conversation Newman gathered Stahl's chief had told him that his rescuer was totally reliable, that he could tell him everything.

Paula was watching Newman as he sagged on her bed, checked his watch. She thought Newman looked at the end of his tether, desperately short of sleep, haggard, and with a drawn face. He leaned towards her, whispered hoarsely as Stahl ended his conversation.

'Tweed is no longer in Paris. Lasalle told me he was on his way to the airport.'

'He was expecting me,' Paula protested. 'Aboard the Alouette.'

Butler had joined them. He listened for a moment, then lowered his voice while Stahl was washing his hands. The sound of the water running into the basin muffled their conversation.

'Tweed said he wouldn't be back from London until some time this evening.'

'Then there's no point in my flying to Paris aboard the chopper,' Paula decided, still watching Newman who had stifled a yawn. 'Harry, you'd better call Lasalle and tell him to send the chopper to land at dawn twenty-four hours later.'

'I *have* to drive to the *Landes*,' Newman commented, spacing out his words, talking with an effort.

'Like hell,' Paula snapped. 'You're flaked out. Anyone can see that. You'll end up driving the car into some ditch.'

'Have to collect the witness . . . Martine . . .'

'Yes, we do,' Paula continued briskly. 'So I'll share the driving with Harry and Pete. You can sleep in the back.

Then you'll be fresh enough to guide us when we get close to the witness.'

She used the last word because Stahl, adjusting his glasses and smiling, had come close to them. He stared at Newman, then at Paula.

'I'm OK,' Newman growled. He propped himself against the headboard to stop falling asleep. 'You stay here, Paula. The Landes . . . dangerous.'

'It would be for you,' she snapped and stamped her foot. 'You say you're OK, you haven't slept for ages, and you can't even keep your eyes open now.'

'And,' Butler reminded him, 'Pete and I have to stay next to Paula. Remember?'

Stahl intervened. 'You have a problem? Maybe I could help? I slept during the day and I'm fresh.'

'You wouldn't have a weapon of sorts?' Butler enquired.

'Would these help? Give you confidence?' Stahl replied.

In his eager beaver manner he unzipped his leather bag. Butler stared as he produced a Heckler and Koch sub-machine-gun. Newman recognized the type used by the SAS that had a collapsible stock. As he went on talking Stahl was careful to aim the muzzle at the ceiling.

'This 9mm sub-machine-gun has a rate of fire of six hundred and fifty rounds a minute, a range of almost five hundred feet. I have a lot of spare mags, as you see. Also I have grenades, a lot of them. Like this one.'

'You're carting around a ruddy armoury,' Butler commented.

'But I was trapped in that building before Mr Newman and the girl, Isabelle, brought me out. I couldn't have tried to escape without transport. The patrols in the streets keep stopping people at night – especially those on foot. I could come with you.'

'You're hired for the duration,' Paula decided without consulting anyone. Newman blinked at her.

'You've taken charge?' he enquired.

436

'Yes. Someone has to until you're fresh. I just elected myself. Harry, you'd better call Lasalle now, turn back that Alouette.'

Butler told Newman they were moving base to Isabelle's apartment before they left, went to the phone. Newman raised a hand, dropped it.

'I'd better tell Isabelle that . . . ask her, I mean.'

'No!' Paula's tone was firm. 'I'll talk to her briefly before we set out for the Landes. Won't tell her where we're going, but I'll check to see whether she can cope with this lot. I can handle her.'

'Still don't think you should come with us to the Landes, it could – will be – a damned dangerous undertaking,' Newman protested again.

'It's decided,' Paula told him. 'And try not to go to sleep before we carry you into the back of the car. It will be a full house,' she added, glancing at Stahl, 'but we'll manage. And both of you should have a shave. If you don't mind.'

Victor Rosewater, clad in a British warm camel-hair, arriving on the flight from Switzerland at Bordeaux Airport, walked across the concourse. Stopped by an Army patrol, he waved a pass at them.

'Get out of my way, I'm in a hurry.'

He hastened to where he'd left his car parked. Two minutes later he was roaring away confidently. His destination was Arcachon and, as usual, he wanted to get to where he was going quickly.

To avoid registering at a hotel he had hired a small cabin cruiser moored at the edge of the *bassin*. He bought food from a supermarket, cooked it himself in the cruiser's galley, or ate out at restaurants. Rosewater was expert at evading a country's regulations designed to record who had arrived from abroad.

When he'd checked his vessel his first call was planned

for the Bar Martinique. He was determined to trace the movements of the talkative Irishman who frequented the bar. Then he hoped to meet Paula Grey again, even if it meant exercising patience.

Carrying his hold-all, Marler disembarked from the Air Inter flight at Orly, Paris. Once again he avoided the waiting taxis: cab drivers had good memories.

He used the anonymous Metro to reach the station nearest his shoddy apartment close to the rue du Bac. On his way up to his room, the key in his pocket, he doled out more francs to the reception clerk – enough for another two weeks' stay.

'Business good?' the clerk enquired, accepting the tip.

'So, so . . .'

Inside his room Marler checked for any indication that it had been searched. If so, he'd move to the other apartment he'd reserved a few streets away. There was no sign of any intrusion.

Taking off his trainers, he sat on his made-up bed and took the mobile phone from his hold-all. Dialling the Ministry of the Interior, he asked for Tweed by using a codename. After a delay Lasalle came on the phone, told him the man he wanted was abroad for the whole day.

'Thank you. I'll call him later, René.'

46

Tweed was on the warpath at Park Crescent. Arriving on the first flight from Paris, he had found Howard waiting for him in his own office. Monica greeted him, looked grim, then buried her head in a file.

'You bought yourself a new suit in the States?' Tweed suggested with a straight face.

'You must be joking.' Howard was indignant. 'This came from Harrods. Chester Barrie. The best money can buy off the peg.'

Plump-faced, his complexion pink, clean shaven, six feet tall and with a well-fed look, the Director was at his most pompous. He stood by Tweed's desk, shot his cuffs to expose jewelled links and smoothed one of the lapels of his dark grey suit with a thin chalk stripe. The trousers had the fashionable turnups. He placed a hand on his right hip.

'I called you back to find out what is going on in France. And I've had an interview with the PM since I returned. I understand that, like his predecessor, he gave you one of those damned personal directives.'

'Yes, he did,' Tweed said tersely, seating himself behind his desk.

'Well, did he tell you that he's working on a twin-track basis?'

'What does twin-track mean?' Tweed enquired, polishing his glasses on the corner of his handkerchief.

'It means . .' Howard paused, took up his favourite pose, sprawling in the armchair with one leg propped over the arm. His black leather shoes gleamed like glass. 'It means,' he repeated, 'that the PM has another unit in the field of which we have no knowledge.'

Of which . . . Typical of the Director's liking for pedantic phraseology. Tweed began drumming his fingers slowly on the desk, a sign that he was in a mood of cold fury. Monica looked up, intrigued at the prospect of battle.

'Doesn't he realize,' Tweed demanded, 'that a manoeuvre like that can cause total disaster? Two different units stumbling around on the same territory without any idea of the other's existence? Didn't you point out that it could lead to a catastrophe?'

'Well . . .' Howard adjusted the display handkerchief in his breast pocket. 'He is the new boy. We need his support so we have to give him some licence.'

'In other words you're telling me you didn't have the guts to object,' Tweed growled.

'I deeply resent your insubordinate language.'

'Resent away.' Tweed showed no contrition. 'Did he by any chance give you a hint as to who the other unit is?'

'None at all.' Howard's manner was stiff. 'And I most certainly didn't ask him. We are talking about the new PM. He has a right to his own ideas.'

'He struck me as a man who appreciates straight talk.' Tweed was disgusted. 'He was waiting to see if you'd press him, insist on being given the information.'

'You weren't there . . .'

'He was testing you,' Tweed insisted.

'My dear chap.' Howard ran a manicured hand over his perfectly brushed dark hair. '*We* are the ones who are on trial. My guess is he's simply not relying on one organization. The situation is serious. By the way, how serious is it?'

Tersely, Tweed brought him up to date. He concluded by revealing he'd made a quick call from a London Airport public phone to Lasalle – that Lasalle had received a late call from Butler saying they were moving south to bring back a witness.

'South?' Howard sounded appalled. 'South from Arcachon? My God! Straight into the jaws of the lion's den. The den of General Charles de Forge. Whereabouts exactly are they going to?'

'The Landes, I expect.'

'Heavens, man! Are you crazy?' Howard swung his leg on the floor, jumped up, buttoned his jacket. 'You've just told me about this hideous burial ground of de Forge's. In the Landes. How could you let our people venture near there again?'

'I let my people in the field have wide latitude as to how they react in an emergency. You know that,' Tweed said quietly. 'They took the decision themselves and I am backing them to the hilt. If you think you can run an operation from an armchair here, then you've spent too long in the States.'

The quiet vehemence of Tweed's attack threw Howard off balance. He pursed his lips, looked at Monica, who looked back at him.

'What are your next plans?' Howard asked eventually in a reasonable tone. 'I mean you personally.'

'Before I return to Paris tonight I am driving to Aldeburgh. That's where it all started – with the murder of Karin Rosewater. If Lord Dawlish is at home I'm calling on him.'

'For what purpose, if I may ask?'

'You may. He's up to his neck in this thing, I'm sure now. I want to rattle his cage.'

'I insist you take protection. No, hear me out.' He held up his hand as Tweed opened his mouth to protest. 'What about Fred Hamilton? Be good experience for him. And he scored tops on the target range I understand.'

'He's very promising,' Tweed admitted.

'Then that's settled.' Howard beamed his broad smile. 'I

441

shall feel far less worried as you're going there with Hamilton by your side. Must get on. Piles waiting for me to deal with . . .'

Monica stared at Howard's back as he left the room. She looked furious and burst out as soon as she judged Howard was well clear.

'Piles, indeed! I dealt with everything that came in for him while he was away. All he has to look at are copies of my replies.' She calmed down. 'Still, you could have knocked me down with a feather when he insisted Hamilton accompanied you. He sounded really concerned.'

'He was,' Tweed agreed. 'And it will take him time to learn to cope with the different style of the new PM.'

'What are you doing in France to cope with de Forge?' she asked.

'I'll tell you.'

Tweed clasped his hands behind his neck, stared at the ceiling after checking his watch. He began to talk.

'In my temporary office in the Ministry of the Interior I have pinned a photograph of de Forge Lasalle found for me on the wall. It faces my desk. I study my enemy, try to put myself in his shoes.'

'I read that General Montgomery did that – had a picture of Rommel pinned up in his caravan so *he* could get inside the mind of his opponent.'

'That very much over-dramatizes what I'm doing. Maybe there is a similarity – I wouldn't know. To get down to brass tacks. I'm convinced de Forge has set the stage for a *coup d'état* to make himself President of France. All the riots, the absurd – but highly effective – use of men in Ku-Klux-Klan garb. I'm convinced he's waiting for just one more development before he makes his move.'

'Which is?'

'The arrival of more funds – and especially sophisticated

442

weaponry – from Lord Dawlish, armaments king. In short, the berthing of the *Steel Vulture* at Arcachon. Brand, his deputy, is already there.'

'Where is the *Steel Vulture* now? Can't it be stopped?'

'Answer One, I'm driving up to Aldeburgh to shake Dawlish. Then on to Dunwich to try and trace the vessel. Answer Two, no we can't stop the vessel. We have no proof it's carrying arms.'

'You mean General de Forge is going to start a war?'

'Definitely not,' Tweed replied. 'He's going to try and use the threat of overwhelming force to subdue Paris and the present government. I predict there will be rumours that his troops are armed with nerve gas.'

'And what are you doing to stop him?'

'Two things at the same time. Rattle him by using psychological warfare tactics – to cause him delay. Rather unusual techniques. The second thing is to get evidence which will discredit him before he strikes.'

'This is serious, then.'

'The worst threat to the stability of Western Europe since the Berlin Wall collapsed. A military dictator in Paris would upset the whole of Europe. Now I must get moving. There's not much time left for me to drive to Aldeburgh and Dunwich, then drive back in time to catch a late flight to Paris.'

As he stood up Monica brought to his desk a copy of the *Daily Mail*. She laid it down flat and pointed to the headline and the main story.

MANTEAU – 'THE CLOAK' – MASTER ASSASSIN

As he put on his Burberry, Tweed glanced at the story which had now crossed the Channel. *Manteau* was 'credited' with having killed the Prefect of Paris, with the assassination of the President and the Prime Minister by blowing up the TGV Express, and also with the killing of an Englishwoman, Jean Burgoyne.

In each instance, the article continued, the assassin had

443

left behind his trademark. The Cloak. In the case of the Paris Prefect a cloak had been found stuffed in a nearby litter bin. When the TGV Express was wrecked DST men had found another cloak in a nearby village. And now, with the strangulation of Burgoyne, DST men had discovered a discarded cloak inside the boathouse in the vicinity of Arcachon.

'This *Manteau* is very sinister,' Monica observed.

'And mysterious,' Tweed agreed impatiently. 'Hamilton is waiting with the car?'

'Yes. Have a care. Kalmar may still be in the Aldeburgh area.'

'Or do you mean *Manteau*?' Tweed commented as he left.

Fred Hamilton sat behind the wheel of the Ford Escort. Marler mockingly had nicknamed the new member of the team the RSM: he thought Fred took life desperately seriously.

'I'll take the wheel,' Tweed said brusquely.

Hamilton transferred his tall figure to the front passenger seat. Twenty-eight years old, he sat like a ramrod, glancing round as they moved through the London traffic to check whether they were being followed. He was clean-shaven with brown hair trimmed short and an aquiline nose. They were well clear of London, driving through Essex when Tweed asked his question after glancing at Hamilton's trenchcoat.

'You're carrying a hand-gun, aren't you?'

'A Colt .455 automatic pistol. Magazine capacity seven rounds. Plus spare mags.'

'I don't think you'll need that.'

'Mr Howard insisted. And, with respect, sir, it's when you don't expect to need a firearm that you find it saves your life.'

444

'No need to call me "sir". Just Tweed will do . . .'

He drove like the clappers across Suffolk, just inside the speed limit. Ignoring Aldeburgh, he slowed down as they passed Snape Maltings, turned on to the country road for Grenville Manor. He was on the point of turning left down the last stretch to Iken, the river Alde a calm lagoon below them, when a car parked on the grass verge started up, followed them, with the Volvo's horn tooting.

Hamilton slipped his hand inside his trenchcoat. Tweed looking in the wing mirror, shook his head, swore inwardly, pulled up, and the Volvo parked behind them.

'I know these people. The Yard,' Tweed warned Hamilton.

It was, of course, Chief Inspector Buchanan and Sergeant Warden. Tweed sat gazing ahead as Buchanan got out and strolled up to his window.

'A small world, Tweed,' he said, his grey eyes glancing at Hamilton. The tall man had bodyguard written all over him. 'We were taking a rest,' Buchanan continued genially, 'before keeping an appointment to interrogate Lord Dawlish.'

'My intention too,' Tweed replied stiffly.

'Then why don't we combine our visit? What colours are you sailing under this time?'

'Special Branch.'

'Then together we could possibly exert more pressure on his Lordship. I'm sure you'll have no objection . . '

It was a grey weepy day. Inside Grenville Grange, Lord Dawlish gazed out of the windows down over the lawn to the landing stage. Over the lawn where once – it seemed a hundred years ago – he'd held his shooting party. His yacht, *Wavecrest V*, moored to the landing stage, rested motionless in the still water. Rain streaks slashed the windows, speckled the turgid surface of the Alde.

Dawlish was in a blazing fury. He had recently returned from the *Steel Vulture*, still stationed off Dunwich, and he could have strangled the skipper, Santos. Arriving on the bridge he'd asked the vital question.

'When can we sail? I want a straight answer. Now!'

'The loading—' the swarthy-faced Santos had spread his hands — 'it is still proceeding.'

'For God's sake, man, how long is it going to take?'

'Señor, it is a dangerous cargo we are loading. A very large cargo – the largest yet. You would wish us not to risk an accident which might damage vessel.'

'I'm interested in results. Conditions are ideal. A calm sea – and the met forecasts for the Bay of Biscay are good. How long do you expect that to last?'

'My first consideration is the safety of your beautiful ship, Señor . . '

'It's not a cruise liner. Of course I'm concerned for its safety.' Dawlish waved a thick forefinger under Santos' nose. 'But I'm also seriously behind schedule. Put more men on the job, you cretin.'

'All available divers are working round the clock. Is that right – round the . . .'

'I don't give a damn for your fractured English. Give me a straight answer,' Dawlish had stormed. 'When will we be ready to sail?'

'The night after this night we will be ready. You will see . . .'

'That's a deadline,' Dawlish had raged. 'And if not kept maybe you'll be dead.'

He had attended to two more things before leaving. Rushing to his cabin, he had coded a message. It was phrased carefully.

Expected cargo will be delivered agreed destination within seventy-two hours. My next signal will be the last, will give ETA. Oiseau.

After taking it himself to the radio op. room he went on

446

deck aft of the bridge. The specially designed aircraft which could land on ground or water – equipped with floats it also had a retractable undercarriage fitted with wheels – sat on the pad.

'I want to see you take off and land again on this vessel,' he had ordered the pilot.

Constructed as an adapted miniature version of the Harrier jump jet, the machine's jets began building up power. He watched it as the pilot lifted off vertically, hovered above the vessel, then landed with pinpoint precision on the pad. Satisfied with that at least, he had returned to Grenville Grange. Only to find a message waiting for him that Chief Inspector Buchanan of Homicide would be calling later in the morning.

'What the hell could this flatfoot want?' he asked himself aloud as he stared across the lawn.

Dawlish had convinced himself they had given up investigating the murder of Karin Rosewater. Someone tapped nervously on the panelled door. Dawlish bawled out for the intruder on his thoughts to come in. A manservant entered.

'A Chief Inspector Buchanan and a Sergeant Warden have arrived. They say they have an appointment.'

Dawlish told him to stay where he was. Opening up the cocktail cabinet, he poured himself a stiff neat whisky. He downed the drink in two long gulps, licked his thick lips, closed the cabinet.

'Send the bastards in.'

Entering the room Buchanan noted that Dawlish favoured an outfit of riding kit, which seemed bizarre at the end of November. He even wore a hard hat as he stood with his back to a large brick alcove fireplace where a log fire crackled. In one hand he held a coiled riding whip. He used it to gesture.

447

'Kindly sit there.'

Buchanan smiled to himself as he sat on a couch facing the light from the window and Warden perched uncomfortably beside him. An old trick: stand in the shadow yourself and plant your visitors with the light on their faces.

Dawlish frowned as a third man entered, paused, looking carefully round the room. He seemed to be examining every piece of furniture – everything except the owner.

'Who the blazes are you?' Dawlish snapped. 'I was told two men from Scotland Yard would be coming.'

'Special Branch.'

Tweed held up a card forged by the experts in the Engine Room at Park Crescent. He took his time putting the card back in his wallet before replying.

'Obviously the message was garbled. But it is important that I ask you some questions later. Chief Inspector Buchanan takes precedence.'

'I don't understand any of this. Sit down. There.'

The whip gestured towards the large couch where there was space for a third visitor. Tweed ignored the suggestion. Walking to a carver chair placed against the same wall as the fireplace, he sat down. It placed him sideways on to Dawlish, who had to turn round to observe him. Buchanan smiled to himself again, guessing the reason for Tweed's manoeuvre.

'I prefer a hard chair,' Tweed said neutrally. 'I now leave the floor to the Chief Inspector.'

'Who has not yet shown any identification,' Dawlish snapped.

Buchanan saw his chance. Standing up, he strolled over to Dawlish, showed him his identity card, remained where he was, leaning an elbow on the mantelpiece, several inches taller than his host. He produced a photograph.

'Do you recognize her?'

'No.'

'Come, Lord Dawlish, the photo is a trifle blurred and you hardly glanced at it. I repeat, do you recognize this lady?'

'Who is she?' Dawlish asked, studying the print handed to him.

'You tell me. You seem to be having trouble answering the question. She is familiar then?'

'I've never seen her in my life. What is this about?'

Dawlish thrust the photo back at Buchanan. He glanced at Tweed who sat, knees together, hands clasped in his lap as he watched Dawlish. His Lordship seemed unsure whether to move away from the two men flanking him. He threw the whip on to a table, tossed his hard hat after it, thrust his large hands into the pockets of his jodhpurs.

'This,' Buchanan informed him in the same level tone, 'is about the brutal murder of Karin Rosewater on the marshes at Aldeburgh. Not so far from here.'

'So why come to me?'

'Because a witness to the murder of Rosewater, Paula Grey, saw at least five heavily-built men wearing Balaclavas, armed with rifles, pursuing them after following the two girls in a dinghy from Dunwich. You have divers aboard the *Steel Vulture*, I understand, Lord Dawlish,' Buchanan added conversationally.

'That's what my philanthropic project is all about – using divers to explore the sunken village overwhelmed by the sea years ago.'

'So, you admit you employ divers.' Buchanan made it sound like an accusation. 'My problem is to find the members of the murderous gang who chased the two girls, one of whom was brutally strangled.'

'I still don't follow why you're bothering me.'

Dawlish's tone had become aggressive. Ostentatiously he checked his Rolex watch.

'Because,' Buchanan continued in the same calm manner, 'I am having trouble locating men who could have

449

formed that gang. You check your divers' background before you hire them?'

'Meticulously.' Dawlish found Tweed's unblinking stare irritating, turned to face him. 'What do you want to know?'

'In addition to your *philanthropic* activities you made your fortune out of armament deals. You supply arms to France?'

'France has its own armaments industry,' Dawlish barked.

'You haven't answered my question. Does your ship the *Steel Vulture* ever visit French ports?'

Dawlish rounded on Tweed. 'Look, I've had enough of this. A man with my interests – which, incidentally, are mainly supermarkets – needs some relaxation. That may surprise you, ' he said sarcastically. 'But I cruise all over the world in the *Vulture*.'

'A dual-purpose vessel, then,' Tweed remarked.

Dawlish froze. His hard black eyes gazed at Tweed with vehemence. If looks could kill Tweed would have dropped dead.

'What the hell do you mean by that?' he demanded.

'Did I touch a raw nerve?' Tweed enquired innocently. 'I referred to the fact that the *Vulture* is used to explore your sunken village. Also for jolly trips off to foreign parts.'

Buchanan intervened, handing his card to Dawlish.

'I'd like a complete list of your divers sent to me at the address on my card. I could, of course, investigate their backgrounds in other ways. Thank you for giving us some of your valuable time, Lord Dawlish. I think that's all. For now at any rate. Tweed?'

Merely nodding, Tweed stood up and followed Buchanan and Warden. They were leaving the room when Tweed paused, turned round in the doorway to address Dawlish.

'I've heard that Brand is always with you. A kind of Siamese twins act. He's abroad on his hols?'

Dawlish aimed a stubby finger at Tweed's chest like a gun.

'The front door is behind you.'

47

Running up the wide staircase, Dawlish went into a front bedroom and watched the two cars leaving together – the Volvo in front – watched them until they vanished round a curve in the drive. He walked down to his room over-looking the lawn more slowly. Opening his cocktail cabi-net, he poured himself another neat double Scotch.

Settling his bulk in an armchair, he swallowed half the Scotch, put the glass down on a table. He didn't give a damn for the lofty Chief Inspector from the Yard. It was the enigmatic intruder from Special Branch which had shaken him.

First, his reference to France, to French ports. Second, his ambiguous phrase 'dual purpose' about the *Steel Vul-ture*. And third, that last question about Brand. The way his eyes had studied Dawlish's when he mentioned the name.

'May he rot in hell,' Dawlish said aloud.

He drank the rest of his Scotch in one quick gulp.

Tweed followed Buchanan's Volvo until they reached the A12. Here Buchanan turned south for London. Tweed swung right, accelerated along the highway. North for Dunwich.

'Satisfactory, sir?' Hamilton asked when they had driven many miles.

'I think so.'

Tweed said no more, concentrating on maintaining the maximum speed along the highway which was comparatively free of other traffic. Impatiently, he had to slow down when he turned off east along the country road to Dunwich. Arriving at the coast, he left his Escort in the car park next to the Ship Inn.

Getting out of the car, Tweed took a deerstalker hat from the rear seat, crammed it on his head. He looped a pair of binoculars round his neck. It gave him the appearance of a man on holiday, probably a birdwatcher. He looked at Hamilton.

'Try and look more relaxed. We're tourists.'

Hamilton's reluctant concession to Tweed's request was to shove both hands inside the pockets of his trench coat. He liked his right hand free to grab for the Colt. Tweed led the way out of the car park, turned right and made his way up a steep winding path past a signpost. *Cliff Path.*

'You've been here before, sir?' Hamilton enquired.

'A long time ago. It's one of the few places which never changes.'

Tweed hustled up the difficult path, emerged on to a grassy plateau on top of the cliffs. A wooden seat stood facing the rippled grey of the calm sea, as though waiting for someone to sit on it. Tweed saw what he wanted to see without binoculars, but he pressed the lenses to his eyes, focused them.

The *Steel Vulture* came up clear as described by Paula, motionless about half a mile out. Tweed swept the vessel with his glasses. A lighter was moored to the platform suspended just above the water – presumably for carrying supplies. A large dinghy with an outboard motor was attached to the lighter. Was it the dinghy which had carried men in Balaclavas in their cold-blooded pursuit of Paula and Karin? He pressed the lenses closer to his eyes, adjusted the focus with care.

Aft of the bridge was a strange-looking aircraft. No one had reported that. So, once aboard, Dawlish had great mobility. Tweed saw several men descending into the dinghy, probably prior to coming ashore.

'We'll get away from here fast . . .'

He had hardly completed the brief instruction before he was hurrying back down the winding path back to Dunwich. Hamilton had trouble keeping up with him. Tweed already had the car engine started as he dived into the passenger seat beside him. Taking one last look at the anchored vessel beyond fields spreading down a slope towards the beach, Tweed drove off.

He was speeding back down the A12 when he suddenly slowed, turned on to a wide grass verge and stopped, leaving the engine running. He sat like a man in a trance, hands quite still on the wheel. Hamilton glanced at him, saw his glazed look, was careful to keep quiet.

Butler had once warned Hamilton that if he was with Tweed when this happened he should keep quiet. It meant that something of great significance had struck him.

Twin-track.

That was the phrase Howard had quoted the PM as using in their conversation. Two different units in the field – and Tweed hadn't been told which other unit was operating. It simply confirmed to Tweed that he had been right about the identity of Kalmar, the assassin.

He resumed the drive to London at top speed.

'Have you had anything to eat?' Monica asked the moment Tweed entered his office. 'I thought not,' she said as he shook his head. 'Ham sandwiches on your desk and a flask of freshly made coffee.'

'Thank you. Most considerate.'

Tweed checked the time as he sat at his desk. Half an hour before he had to leave to catch his flight back to Paris.

Unwrapping the foil, he bit into a ham sandwich and realized he was ravenous. Monica came over, poured coffee from the flask into a mug.

'You're going to stay in Paris until it's over one way or the other?' she asked.

'No. To Paris first, yes. Then I fly south to Arcachon to take charge at this critical moment.'

'Porton Down phoned again,' she said grimly. 'They did find one flask among some rubbish. Their top expert returned from holiday. He says the flask shows positive traces of nerve gas. From Dawlish's factory near Oxford.'

'Which makes my visit to Arcachon even more vital.'

'Won't it be dangerous?' Monica pressed.

Tweed devoured another sandwich. 'Probably. But my team is in the danger zone. I must be there with them.'

'You know something you're not telling me,' she accused.

'If I do, I haven't told anyone else. Don't feel out of it.'

'General de Forge is about to move, isn't he?'

'Within the next two or three days. He's waiting for one more development. I want to be there when that development happens.'

The phone rang. Annoyed, Monica ran to her desk, picked up the phone, listened, said she'd see if he was still in the building.

'Chief Inspector Buchanan on the phone . . .'

'Tweed here.'

'I think we make a good team. I detected signs of alarm in his Lordship. I'm tracing those divers.'

'Good idea. A better one would be to check all the hotel registers in Aldeburgh for the night Karin Rosewater was murdered. Concentrate on the names of the people involved in this thing. Should lead you to the murderer. Sorry, must go now . . .'

PART THREE

Cross of Fire

48

'Operation Marengo – the seizure of Paris – has begun.'

General Charles de Forge had taken his decision in the middle of the night. He was poring over a large-scale map of France spread over his desk. By his side stood Major Lamy.

'The advance elements of the First Armoured Division are approaching the outskirts of Angoulême,' Lamy reported. 'They are moving at speed under the cover of darkness. Motor-cycle patrols have already reached the outskirts of Angoulême. The Division will then proceed north tomorrow night – to outflank Paris and move on the capital from the north. According to plan.'

'No!' de Forge contradicted. 'That is the official plan. There is a spy in our midst who has to be caught.' He glanced at Lamy. 'From Angoulême the Division, followed up by heavy reinforcements, will turn north-east, racing via Argenton for Chateauroux and beyond up the N20.'

'The plan has been changed?' Lamy asked in surprise.

'No! The plan I have distributed is a cover plan. If rumours of our movements leak to Paris they will think we are going to keep west of Paris until we can swoop on it from the north.'

'And the real plan?'

'Has been handed as sealed orders to each commander – orders to be opened and acted on only on receiving a personal signal from me. I have sent the signal.'

'Should I now activate Austerlitz in Paris?'

457

'Not yet. What you can do, Major, is to contact Kalmar and tell him to finish the job. Paula Grey. She has to be a spy. That's it.'

'But Kalmar is pressing for payment – pressing hard.'

'Then pay him.' De Forge's tone was silky. 'I am sure you can lay your hands on the necessary funds.'

Lamy left the presence, his mind in a whirl of calculation. De Forge had refused to reveal to his Chief of Intelligence the real Marengo plan. And only on rare occasions did he address his subordinate by his rank – instead of by name. De Forge was distancing himself.

In his office the General continued to study the detailed map. The sealed plans ordered his commanders to continue north up the N20 – to head point blank for Paris by the most direct route. The last strategy Navarre would expect from a general noted for his devious manoeuvres. He would be in Paris before the government woke in their beds.

And Austerlitz, the infiltration operation, would throw the government into a panic when commando groups started to take over key centres of authority – only hours before de Forge's advance units entered Paris.

Paula was behind the wheel well south of Bordeaux, heading for the Landes, when the catastrophe occurred in deserted open countryside. At a garage they had exchanged temporarily the Renault for a much more spacious Renault Espace, leaving the original vehicle and a large sum of French francs as collateral.

Butler sat beside her, navigating. Immediately behind them were seated Nield and Stahl. Newman was sprawled at the back of the car, fast asleep. At the entrance to an abandoned farm with a large barn the car stopped.

Paula repeatedly turned on the ignition, used the accelerator. It was no use: the engine refused to come alive. Butler got out to examine the engine and Stahl followed him.

'I don't know much about these engines,' Butler remarked.

'That's great,' said Paula, who had also got out.

'But I do,' Stahl told them eagerly. 'I have spent much time in France. I have driven one of these. Let me take a look . . .'

They waited half an hour while Stahl checked the engine. Paula looked round, was conscious of how exposed they were on the deserted country road. Apparently Stahl had the same thought.

When the half-hour was up he raised a hand, indicating they should stay where they were. He trotted off up the short track leading to the farmhouse which had a crumbling roof, exposing the rafters where tiles had slid away.

The barn was made of stern stuff. The roof was intact and the huge doors swung outward, held firmly on hinges, as Stahl opened the barn, investigated the interior briefly, ran back to the road.

'We must push the Espace into that barn so I can work on the engine. Paula, you handle the wheel. Get out, everyone.'

'Why?' Paula demanded.

'Because,' Stahl explained patiently, 'I can see it will take me several hours to repair the engine. I must dismantle, then put it together again. We were sold a pup. Is that right?'

'Yes,' Paula snapped impatiently. 'Are you sure you can get it going?'

'Absolutely. But I need the time. And we are in a very exposed position here. We have already seen tanks in the distance. Please! We all push.'

Nield was already standing beside Butler but Newman was unaware of anything. He flopped fast asleep, exhausted. Paula climbed behind the wheel while Stahl, Butler and Nield pushed the vehicle up the level track inside the huge empty barn, its floor deep with straw. The glass of windows on three sides were coated with a thick layer of grime. At the back a ladder led to a loft with an equally grimy skylight. Stahl closed one door, Butler the other. While Nield held a pencil flashlight, Stahl began work on the engine.

'Do you really think you can manage it?' Paula persisted.

Stahl grinned. 'I used to be a mechanic before I took up my present occupation. But please do not expect quick results . . .'

During all this activity Newman had not moved an inch – let alone opened an eye. He was in a very deep sleep. At lunchtime Paula collected the basket with sandwiches wrapped in foil and two flasks of coffee. When she had visited Isabelle just before they left Arcachon the French girl had asked Paula how many people there were, how long they would be away.

'Four people,' she lied, omitting Stahl. 'And two or three days,' she lied again.

'Then you'll need food and drink to see you on your way.'

Isabelle had insisted, had prepared sandwiches in a few minutes, her knife flashing while Paula prepared coffee. At the time Paula had cursed the delay: now she blessed Isabelle's consideration. Handing round sandwiches after unwrapping the silver foil, she then poured coffee and they shared the same makeshift cup – the top of the flask. Newman slept on.

While Nield held the new flashlight provided by Paula, Stahl, arms and hands covered with oil and muck, worked away. Half the engine seemed to be on the floor and Paula wondered whether he'd ever assemble it again. The alarm came in the early afternoon.

Butler had made it his business to keep a watch through

the windows, resisting the temptation to clean a hole in the grime. At other times he climbed the ladder and peered over the countryside through the skylight. He was in the loft, Paula was scrunching restlessly over the straw, trying to ignore the rising dust, when Stahl waved the screwdriver he'd found in the vehicle's toolkit.

'It's OK. It will go first time. I promise you . . .'

'Trouble. Big trouble. And coming this way fast.'

It was Butler interrupting the German. Paula stiffened as Butler scrambled down the ladder. For a brief second she'd half-believed Stahl: he spoke with such assurance. Now her hopes that they could get away from this musty-smelling barn were dashed. Whatever the situation Butler usually kept his cool, but there had been urgency in his warning. She glanced at Newman in the back of the vehicle. Still out cold.

'What is it, Harry?' she asked.

'See for yourself. Through this window. Tanks. De Forge's tanks. A whole squadron of them . . .'

She peered through the window from the side with Butler staring over her shoulder. Coming over a low ridge towards them were three large tanks, gun barrels elevated. She tightened her lips. Of all the bloody bad luck. Butler gripped her arm.

'Come with me. Take a better look.'

He shinned back up the ladder to the loft and she followed him. Heaps of straw in the loft. Dry as a bone. The barn was pretty waterproof. He took her to the skylight, stood back so she could look out. From that height she had a much better view – a panoramic sweep – over the low-lying countryside. A spread of fields as far as the eye could see. No trees. And a horde of tanks advancing in the direction of the farm.

'Doesn't look too good,' she commented.

'They are on manoeuvres.' It was Stahl speaking. He'd followed them up the ladder. 'We are at least under

461

cover. Maybe they will change direction before they get here.'

Paula's stomach muscles tightened as she watched. Here and there veils of cold grey mist floated across the landscape, drifting over the ground. The tanks slid though the veils, emerging like land-bound sharks seeking prey. Stahl, as always, was for action.

'The Espace will go now,' he pressed. 'Let us drive to the north, back the way we came.'

'Better take a look to the north,' Butler advised.

Stahl and Paula turned their heads. More tanks were advancing from that direction. They all seemed to be making for the farm from three points of the compass. West, south, and north. Only the east was clear. And the road ran roughly north to south.

Butler ran down the ladder, followed by the others. He peered out of the window which looked on to the separate farm building. About thirty feet divided the barn from the wreck of a farmhouse. As he turned round there was movement from inside the vehicle. Newman had at long last woken.

He staggered out, stared down as his feet crunched straw, shook his head as dust rose. Staring round with heavy eyes, his gaze fixed on Butler.

'What the hell is happening?' He looked at his watch. 'It's mid-afternoon. We should be in the Landes . . .'

Paula poured him lukewarm coffee. He swallowed it greedily, held out the container for a refill as Butler tersely explained what had happened, their present situation. The report galvanized Newman.

Handing the container to Paula, he shinned up the ladder to the loft to see for himself. Butler and Stahl followed him. On the barn floor Nield stood alongside Paula as they stared at the incoming tanks which now looked like leviathans. Mobile power at its most terrifying.

'We stay put,' Newman decided. 'Nothing else we can

do. Try to make a run for it and they'll use us for target practice.'

'If it comes to it we can take some of them with us. The tank commanders are exposed in their turrets,' Stahl observed.

As he spoke he extracted the Heckler and Koch sub-machine-gun from his bag. He had cleaned his arms and hands on cloths found in the rear of the Espace.

'Put that away,' Newman snapped. 'We can only wait and hope for the best.'

'Or the worst,' Butler added under his breath.

Paula had run up the ladder to join them. She stared at the tanks as though hypnotized. A unit of three large machines was heading straight for them. Suddenly the lead tank increased speed, rumbled forward. She could hear the grind and clatter of its caterpillar tracks rumbling over the stony field.

'Oh, my God!' she gasped.

She could see clearly in the turret of the lead tank a sergeant wearing a helmet, waving his arms ecstatically, in his early twenties. The tank forged remorselessly on, slowed as it reached the farmhouse, mounted a wall. The wall collapsed, the entire farmhouse fell inwards under the impact as the caterpillar tracks ground over the rubble of the wreckage. The young tank commander swept his gloved hand in a sideways gesture, shouting into his microphone. Paula heard the command clearly.

'Now the barn. Flatten it . . .'

Her last thought was that she had made a brief call from Isabelle's apartment, telling Lasalle they were driving south, giving him the apartment's number and its occupant. She'd seized the chance to make the whispered call while Isabelle was preparing the sandwiches.

* * *

Tweed had arrived back at the Ministry of the Interior in the early hours of the morning when Newman and his team had left Arcachon for the Landes. He had been delayed for hours at Heathrow due to a bomb scare. His flight had left five hours after scheduled take-off.

Lasalle, just returned from rue des Saussaies, sat in his office. He was studying his map when Tweed walked in, his manner urgent as he took off his Burberry.

'Navarre,' Tweed said immediately. 'Where is he?'

'At an emergency Cabinet meeting. Impossible to get to him. Why?'

'I estimate he has a maximum of sixty hours before de Forge launches his bid for power. I heard at the airport here that Dubois addressed a huge rally in Bordeaux yesterday evening, that he said what he called "the people" would soon be in power. Which means himself as Prime Minister, I assume.'

'I have heard about that ominous speech. Why no more than sixty hours?'

'Because de Forge is waiting for a delivery of weapons – nerve gas missiles I suspect – before he strikes. The weapons will come aboard the armament manufacturer Lord Dawlish's vessel, the *Steel Vulture* . . .'

'The catamaran you told me about before leaving for London?'

'Exactly. I think I know where the weapons are hidden. Something Paula told me eventually came back. It all links up with Kalmar, as I've always thought.'

'Where is this vessel now?'

'Anchored off a nowhere place called Dunwich on our east coast.'

'Then why not impound – search – the vessel?'

'Because I have no proof of my theory.' Pacing restlessly, Tweed thought that must sound strange to Lasalle. 'The trouble is the catamaran is based at Harwich. While there at different times recently it was searched – for drugs. Nothing was found. Dawlish has clout in high places, contributes large sums to party funds. I know I'm right but, as I said, I can't prove it.'

'We could send aircraft to patrol offshore. If we knew which areas to concentrate on.'

'The approaches to Arcachon. The Bay of Biscay,' Tweed said promptly.

'I will put the idea to Navarre as soon as I can. I do not have the authority. You mentioned Paula. She called a few minutes before you arrived . . .'

He paused as Otto Kuhlmann, in shirt sleeves, looking rumpled, appeared. The German held an unlit cigar in his hand as though he felt lost without it. Lasalle waved to a chair, continued.

'I was telling Tweed that Paula Grey called from Arcachon just before he got here. She was speaking in a low voice as though not wishing to be overheard. She said the team, including Egon, was driving south . . .'

'That damn bomb hoax,' Tweed burst out. 'Where was she calling from?'

'Isabelle Thomas's apartment. She repeated the number.'

'Get it for me, please. Urgently, René,' Tweed requested. 'I might catch them before they leave.'

'Stahl will be an asset,' Kuhlmann reassured Tweed.

'I'm sure he will. But we need the information Jean Burgoyne obtained. More urgently now . . .'

He took a deep breath as Lasalle handed him the phone. He was deciding how to talk to Isabelle if she had come on the line. She had. Odd, Tweed thought, to be answering the phone so quickly in the early hours.

'Is Paula there?' he asked.

'Paula? Who is that? And who are you?'

'A close friend – an associate – of Robert Newman's.'

'I have seen Newman's picture in the papers – if you refer to the foreign correspondent. You have not given me

465

your name. Can you describe Mr Newman? Very accurately.'

Tweed swore to himself, but was impressed by Isabelle's caution. He could be anybody. She'd had enough trauma with phoney DST men. He gave her a detailed description of Newman but she hadn't finished with him yet.

'Let us assume he is carrying a weapon for self-protection. What weapon would that be?'

'A Smith & Wesson .38 Special,' Tweed said quickly.

'I'm sorry to question you so closely but I had to be certain of your claim to be an associate. Paula Grey is no longer here. No one is except myself. They drove off about half an hour ago.'

'I see.' Tweed was careful not to alarm her. 'They have been staying at a hotel,' he said, testing her.

'I know. The Atlantique. But when they return they will stay here. In two or three days' time. You have my number, so do not hesitate to call me again.'

'May I suggest you stay in your apartment as much as you can?'

'Bob – Mr Newman – has already told me that. Please do not hesitate to call me again,' she repeated.

'We are going to have to do something drastic, René,' Tweed said as he put down the phone. 'I'm alarmed – very alarmed. Because my whole team is heading for the Landes. Tell me, that map you're studying. It's festooned with crosses. Do they indicate areas where de Forge's troops are manoeuvring?'

'Exactly. From reports received so far . . .'

'And there are crosses in the Landes region.'

'You can read upside down. Ah! I see your point. Your people are moving straight into the danger zone. I am afraid so.'

'I repeat, we are going to have to do something drastic. I have another idea. Are the drivers of French petrol tankers likely to be sympathetic to de Forge?'

466

'My God, no! They're an independent gang. Very tough. They didn't even like de Gaulle. They loathe de Forge. Any breath of military rule is their idea of hell.'

'And the farmers,' Tweed went on. 'The farmers in the centre and north of France. Do they think de Forge is a saviour of France – like their compatriots in the south?'

'No. They deeply mistrust the Army. De Forge has successfully cultivated the farmers in the south by helping them to bring in their harvest. Farmers further north would chase a soldier off their land with a pitchfork. Why? Ideas seem to be tumbling out of your head.'

'I'm an owl,' Tweed said with a dry smile. 'Are you still worried that de Forge has a network of informants here in Paris reporting back to him?'

'Yes. I told you. I know he has. I just can't locate his network.'

'Then tomorrow I will accept Josette de Forge's invitation to see her again.'

'And your references to petrol tankers, to farmers?'

'This is what I suggest you do with lightning speed . . .'

49

'Get down the ladder quick!' Newman ordered.

Paula almost slid down it from the loft, followed by Stahl and Newman. The loft would hardly be the safest place when the tank crashed into the barn. They ran to the side window overlooking the carnage which had been a farmhouse. Paula kept to one side of the window with Newman, Stahl stayed on the other side.

Like the others, Paula felt she had to see what was

467

happening before they ran for it. Ran where? She had a horrible vision of the walls toppling from a great height, caving in and burying them. They heard someone shouting in French as the young tank tearaway aimed his metallic monster at the barn.

A second tank appeared, broadside on, almost scraping the wall of the barn. Peering up, Paula saw the tank commander, a lieutenant. He had torn off his headset, was roaring at the top of his voice, waving his clenched fist. Through the glass of the window they could hear every word he said.

'I'll have you up on a charge. No! It will be a court martial. You crazy idiot! You have wantonly destroyed a farmer's property. We need the farmers on our side. You will also be accused of attempting to smash down the barn. You are relieved of command of your tank, Sergeant! My own NCO will take control. Get down immediately. You will be a prisoner in my tank . . .'

The engines of both machines had stopped. Inside the barn they froze, gazed at each other in disbelief. Outside they heard the sound of boots descending – presumably the sergeant leaving for the other tank. Newman gestured and they withdrew from a window, sliding back along the roughened wall.

Paula looked at Nield who had remained at the other side of the barn, cool as a cucumber, holding his handgun. With his other hand he gave her the thumbs-up sign and winked. She managed a smile.

The roar of the tanks' engines was resumed, the grinding clatter of their caterpiller tracks. Newman held up a warning hand to ensure everyone kept still. He waited until the sounds had receded some distance, then dived back up the ladder with Paula at his heels.

From a skylight he surveyed the landscape. It was not encouraging. The tanks were coming together in compact formations, manoeuvring across the distant terrain, conducting some mock battle. He shook his head.

'We're not out of the woods yet.'

'So how long do you think we may have to stay here?'

'Until we're very sure the coast is clear. And I see Pete is munching a sandwich. I hope you kept some for me . . .'

In the late morning of the same day Tweed arrived at the Passy home of Josette de Forge. He had phoned in advance, using the same pseudonym, Prentice of the *Daily World*, explaining that his editor was enthusiastic for more information.

'*Information*, Mr Prentice?' she had purred, giving the word an ambiguous inflexion. 'If you come now I shall be available for you . . .'

Available? When she opened the door herself she wore a fluffy housecoat, open at the front, and underneath a flimsy chiffon slip which was very revealing. As she led him upstairs her housecoat swung wider while she mounted the curving steps, exposing a magnificent long leg. Tweed was relieved when she led him into a bedroom at the front. She turned to face him, taking his Burberry, her dark eyes peering at him through long lashes. She looked towards a large canopy bed draped with the most expensive and laced-edged linen.

'I thought we would be more comfortable up here. And we shall not be bothered by the servants. Just a pleasant tête-à-tête.'

'I do have some questions to ask,' Tweed insisted.

He walked over to a *chaise-longue* and perched at one end. Not the piece of furniture he would have chosen but there was no chair in the elaborately furnished room. Hanging his Burberry in a dressing room, she came and sat close to him, crossing her legs.

'Do we have to waste time on boring questions? And

when will your long article on my husband appear in your so respected paper?'

'Soon. That is a very fine bust over there.'

In case she was tempted to interpret the word 'bust' in another way he pointed. On a half-round table against one wall was a head-and-shoulders bust of Napoleon. He thought, apart from other factors, his visit had been worthwhile to observe the presence of the bust. He waited for her reaction.

'Charles brought that here. Maybe at the moment he is only Bonaparte, but in the future . . .'

'I heard a rumour that General de Forge's army is nearing Paris. Will Navarre permit that?'

'A delicious question, *chéri*. Navarre is a nobody who will be swept aside by the tidal wave of history.'

'You mean you expect your husband to occupy the Elysée?'

She patted his right cheek. 'Now, I did not say that.'

'But he is a clever man. I hear he has extraordinary Intelligence sources here in Paris. When I was last in this house for your salon I observed some influential guests. General Masson, for example. It occurred to me that your salons would be ideal occasions for passing Intelligence from GHQ Third Army to Paris, and the other way round.'

She was inserting a cigarette into an ivory holder as he spoke. Her hand slipped, broke the end of the cigarette. Her full lips tightened and for a moment she didn't look at him while she recovered her poise.

'You do have a lively imagination,' she retorted with an edge to her voice.

'Have I? Most of your important guests have been linked with de Forge's views.'

'It was a mixed gathering. Artists, intellectuals . . .'

'Together with generals and other key officers.'

'My salons are artistic gatherings . . .'

'Which would be excellent camouflage for Intelligence-gathering operations.'

'You are not putting these lies in your paper, I hope?'

'Only the truth, Madame de Forge,' Tweed replied.

'We are wasting time.' She dropped a fresh cigarette and the holder into a crystal ashtray. Turning to him, she leaned forward and he caught the aroma of expensive perfume as she wrapped her long bare arms round his shoulders.

He smiled, reached up, removed her hands just before she embraced him. Standing up, he walked to the front windows, draped with heavy net curtains. He moved one as though peering into the street, let it drop.

'What is it?' Josette asked, her expression bleak and cold. 'No one is watching this house, if that is what worries you. I thought I'd told you. My husband has his own dalliances. So why shouldn't I?'

She had left the door slightly ajar and suddenly there was a continuous ringing of the bell accompanied by non-stop hammering of the bronze knocker. Tweed went swiftly to the door.

'Excuse me, Madame.'

He ran down the staircase as a woman wearing a black shawl over her head and a black dress which draped her ankles appeared in the hall. The housekeeper. Brushing past her, he turned the security handle as he had observed Josette close it, flung open the door. There were six men in business suits and open trench coats outside. Beyond them two black limousines were parked at the kerb.

'The front bedroom upstairs,' Tweed said.

Lasalle and three men rushed up the staircase. As he entered the room Lasalle saw Josette holding an old-fashioned gold telephone to her ear, working the cradle up and down furiously. He placed a hand on her arm.

'DST. You have to come with us. And the phone wire has been cut. Please, we must leave at once, even if we

471

have to carry you. Which would be undignified.'

They hustled her down the stairs, protesting. In the marble-floored hall two more men stood by the housekeeper. Lasalle walked up to her, excused himself politely, removed her black shawl. Turning, he wrapped it round Josette's head.

'What are you doing, you shit?' she screamed.

'Treating you like a lady. You wouldn't want scandal, the neighbours talking. You will leave as though you are the housekeeper. We are taking you to a comfortable residence well outside Paris. No, Madame. You have no say in the matter. Treason is an offence that carries a heavy penalty. Make a scene,' Lasalle continued genially as they escorted her to a limousine, 'and I will give the papers a list of twelve of your lovers – eight of them married men. There is bound to be one wife who will shriek her head off in public, which would be a shame. Spoiling your eminent position in Parisian society . . .'

Holding her arm, he had seen her into the limousine where two men joined her. He closed the door, bowed for the benefit of any prying eyes. Josette had preserved – for her – a rare silence. The limousine moved off.

Tweed, who had watched, was full of admiration for Lasalle's skilled performance. Only a Frenchman could have pulled it off. He walked to the other limousine, climbed in the back as Lasalle joined him and the chauffeur pulled away.

'I have left men inside the place to search it,' Lasalle informed him. 'She will simply disappear. You see, I also know how to practise psychological warfare. Imagine the effect on de Forge.'

'Very good,' Tweed agreed. 'I had a nasty moment when I thought she might take me into a back bedroom. You saw my signal with the curtain, of course.'

'We left our cars the moment we saw the curtain move. I think you handled your part well.'

'I saw something which tells me the route de Forge will adopt to march on Paris – if it ever comes to that. Now we must launch Phase Two.'

'What did you see in that apartment?'

'A favourite bust of de Forge's. Of Napoleon. Remember Waterloo,' Tweed ended cryptically.

At Arcachon Victor Rosewater stood on the deck of his cabin cruiser, scanning the front with binoculars. He switched his survey to the craft in the port where the masts of a cluster of vessels swayed slowly under the gentle swell entering the *bassin* from the Atlantic.

Dressed in a polo-necked sweater under an oilskin he looked the typical sailor. A fine drizzle of rain was falling. The sky was like grey porridge. Everything looked grey. Satisfied that he was not observed, he ran down the companionway into a large cabin.

Throwing off the oil-skin, he pressed a secret button. A section of the galley wall slid back, revealing a radio telephone and a transmitter. He pressed another button and on deck a tall aerial elevated alongside the mast.

Within minutes he was speaking to his contact, Oscar, at Kriminalpolizei HQ in Wiesbaden. They exchanged code words and Rosewater gave his message.

'Soon I will be able to supply a list of the addresses where our friends are staying in the Federal Republic. That is all . . .'

In Wiesbaden Oscar immediately transmitted the signal to Kuhlmann in Paris.

Despite Rosewater's careful surveillance of the *bassin* he had overlooked a broad-shouldered man dressed in a pea-jacket. Brand was crouched behind the wheelhouse of a smaller cabin cruiser moored in the port.

He was also using binoculars and had seen Rosewater scanning the anchorage. He continued watching as the Englishman disappeared inside the cabin. Through his binoculars he saw the elevation of the aerial. He stood up, stepped ashore and strolled along the waterfront to a public call box. Shoulders hunched, a cap pulled down over his forehead, he appeared to be just an ordinary seaman. He entered the call box, dialled the number from memory, announced himself as Bird Two. It was fortunate the girl who came on the line spoke English.

'Is that you, Yvette? Listen. You know where I am. There's a British spy ship in the harbour. The Red Ensign at the mast. Cabin cruiser. The *Typhoon IV*. Got that? Repeat the name. Yes, that's it . . .'

General de Forge was in a rage. Summoned to his presence, Major Lamy found him in a storming mood, unable to keep still. He looked at his subordinate with a piercing stare.

'You know what's happened now? I can't contact Josette. The operator says the line has been disconnected. My main pipeline into Paris has been cut. Just as we are about to launch Austerlitz within hours. Find out what the hell is going on. Why are you still standing there?'

'Yvette has reported a call from *Oiseau Deuxième* . . .'

Reluctantly he gave de Forge more bad news. As he feared, it did not improve the General's temper. De Forge hammered his fist on the desk.

'Send a team to clean out Arcachon. You know how important the place is. First this Paula Grey, who is still on the loose. Now this new spy. Include in the team Sergeant Rey. A boobytrap may be the answer for this cabin cruiser, *Typhoon IV*. And Kalmar has to liquidate the Grey woman at the earliest opportunity.'

'There is our problem of paying Kalmar . . .'

'*Your* problem! Flood Arcachon with men posing as DST. And don't forget Isabelle Thomas, mistress to Henri Bayle. Wipe the lot out. One more thing. I have a report from the Landes that the attempt to kill Moshe Stein misfired. Find him. There has been no report from Paris of his arrival – and if he had got there they would have put him on TV to moan on about the so-called Tarbes massacre. I'm worried about the Landes. Dispatch another team by sea to remove the remains of the criminal elements from the graveyard in body bags. Take them out to sea, weight the body bags, and throw them into the Atlantic.'

'You don't wish me to be involved in this?' Lamy protested.

'No. Put Lieutenant Berthier in charge of the team. And tell him to wait until Sergeant Rey is available to join the unit. It may be easier and more effective to blow up the relics well out at sea. Act now . . .'

De Forge waited for a few minutes, then summoned Sergeant Rey to come and see him. When the gnome-like boobytrap expert appeared, képi under his arm, head bent respectfully, de Forge greeted him warmly by his real rank.

'Sit down, Captain. Recently I had a telephone engineer in our pay come and tap the phones of every officer among our inner circle. I have discovered the traitor who has informed Paris of some of my plans. I will play the tape in a moment.'

'Every officer?' Rey enquired.

His nominal role of sergeant enabled him to mix with the troops, to inform de Forge of what they were saying. Guile was one of the General's favourite weapons.

'Yes. Yourself included.' De Forge smiled cynically. 'I am noted for thoroughness. Now, this is what I want you to do . . .'

*   *   *

475

Newman and his team were still trapped inside the barn. It was early evening, a grey dusk was descending over the surrounding landscape. From the skylight window in the loft Newman watched distant tanks lining up behind each other in columns. They had their rear lights on but no headlights, and they were moving very close together. It reminded Newman of accounts he'd read of General Guderian's panzer breakthrough into France during World War II. *His* tanks had moved through the defiles of the Luxembourg Ardennes at night nose to tail, each German tank commander following the vehicle ahead by watching its rear lights. He descended the ladder.

'Are we still stuck here?' Paula enquired.

'I'm afraid so. Let's hope the manoeuvres don't go on all night. You look worried.'

'I was thinking of Moshe Stein. Where is he?'

'Still in his room at the Atlantique. He has food sent up and I warned him not to venture outdoors. As soon as we can, one of us must escort him to Paris.'

'Will he do that? Just stay in a cramped room?'

'He once spent six months in a small cellar as a boy during the Second World War. Somewhere in the Balkans. He'll stay put.'

'Thank heavens,' Paula said with feeling. 'Then he will be quite safe.'

50

France was ablaze. In Toulouse, in Marseilles, in Toulon, in Bordeaux, men in Balaclavas marched holding aloft slow-burning Crosses of Lorraine. They were joined by aggressive youths, small shopkeepers, market stall hold-ers. The same chant built up to a crescendo, started by the hooded men in Balaclavas.

Pour France! Pour France! Au Pouvoir! Au Pouvoir!

For France! For France! To Power! To Power!

The conflagration was spreading to smaller towns, caught up in the frenzy. It was dark now and the symbolic crosses burned like menacing daggers.

On the hillsides bonfires were lit. Great beacons seen from miles away. Spreading the message further and further north. In Bordeaux Dubois was addressing an assembly of massed people crowding to listen as he orated at the Place de la Victoire.

'Frenchmen! Your hour has struck. The little people will at long last have their say. We will sweep aside the vested interests which have for so long used you as serfs. You will become the pride of all Europe. Paris will be cleansed of the filthy exploiters, the corrupt ministers, the men who buy you for a miserable handful of francs . . .'

'*Pour France . . .!*'

Not everyone joined in the manic orgy of mob violence. Some stayed indoors, the shutters firmly closed. In one apartment a lawyer turned to his wife, his voice full of foreboding.

'Louise. This reminds me of what I've read of the early days of the Revolution in 1789. The prelude to the Reign of Terror . . .'

In central France and towards the north rather different scenes were taking place. Farmers were working in the night, hauling out of storage bales of hay. Their wives were helping too – helping to carry the bales to open trucks waiting to receive the loads.

DST officers were overseeing the operation. They were carefully listing the quantity and numbers of the bales, preparing records for future compensation by the government.

Many of the bales were ripped open once aboard a truck. Once a vehicle was full, tough young farmers armed with pitchforks jumped inside the truck, resting on the hay as the vehicle moved off to its pre-arranged destination.

Close to the main highways groups of petrol tankers were parked in laagers. Often as many as half a dozen. The drivers were content to sit in their cabs: they were being paid full wages without the stress of driving their mammoth loads through the night. Each driver had concealed in his cab a long coiled stretch of hosepipe. And each man had been supplied with a walkie-talkie and instructions by DST officers.

Wherever possible they were laagered inside evergreen woods. This meant they were invisible to observation from aircraft. It was now a matter of waiting for the orders to come over the walkie-talkies.

News of the fiery crosses burning in the south, of the crowds massing and chanting had reached Paris. Lights were burning late in the Ministry of the Interior which Navarre had now made his emergency HQ.

For one thing, the ministry was heavily guarded. For another it was equipped with the most sophisticated communication facilities in France. Navarre, in his shirt sleeves, had called a meeting in his large office. Round the table sat Tweed, Kuhlmann, and Lasalle. The only men he could fully trust.

'I have,' Navarre began, 'informed the Cabinet it will meet next in three days' time.'

'Why?' asked Lasalle.

Navarre smiled grimly. 'It is a trick. Within three days the crisis will be settled. One way or the other. I am sure de Forge has already heard the news. He will think we believe

478

we have plenty of time, that no action will be taken against him in the meantime.'

'Are the measures we talked about being activated?' Tweed asked.

'The measures *you* suggested,' Navarre corrected him. 'Yes. Both with the farmers and the drivers of a whole fleet of petrol tankers. The trouble is we need to know the route de Forge's forces will take.'

'The N20,' Tweed said. 'The direct route to Paris. But I emphasize that is my educated guess. We need the data Stahl compiled, the data Jean Burgoyne obtained. And my people, who have the documents, are on their way to the Landes. That was a mistake, but I can't blame them. I'm sure they want to give us a complete package – including a witness we can put on TV.'

'Time is running out,' Lasalle said quietly.

'You still have an informant inside de Forge's camp?' Tweed enquired. 'Even after the murder of Jean Burgoyne?'

'That murder I mourn,' Lasalle replied. 'She was a brave woman. To answer your question, yes I still have one informant. I received a brief message early this afternoon. The *Cercle Noir* is holding one final meeting just after dusk today. That is why I say time is running out.'

'I think we must do something about that,' Navarre decided. 'At the Cabinet meeting General Masson said he would be away from Paris visiting a unit.'

'I think I would suggest that we do *two* things if you are agreeable. A double-pronged attack. Plus more psychological warfare. The first prong of the offensive should be . . .' Tweed elaborated.

Arriving in Arcachon, Sergeant Rey worked quickly. He had little time before he had to join Lieutenant Berthier's seaborne landing in the far south.

Rey was dressed as a fisherman. He wore an oil-skin with the hood pulled well down over his face. He trudged in a mist of drizzle, plodding in his gumboots, carrying a fishing rod. Over his shoulder was slung a canvas bag, presumably for his catch. Inside the bag was the time bomb.

He had earlier sat on a stone jetty, fishing line in the water dappled with the rain, watching the *Typhoon IV*. He saw no sign of activity and the curtains were drawn over the cabin windows. The owner was undoubtedly enjoying an afternoon nap.

Rey made no sound as he stepped from the shore on to the wet deck. He took one final look round to make sure he was not observed. Extracting the small limpet-shaped bomb, he pressed a button, activating the magnetic legs. Crouching down, he attached it to a band of metal running round the outside of the cabin. He pressed a second button. The timer was now operating, the silent clock ticking away. Rey had five minutes to get clear.

He walked rapidly to his car as though fed up with the drizzle which had developed into steady rain. Dumping his fishing rod with the canvas bag on the back seat, he climbed behind the wheel, started his engine, waited.

He had parked his car in a position where he could see *Typhoon IV*, moored by itself. He was several hundred yards away from his target. He checked his watch. One more minute . . .

The explosion was muffled by the rain but still loud. The *Typhoon IV* was ripped apart. The hull soared above the *bassin*. It shattered into pieces which fell back into the water, some pieces causing huge eruptions of water like fountains. Smoke rose from the portion of the hull still at the mooring point. Flame flared briefly, was quenched as the remains of the vessel disappeared.

'Another job dealt with,' Rey muttered to himself callously.

480

He drove off to the rendezvous with Berthier at a lonely point on the coast south of Arcachon. They should reach the Landes by mid-afternoon.

Aboard another cabin cruiser, his reserve base, Rosewater saw the explosion. He had expected something like this. All essential equipment had been moved to the cruiser he watched from through binoculars.

Earlier, while transmitting his brief message to Oscar in Wiesbaden, he had watched through the net curtains masking the windows of his cabin. He had seen Brand appear suddenly, hurrying along the waterfront. Too suddenly after Rosewater had scanned the area for any sign of activity.

It could have been a coincidence, but Rosewater had survived so far by never believing coincidences. And wherever he was stationed even for a few days he always had a second secret base. As the fountains of water vanished he shrugged his shoulders. He was not disturbed – his occupation assumed risks all the time.

Newman was driving the Renault Espace through the night. Paula sat beside him, checking her map. Behind them were seated Stahl and Nield. And in the back, staring constantly through the rear window, was Butler.

Taking a risk – because they had lost so much time – Newman was racing down the N10, the main highway towards the Spanish border. He had stopped at a truck drivers' café earlier to check the situation. Strategically situated by the side of the N10, the eating place was filled with the smoke of cheap cigarettes, so much so he paused inside the entrance of the long cabin-like structure to get used to the blue haze, the stench of over-cooked food mingling with beer fumes.

Drivers from the trucks parked outside occupied all the tables. Others were standing. He pushed his way to the bar, ordered a Pernod, started chatting to a burly driver in French.

'We're on our way to the border from Paris on holiday. I'm wondering whether to turn back. Bloody Army seems to be everywhere.'

'Keep going south,' the driver advised. 'I'm up from San Sebastian. The tanks have all gone north. You'll meet nothing. You think this Dubois is any good? Don't believe a word he says. He's after a fat job in the Cabinet – to keep him quiet. That's politics for you.' He spat on the straw-covered floor. 'You take your holiday, mate . . .'

They drove on, reached the Landes, the sinister walls of the forest closed in on both sides. Here and there a massacre had taken place. Trees chopped down, the head-lights of the Espace swept over vast clearings with ugly tree stumps left like the amputated limbs of giants.

Dawn was not so far away when, guided by Paula, Newman turned off the N10, swung west on to the D42 at Castets. Soon they reached St Girons, the village where their witness, Martine, lived. It took them a while to locate her tiny cottage on the edge of the village as Moshe Stein had described. Newman was disturbed to see lights in every window of the dwelling.

The first grey streaks of dawn filtered from the east as he took Paula with him and pressed the ancient bell. He heard nothing inside so he hammered on the woodwork. A shuffling sound like someone walking in clogs approached the door. It was opened on a heavy chain. Martine, fully dressed, peered out.

'Remember me?' Newman asked quietly. 'This is Marie. We have other friends outside.'

'Are you armed?'

The question shook Newman, unsure which answer would reassure her. Then he realized she was frightened.

'Yes, we are . . .'

'Come in!' She couldn't open the door quickly enough and talked non-stop in an urgent gabble. 'You may be in time. You may be too late. Can you remember the way to the graveyard? They are going to kill another one . . . They landed from the sea . . . I was collecting brushwood when I saw them coming.'

'Saw who coming?' Newman asked.

Paula looked round the small living room-cum-kitchen. It was spotless. An ancient stove stood against one wall and a welcome glow of heat met her. It was freezing outside.

'Their rubber boats with engines . . .' Martine was clutching Newman's arm. 'One man had his hands tied behind his back. It's another firing squad. The swines are going to murder another one, then bury him. Hurry! You might be in time. I have just got back. They were just coming in to land when I hurried back . . .'

'We'll go immediately.'

Newman had to abandon the Espace after driving a short distance when he came to where the path leading into the forest was too narrow. The light was growing stronger but it was still not dawn as they ran flat-footed among the trees to prevent stumbling on the soggy earth.

They were very close to the sea: they could hear a surge of incoming waves slapping on a beach and the tang of salt air was strong in their nostrils. This was mixed with the aroma of pine and fir and, normally, Paula would have revelled in the scent. Now she was only hoping they would not be too late.

There had been a brief argument outside the cottage when Newman had told Paula to stay with Martine and she had insisted on coming. Newman had made a mistake in how he worded his suggestion.

'It might be better if someone stayed to guard Martine –

and in any case it would be much safer if you waited for us here.'

'Safer!' she flared up. 'You think I'm just a passenger? Someone you can drop off the train as soon as the journey looks tricky? You're damn well wasting time – and I am coming with you . . .'

Newman found he could remember the way along the path he had previously trod and led the way. Behind him Paula followed and behind her Stahl, nursing his sub-machine-gun. Butler and Nield completed the small column. They had reached firmer ground, were threading their course through the immense tree trunks towering above, when Newman held up a hand to stop them.

'We have reached the graveyard.'

'Is it those humps?' Paula asked, gritting her teeth.

'Yes. I think I heard someone over to the right. A voice, I'm sure.'

'Then whoever it is must be on the beach,' Paula commented. 'We'd better not waste a second . . .'

They crept forward through the trees, Newman in the middle, Paula on his left, Stahl on his right. Behind followed Butler and Nield. All held their weapons in their hands. The forest ended suddenly. They were out in the open and below the leaden sea stretched away, its surface ruffled with the endless waves rolling in.

Paula almost gasped with horror, clapped her left hand to her mouth. They were on an elevated bank of fine sand. Beyond, dunes spread away to the south, those in the distance rising to a considerable height. The tide was out and a belt of freshly washed sand edged the swirling surf from the gentle waves. It was the scene on the beach below which had startled Paula.

A lieutenant stood erect, blindfolded, facing north, his hands tied behind his back to a wooden stake rammed into the beach. Twenty feet away from him, facing south, were ten soldiers holding rifles. Well back, and midway between the target and the men with rifles, stood a hunched figure, also in uniform, a pistol in his hand by his side.

'My God!' Paula whispered. 'It's a firing squad. They're going to shoot Lieutenant Berthier.'

'And that creep with his back to me is familiar. Sergeant Rey. He's going to administer the *coup-de-grâce*. After that squad has shot him.'

'Can't we stop them?'

As she spoke Rey raised his weaselly voice, attempting to assume a commanding posture.

'Take aim . . .'

The rifles were rising when Newman's voice bellowed out. At the same moment Stahl aimed his sub-machine-gun.

'Don't move, Sergeant Rey! We can shoot you all down in seconds. Here is a demonstration . . .'

Stahl pressed the trigger and the sub-machine-gun spattered the beach, spraying close to the feet of the squad.

Fine sand spurted up in the soldiers' faces. In the act of raising their rifles they froze. It was like a waxwork tableau. Newman bellowed again.

'Sergeant Rey! Order them to drop their rifles. Now!'

Stahl aimed his sub-machine-gun again. Bullets sprayed the beach a few feet in front of Rey. He stiffened and gave the order. Ten rifles fell to the beach. For the third time Newman shouted an order.

'Sergeant Rey! Drop your pistol. Now!'

Still not daring to turn round, Rey obeyed. Newman gave him a fresh instruction.

'Order your soldiers to lie on their stomachs in the shape of a fan. A wheel – like the spokes of a wheel. One man facing outwards, the next towards the hub. Get on with it.'

Rey gave the order. The soldiers had to be told three times what was wanted. Newman's tactic was to have the face of one man between the boots of his companions. No communication could then be passed between them.

'Get rid of their weapons, Pete,' Newman whispered to Nield. 'And keep well clear of Stahl's line of fire – just in case someone gets lively.'

Nield collected Rey's automatic pistol first, ejected the magazine, fired the bullet up the spout towards the sea. He then gathered up the rifles, piling them away from the spreadeagled soldiers and near the surf line. Picking up each rifle, he extracted the cartridges, used a piece of hard wood he'd found among the brushwood littering the sand. He used it to damage the breaches. Then, one by one, he Hhurled each weapon as far out to sea as he could.

'Check Rey for other weapons,' Newman called out.

'Clean,' Nield reported after checking the gnome whose face twisted with hatred.

'Rey,' Newman ordered, 'you will now release Lieutenant Berthier from that barbaric stake. Nield, accompany him and keep your gun at the ready.'

As the two men reached the prisoner a strange silence fell over the scene, broken only by the peaceful sound of the surge of the sea. Freed, Berthier eased the ache out of his hands, flexing them, stretched his arms and walked with surprising firmness to Newman.

'Keep Rey where he is,' Newman ordered Nield.

He couldn't understand the furtive expression which had come over Rey's evil face. As though he were waiting for something. Berthier stood in front of Newman.

'Thank God! You saved my life. They turned on me when I was in one of the dinghies. They've dragged them into the undergrowth to avoid surveillance from the air. I managed to phone Paris,' he continued in a low voice, 'just before we embarked. Said I was calling my girl friend. Then I delayed the passage of the dinghies down here before they grabbed me. I kept pretending to see lights of vessels – which meant we had to put out our lights and stop.'

'You phoned Paris? Who did you contact . . .'

Newman got no further. Rey shouted at the top of his voice.

'Don't move. Drop your weapons or you'll be shot down like the trash you are.'

As he completed his threat Rey dropped flat to the beach. Newman glanced behind them. Twelve more French soldiers had emerged from the forest, most of them carrying automatic weapons aimed point blank at Newman's team. Two had shovels sloped over their shoulders. Stahl stiffened, Newman warned him quickly.

'Don't, Egon. We'll be cut down. Drop it. We're outgunned.'

Newman was cursing himself for carelessness. As they'd hurried across the graveyard he'd noticed signs of recent disturbance of the humps. He had hardly registered the fact, so urgently had he wanted to reach the beach.

Obviously – now – another section of troops had been beginning to remove the evidence when they had heard Newman's team approaching. They must have retreated into the forest to observe who was coming. And Rey was now wearing the uniform of a captain. The gnome swaggered after Nield who joined the others with his hands in the air. Rey was grinning, exposing bad teeth, as he stared at Paula.

'We'll have some fun with you before six more corpses are sunk at sea. Your death, Berthier, may be prolonged.'

At the Atlantique in Arcachon Moshe Stein's bedroom door flew open and two grim-looking men in trench coats stared at him. The smaller man had a Luger pistol aimed at Stein's chest. The taller, more heavily-built man seemed to be in charge.

'DST. Moshe Stein? You're wanted for questioning.'

'Where? And why, if I may ask?'

'You may not.' The taller man strode forward and hit

487

him across the face with his clenched fist. The ring on his finger cut Moshe's lip. 'You just come with us, you filthy Jew, and keep your dirty mouth shut.'

Both men gripped an arm, hauled him to the door and down the staircase. The staircase was narrow so the tall man went first, keeping hold of one arm, while his companion followed, also gripping an arm at an awkward angle. The descent was painful. No duty clerk behind the desk, Moshe noted. They frog-marched him into the street towards a waiting car.

51

In Dunwich no one would have recognized the well-known figure of Lord Dawlish as he walked along the beach at half the pace of his normal vigorous stride. He wore gumboots, a pea-jacket underneath his oilskin with the hood pulled over his head.

He had disguised himself as a seaman on his way to the waiting large dinghy hauled up on the sand. No local would realize he was going on board, as he often did before the departure of the *Steel Vulture*.

Seeing his expression, none of the crew aboard the dinghy spoke to him as he settled himself at the stern. The outboard was started after several hefty seamen had pushed the dinghy into the sea and jumped aboard.

The dinghy purred across the calm surface while drizzle continued to fall. The atmosphere was so murky it was several minutes before the catamaran hove into view – weather conditions which gave Dawlish great satisfaction. After dark the *Vulture*, sailing illegally without navigation lights, could depart without anyone in Dunwich realizing it had left its station.

He summoned Captain Santos to his cabin as soon as he went on board. Taking off his dripping oilskin, he thrust it at the skipper.

'Take that and get it dried off. You will be ready to sail tonight? By God, the answer had better be yes this time.'

'Señor, I am most happy to report the loading is almost complete . . .'

'*Almost?*'

'That it will be complete by this evening. Most definitely, Señor. I give you my word . . .'

'And I'll give you the destination when at long last you've got your act together. Get out of here and kick a few backsides to make them work faster . . .'

Alone when Santos had hurried away, he opened the wall safe. Stripping off the pea-jacket, he removed the fat money belt strapped round his waist. He began taking out French and Swiss banknotes in stacks, all high-denomination bills. When he closed the safe it was holding a fortune.

He next took from his wallet the message he had already encoded before leaving Grenville Grange. Making himself comfortable in front of the transmitter, he sent the signal which passed from the aerial alongside the complex radar above the bridge. Decoded, the message was simple.

Expected consignment will arrive agreed destination tomorrow positively. Equipment and finance. ETA 0800 hours. Oiseau.

'Just in time for breakfast in Arcachon,' Dawlish said to himself.

At his GHQ General de Forge read the decoded signal Lamy had just handed him from *Oiseau*. He folded his strong hands and stared at his Chief of Intelligence without

489

speaking. Lamy forced himself not to shift about in his chair. It was another favourite tactic of de Forge's – to use silence to intimidate his subordinates. He had a maxim he sometimes liked to utter at meetings of the *Cercle Noir*. And the final meeting would take place this evening. The maxim was typical of the General: 'There are two ways of ruling men. Through love or fear. I prefer fear.'

'Lamy,' he said eventually, 'you'll have to reply with our own signal. Warn him that we have observed French aircraft patrolling offshore. He should make a broad sweep well out in the Bay of Biscay. We move tomorrow.'

Newman was in a cold fury. The troops were eyeing Paula in anticipation. Rey saw his expression and grinned again, his eyes glowing with lecherous malevolence. He tapped Newman on the arm.

'You can watch. Before we shoot you. Then her.'

Newman glanced at Berthier and almost frowned. Rey was deciding which soldier should take Paula first. Berthier had glanced surreptitiously at his watch. Then his expression went blank.

It was at this moment when Newman's acute hearing caught the sound of engines approaching at high speed. Within seconds the surge of the sea was drowned with the roaring chug-chug of a whole fleet of helicopters. The Alouettes appeared over the tree-tops like a cloud of metal birds. Several vanished out of sight, descending into a clearing, Newman assumed.

More choppers were flying south parallel to the beach. They came in very low. Then they were landing on the sand, spilling out droves of CRS men in leather coats and armed with automatic weapons.

From the nearest machine a swivel-mounted machine-gun fired a warning burst, coughing up bursts of sand. A familiar figure jumped out, ran with an escort of CRS men to where the group was lined up. Lasalle.

'Surrender!' His order was a piercing shout. 'Drop your weapons or every one of you will be shot down.'

Rey suddenly broke away, screened by his recent prisoners, running into the forest. Newman followed him. His feet pounded the earth, surprised at how fleet of foot the horrific gnome was. Ahead other troops were fleeing.

They stopped abruptly. From behind every massive tree trunk – or so it seemed to Newman – appeared a CRS man, aiming his automatic rifle. The soldiers froze in their tracks. Rey slowed, stopped, staring round desperately for an avenue of escape. There wasn't one.

Rey heard the pounding of Newman's feet, turned. He reached for the pistol, which was no longer in his holster. Newman's fist smashed with tremendous force into the side of his jaw, breaking it. Rey sagged against a tree trunk.

'You'd do that to a woman!' Newman was beside himself. He grabbed Rey by the throat, began to strangle him as Rey's fists beat futilely against his chest. Lasalle and Paula caught up with them. CRS men grabbed hold of Newman, pulled him away from Rey, who collapsed.

'He's not worth creating a storm about,' Paula said in a chilling voice. 'You've done enough.'

Berthier appeared at Paula's elbow. He shook hands with Lasalle, thanking him.

'What happened?' Newman asked, breathing heavily.

He remembered then that ages ago he had given Paris the map reference of the graveyard. Berthier shook Newman's hand.

'I told you I called Paris. I warned Lasalle they were going to destroy the evidence of the killing ground.'

'And luckily saved yourself – and us,' Newman commented, rubbing blood off his knuckles with his handkerchief.

'You must have smashed the bone,' Paula observed, staring down at the unconscious Rey.

'All of them, I hope,' Newman said with vehemence.

'We must round up the rest of these killers,' Lasalle said. 'And where is your witness?'

'Give us ten minutes and we'll give you the witness.'

'Tell me where.'

'St Girons . . .'

'So we fly you there in one of the Alouettes. It will pick up your witness and fly you on to Paris.'

'I want to go straight back to Arcachon with my team,' Newman said firmly.

'So,' Lasalle spread his hands, 'the Alouette flies you to St Giron, the witness is put aboard, the Alouette flies you to Arcachon, then proceeds to Paris with the witness Navarre needs so badly.'

'Agreed.' Newman pointed to the sagging figure of Rey who was beginning to stir, groaning. 'What do we do with that? He was going to kill Berthier, was directing a firing squad when we arrived just in time.'

'He will be flown to Paris for intensive interrogation. He'll crack. That sort always does. Follow me . . .'

He led the way back to the beach. They passed CRS men handcuffing the hands of soldiers behind their backs. Paula was relieved to get on to the clean air of the beach. Stahl had collected their weapons, handed them back to their owners, including Paula's Browning.

Lasalle ushered them to the Alouette behind the lead machine he had travelled aboard. He shook the hand of each man as he climbed into the machine – Berthier, Newman, Stahl, Butler, and Nield. He had kept Paula to the last and hugged her before she joined the others.

'You have had an appalling ordeal,' he told her.

'It was a bit tense,' she admitted.

He felt her trembling as she smiled. Reaction was setting in. She took one last look south to where the high dunes rose, where the sea glided in, retreated before another wave rolled in. An idyllic scene – to hide so much horror. As soon as she was inside the door was closed, the rotors began to whirl, the machine ascended.

Outside the Atlantique Moshe Stein had been hustled to the waiting car on the far side of the road. A man inside threw open the rear door. The taller captor took hold of Moshe by the scruff of the neck, prepared to hurl him inside.

There was a sudden screech of burning rubber, of cars braking violently. Four Citroëns were parked in a military-style manoeuvre – one car blocking off the car Moshe was about to enter, a second blocking the rear. Two more cars stopped on the far side of the road and men in civilian clothes holding automatics dived out. A tall, thin man with a streak of a moustache and without a gun, hands in his raincoat pockets, called out as he approached the trapped car.

'DST. Don't move. My men have orders to use their weapons at the first sign of resistance.'

'*We* are DST,' protested the man who had hit Moshe.

The thin man glanced at the coat lapel of the protester. He grinned without humour as the man produced his papers. Glancing at them, he held them up to the grey light, shook his head.

'Forgeries. And that is another offence.' He looked at Moshe's mouth where blood seeped. 'Who hit you?'

'Does it matter? Violence is the only language these people understand.'

'You're Moshe Stein? Good. And I agree with your remark. Come with me, please.'

Taking him out of earshot of the fake DST trio, he led him to the second car on the far side of the road. He opened the rear door, stopped Moshe as he was about to get inside.

'You will be flown to Paris under protective guard. I

understand they need you there urgently as a witness to atrocities. Talking about atrocities, I insist you tell me who struck you.'

Moshe shrugged. 'Since you insist, it was the tall one. And perhaps I shouldn't ask but I'm curious. How did you know those men were not genuine DST?'

'As you're going to Paris, I will tell you. It was the idea of my chief based in Paris. Knowing there were a number of men posing as DST he told us all to wear blue pins in our lapels.'

'Clever.' For the first time Moshe saw the blue pin.

The thin man closed the door, the car drove off. He beckoned to the tall man, opened the rear door of the first car. The prisoner glared at him viciously, bent his head to step inside. The thin man grabbed his collar, pulled him back, then slammed him forward so his face smashed into the top of the car. The prisoner yelped with pain. He had blood all over his mouth and chin, had lost three teeth.

'Tsk, tsk!' the thin man said sympathetically. He moved a foot over the wet street. 'It is very slippery. You should be more careful . . .'

Marler, carrying his hold-all, had disembarked from the internal flight from Paris. He was walking across the concourse when he saw a group of soldiers stopping two scruffily-dressed youths. He immediately changed direction, went to a bookstall, bought a newspaper.

He joined a crowd heading for a departure lounge, trailing in their wake. Looking back he saw the soldiers escorting the youths to a bench where their duffle bags were deposited prior to search. The troops were absorbed in their task.

Adjusting his beret, he turned round again, strolled out of the concourse. The car he had ordered from Paris was waiting for him. A Peugeot. He showed his papers to the girl, paid her a generous sum as though needing the vehicle for a few days, drove away.

Earlier, waiting in his room near the rue du Bac, he had received further instructions from Tweed over his mobile phone.

'Increase the pressure to the maximum. We have not much time left.'

'Don't worry. I have a new idea,' Marler had assured his chief. 'A very tight turn of the screw . . .'

Kalmar sat in his camper concealed in woods outside Arcachon drinking coffee. He was studying a map of the port. The coffee was black and strong and helped him recover his nerve. He had just experienced a frustrating shock.

He had traced Moshe Stein to the Atlantique and had been on his way to strangle the Jew. Arriving a short distance from the hotel, he had carefully parked his motor-cycle inside a small alley. Always station your means of escape within easy walking distance of the target's home or temporary residence. But not so close that it might be seen and remembered by a passer-by.

He drew on his Gauloise, recalling the incident. He had been very close to the hotel, wearing the sort of trench coat favoured by the fake DST men crawling round the town. He had seen his target, Moshe Stein, being dragged from the hotel and had stopped, bending down as he pretended to tie an imaginary loose shoe lace. Then the other cars had arrived, other men had dived out of them.

Kalmar was a professional, so very observant. Before he turned away his sharp eyes caught the glitter of a blue pinhead in the lapel of one of the new arrivals. No similar pinhead in the lapels of the men who had hauled Stein out, who appeared to be arrested by the newcomers.

Kalmar had walked away. He knew exactly the right

shop which sold embroidery equipment. Sure enough, they had a selection of blue pinheads. He had purchased half a dozen. He was wearing one now in the lapel of his trenchcoat. Taking another drag at his Gauloise, he folded up the map. His next target was Paula Grey, who had disappeared from Arcachon. His instinct told him she would soon return.

52

Navarre was holding a battle conference in his office at the Ministry of the Interior. Also present were Tweed and Kuhlmann. The three men were taking final decisions.

'Lasalle has signalled me,' Navarre informed his two confidants. 'He was brief. The graveyard has been discovered and soldiers were there on the verge of removing the corpses. The two witnesss, Moshe Stein and the old woman, Martine, are on their way here.'

'Old woman?' Kuhlmann queried. 'Will she make a convincing witness?'

'Lasalle says she is fiercely anti-de Forge and has all her marbles.'

'What about my people?' Tweed asked quietly.

Navarre ran a hand through his dark hair. His lean face radiated dynamic energy and determination.

'My apologies. I should have told you first. Newman, Paula Grey, and the rest of your team are safe. They are returning to Arcachon. They seem to think something crucial is going to happen there.'

'It is,' Tweed agreed. 'And the air patrols over the Bay of Biscay?'

'Are flying non-stop.' Navarre turned to Kuhlmann. 'I should have told you that your agent, Stahl, also is safe. He has joined Newman's team.'

'Not such a brief signal,' Tweed observed.

'Ah! Lasalle has a short-hand method of communication. He can convey much with few words. Have you news yet of *Siegfried*, Kuhlmann?'

The German smiled cynically at Tweed. 'My informant has reported he will soon have the locations. Soon.'

'And the saboteurs de Forge has infiltrated inside Paris?' Tweed queried. 'Were you able to obtain Balaclavas?'

'Yes,' Navarre replied. 'We now have mobile CRS in small groups stationed near likely targets. That was a clever idea of yours, Tweed. The Balaclavas.'

'I simply pinched the brilliant idea Lasalle had of using blue pinheads to distinguish between real and fake DST.'

'The whole key to victory against de Forge,' Navarre went on, staring at Kuhlmann, 'is the timing of two strikes. Ours against the Paris saboteurs and yours against this *Siegfried* underground organization in Germany.'

'The strike against *Siegfried* should take place first,' Tweed warned. 'Preferably by only a few hours. So the timing will be hair-raising.'

'I'm ready. And I agree,' said Kuhlmann.

'So now we can only wait for news of Lasalle's attack on the *Cercle Noir*,' Navarre stated. 'The precision timing – in the correct sequence – is, as you say, Kuhlmann, hair-raising.'

They were speaking in the common language they all understood: English. Tweed rose from the table, glanced at the clock on the wall.

'I am not waiting for anything. I gather a chopper is standing by to fly me to Arcachon. I propose to leave immediately. Events at that port will decide whether we win or lose . . .'

*   *   *

497

General de Forge was pacing up and down behind his desk. Lamy watched him. It was unusual for the General to be so edgy. Normally he was cool as ice. He guessed that the communications from *Manteau* were getting on his nerves.

'I have been waiting for you, Lamy,' de Forge said grimly. 'I was actually standing at the entrance to this building, wondering where the hell you were when I saw you arrive at the main gate on a motor-cycle.'

'I had another urgent message from Kalmar's woman. I had to ride like blazes to a call box in a remote village in the hills. The phone started ringing just as I arrived.'

'What did he want?'

'Money. Of course. He is going ahead with the assignment to eliminate Paula Grey as soon as he locates her. But he was very aggressive in his demand for payment.'

'I expect large funds to reach me tomorrow.'

De Forge left it at that. He was not ready yet to tell anyone else the *Steel Vulture* was berthing at Arcachon at eight in the morning the following day.

'Kalmar also said *Siegfried* is now in place all over Germany . . .'

'So I hope you stressed we will be ordering him to send the signal for action within hours?'

'As you instructed me to do when he next contacted me. He will be available for me to contact him through the cut-out number of the woman.'

'So,' de Forge mused, 'we shall then have the spectacle of Germany reeling under car bomb explosions. Then when the world's attention is fixed on Germany we act. It will be a model campaign, Lamy.'

'And all planned by yourself months ago. Even down to the Ku-Klux-Klan-style demonstrations, the Cross of Fire riots in major southern cities. Not only a model campaign, a unique campaign.'

'You would be flattering me for some reason . . .?'

498

General de Forge stopped speaking as he heard thudding feet approaching outside. Someone hammered in a frenzy on the door. De Forge nodded and Lamy went to the door and opened it. The sergeant of the guard stood there, fearful and gasping for breath.

The incident had occurred minutes earlier. On the orders of de Forge himself the guard at the main entrance gate had been doubled. Six soldiers on foot patrolled outside the gates, each armed with an automatic weapon carried ready for action in his hands.

On the grass verge a tank had been stationed, the barrel of its long gun aimed up the road to Bordeaux. As zero-hour came close the General had felt it wise to protect GHQ more strongly.

It was an unusually bright afternoon for the time of the year. Across the road from the gates the ground had been cleared of all undergrowth. Trees had been chopped down and taken away with the remnants of their trunks. The flat countryside now spread away for a long distance and made it impossible for anyone to approach without being seen.

Here and there low hills studded with boulders rose up and broke the flatness of the plain running towards the horizon. Behind the hills the landscape was criss-crossed with a series of gullys, often with shallow streams running along their beds. It was a scene of serenity and peace.

The first *cr-a-a-ck* of a rifle shot shattered the silence. A soldier dropped his weapon, stared at his hand streaked with blood. Followed by another *cr-a-a-ck*. A second soldier lost his weapon, gazed down at his own blood-smeared knuckles. *Cr-a-a-ck!* A third weapon hit the road. The soldier fainted with shock.

*   *   *

After listening to the NCO's report of the incident de Forge walked out, made straight for the main gates despite the sergeant's warning. 'You could be a target, General . . .'

De Forge never lacked courage. Ignoring the protests, he marched up to the gates, waved a hand for them to be opened, walked out into the road.

He examined the hands of the three men who had been hit, including the soldier who had fainted and had, fortunately, regained consciousness and stood up before the General's arrival. De Forge turned to Lamy who had followed him.

'More marksmanship shooting. Like the bullet which missed me in the car by five centimetres.'

'I don't understand . . .'

De Forge led him aside so they could not be overheard. 'You are stupid. In all three cases these men's knuckles have been grazed – sufficient to make them drop their weapons. Quite remarkable. I wish we had men who could shoot like that . . .'

He stopped speaking, stared at the distant landscape, at the boulder-studded hills. De Forge was reputed to have sharper eyes than any man under his command. In the windless sky a rope of smoke rose from one of the boulder-strewn hilltops. De Forge pointed.

'That's where he fired from. Lamy, go and investigate.'

'Yes, General. I think I'll get an armoured carrier and take an escort.'

'That's right, Lamy.' De Forge grinned. 'Play it safe . . .'

An hour later de Forge was poring over a battle plan for his advance on Paris. He folded it quickly, put it in a safe when Lamy entered.

'So, you survived,' de Forge remarked, sitting in his chair.

'The fire was caused by someone who had collected bracken and wood. We also explored the area. We found

500

tracks of a motor-cycle in one of the gullys. And we found this.'

Lamy produced something from behind his back, laid it on the desk and sat down. It was a large rumpled piece of cloth. De Forge opened it, spread it across his desk. It was a grey cloak. He felt a tingle of apprehension as he gazed at it.

When the phone rang de Forge knew who it was before he picked it up. His expression was blank as he asked who was on the line.

'*Manteau* speaking, General. Recently I shot three of your guards. I aimed to scrape their hands, make them drop their weapons. I think I succeeded.'

'You did.'

'So, General,' the voice continued respectfully, 'it was a last reminder that I'm short of one million Swiss francs for the killing of Jean Burgoyne. I called Major Lamy to give him instructions and he slammed the phone down on me. I dislike bad manners. I dislike people who don't pay up. You have three hours to remedy the situation. I will call Lamy one more time. After that, you are the target.'

The connection was broken. De Forge replaced the received, relayed the gist of the conversation to Lamy.

'That was more than a crime, it was a blunder, as Talleyrand once said – slamming down the phone on him.'

'Kalmar is the man we deal with,' Lamy insisted obstinately. 'He is the man we paid three million francs to for organizing *Siegfried*.'

'Which, in retrospect, may have been a mistake. Handing that task to a man whose identity I have no idea of. I suggest that when *Manteau* calls again you pay him.'

'We haven't the money,' Lamy protested. 'Only enough to pay the troops. And pay-day is today. At this moment we can't afford not to pay them. So what do we do?'

'What do *you* do?' de Forge corrected him with a dreamy look as he stared over his subordinate's shoulder.

'Kalmar has always delivered,' Lamy said with renewed obstinacy.

'Whoever Kalmar may be.' De Forge gave Lamy a piercing stare. 'Have you heard yet from Captain Rey? The traitor, Berthier, should be dead by now. The graveyard cleaned out.'

'No news so far, General. But Rey may be careful about sending even coded signals concerning such a matter. He could be waiting until he returns here to report personally.'

'If you say so.' De Forge rose and his action indicated dismissal. 'And find the money for *Manteau*.'

'There is nowhere I can . . .'

Lamy stopped in mid-sentence. De Forge was leaving the room to inspect the troops.

Brand came out of the phone box on the windswept front at Arcachon. The weather had changed suddenly and the *bassin* was a heaving mass of turbulence as waves crashed on to the promenade. Brand threw away his cigarette.

Today he had dispensed with the seaman's outfit he had previously worn. Now he sported a blue blazer with gold buttons and knife-creased grey slacks under his trench-coat. On his head he wore a naval cap rammed down over his forehead. He looked the typical British yachtsman abroad.

He hurried round a corner to where he had parked his motor-cycle. He had been using it to search Arcachon with great thoroughness. Settling himself in the saddle, he tucked his trouser ends inside his leather boots, pressed the starter button, and rode off to continue his search.

*   *   *

The Alouette transporting Newman, Paula, Berthier and the other passengers, including their witness, Martine, descended to the almost deserted airfield near the *étang* south of Arcachon. The waters of the lake were seething as the wind increased in ferocity. The pilot showed great skill in landing them. Paula breathed a sigh of relief as the skids touched firm ground.

'We haven't seen a sign of de Forge's troops,' she said to Newman as the rotors slowed to a stop.

'That's because he's massing his forces to the north,' Newman replied grimly.

'It's wonderful to get away from the horrible Landes,' she commented.

The door was opened, cold air flooded inside the machine, the exit ladder was lowered. Approaching the airfield Newman had observed the Renault Espace parked at the edge of the perimeter. Once airborne above St Girons, he had remembered they'd need transport. The co-pilot had radioed his request to Lasalle who received the signal inside his own radio-equipped Alouette on the beach.

'What type of transport most desired?' he had radioed back.

'Preferably a Renault Espace. But any vehicle large enough to take us all.'

He had been surprised to see it *was* an Espace waiting for them. Lasalle must have made a great effort to provide him with what he needed. The driver stood outside the vehicle, waving a welcome as they landed.

Newman had joined Berthier at the open door when he stiffened. From their concealed positions a troop of soldiers was running towards the helicopter. One man aimed an automatic weapon at the pilot's cabin. Paula, gazing over Newman's shoulder, trembled.

'Oh, my God! Just when I thought we were safe. De Forge's men . . .'

*　　*　　*

Major Lamy drove into Arcachon in the middle of the afternoon. He drove the Citroën slowly along the front, stopping frequently while he scanned the ships at their moorings swaying under the impact of the large waves sweeping inside the anchorage.

He wore the same clothes he had dressed in when visiting Aldeburgh. A shabby Aquascutum raincoat with a well-worn buckle and underneath an English sports jacket and trousers. His suede shoes were English, as was his tie and his striped shirt. Lamy was a thorough man.

After exploring the front and the port area he drove out of Arcachon to where a road edged the *bassin*, close to the boathouse where Jean Burgoyne had been strangled. A fleet of camouflaged canvas trucks, large vehicles, was parked near a wide slipway leading across the marshes to the edge of the *bassin*. He stopped again. A moment later two soldiers carrying rifles appeared on either side of his car.

'You can proceed no further,' the soldier next to his window said in French.

'I am English,' Lamy drawled in that language. 'Sorry, but I do not understand French. *Anglais.*'

'No go. No go,' the soldier ordered in heavily-accented English.

'No go where?' asked Lamy.

'Back.' The soldier waved a hand away from the boat-house. 'You go. *Zone militaire.*'

'I'm frightfully sorry.' Lamy smiled from under his deerstalker hat. 'I go back? OK?'

'OK. *Maintenant!*'

Lamy reversed his car up the track he had driven down to the road. Waving to the soldier, who did not respond, he drove back to Arcachon. He began driving round the town slowly, patiently criss-crossing Arcachon, slowing even more when he passed a pedestrian.

*   *   *

504

On the bridge of the *Steel Vulture*, anchored off Dunwich, Dawlish was consulting Captain Santos. In his pocket he had the signal warning him of air patrols.

'Santos, I have reason to believe there will be French aircraft patrolling off the coast, searching for us. We must elude them.'

'Elude, Señor?'

'Make sure they don't find us, you damned fool.'

'In that case we do two things. We change course, sail further out to sea. And we sail through night, reaching Arcachon sometime after dawn, I think. Please wait.'

Santos sloped over with his seaman's roll to his chartroom. Dawlish followed impatiently. Surely he could calculate a thing like that in his thick head. Santos would not be hurried. He used a ruler to take measurements on his chart, grunted, tapped the chart with the ruler.

'Yes, but it has to be a rough estimate. We can probably arrive a few hours after dawn.'

'See that we do.'

Furious with the delay, Dawlish returned to his cabin to compose a further signal, to code it, to transmit it.

De Forge swore inwardly when he read the fresh signal from *Oiseau* handed to him by the unattractive Yvette. But his expression showed no reaction. He might have to delay sending the order to his commanders to open their sealed orders, might have to delay Austerlitz. Decide at the last moment he told himself. Looking at Yvette, he had an idea.

'That night you followed Jean Burgoyne to the boat-house. I recall you said you saw a man and a woman in the headlights of their car?'

'Yes, General. The man was Robert Newman, the foreign correspondent. I recognized him at once from

505

pictures I have seen in newspapers. And I had a good look at the woman.'

'Good enough so you'd recognize both again?'

'Absolutely.' Yvette spoke proudly. 'I have a perfect memory for faces. I would recognize both of them.'

'Then take your old car and drive round Arcachon. Keep on driving, looking for them. If you spot either – or both – call me over your radio telephone.' He smiled and she glowed. 'I am relying on you, Yvette.'

Standing at the open door of the Alouette, gazing down at the soldiers surrounding the machine, Lieutenant Berthier whispered to Newman.

'Leave this to me. I think I can handle them. With a bit of luck.'

Straightening his képi, his expression stern, Berthier descended the ladder slowly. The unit's commander, a sergeant, looked uncertain as he held his automatic weapon still pointed at the officer.

'You normally point your weapon at an officer?' Berthier asked quietly. 'If you do not lower the gun at once I'll have you in the guardhouse, prior to demotion to corporal, maybe private.'

'Sir, we have been instructed to guard this airfield. To escort anyone landing here to GHQ,' he added nervously.

Berthier decided on the big bluff. He doubted whether de Forge had spread the news that he was due to be shot by firing squad.

'You mentioned GHQ,' he went on in the same even tone. 'You have heard of Major Lamy?'

'Oh yes, sir. He is . . .'

'Chief of Intelligence,' Berthier completed for him. 'I am Lieutenant Berthier, Major Lamy's aide. I have with me several very important people I am accompanying to Arcachon. A secret mission for GHQ. And you are

506

running counter to orders from the very top.'

'We were not told . . .'

'Of course not, cretin.' Berthier's tone was harsh. 'I have just told you this is a secret mission. Why do you think the Espace is stationed over there waiting for us? There are checkpoints on the way to Arcachon.'

He made the last statement sound as though it could be an assertion or a question.

'As you say, sir, there are checkpoints.'

'So your unit, which is sloppily dressed, can serve GHQ some useful purpose. First, have you motor-cycles?'

'Yes, sir . . .'

'Then four of your unit can act as outriders to escort the Espace through the checkpoints. You will be one of them. Once we have passed through the last checkpoint you turn round and ride back here. Meantime, withdraw all your men out of sight. The passengers aboard are so important they must not be seen. Now, get moving. We are late . . .'

When all the soldiers had disappeared Berthier beckoned to the Espace. It drove to the foot of the ladder and the driver looked scared. The passengers filed down the ladder, entered the vehicle. Berthier sat in front beside the driver, told him to make for Arcachon at high speed. The four outriders joined them as they left the airfield – two in front, two bringing up the rear.

'I wonder why I am sweating,' Berthier remarked.

Kalmar sat astride the saddle of his motor-cycle parked by the kerb on a quiet street near the front in Arcachon. He wore a black leather jacket and a Martian-like helmet. Adjusting his goggles, he prepared to continue his search of the town.

He had been cruising the streets for an hour and had stopped for a rest. A farm tractor crawled along the front. At the same low speed a Renault Espace followed it, the

507

driver obviously waiting for the moment to overtake.

Through his goggles Kalmar stared hard. As the Espace crawled along he saw a woman peer out of the window midway along the vehicle. Paula Grey. He left the kerb, turned on to the front, keeping well back. The tractor proceeded further along the front, the Espace turned into a side street.

Kalmar could hardly believe his luck. Once again his instinct had proved right: Paula Grey had returned. When the Espace turned again into another side street he overtook it, careful not to glance at the windows. In his wing mirror he saw it pull up. He slowed down.

Newman jumped out first, helped Paula down, ran to the entrance to the apartment, inserted the key Isabelle had loaned him, threw open the door into the lobby. The other passengers jumped out, filed inside quickly. Newman went back to the driver who had also jumped out. Locking the Espace, the driver handed the keys to Newman, walked away towards the front.

Kalmar watched all this in his wing mirror, counted up five men, including Newman. One had bushy hair and another, to his surprise, appeared to wear the uniform of a French officer.

Newman closed the door as the others climbed to the first floor. To the side of the lobby the door to the ground-floor apartment was open a few inches. A woman with sharp eyes and a beaky nose closed it. She opened it a few minutes later when someone pressed the bell. A man in a black leather jacket, holding his helmet under his arm and a package in one hand, showed her a cutting from a newspaper of Newman. He explained he had to deliver the package to Mr Newman. Which floor?

'Floor One,' Beaky-Nose replied. 'Now she's got five men up there.' She smirked. 'If you see what I mean.'

Kalmar began to mount the stairs, pulling his helmet back over his head. The moment he heard her close the door he slipped quietly back to the lobby, the skeleton key he'd used to open the front door in his pocket.

He closed the outer door quietly. Again he couldn't credit his luck. He had located where his target was staying. Paula Grey wouldn't have much longer to live.

53

The telephone van pulled up outside the apartment block. Four men in boiler suits jumped out, walked to the front door. One of them had a bunch of keys in his hand. The third key fitted, he opened the door and went inside the lobby. A short heavily-built man, he immediately spotted the apartment door open a few inches, the beady eyes and beaky nose of the woman staring at them. He went to the door.

'You want a good man, you old bag? Better still, a bad one?'

'How dare you . . .'

She slammed the door in his grinning face. They ran up the staircase and the second, slim man, knocked on the door of Isabelle's apartment. Newman opened it a crack, his right hand concealing his Smith & Wesson. He stared at the thin man in the boiler suit. Lasalle.

'Are you going to be like Old Nosy downstairs?' Lasalle joked in English.

Newman let the four men in. Lasalle introduced his companions as DST officers. They had blue pinheads stuck in their boiler suits. Lasalle smiled at the surprise on Paula's face.

'I know what you're wondering. I've dispatched

509

Martine and Moshe Stein by air to Paris. Rey and the rest of the thugs called soldiers are also on their way there for interrogation. We landed on the island in the *bassin* where a boat was waiting to bring us ashore. The telephone van was waiting. Precision organization. This town is crawling with de Forge's troops.'

'Quite takes my breath away,' Paula said with a grin.

'Now, no time to waste. You have those papers taken off poor Jean Burgoyne's body?'

'Here in my bag. They appear to be notes of dispatches outlining a military campaign. There you are.'

'Thank you.' He turned to Stahl. 'Kuhlmann told me you have vital information. Otto is in Paris where I go now.'

Stahl produced a small notebook from somewhere under his jacket. He handed it to Lasalle.

'I disguised myself as a DST officer,' he said in English. 'I got inside GHQ, then inside de Forge's office. He had rushed out during some emergency – leaving on his desk the order of battle. For an attack on Paris. The notebook has the details.'

'Thank you. A remarkable feat. Kuhlmann – and others – will be relieved to lay their hands on this.' Lasalle looked at Berthier. 'I am glad to see you escaped from de Forge. You have done wonders for your country. We can talk properly when you return to Paris.' His voice became casual. 'Is Isabelle about?'

'In the kitchen,' Newman said. 'I'll bring her out if that's what you want?'

'Please. A remarkable woman, from what you've told me. Just tell her we are from the DST. But hurry!'

'First, this is Henri Bayle's notebook. Inside is a list of de Forge's units he identified in Bordeaux.' After handing over the notebook for which Francis Carey had died, Newman brought Isabelle out after she'd hastily whipped off her apron. She had been preparing a pile of sandwiches.

She shook hands with Lasalle. He gazed at her with a quizzical expression Newman found odd. Then the DST team were gone.

Berthier began speaking as they all sat round the large table, devouring the sandwiches. Isabelle frequently stood up with the coffee pot to refill cups. Paula had tried to help her in the kitchen but she had refused politely. Newman had told the others they could trust Isabelle, had recalled how she had accidentally killed two of de Forge's fake DST men – and had come with him on his dangerous mission to bring out Stahl.

'I was working for Lasalle for many months,' Berthier told them, 'once I realized de Forge was a menace to France. As an Intelligence officer, working under Major Lamy, I pretended to de Forge that I was fooling Lasalle, *pretending* to work for the DST. If you follow my meaning. Lasalle provided me with misleading information to hand on to GHQ. He also gave me a listening device I could attach to the wall of my office, next door to Lamy's. I overheard many phone conversations. When I called Lasalle I used a public call box in different nearby villages.'

'So what went wrong?' Newman asked. 'They were going to shoot you on that beach.'

'Later on no one was allowed to leave barracks at GHQ. I made the mistake of using an internal phone to report something vital to Lasalle. That bastard de Forge had had all phones tapped. I was overheard. Captain Rey took delight in telling me that on the beach.'

'But what were you doing in Aldeburgh,' Paula asked him, 'posing as James Sanders, salesman of marine spares?'

'General de Forge sent me with a message to Lord Dawlish. That is another evil man.' He looked at Newman. 'His only ambition is to establish close relations with the

511

French High Command so he can sell arms to certain middle eastern countries. Especially those where arms sales are officially banned. That is my story.'

Newman looked at Paula who had left her seat to gaze out of the window. It was the second time she had done so.

'What are you nervous about, Paula?'

'Shortly after we arrived I looked out of this window. A man on a motor-cycle was riding down the street. He wore a helmet and was hunched over the handlebars. I am sure I know that man. Something about his movements as he turned the corner. It will come back to me.'

'Get on with your meal. Then I want to drive round Arcachon. I have the feeling something important is about to happen here.'

General Charles de Forge stood erect in the turret of his tank. Before him on the vast parade ground at GHQ were drawn up line upon line of tanks of the Second Armoured Division. Their commanders and crews stood at ease beside their leviathans, gazing at the General as he began his hypnotic speech.

'Soldiers of France! Zero hour is close! It is your duty to save the Republic from the corrupt politicians in Paris. Mob rule is rampant in Toulon, in Marseilles, in Toulouse, in Bordeaux itself, in Lyons, in half a dozen other cities. How long before Paris collapses into chaos?

'Soldiers! Who is behind this anarchy? There are three and a half million Arabs in France. Arabs! They have raped our French women, have wrecked shops, have set fire to French homes. The Jews are also rising – seeing their chance to take control. Algerians! Go home to where you came from! The slums of Africa, riddled with disease they bring here.

'Soldiers, *you* will be the saviours of France! Hordes of refugees threaten to overwhelm Europe from the East.

France must resume its rightful role. Only France has the will to stem this tide of aliens. Are you ready?'

A storm of cheering broke out. A thunderous shouting of men whipped to hysteria.

'De Forge to Paris! To Paris! De Forge to the Elysée!'

As the roar eventually began to die down a captain turned to a lieutenant.

'What a great orator. He makes Dubois look like some amateur . . .'

De Forge waved, acknowledged the acclamation. Jumping from his tank he marched swiftly along the front line, shaking the hands of officers, of private soldiers. They were ready.

54

Tweed had arrived in Arcachon. It was now December.

The Alouette which had brought him from Paris was descending over the triangular-shaped *bassin* – prior to landing on the beach at the tip of the Île aux Oiseaux, the island north of Arcachon. A second Alouette was stationary on the sand. The flight had been timed for low tide. Tweed spoke to the pilot through his headset microphone.

'Could you please cruise over the front at a low altitude. I want to get my bearings.'

'What's the idea?' asked Fred Hamilton, sitting next to him.

Back at Park Crescent Howard had insisted that Hamilton should accompany Tweed as bodyguard. Reluctantly, Tweed had agreed.

The Alouette lost more height, changed course. It flew

south almost to Cap-Ferret, located on the peninsula which blocked off the full fury of the Atlantic. A short distance further south was the narrow entrance to the *bassin* from the ocean – the entrance the *Steel Vulture* would have to pass through before berthing at the port.

'The idea,' Tweed said as the machine began to approach the front, 'is to see if I can recognize anyone.'

He had lifted a powerful pair of field-glasses and scanned the front, the boats moored offshore. He adjusted the focus on a man swabbing down the deck of a cabin cruiser. Victor Rosewater. Always present at the new trouble spot.

Near the port he frowned, focused afresh. A man wearing a naval cap was stepping ashore from a vessel, walking towards a motor-cycle. Dawlish's right-hand man. Brand. Tweed had rather expected he would be in the area. His mouth tightened as he watched Brand exchange the naval cap for a yellow helmet, start up his machine, riding away from the shore into the town. He gave the pilot a fresh order.

'Please follow that motor-cycle – without him realizing what we're doing if you can. Even if it means gaining some altitude.'

The Alouette climbed a little higher. The pilot showed great skill keeping his target in sight from a distance. Using his field-glasses, Tweed was struck by the intricate network of streets making up the town.

Brand was threading his way in and out of the maze. He seemed to have no particular destination. Then it dawned on Tweed the rider was searching the town. Looking for what? A few minutes later he saw the second motor-cyclist.

He was riding down a street in a different part of the town from Brand. Tweed adjusted the focus as the rider turned into an alley, stopped, swung his machine round. From the way he took off his helmet, stretched his neck, Tweed guessed he was taking a breather.

In a town like Arcachon a motor-cycle was a good way to

514

get about but it seemed odd to spot two in such a short space of time. Tweed adjusted the focus while the rider was stretching aching muscles. A familiar face jumped into his lenses, a face Tweed recognized from one of the photos Lasalle had shown him. The face of Major Lamy.

Receiving a fresh instruction from Tweed, the pilot followed a new course along the southern and eastern shores of the *bassin*. They had left the town behind, marshes were stretching down to the water's edge, when Tweed saw military checkpoints on the roads inland. De Forge had the port sewn up tight.

He pressed the glasses close to his eyes as he saw the oblong of a slipway slanting down from firm ground into the water. Behind the slipway was a fleet of camouflaged trucks. He frowned, swept the whole area. It had manned checkpoints guarding every approach road.

Tweed nodded to himself, lowered his glasses, ordered the pilot to land on the island immediately.

'You've seen something, sir?' Hamilton enquired.

'Yes. I have been surveying the coming battlefield.'

A boat was being drawn up on the beach as Tweed descended the ladder agilely from his Alouette. He was in a hurry. A slim man in a telephone company's boiler suit came towards him.

'Welcome to the Île aux Oiseaux,' said Lasalle.

Tweed came out immediately with what was on his mind while they shook hands. He described tersely the slipway across the marshes, the waiting fleet of Army trucks, the checkpoints.

'Hamilton, my aide here,' he went on, 'visited Dunwich before he joined me at Heathrow *en route* to Paris. It was misty, he couldn't even see the *Steel Vulture*. I'm convinced that vessel – which moves at high speed – will be arriving here to deliver weapons to de Forge. Within hours. Maybe in the middle of the night. Or at dawn.'

'Not in the middle of the night,' Lasalle objected. 'It is a difficult passage into the *bassin*. The skipper will need daylight. It is a problem – the whole area is infested with his troops.'

'Then the *Steel Vulture* must never land. Contact Navarre. He has the authority . . .'

'To do what?'

'To issue a warning that mines from the Second World War are floating off Arcachon. No vessel must approach within ten miles.'

'That will stop Dawlish?'

'Having met him, I doubt it. He'll think it's a bluff. So get aircraft to drop real sea mines. I hear there is a type which has a beeper signal – makes them easy to locate, pick up afterwards.'

'That is so. You are ruthless,' Lasalle commented with a wry smile.

'So is General de Forge. I know the enemy now. I wish I could see him, face to face.'

'It might be arranged, with a safe conduct. But I would have to be present.'

'Then arrange it. I see you have another boat concealed in the undergrowth. Can I use it to visit Arcachon?'

'You have sharp eyes.' Lasalle smiled again. 'It is supposed to be concealed. But it cannot be seen from the air . . .'

'Where are Paula, Newman, and the others?' Tweed hurried on.

Lasalle explained that they'd returned from the Landes, their experience there, that they had moved from the Atlantique to Isabelle Thomas's apartment. Tweed shook his head.

'That so-called safe house could be traced. They simply must move at once. But where to?'

'I can help there,' Lasalle assured him. 'I have hired a large cabin cruiser, *L'Orage V* . . .'

'"The Storm". Appropriate for what is coming,' Tweed commented.

'It is berthed at the edge of the *bassin* away from other craft.' As he spoke Lasalle took out a map, marking a position with a cross. 'It is the HQ of my DST team operating in the town. Also well away from any checkpoint. There would be plenty of room for all of you.'

'Then get me ashore fast.'

Newman had just arrived back at Isabelle's apartment. He had driven the Espace round Arcachon, had decided he was taking too many chances. As soon as he came near the outskirts he saw a checkpoint manned with troops. He parked the Espace further up the quiet side street. They had stayed with one vehicle too long.

Tweed arrived a few minutes later, riding a bicycle provided by Lasalle from several stored beneath the undergrowth on the island. He had also marked Isabelle's address on the map.

'A man on a cycle is never noticed,' he had remarked.

Tweed had to press the bell. After a minute a large woman with a beaky nose and inquisitive eyes opened the door.

'I have to visit someone on the first floor,' he explained in French.

'The stamina of that girl,' the woman sneered. 'She has five men up there already. I expect she'll cope with you.'

'Would you repeat that comment?' Tweed demanded.

She wilted under his icy stare. Contemptuously, he pushed past her ample form into the lobby, ran up the

517

stairs. Newman opened the door to him, unable to hide his surprise.

'All of you have to get out of here,' Tweed announced without ceremony as he entered the room. 'Immediately!'

He took in Butler, Nield, Berthier, Stahl, and Paula with a quick glance. His gaze rested longer on Isabelle, introduced to him without a name as a friend by Newman.

'Just why do we have to leave so quickly?' she demanded, her chin tilted, her eyes studying him.

'Because the town has practically been taken over by de Forge. I can give you five minutes to clear up, collect some things. Less would be better.'

'We have been safe so far,' she persisted and he realized she was challenging him, which he found intriguing. 'Kalmar, a top professional assassin, is in Arcachon. He strangled a girl in England. He has since strangled another woman not three miles from here. He seems to specialize in strangling attractive women. I think you're on his list. So is Paula. Pack your things. Quickly . . .'

L'Orage V was a very large cabin cruiser. It was moored part way up a creek outside Arcachon, shielded from the mainland by a copse of pine trees. Leaving the Espace, which Newman had parked inside the copse, Tweed insisted on exploring the apparently deserted vessel alone.

Walking gingerly along the gangplank, he stepped on to the deck. The *bassin* was still calm, its surface hardly ruffled by wavelets, but approaching from the ocean was an army of low black clouds.

The *Orage* had the wheelhouse for'ard, a companionway leading down to a saloon. Tweed's first warning that someone was aboard was as he stepped into the large saloon equipped with a long table. A hard object like the barrel of a gun was rammed into his spine. He stood quite still.

'Pierre?' he enquired.

'Who the devil are you?' a harsh voice rapped back.

Tweed held up the folded letter of introduction Lasalle had given him. A hand snatched it over his shoulder. The gun stayed pressed into his spine. Then the invisible man spoke in French again.

'Stand quite still while I check you.'

'Check away. I rarely carry a weapon,' Tweed said in French.

A hand expertly patted him in all the right places. He felt the gun leave his back, turned round cautiously. A six foot tall, well-built man in his thirties faced him. Fair-haired, with humorous eyes, he wore a trench coat with a blue pinhead in the lapel.

'I was expecting you,' he greeted Tweed. 'Can't be too careful. De Forge's men are everywhere. I have to leave now you've got here. A job to do. How many of you in the Espace?'

'Five men and two women, excluding myself.'

'You should be all right. There are eight decent bunk beds in the foc'sle. A well-equipped galley, a ton of food, and plenty to drink.'

'Before you go, could I have a glass of water?'

Tweed had a horror of ships and the sea. Everything was always moving unpredictably. Even inside the creek he didn't trust the cruiser: the *bassin* was tidal. Before bringing the others aboard he swallowed a Dramamine with some water. Better bc safe than sorry . . .

Five minutes later Pierre had gone, after telling Tweed he had sole use of the vessel. Tweed had hustled his team aboard with their kit and they were settled in. Paula offered Isabelle the lower bunk at the end of the sleeping quarters but Isabelle insisted she would take the upper one. They hurried into the galley, together checked the food supplies, the cooking arrangements. Newman noticed how well they were getting on together. Tweed then summoned them into the saloon, asking Nield to keep guard on deck and seating the others at the long table. He sat at the head, his expression grim.

'There are rules. One, no one leaves this vessel without my permission. Two, I will establish a guard roster . . .'

'Which will include us.'

Isabelle and Paula had spoken together. Tweed glared.

'I'll decide that later. Lasalle will be coming to take me somewhere just before dusk. Newman will come with me. In our absence Egon Stahl will be in charge. Three, we take meals at regular hours . . .'

'We shall want to know the times in advance,' Isabelle said firmly.

'Well in advance if we're cooking,' Paula agreed.

'Why,' Newman asked, 'have you assembled us all together here?'

'Because the time has come for me to have complete control. And Isabelle's apartment had been used long enough.'

'Those are the only reasons?' enquired Stahl.

It was a shrewd question. Tweed had swiftly summed up the German as capable and resourceful. He must be to have survived in Bordeaux so long. Before Tweed could answer Newman put a question which had been intriguing him to Stahl.

'How on earth did you penetrate de Forge's GHQ?'

'Planning.' Stahl gave his infectious smile. 'I travelled inside the van which delivers daily bread to the officers. Hid inside the back, unknown to the driver. Locating where he loaded up took some research, but forget that. While he was delivering I left the van. Earlier in Bordeaux I picked the pocket of a fake DST officer who was checking my papers. I took his identity card.'

'Where did you learn to pick pockets?' Paula asked.

'Oh, that's how I started out in life.'

It took Paula a moment to realize he was joking. Stahl patted her hand, went on.

'I was stopped by a sergeant behind a cabin. I showed him the DST card, knocked him out, tied him up with rope, hid him in a large rubbish bin, which seemed appropriate. Then I waited a long time near General Charles de Forge's office. When he rushed out I marched inside. I told you the rest.'

'Interesting,' said Tweed.

'And you haven't answered my question,' Stahl reminded him. 'The other reason why you brought us all here?'

Tweed paused. He looked all round the table. He wanted his reply to have the desired effect: to make them more alert.

'Because when I was flying over Arcachon in the Alouette which brought me from Paris I saw Kalmar.'

55

Lasalle arrived in a large powerboat half an hour before dusk. The craft edged its way up the creek, filling with the incoming tide, bumped against the hull of *L'Orage V*. There were already several DST men aboard, armed with automatic weapons. Lasalle was impatient.

'Join us quickly,' he called up to Tweed. 'We are on a tight time schedule. Berthier, you come too . . .'

'Newman is coming as well,' Tweed told him.

The powerboat turned round beneath the hull of the cabin cruiser, raced out of the creek. Paula was standing on deck, anxiously watching the wake of the craft heading for the Île aux Oiseaux. Butler took her by the arm.

'Below decks. Now. You're a target out here.'

'I sense it's a dangerous mission they're going on.'

'Probably.' Butler followed her down the companion-way. 'But surely you always realized when it came to a climax it would be just that. Dangerous . . .'

Thanking heaven that he'd taken Dramamine, Tweed hung on to the rail as the powerboat whipped over the waves which were now rolling in. A storm was imminent.

Reaching the island, Lasalle bundled them aboard a waiting Alouette. It took off almost before they had time to fasten their seat belts, put on their headsets. The machine headed east – inland and away from Arcachon.

'Is this when I meet de Forge?' Tweed asked.

'That's part of the idea,' Lasalle replied. 'In fact you're going to meet the whole of the *Cercle Noir* – now assembled for its final meeting at the Villa Forban.'

'How do you know that?'

'Berthier informed me.'

'From a phone inside GHQ?' Tweed queried.

'No. He phoned from a call box in a small village. That last call which nearly cost him his life told me de Forge was massing his Second Armoured Division at GHQ. This raid will be a complete surprise. We grab the lot . . .'

As they flew at top speed further inland Tweed, peering out of the window, saw other Alouettes rising up out of small clearings in woods, from inside huge barns. Beyond his window a whole fleet of Alouettes was flying at the same height. Another small armada could be seen through a window on the other side.

'Who is aboard those machines?' Tweed asked.

'Heavily armed, reliable units of the CRS. De Forge will be thinking any CRS are still stationed in the trucks at the Bordeaux Prefecture. In fact they were all flown down in Alouettes which made the trip one by one, landing in preselected sites chosen by a DST deputy who knows the area. I think I can see the lights of the Villa Forban.'

Dusk, a smoky grey dusk, had descended. The Alouettes were circling. Ahead Tweed could see a walled estate, a winding drive leading to a large villa with lights on. As they drew closer he saw limousines drawn up in front of the villa. Where poor Jean Burgoyne had spied.

The swoop from the sky had been well organized. Tweed watched large numbers of the choppers moving ahead of their machine, landing on all sides of the estate. The *Cercle Noir* was surrounded.

'No one can escape this cordon,' Newman remarked.

'And they've neutralized the guard at the gate,' Tweed pointed out.

As their machine flew below tree-top height he had seen guards – uniformed soldiers – holding up their hands at the entrance. An Alouette equipped with a swivel-mounted machine-gun had touched down on the grass verge opposite the closed gates.

Lasalle's Alouette landed in front of the villa next to the parked limousines. Pistol in one hand, keys in the other, he was the first out of the machine, followed by several CRS men in leather jackets who had sat at the rear of the chopper. Tweed, Newman, and Berthier jumped out and followed him to the door. Lasalle inserted and turned each key, nodded to the CRS.

'Where did he get those keys?' Tweed whispered.

'I gave him a bunch of keys I found in Jean Burgoyne's handbag,' Newman told him. 'Two were engraved with the Cross of Lorraine – like the emblem on the door . . .'

Lasalle had rushed inside the large hall. He seemed to know just where to go. Aiming his pistol he threw open a door to the left. Inside everything was confusion.

Tweed recognized General Masson, Chief of the Army Staff, hastily stuffing papers into a briefcase. General Lapointe, commander of the *force de frappe*, standing erect by a chair. Louis Janin, Minister of Defence, ashenfaced, sat petrified at the long table. Dubois, dressed again in a rumpled black suit, soiled white tie, shaggy hair awry, looked desperate.

But what attracted Tweed's attention was the chair at the head of the table, pushed back. And no sign of General Charles de Forge. Lasalle, standing at the near end of the table as CRS men crowded in, weapons aimed, addressed Masson.

'Where is de Forge?'

'General Charles de Forge, do you mean?'

Masson's manner was cold, brusque. He stared at Lasalle with undisguised contempt.

'I repeat, where is de Forge?' Lasalle snapped. 'You are all under arrest. The charge? High treason. And that applies to General Charles de Forge – who was sitting in that chair. Where is he?'

'The General has never been here. Who are you? Address me as General . . .'

'Lasalle, Chief of the Paris DST . . .'

'You won't hold that job much longer!' Masson stormed. 'I will personally see you are thrown into the street . . .'

'You are a liar. Come with me this instant. All of you,' Lasalle ordered.

He went to a side door half-way along the room, opened it, walked into the next room which was furnished like a study with a large desk. Newman and Berthier watched as two CRS men had to grab Masson by the arms. He raged as they frog-marched him into the study.

General Lapointe, thin and grave-faced, needed no encouragement to do as he was told. With a certain dignity he moved into the study: he struck Newman as the

524

most intelligent man in the *Cercle*. Dubois also offered no resistance. He pulled at his untidy moustache as he slouched after Masson with dropping shoulders. Lasalle was seated behind the desk, had used a key to open a deep bottom drawer. Newman glanced inside: it held a modern tape recorder. Lasalle had pressed the rewind button and the reels were spinning. The members of the *Cercle* were lined up against the wall as he pressed the play button, sat back, listened.

'Gentlemen, I will not waste words. Tomorrow we take Paris. I shall send the Austerlitz signal to destabilize the capital early in the morning . . .'

De Forge's crisp commanding voice. Unmistakably.

'Are you quite certain Austerlitz will work? Only that gives us the excuse that you are needed to restore order.'

Masson's voice, showing a trace of nervousness.

'Masson, you really must trust me. There can be only one commander of an operation. I, General de Forge, am that commander.'

Masson's normally ruddy face had lost colour. He stood like a frozen statue as the tape continued to relay the conversation.

'Of course we all accept you as commander of the operation, General. Soon I shall be addressing you as President. But how soon can we remove Navarre so I can take over his position?'

The oily voice of Dubois. His eyes shifted uncertainly from the CRS man on his left to the one on his right. Lasalle stopped the tape, stared at the three men.

'Do I have to play any more? I said high treason, Masson. You have only one alternative, not open to the others . . .'

While he had played the tape Newman had moved to the other side of the room, walled with glass-fronted bookcases. He noticed one case where the books inside had toppled. He ran his fingers down the hinges of the glass-fronted door. As he pressed one hinge there was a click. The edge of the bookcase slid an inch or so open all the way to the floor like a door. He hauled at it and the concealed door opened, exposing a flight of stone steps.

The Smith & Wesson was in his hand as he ran down the steps and down a long corridor under the house. He was stopped by a steel slab he couldn't shift. He ran back and Lasalle turned in his chair.

'De Forge got away through an escape tunnel,' Newman reported. 'I've no doubt it comes out well beyond the walls round the estate. Probably had a car waiting for him.'

'Pity. Our troubles are not over.' Lasalle gave the order to one of the CRS men. 'Handcuff the prisoners, escort them to separate helicopters. They will be flown to Paris.'

'This is outrageous,' Dubois protested.

General Lapointe made no protest. He simply extended both hands, wrists close together. Lasalle shook his head as the DST man next to Lapointe produced handcuffs.

'No cuffs for General Lapointe. Simply escort him.'

Tweed had kept quiet up to now. This was, after all, Lasalle's affair, but he was curious about Lapointe. He asked his question as Masson was shown into another room and Dubois was taken away.

'General, your voice is on that tape?'

'Yes.' Lapointe smiled drily. 'You'll find you have the evidence you need on me.'

'You supported de Forge's plan?' Tweed pressed.

'He never told us his battle plan. He is a very careful man.' He paused. 'Oh, well, it is on the tape. I urged him to do nothing rash, to go and see Navarre to get his views. I still take full responsibility for my actions. Good evening, gentlemen . . .'

'Now for Masson,' Lasalle decided, jumping up.

'Before that how did you know about this tape

recorder?' Tweed asked. 'You installed it yourself?'

'It was Jean Burgoyne's idea. A wire runs from the recorder under the carpet here.' Lasalle went to the wall adjoining the room where the *Cercle Noir* had always met. He pulled aside an escritoire. 'One of my technicians drilled a hole in the wall. A small powerful microphone was inserted – voice-activated. It picks up everything said in there. Jean always knew when they'd be meeting – de Forge would invent an excuse for her not to be here during the evening. She put on a fresh tape. Later she sent the tapes to me. One reason why I knew so much. Bless her. I came here earlier today with a new tape. Now for Masson . . .'

They entered the living room where Masson sat gazing at the wall. Lasalle drew up a chair, facing the general.

'You have two options. Proposed by Navarre. You will be guarded night and day in Paris – a rumour will be spread that *Manteau* has said he is going to kill you. You keep your present post until this problem is settled. You make only public statements sanctioned by Navarre. Later you retire – for reasons of ill health – on a full pension.'

Lasalle paused. He stared at Masson who gazed back with an icy expression.

'The other option,' Lasalle continued, 'is public disgrace, a court martial, maybe even a prison sentence.'

'I will co-operate,' Masson said immediately.

There was a strange gleam in his eyes. Lasalle smiled to himself: Masson had fallen for it. He was banking on de Forge winning. When Masson had been escorted from the room Lasalle turned to Tweed and Newman.

'Janin will be offered the same terms. He will accept. We are gambling. Nothing is solved. A great pity de Forge was able to escape. He will move fast. The final crisis is imminent. You had better fly back with me to Paris. Navarre has agreed to the laying of old mines.'

527

'Not yet,' said Tweed. 'We are staying in Arcachon for the moment. I want to see what Dawlish does. And I'd say now is the time for Kuhlmann to round up *Siegfried* – before they break loose.'

Kuhlmann's dragnet – spread out all over Germany – struck at 1 a.m. the following morning. Police units stormed into addresses in Hamburg, Frankfurt, Munich, and many other cities. The addresses supplied by Helmut Schneider, Rosewater's informant.

They surprised the *Siegfried* organization everywhere. By 3 a.m. in Paris Kuhlmann had received reports of several hundred pounds of Semtex, bombs with timer devices, large numbers of rocket launchers, and an armoury of weapons being seized.

'Enough to start a small war,' he remarked to Lasalle who had returned to Paris.

'And the men who were going to use this equipment?'

'Mostly from Alsace. Presumably because they can speak some German down there. Even members of a crank movement which wanted Alsace taken over by Germany. The media has no idea of what happened. A model operation.'

'Austerlitz in Paris will be different,' Lasalle commented grimly.

The *Steel Vulture* had sailed from Dunwich as soon as it was dark. Instead of riding the rollers in Biscay the twin hulls sliced through the waves like a knife through butter.

Dawlish was on the bridge as Santos – for the umpteenth time – checked the sophisticated radar himself. No sign of any vessel ahead. Earlier he had briefly registered aircraft flying out from the French coast but they had turned away, mere blips a long way off.

The *Vulture*, on Dawlish's direct orders, was completing its great sweep across the Atlantic without navigation lights. Santos had expressed reservations.

'I have never sailed without them before.'

'So it's time you learned to live dangerously,' Dawlish had snapped. 'We have radar. Best in the world.'

'No radar is foolproof . . .'

'Then make sure no fool is using it. Check yourself. That is what a skipper is for. No more crap. That is, if you want that promised bonus . . .'

Santos had shrugged. And he did want that large tax-free bonus paid in cash. Now they were approaching Arcachon and the first blood-red streaks of dawn were splashed across the eastern sky. Santos stood alongside Dawlish on the bridge when the wireless operator dashed up the companionway. He looked scared out of his wits, was waving a piece of paper.

'Captain! I've just received this signal from the shore. There are old wartime mines which have appeared! We are ordered to turn round immediately before it is too late.'

'My God . . .!' began Santos.

'Bluff,' Dawlish barked. 'Sheer bluff. Mines, my foot. It's a Navarre trick. Maintain your present course . . .'

'But if they are right . . .' Santos began again.

'I said *maintain your present course*, damn you!'

Aboard *L'Orage V* the tall DST officer they had met when they arrived on the vessel stood crouched over a powerful transceiver. Crowded behind him were Tweed, Newman, Paula and the others. The DST man looked at Tweed.

'They've sent the warning signal repeatedly. No reply.'

'And there won't be,' Tweed replied. 'I know Dawlish. He will try to bring in the *Vulture*. He'll think it's just a trick. Nothing gets in the way of Dawlish. I'm going to take a look . . .'

With binoculars looped round his neck he ran up the companionway. On deck he climbed to the roof of the wheelhouse, then mounted the ladder alongside the radar mast. Below, Paula watched anxiously: Tweed had been known to suffer from vertigo.

Perched at the top of the mast, Tweed could see beyond the entrance to the *bassin* the *Vulture* cutting through the waves with its twin hulls. He kept the night glasses pressed to his eyes. It really was an amazing vessel. Could it, with the luck the wicked so often possessed, dodge the mines and make its owner's landfall?

Dawlish walked to the port side of the bridge. He stared down. A metal sphere with protruding prongs was drifting a yard or so away from the hull. He left the bridge, ran to the small aircraft aft of the bridge where a pilot was always at the controls.

Climbing the ladder to the inside of the machine, he shouted his order. At the same time he pressed the button which automatically retracted the ladder, slammed the door shut.

'Lift off! Get this bloody toy in the air before we are blown to pieces. Course? I'll tell you later. Get her up now, for Christ's sake!'

Watching through his glasses, Tweed saw the *Vulture* slowing down prior to entering the *bassin*. He pursed his lips. It looked as though Dawlish was going to make it. Nerve gas in the hands of a man like de Forge. The mere threat would clear the way straight into Paris.

Then he saw the small aircraft appear, jumping clear off the deck, climbing vertically, and he guessed Dawlish was escaping. One hundred feet up, the machine hovered above the vessel below, ready to fly away.

Seconds later the *Vulture* detonated the mine. There was a dull thudding *b-o-o-m!* which echoed round the *bassin*. An immense geyser of water rocketed upwards to a great height, carrying with it huge chunks of metal debris. It enveloped the hovering aircraft, which briefly vanished in the dense spray cloud. The geyser sank back. The aircraft sank with the geyser, toppling with a slow windmilling motion. Below, one of the twin hulls split off, skidding across the ocean surface. The other hull went down like a high-speed elevator. As the tumbling aircraft hit the deck the vessel fragmented. Massive pieces of the hull and bridge were hurled out to sea. There was an ear-splitting dull roar as the relics of the *Vulture* dived beneath the waves. The missiles had exploded. A new eruption of water soared upwards, a gigantic fountain infested with the wreckage of what had been one of the most advanced vessels in the world. Tweed consoled himself with the knowledge that nerve gas would swiftly disperse in the ocean, would become harmless. He braced himself and the shockwave shook the mast. Then silence. He climbed down, looked at his team.

'Dawlish is no more. The weapon delivery is destroyed. I don't think for a minute this will stop de Forge.'

56

Marler had received his fresh instructions before Tweed had left Paris for Arcachon. For the first time he was not travelling Air Inter. He had waited for hours in the cabin of an Alouette parked on a small airfield outside Paris.

In the seat beside him rested his large hold-all containing his Armalite rifle and sniperscope. He ate the meals brought to him by a girl who said little. Between meals he dozed quite a lot of the time. But when the pilot came to shake him awake he was instantly alert.

'News?' he asked abruptly.

'They're on the move. All hell has broken out in the streets of Paris. We're flying south now . . .'

All hell had broken loose in the streets of Paris. But the hell was being endured by the saboteurs infiltrated into the city and activated by Austerlitz.

A group wearing Balaclavas threw open the rear doors of a furniture van parked close to the main telephone exchange and spilled out gripping automatic weapons. As they approached the entrance other men clad in Balaclavas swarmed round them carrying rifles.

The leader of the attackers, bent on capturing the communications centre, was confused. Were these reinforcements he hadn't been told about? He was making up his mind when a rifle butt descended on the back of his head and he slumped to the ground.

With no leader, his troops were even more confused. The next surprise was when tear gas shells burst at their feet. None of the saboteurs noticed that the newcomers in Balaclavas wore a thin green band on their right arms.

The battle for the exchange was brief and rough. The CRS paramilitary troops – able to distinguish friend from foe by the green armbands – rounded up the Austerlitz attackers. They were bundled into waiting Berliet trucks hidden in side streets. Many of the defeated were carried aboard unconscious. The whole counter-operation lasted exactly five minutes.

Similar scenes were taking place all over Paris. Lasalle

had skilfully predicted the likely targets, had distributed his CRS men disguised in Balaclavas close to every key objective.

The main assault was mounted against the Ministry of the Interior. A hundred Austerlitz troops surged out of various stolen tradesmen's vehicles. To their surprise and delight the gates were not locked leading into the courtyard from the Place Beauveau. Brushing aside the guards, they stormed into the spacious courtyard, heading for the inside of the ministry. General de Forge had pinpointed this as the prime objective – on the advice of his wife, Josette, who had since disappeared.

They stopped suddenly as large forces of other men in Balaclavas appeared in front of them. Behind them the gates were closed and they were trapped. Before they could decide what was happening the CRS in Balaclavas were on them, wielding rifle butts, rubber truncheons, cracking skulls, felling the invaders. The CRS are not noted for their gentlemanly behaviour. Any man without a green armband was a target.

Navarre watched the violent mêlée from the window of his office on the first floor. Again the vanquished attackers were carried, thrown into a fleet of Berliet trucks which edged their way through the opened gates.

An hour later the CRS unit commanders from all over the city had reported they'd done the job. Navarre acted immediately. Special CRS units had kept TV vans and reporters well away from the onslaughts. Navarre appeared on television. He briefly reported that 'terrorists' had been detained, that the city was now quiet.

General Charles de Forge was a resolute commander. When he received the call from Major Lamy in Arcachon he listened.

'It is a complete disaster, General!' Lamy sounded

shaken. 'The *Steel Vulture* was almost inside the *bassin* when it blew up – exploded into the sky. It was reported that wartime mines had been seen floating offshore. I thought it was bluff. The extra weapons you were waiting for will never reach us . . .'

'Thank you, Lamy. Report back to GHQ.'

De Forge put down the phone. He stood up to address the officer awaiting instructions.

'We move now. Operation Marengo is launched. I intend to travel in the lead tank of an Armoured Division. I ordered the other commanders to open their sealed orders one hour ago. Victory will be ours – before the day is out . . .'

Aboard *L'Orage V* Tweed read the statement de Forge had issued the night before – timed to catch the next day's edition of *Le Monde*.

Exercise Marengo is being extended to Central France. The exercise will move no further north than Chateauroux. The population is warned to keep clear of where the exercise is taking place. Under certain conditions live ammunition may be used.

'What does it mean?' Paula asked.

Tweed looked out of the porthole. It was mid-afternoon and the cabin cruiser was swaying like a ballet dancer. He had taken another Dramamine.

'Note the use of the word "exercise",' he pointed out. 'Repeated twice. An attempt to confuse Navarre. And from Chateauroux the N20 runs due north to Paris. As I predicted that will be his route. Not a devious flanking movement to the west as they thought in Paris.'

'I am sure you are right,' said Berthier. 'He'll move at top speed through the night. When Paris wakes up de Forge's forces will be on the Champs-Elysées. He has won.'

'What made you predict his route up the N20?' Paula asked.

Tweed smiled drily. 'When I was visiting Josette in the Passy house I noticed a bust of Napoleon. One of de Forge's heroes. He'll have studied his campaigns. When Napleon was advancing against Wellington he drove his army at top speed direct for Brussels, surprising Wellington when his enemy reached Quatre Bras. Paris is de Forge's Brussels – the direct thrust by the shortest route.'

'And nothing to stand in his way,' Newman said grimly.

'Not a lot,' Tweed agreed. He looked at the DST officer in charge of the vessel. 'I think we should all return to Paris. There is an Alouette waiting for us on the island? Good . . .'

He paused as they heard someone crossing the gangplank. Newman moved to the side of the bottom of the companionway, the Smith & Wesson in his hand. Footsteps clumped noisily down the wooden steps. Victor Rosewater stopped at the bottom, smiled at Paula and the others.

'I thought you'd be somewhere in Arcachon. Well, it's the big goodbye to Lord Dane Dawlish.'

'We're all drenched in tears,' said Newman.

Rosewater looked at Tweed. 'I thought you should know Major Lamy is still in Arcachon. Why isn't he with de Forge?' He glanced at Paula. 'Some unfinished business in Arcachon?'

'I also saw Brand in a bar in Arcachon late this morning,' Rosewater told Tweed.

'Brand. I've been wondering about him.'

Tweed said nothing more as he peered down out of the window of the airborne Alouette. Aboard the machine were Isabelle and Paula, chatting to each other, Stahl, Newman, Butler, Nield, and Berthier. All on their way home via Paris.

Tweed, in a hurry, had been irked by the long delay on the island. Some mechanical defect in the Alouette's engine which had to be remedied. It was still daylight, but only just, when they caught up with the Third Army beyond Chateauroux.

Tweed asked the pilot to fly lower. First there were truck-loads of infantry, armoured personnel carriers, motor-cycle outriders. Then they saw the endless columns of huge mobile 155mm artillery. And ahead of the guns, also proceeding up route N20, more endless columns of heavy tanks. Raising his field-glasses, Tweed focused on the lead tank behind a swarm of motor-cycle outriders.

General de Forge stood in the turret of his Le Clerc tank. Disdaining a helmet, he wore his képi and slung round his neck was a pair of field-glasses. Spotting the Alouette, he raised his own glasses and Tweed had the oddest sensation that they were staring at each other. Lowering the glasses, de Forge gave a jaunty wave as his tank thundered on.

'He's now well north of the so-called exercise line,'

Tweed said coldly. 'The line he laid down. The exercise to be confined *south* of Chateauroux. And it is the N20. How on earth is he clearing the highway to give that army of steel through passage?'

'I've no doubt he'll find a way,' Rosewater replied. 'And what was Brand doing in Arcachon? Waiting for the *Steel Vulture*?'

'That, yes. And he may have had another objective. We have not seen the last of him.'

Marler stood behind the pilot in the chopper flying south over the N20. It was still daylight and a shaft of sunshine like a searchlight had broken through the high overcast.

'Here they come,' said the pilot in French.

'To liberate Paris,' Marler replied cynically in the same language.

Holding on to the back of the pilot's seat with one hand, he raised his binoculars. A group of outriders had stopped at an intersection. Behind them men were carrying signs from a civilian truck. Through the lenses Marler read the signs.

Diversion. Do not miss! Army manoeuvres!

'De Forge is taking over highway N10,' Marler commented. 'Keep following it. He can't be far behind.'

'And the bastard is marching on Paris . . .'

The pilot maintained the same low altitude. Marler was watching the light. Soon it would be dusk, then dark. Which would mean accomplishing his mission could turn out to be impossible. He raised his glasses, saw a clutch of outriders speeding up the highway. Behind them rolled the tanks.

Feet wide apart, bracing himself to keep steady, Marler refocused his glasses. He couldn't believe it. The erect figure of General de Forge was standing in the turret of the leading Le Clerc tank. Marler lowered the glasses,

537

scanned the countryside. To the east of N20 a small hill rose. Mentally he checked the range.

'Can you land on that flat-topped hill?' he asked the pilot through the microphone slung below his headset.

'Perfect place to put down.'

'Don't stop the engine . . .'

The machine swooped away from the highway in an arc. As it hit the summit Marler, who had taken off his headset, grabbed his hold-all, threw open the door, jumped to the ground, crouching below the whirling rotor. Running to a rock embedded in the earth, he dropped flat, hauled out the Armalite, screwed on his sniperscope, perched the weapon on the rock, adjusted the sniperscope when he had the leading Le Clerc tank in his crosshairs.

De Forge had a sensitive instinct for danger. He watched the chopper land. He turned once again and waved on the tanks coming up behind him with a confident gesture. He then gave the order to his gunner through his microphone.

'Target chopper just landed hilltop to the east. Fire when ready!'

The computer raced through its calculations at the speed of light. The huge barrel swivelled through ninety degrees. The elevation began lowering to bring it dead on target.

Marler pressed the trigger two seconds before the tank's gun sent a shell crashing into the chopper, blowing it to tiny pieces. The special explosive bullet blasted the front of de Forge's skull clean away. His body sagged down on to the crew below, fountaining blood, splashing into the eyes of the gunner who automatically pressed the button.

The shell curved a dozen feet above the chopper,

landed on a farmhouse, killing the farmer, his wife, and three children, who were eating a meal.

Marler switched his aim, fired three times over the heads of the outriders who had sat stunned on their machines. They leapt out of the saddles, gripped their automatic weapons, began firing at random towards the chopper now climbing rapidly off the hilltop.

Inside the tank there was panic. De Forge, a grisly sight, was sprawled over them, still spraying blood. Five tanks behind the stationary vehicle, unaware that their General was dead, obeyed his last hand wave and trundled forward, their caterpillar tracks clanking and grinding like some huge stamping mill.

Immediately ahead was a copse of trees and behind them drivers of petrol tankers held hoses, were drenching the highway with petrol which spread like a lake. A farmer held a torch made of straw. He flung the burning brand, the petrol lake ignited, the five advancing tanks rolled towards a curtain of flame.

Confusion. Chaos. Tanks swivelling round, colliding with each other in their desperate flight from the wall of fire. Two tanks rumbled past either side of the tank where de Forge lay, crashed headlong into three Le Clercs moving up the highway. Soon the whole column ground to a halt, zigzagged across the highway. An army without a leader, without orders, with nowhere to go.

The Alouette carrying Marler back to Paris was a grey dot in a grey sky as dusk fell and a sheet of flame spread across the fields on either side where bales of hay soaked in petrol had ignited.

58

'There is still the hunting down of Kalmar – identifying who Kalmar is,' Tweed said firmly.

It was twenty-five hours later and they were all assembled in Navarre's office at the Ministry of the Interior. Navarre had just spoken.

'We are cleaning up the mess rapidly,' he had announced. 'As you'll have seen from this morning's news-paper headlines, General Charles de Forge died tragically during an exercise when he insisted live ammunition should be used. We'll never know who accidentally shot him during that panic on route N10.'

'One of his own troops?' Marler suggested.

'That is the assumption,' Navarre had agreed. 'Then a large petrol tanker overturned, the petrol caught fire. As I said, a major tragedy.'

'Yes, indeed,' Lasalle said with a blank expression.

'The military exercise has been cancelled,' Navarre had continued. 'All troops have returned to barracks. There will be no reports of that mysterious graveyard Newman discovered in the Landes.'

'Just one of those things?' Newman had commented cynically.

'De Forge had earlier reported all the deceased as deserters. There's no point in upsetting the relatives. A logical outcome,' Navarre had remarked with typical Gallic realism. 'And the recordings for TV of the two witnesses, Martine and Moshe Stein, will never be relayed. The cassettes have been destroyed. The old lady, Martine, seems satisfied now she has heard of the death of de Forge. Moshe Stein is philosophical.'

'And the smashing of the *Siegfried* organization is completed,' Kuhlmann commented. 'Which just about wraps it up.'

Which was the point at which Tweed had intervened.

'There is still the hunting down of Kalmar . . .'

'How would we know where to start?' Rosewater asked. 'We haven't a clue as to his identity.'

'I'm not so sure about that,' Tweed insisted. 'I made a phone call to Jim Corcoran, chief of security at Heathrow. He reported seeing Major Lamy arriving by direct flight from Bordeaux.'

'With a lot on his conscience,' Navarre rapped out.

'Corcoran followed him,' Tweed went on, 'got the number of the car he'd hired. I phoned the firm. Lamy was driving to Aldeburgh.'

'I want to go back there,' Paula told him.

'Too dangerous,' Tweed contradicted her. 'I also phoned Grenville Grange. Imagine who answered the call. Brand. He also is back in the Aldeburgh area.'

'I have leave due,' Paula persisted. 'I'll go there in my own time. I want to lay the ghost of what happened there.'

'Not a good idea,' Newman snapped.

'So I don't want you coming with me. It's a personal pilgrimage.'

'What about the trouble in the south of France?' enquired Tweed, changing the subject.

'Dubois was given two options,' Navarre explained. 'One, he could disband his vicious racist movement, *Pour France*. Two, he could stand trial for high treason as a member of the *Cercle Noir*. He was reminded we have that tape with his voice on it. Guess which option he chose.'

'He copped out,' Newman replied. 'That louse with the soiled tie has no guts.'

'You are right. He has agreed to dissolve his party. He

will return to his old job of grocer in Provence, selling rotten fruit at extortionate prices. Without leadership the racists are impotent.'

'And we have to return to London,' Tweed said.

'Then I can visit Aldeburgh again,' Paula asserted.

It was late afternoon, a December afternoon, when Paula stood by the window of her bedroom at the Brudenell Hotel in Aldeburgh. Below her was the narrow Parade of the front. A storm of grey clouds was flooding in from the north east. Giant waves surged in, crashed against the sea wall, hurled spray as high as her window. A little wilder than the day when she had fled across the marshes with Karin but the atmosphere was similar. Time to go for her walk before it was completely dark.

She checked the contents of her shoulder bag, tightened the belt of her raincoat, tied a scarf round her head and left her room. Hardly anyone about downstairs. She smiled at the receptionist, ran down the stairs to the rear entrance, turned left and walked towards the bleak marshes.

Crossing the deserted public car park, her feet crunched the gravel of the road leading to the sea defences which were still being reinforced. At that hour the site was closed: all the workmen had gone home. Passing the Slaughden Boat Storage yard she turned down the steep grassy path on to the marshes.

The light was fading faster than she had anticipated. She found herself thinking of Kalmar, the brute who had strangled poor Karin. It seemed ages ago. The ground was more mushy than it had been the last time she had taken this walk. She reached the point where the path forked – left back up to the road, right up the steep path to the dyke overlooking the yacht anchorage.

She took the right-hand fork, picked her way along the narrow twisting footpath running along the ridge of the dyke. The tide was coming in, funelling its way up the narrow channel parallel to the coast from the opening to the sea almost twenty miles to the south. That was when she heard the steady tread of footsteps coming up behind her at speed.

Tweed parked his Ford Sierra in a slot by the wall of the Brudenell. Jumping out, he locked the car, ran to the entrance. Half-way up the stairs he stumbled, swore aloud. As he hauled himself up the rest of the steps, clinging to the banister rail, the receptionist appeared.

'Is there something wrong, sir? Oh, it's you, Mr Tweed.'

'I've twisted my bloody ankle. Sorry. Is Miss Paula Grey in the hotel?'

'She just left. Went for a walk over the marshes . . .'

'Not by herself, I hope?'

'Yes, no one was with her.'

Victor Rosewater appeared from the direction of the bar. He stared as Tweed collapsed into a chair, stretched out his right leg with the ankle turned at an awkward angle.

'Is there a problem?' he asked. 'Paula phoned me at my town flat to say she was coming here. Would I like to keep her company.'

'So why aren't you doing just that?'

'Because I didn't know she had arrived. I've been waiting for her in the bar.'

'Isn't Robert Newman here?' Tweed asked the receptionist. He appeared agitated. 'He told me he was coming here.'

'He arrived earlier, sir. He said he was driving over to Grenville Grange.'

'Oh, no!' Tweed looked at Rosewater. 'He's convinced Kalmar is back in Aldeburgh. He must have gone to Grenville Grange to tackle Brand. He'll find Brand isn't at the Grange.'

'What gave Newman that idea?' Rosewater pressed.

'Because both Major Lamy and Brand are back in Aldeburgh. Now Paula has gone gallivanting off across those marshes. I'm really worried. By herself. She's in great danger. And now all I can do is hobble a few feet.'

'I'll go and find her,' Rosewater assured him. He lowered his voice. 'And I have my Service revolver with me.'

'Then why the hell are you wasting time?' Tweed looked at the receptionist. 'Can you say how long ago she left here?'

'A good fifteen minutes ago . . .'

'I'll get after her now. You nurse your ankle.'

Rosewater had dashed down the stairs, clad in a trench coat, and had disappeared before Tweed could reply.

'Is she really in danger?' the receptionist asked. 'I am thinking of what happened on the marshes once before.'

'So am I. Pray God he's in time.'

Paula could hear the incoming water lapping across the marshes below the dyke. It was coming in like a flood. Yachts moored to buoys were rocking under its impact, their masts swaying back and forth. She turned as she heard the hurrying footsteps. It was Victor Rosewater.

'Thank God it's you, Victor. I wondered who it might be. I felt I had to come and take one last look at where Karin died. A pilgrimage, as I said in Paris.'

Rosewater clenched his gloved hands together. He looked out across the anchorage where a yacht swathed in blue plastic for the winter was drifting in fast on the tide. It must have broken loose from its buoy and was now drifting through the reeds close to the dyke.

'Tweed has arrived at the Brudenell,' he told her. 'He's worried sick that you're out here on your own.'

Paula had one hand inside her shoulder bag. She smiled at him.

'But that suits you, doesn't it, Kalmar?'

'What the hell are you talking about?' Rosewater demanded roughly.

'Oh, I should have known much earlier. Remember the night when we paid a second visit here with Newman – at your suggestion. You said you thought maybe the police had overlooked a clue. As we passed the Slaughden Boat Yard on the road you said: "Which way now?" You made out you had no idea of the route here. Then when we came to where the path forks – one way back up to the road and the other less obvious path up to the dyke? I slipped. You were in the lead. You hoisted me *straight up on to the dyke*. I only realized what that meant recently. You knew where Karin's body had been found.'

'You, my dear, are a bit too clever for your own good. In any case, I've been worried you might have seen me strangling that silly bitch from your tree-top view.'

'Silly bitch? Karin was your wife . . .'

'And getting very tiresome. Just like you . . .'

'Jean Burgoyne was a friend of mine. You choked her, you bastard. Choked her to death.'

'For a big, fat fee. That was a near run thing – at that remote boathouse outside Arcachon. But I'd done the job and got clear before your lot turned up.'

'You cold-blooded bastard. God knows what else you have done.'

'Organized *Siegfried* in Germany for one thing. As an Intelligence officer supposedly after IRA I had the contacts. For another big fee. Now you're the only one left. Isn't it ironic? You're going to die where your friend, Karin, did. Might give you some comfort . . .'

He moved closer to her. She had half dragged out from

her shoulder bag the Browning automatic when his right hand grasped her wrist in a grip of steel, twisted it. The gun dropped to the path. His gloved hands shot up to her neck, thumbs aimed at her windpipe.

'You'll never get away with it,' she gasped.

'Why not? Tweed has two suspects in the area. Foxy Major Lamy and tough guy Brand. Say goodbye, Paula . . .'

The thumbs pressed hard into her windpipe. She tried to knee him in the groin, but the tall figure looming over her turned sideways. Her knee hammered futilely against the side of his leg. His image was becoming blurred.

The plastic cover over the nearby yacht had been ripped aside. Newman had jumped out, rushing over the ooze and clumps of grass, up the side of the dyke. He grasped a handful of Rosewater's hair, jerked savagely. Rosewater grunted, released Paula, swung round. The two men grappled, lost their balance, rolled together down the side of the dyke on top of the remnants of the craft where Karin had been found. Newman felt hands round his neck, used his shoulders as leverage to roll his body from under Rosewater, ending up on top of him. His own hands gripped Rosewater by the throat, forced his head down under the water below the wrecked boat. He held on. Rosewater's head was a dim silhouette under the surface. He opened his mouth to breathe and swallowed lungfuls of sea as he struggled to get free. Rosewater's head, hair matted to his skull, jerked above the surface. A hideous sight. Newman hung on, his hands squeezing tighter as he forced his antagonist deeper under the tide. Ignoring the desperate thrashing of the body, he held him down. Newman felt the hands round his own throat slacken, fall away. He relaxed his grip cautiously. The submerged body was lifeless.

Soaked to the skin, dripping water, Newman clambered unsteadily to his feet. He managed a little wave to Paula, staring down, one hand massaging her throat. He climbed Everest, hauling himself up the side of the dyke, stood by Paula who was now gazing over the marshes.

Newman heard the sound of an engine approaching. He saw a vehicle – a buggy with enormous tyres – bouncing towards them with blinding headlights. Shielding his eyes with his wet hand, he saw three men in the buggy as it stopped on the landward side of the dyke. Chief Inspector Buchanan, Tweed beside him, Sergeant Warden driving.

'Look . . . Bob,' Paula croaked.

She was pointing to the other side of the dyke. The tide was receding. Rosewater's body, his shoes protruding briefly above the water, was being sucked rapidly down the creek, into the anchorage with the debris of the wrecked craft. Relics of the boat floated rapidly south. Tweed, showing no signs of an injured ankle, was the first to stand beside them.

With his clothes clinging to him, Newman explained to the three men what had happened, kept it brief.

'We always thought it was Rosewater,' Buchanan told him. 'That business of discovering the ring with the Cross of Lorraine – pointing us away from Rosewater to France. Warden supervised an expert team searching the scene of the crime earlier. They would never have missed it. Problem was, no proof. But when a wife is murdered the first suspect is the husband.'

'I think we should get these two back to the Brudenell and a hot bath,' said Tweed. 'And a freak high tide was forecast. The body may be washed all the way into the North Sea.'

Epilogue

A week later Tweed gathered all his team into his office. The bruises on the throats of Newman and Paula – which had convinced Buchanan of the truth of their story – had healed. Marler stood against a wall, smoking a king-size. Butler and Nield perched on Paula's desk while Newman occupied the armchair.

'Who was *Manteau*?' Paula asked. 'I couldn't understand why there were two assassins.'

'There weren't,' Tweed said, leaning back in his chair. 'Marler was *Manteau*. Only three people knew. Navarre, myself, and Lasalle . . .'

'But why?' Paula persisted.

'If you'll keep quiet I'll tell you. It was my idea – part of the psychological warfare against de Forge. We knew he was using Kalmar, so I invented another assassin to throw de Forge off balance. Berthier had supplied Lasalle with the private phone numbers of Lamy and de Forge. It was really very straightforward.'

'Straightforward? But *Manteau* was supposed to have engineered the wreck of the TGV express, the assassination of the President and the Prime Minister. And his trademark, a cloak, was found in a nearby village. A cloak was also found near the Paris Prefecture when the Prefect was murdered. And a third one near the boat-house when Jean Burgoyne was strangled. Marler couldn't have known those murders were going to take place.'

'Agreed.' Tweed smiled drily. 'So before *Manteau*

548

came on the scene Lasalle purchased a number of cloaks from a theatrical costumier in Paris. Trusted DST officers were given the cloaks, stuffed one in a litter bin near the Paris incident. The Paris Prefect, incidentally, was never killed. He went on the holiday he'd planned under an assumed name to Martinique. Officially, he recovered from the bullet wound recently, resumed his duties. It was hours after the TGV tragedy that a cloak was found in the village. Plenty of time to fly one to Lyons. Then the DST bribed an old man in a nearby village to tell the press he'd seen a man in a cloak on the viaduct. Another cloak was flown to Arcachon. Marler, in the role of *Manteau*, kept phoning de Forge demanding large fees for doing the jobs. When a large sum was delivered we obtained Swiss francs from a Paris bank, many in numbered sequence, and a lot of them counterfeit seized by the Paris police months ago. Marler returned the money to confuse de Forge even more.'

'But who killed de Forge?' she asked.

'My dear,' Marler drawled, 'don't you read the papers? It was a random shot when de Forge's own troops panicked during the overturned petrol tanker incident.'

'Really?' she queried, and Marler nodded amiably.

'Berthier, Lasalle's spy inside de Forge's GHQ, played a vital part,' Tweed continued. 'With a listening device he overheard Lamy's phone calls with Kalmar's contact in the office next door. Including the new targets – which is how we knew *you* were a target.'

'Shivery,' she remarked. 'And for a while I liked Rosewater.'

'Which is why,' Tweed emphasized, 'Butler and Nield stayed by your side – with orders never to leave you alone.'

'When did you suspect Rosewater?' she asked.

'I wondered about him from the first. Remember when we met him at the Hotel Drei Konige in Basle? He gazed with lecherous interest at an attractive woman in the dining room. To cover up, he suggested she was a spy. I'm sure Karin, working for Kuhlmann, began to suspect her own husband. He realized it, strangled her on the Aldeburgh marshes. From what he said to you he wanted to get rid of her anyway – so he could pursue his Casanova ways.'

'Hideous man. But just that? Looking at another woman?'

'No, far more. Newman caught on early. Remember he was with you that night the two of you took Rosewater across the marshes? Newman saw Rosewater hoist you on to the dyke without hesitation when you slipped – Rosewater who wasn't supposed to have a clue as to where Karin had been killed. He told me. From that moment you were guarded. The next thing which pointed the finger at Rosewater was Kuhlmann telling me his informant, Heinrich Schneider, had passed via Wiesbaden a list of addresses where *Siegfried* was based in Germany. But not a word from Rosewater even though Schneider had first told *him*. And when you came out of a restaurant in Arcachon after having dinner with Rosewater you later told me he'd suggested a ride in his car.'

'That's right,' Paula agreed. 'Butler stopped me going with him, thank God.'

'There was a red Porsche parked down the street. Rosewater turned away from it when Butler joined you. After you'd driven off Nield stopped the car so he could go back to find his wallet which he said he must have dropped . . .'

'I remember . . .'

'Nield went to the corner, saw Rosewater climbing behind the wheel of that Porsche. What captain in the Intelligence Corps can afford a Porsche on his pay? There were other strange coincidences.'

'Did they find Rosewater's body?' Paula asked.

'No, which was a relief to the MOD. Think of the

scandal. They've just posted him as missing in Germany. His body is probably at the bottom of the North Sea.'

'You took a chance,' Marler remarked, 'using Paula for live bait.'

'I agreed,' Paula replied. 'Insisted when I caught on it was Rosewater. I'd been rather a fool about him. But Tweed had Butler and Nield concealed behind the dyke in case Newman didn't reach Rosewater.' She looked at Tweed. 'But how did Dawlish smuggle those missiles?'

'You told me, but only when I watched the *Vulture* coming into Arcachon was I able to recall it. At the beginning, describing your underwater swim with Karin at Dunwich, you said, "I thought I saw a great white whale." Unlikely in that part of the world.'

'Then what was it?'

'A dracoon – one of those very tough and large containers made of plastic they used to transport extra oil, dragging them on the surface behind tankers. Like a sausage. Dawlish was clever. The missiles, I guess, he brought in from a factory abroad, anchored off Dunwich, then stored the dracoons carrying missiles in the sunken village – hence his interest in underwater exploration. The *Vulture* could then sail safely into Harwich.'

'So all is well?'

'It is in France.' Tweed looked round the gathering. 'I think you all did very well. We helped to stop a military dictator taking power in Paris, which would have wrecked the new Europe. Major Lamy, who often supervised those hideous executions in the Landes, has been found dead in an Aldeburgh hotel. Shot himself. Captain Rey was found hanging in that horrible punishment well. Not popular with some of the troops, I assume. Now I think you'd all better go home.'

'I'd better call on Isabelle,' Newman said, standing up. 'Just to make sure she's settled in the temporary flat we've given her in South Ken.'

'Which is conveniently close to your pad,' Marler observed.

'Pure coincidence,' Newman snapped.

'And maybe Paula would like to join me for dinner,' Tweed suggested.

'What a lovely idea.' Paula jumped up. 'I'll just go and fix my face.' She walked past Newman without a glance in his direction.

Monica, who had said nothing from behind her desk, waited until everyone except Tweed had left.

'Isabelle might just be joining the SIS,' Tweed remarked. 'She was one of Lasalle's trained agents.'

'And your interview with the new PM before you opened the meeting here?' Monica enquired.

'He apologized handsomely and without reservation to me. You remember Howard was told the PM was experimenting with a twin-track policy? Testing us, so to speak? He left it to the MOD to choose someone from Military Intelligence. They chose Victor Rosewater! The PM won't do anything like that again. Now, I must go and freshen up.'

'Isabelle,' said Monica. 'That's dangerous. She may have the training – Lasalle is a pro. But Isabelle and Paula working together? Trouble.'

'They got on well enough in Arcachon. I saw it myself.'

'Men!' Monica cast her eyes heavenwards. 'That was for a brief time in a dangerous situation. You've a lot to learn about women.'

'You're imagining it . . .'

'Am I? Didn't you see how Paula walked straight past Newman without so much as a good-night? All right, bring in Isabelle. And watch the fur fly.'